Praise for Rhys Bowen's Molly Murphy Series

"Entertaining . . . Molly Murphy is endearing, and her quick wit and sharp mind make her a protagonist to root for. . . . Well written and fast paced, with a twist that will leave readers truly surprised. This novel is not to be missed."

—*RT Book Reviews* (4 stars) on *The Edge of Dreams*

"Bowen shrewdly explores the tension between a husband and his very independent wife as they both work to solve a complicated series of murders. One of Molly's best."

—*Kirkus Reviews* on *The Edge of Dreams*

"The extremely tricky plot of Bowen's fourteenth Molly Murphy mystery will keep even veteran whodunit readers guessing. . . . Bowen makes Molly's continued sleuthing plausible, even under her changed personal circumstances, and deftly plants clues so that the surprising final revelation makes perfect sense."

—*Publishers Weekly* on *The Edge of Dreams*

"Once again Rhys Bowen proves why she's one of the great mystery writers working today. . . . Atmospheric, tightly plotted, heart pounding, this is Bowen at her best."

—Louise Penny on *City of Darkness and Light*

"What could be more fun than a new Molly Murphy adventure? A Molly Murphy book set in Paris's avant-garde art world just after the turn of the century! A beautifully rendered portrait of the city and the period, seen from Molly's eyes as she deals with one of her most challenging cases yet."

—Deborah Crombie on *City of Darkness and Light*

"Highly entertaining . . . [Molly] pieces together a complicated mystery set against a rich historical backdrop."

—*RT Book Reviews* (4½ stars) on *The Family Way*

"[A] well-paced twelfth mystery featuring feisty and endearing Molly Murphy . . . The usual full-blooded characters will keep readers engaged."   —*Publishers Weekly* on *The Family Way*

"The latest addition to Molly's case files offers a charming combination of history, mystery, and romance."
                    —*Kirkus Reviews* on *Hush Now, Don't You Cry*

"Engaging . . . Molly's compassion and pluck should attract more readers to this consistently solid historical series."
                    —*Publishers Weekly* on *Bless the Bride*

"Winning . . . The gutsy Molly, who's no prim Edwardian miss, will appeal to fans of contemporary female detectives."
                    —*Publishers Weekly* on *The Last Illusion*

"This historical mystery delivers a top-notch, detail-rich story full of intriguing characters. Fans of the 1920s private detective Maisie Dobbs should give this series a try."   —*Booklist* on *The Last Illusion*

"Details of Molly's new cases are knit together with the accoutrements of 1918 New York City life. . . . Don't miss this great period puzzler reminiscent of Dame Agatha's mysteries and Gillian Linscott's Nell Bray series."   —*Booklist* on *In a Gilded Cage*

"Delightful . . . As ever, Bowen does a splendid job of capturing the flavor of early-twentieth-century New York and bringing to life its warm and human in habitants."
                    —*Publishers Weekly* on *In a Gilded Cage*

"Winning . . . It's all in a day's work for this delightfully spunky heroine."   —*Publishers Weekly* on *Tell Me, Pretty Maiden*

"Sharp historical backgrounds and wacky adventures."
                    —*Kirkus Reviews* on *Tell Me, Pretty Maiden*

"With a riveting plot capped off by a dramatic conclusion, Bowen captures the passion and struggles of the Irish people at the turn of the twentieth century."

—*Publishers Weekly* on *In Dublin's Fair City*

"Molly is an indomitable creature. . . . The book bounces along in the hands of Ms. Bowen and her Molly, and there is no doubt that she will be back causing trouble."

—*Washington Times* on *In Dublin's Fair City*

"The feisty Molly rarely disappoints in this rousing yarn seasoned with a dash of Irish history."

—*Kirkus Reviews* (starred review) on *In Dublin's Fair City*

"Readers will surely testify that Murphy has become one of their favorite characters. . . . This book is a keeper."

—*The Tampa Tribune* on *In Dublin's Fair City*

"Its enjoyable charm and wit will appeal to a cross section of mystery fans."   —*The Baltimore Sun* on *Oh Danny Boy*

"A lot of fun and some terrific historical writing. Fans of the British cozy will love it, and so will readers of historical fiction."

—*Globe and Mail* (Toronto) on *Oh Danny Boy*

"Bowen parcels out bits of her plot with an impeccable sense of timing and . . . has written another outstanding mystery."

—*Library Journal* on *Oh Danny Boy*

Also by Rhys Bowen

The Molly Murphy Mysteries

The Constable Evans Mysteries

In Like Flynn

Rhys Bowen

Minotaur Books ❧ New York

IN LIKE FLYNN. Copyright © 2005 by Rhys Bowen. All rights reserved. Printed in the United States of America. For information, address St. Martin's Press, 175 Fifth Avenue, New York, N.Y. 10010.

www.minotaurbooks.com

The Library of Congress has cataloged the hardcover edition as follows:

Bowen, Rhys.
    In like Flynn / Rhys Bowen. — First edition.
        p. cm.
    ISBN 978-0-312-32815-3 (hardcover)
    1. Murphy, Molly (Fictitious character)—Fiction. 2. Women private investigators—New York (State)—New York—Fiction. 3. Irish American women—Fiction. 4. Legislators' spouses—Fiction. 5. Women immigrants—Fiction. 6. Spiritualists—Fiction. 7. Kidnapping—Fiction. 8. New York (N.Y.)—Fiction.
    PR6052.O848 I5 2005
    823'.914

                                                        2004057031

ISBN 978-1-250-07518-5 (trade paperback)

Minotaur books may be purchased for educational, business, or promotional use. For information on bulk purchases, please contact the Macmillan Corporate and Premium Sales Department at 1-800-221-7945, extension 5442, or write to specialmarkets@macmillan.com.

First Minotaur Books Paperback Edition: September 2015

10   9   8   7   6   5   4   3   2   1

This book is dedicated to my friends in the mystery community, especially to my not-so-evil twin Meg Chittenden, who has to suffer being mistaken for me, and to Lyn Hamilton, with whom I have shared touring adventures ranging from pigs to lobsters.

The mystery community is composed of warm, witty and incredibly generous people. I consider it a privilege to be part of it.

As always my special thanks to Clare, Jane and John for taking the time and trouble to help me polish my work.

☙ One ☙

Spring? Was there any spring this year?" the man in the jaunty brown derby asked. "Oh, that's right. I remember. It was on a Wednesday, wasn't it?"

This remark produced titters of laughter from the women standing in line at Giacomini's Fine Foods. The speaker was the only man in the store, other than old Mr. Giacomini behind the counter. He stood head and shoulders taller than the rest of us and his presence had caused quite a stir. It was unusual to see a man in a grocer's shop, seeing that cooking was women's work. He was well turned out too, with a smart hounds-tooth jacket, white spats and well-polished shoes, unlike the short, round peasant types who frequented this little store in what was still mainly an Italian neighborhood just south of Washington Square. However he seemed quite happy to join in the chitchat as we waited our turn to be served.

"He's right," the woman ahead of me said, nodding her head. "There was only one springlike day that I remember this year. In my recollection we had howling gales until the middle of April."

"Then overnight it got hotter than Hades," the man finished for her.

There was general agreement to this last remark, although there was also a gasp from some of the ladies at this almost-cuss word. It had been a terrible spring, followed by a hot spell for which we

1

were unprepared. Usually I didn't mind waiting in line in Giacomini's cramped little store where the smell of spices and herbs stirred half-forgotten childhood memories. But today it was almost too hot to breathe and the smells were overpowering, especially when mixed with the not-so-pleasant odors of stale perspiration and garlic.

"They say there's typhoid over on the Lower East Side," one woman said, lowering her voice.

"You wouldn't catch me going over there, even when there's no epidemic," another woman muttered. "Packed in like sardines they are in those tenements. And they never wash. Serve them right if they get sick."

Mr. Giacomini poured sugar into a paper triangle, twisted it shut and handed it to the woman at the front of the line. "Anything else then, Signora? That will be one dollar forty-five, please."

Money exchanged hands. The stout lady loaded her purchases into her basket, then attempted to squeeze past us down the narrow center aisle. Good-natured chuckles were exchanged as close contact couldn't be avoided. As each person in turn attempted to flatten herself against the bins and shelves, I saw something I could scarcely believe. That man had reached into the open basket of the woman just behind him in line and taken her purse. My heart started racing. I wondered if I had imagined it and what I should do next. He was clearly too big and strong for any of us to tackle.

The line moved forward. The next customer made her purchases. I had to act soon or the man would reach the front of the line and be out of there before the poor woman discovered her purse was missing. I couldn't just stand there and do nothing. It went against my nature, even though similar bold and imprudent actions had landed me in hot water more than once in my life. I leaned across to the woman and tugged on her arm. She turned and stared at me in surprise.

"That man just stole your purse," I whispered.

She looked at me incredulously, then down at her basket.

"You're right. It's gone," she whispered back in a horrified voice. "Are you sure he took it?"

I nodded. "I saw him."

"What should I do?" She turned to stare up at the big fellow.

"You stay where you are. I'll go and find a constable and we'll have him trapped like a rat." Before she could answer, I muttered an excuse about leaving my shopping list at home, then I pushed my way out of the store and ran all the way to Washington Square. There were always policemen to be found on the south side of the square, because that was the home of New York University, and students were known to be of unpredictable behavior. I found one easily enough.

"Come quickly," I urged. "I've just witnessed a man stealing a lady's purse. If we hurry he'll still be in the store."

"Looks like another pickpocket, Bill," he called to another constable who was standing across the street. "Back in a jiffy. Listen for my whistle in case I have trouble with him. Is it far, miss?"

"Giacomini's on Thompson. Hurry, before he gets away." I fought back the desire to grab his arm and drag him. But he set off with me willingly enough at a trot. Sweat was running down his round, red face by the time we reached Giacomini's. We stepped into the warm, spicy darkness of the store just as the man was paying at the counter.

"Is that him, miss?" the constable whispered.

This was hardly a necessary question as he was still the only man in the store, but I nodded. "And the lady behind him—the one in the blue skirt—she's the one whose purse he took. I told her to act naturally until I came back with you."

"Nice going, miss. Don't you worry. I'll surprise the blighter on the way out." The constable positioned himself in the doorway just as the big fellow turned and made his way past the queue.

"Not so fast, sir." The constable stepped out to block his progress. "I think you have something on your person that doesn't belong to you."

"I do? Now what might that be?" the man asked with feigned surprise.

"You were seen taking a lady's purse."

"A lady's purse? Me?"

"My purse," the woman in the blue skirt said.

The remaining women in the store spun around to stare.

"Ridiculous. How dare you suggest such a thing." The man attempted to force his way outside.

"Well, my purse has gone from my basket and this young lady says she saw you take it," the woman said. The man's gaze fastened on me.

"She did, did she? And did anybody else see this brazen act? Did any of these other women standing in line with a good view of me?"

Nobody answered. Some women averted their eyes. The man turned to glare at me again.

"I don't know what you hope to gain from this," he said, "but you can wind up in serious trouble from making false accusations against upright citizens. Go on then, Officer. Search me if you must."

"If you'd just step outside, into the light, sir, and don't think of making a run for it. There are plenty of other officers close by."

"I'm certainly not about to make a run for it until I've cleared my name." The man stepped out through the door and spread out his arms. "Go ahead then. Search me."

His complete confidence unnerved me. He had an insolent smirk on his face as the constable began searching. He knows the purse isn't on him, I thought. And then in a flash it came to me: He must have already hidden it somewhere, to be picked up later.

I slipped inside the store and looked around frantically. If I were he, where would I stash a stolen purse? He could have dropped it on the floor easily enough and kicked it under one of the shelves, but he'd have to get down on all fours to look for it—which would make him most conspicuous. So he must have made good use of his height. On the right side of the aisle there were shelves of bottles and cans right up to the ceiling. I stood on tiptoe, reached up with my right hand to the top shelf that contained canned tomatoes and was rewarded as my fingers touched a softer, slimmer object. I stretched and reached even harder and managed to knock it down. Then I pushed past the women and ran outside, waving it triumphantly.

Only just in time too.

"There. I hope you're satisfied," the man was saying. "And believe me, your chief's going to hear about this."

"I'm sorry, sir, I was only doing—" the constable began as the man turned on his heels.

"Don't let him go," I shouted. "Here's the purse." I waved it at the constable, who grabbed the man by the arm. "He put it up on the top shelf where it was too high for anyone else to see it. He was going to come back for it later."

"Very smart," the constable said. "Unfortunately for you, this young lady was smarter." His grip tightened on the fellow, who wasn't looking smug any longer.

"You can't pin anything on me. You've only got her word. Anyone could have taken it and put it there. She could have taken it herself," he blustered.

"Nobody else in the store could have put it on that shelf," I said. "I was the tallest woman in there and I had to stand on tip toe to reach that high. Everyone would have noticed me if I'd tried to reach up there. But you—all you needed to do was pretend you were adjusting your hat or brushing your mustache."

"Come on. I'm taking you in," the constable said. "Jefferson Market Police Station is where you're going."

"I'm not going anywhere with you." The man broke away, shoved at the constable and started to run off. Instantly the constable blew his whistle. Two other policemen appeared from the direction of Washington Square. There was a scuffle and the man was grabbed and held fast.

"What's he done, Harry?"

"Tried to steal a lady's purse in the grocer's shop," my constable said, "only this young lady was onto his tricks. She's a sharp one if you like."

"All right, get him back to the station," one of them said, looking at me appreciatively. "And you'd better come along too, miss, to report to our sergeant."

I didn't like to admit that I was loathe to go anywhere near the Jefferson Market Police Station, as I had once spent a night there, having been mistaken for a woman of a very different profession. I trotted along beside them, feeling pleased with myself. I was getting rather good at this investigation business, wasn't I? More observant than the average person, with sharper senses and quicker reactions. It was about time the police realized how useful I was. It was a pity that I couldn't tell Daniel Sullivan of my expertise.

"You guys is wasting your time," the pickpocket said, reverting to a more common way of speech. "Ain't no way you'll make this stick." And he glanced back at me as if giving me a warning. I met his gaze and gave him my famous Queen Victoria stare, still feeling rather proud of myself.

We crossed the square and made for the market complex on the far side of Sixth Avenue. Squashed fruit and straw littered the sidewalk and a barrow was pushed past us piled high with cabbages. In the afternoon heat the smells of rotting produce and manure were overpowering. The triangular complex housed a fire department and the police station beyond it. We were about to go in to the latter when the door opened and a couple of men came out, so deep in conversation that they didn't notice us until they almost collided with us.

They were not wearing uniforms, but they reacted instantly to our little procession.

"What have you got here then, Harris?" one of them asked.

"Caught the fellow stealing a lady's purse," my constable said.

I noticed the half-amused look on the plainclothes officer's face as he observed the prisoner, held firmly between the other policemen. "Been a bad boy again, Nobby?" he asked.

"Go boil your head," the man said easily enough. "No way youse guys will pin anything on me. It's only her word against mine."

Then they noticed me for the first time. I tried to remain calm and composed, even though I had been very aware of one of them from the moment he stepped through the door. It was Daniel Sullivan, my ex-beau. Captain Daniel Sullivan, of the New York Police. I saw his eyes widen as he recognized me.

"The young lady spotted this gentleman helping himself to another lady's purse," my constable explained. "And she was smart enough to figure out where he'd stashed it."

"Was she now?" I could feel Daniel still looking at me, although I didn't meet his gaze. "All right. Take him inside and book him, boys. I'm sure he knows the way as well as you do."

When I went to follow them inside, Daniel grabbed my arm. "Are you so cocky about your skills as a detective that you've decided to take over the duties of the New York Police?" he asked in a voice that wasn't altogether friendly.

I looked up at him. "I was in a store. I witnessed a pickpocket at work. Luckily I used my wits and was able to get him arrested."

"Not so luckily for you," Daniel said. "Do you know who the man is?"

I shrugged.

"He's one of the Hudson Dusters, Molly. You do know who they are, don't you?"

I did know, only too well. There were three gangs that ruled lower Manhattan and the Hudson Dusters was one of them. I had experienced an encounter with a rival gang a few months previously and had no desire to repeat it.

"I don't need to remind you what they're like, do I, Molly?" Daniel went on. "And this character, Nobby Clark, is known to carry a grudge. He took a pot shot at one of our men who arrested him once before, you know."

He continued to stare at me while I digested this. "I don't want you to testify if it comes to trial, is that clear? I want you to make yourself scarce before he is released. He doesn't know your name, does he?"

I shook my head.

His grip on my arm tightened. "Molly, when will you learn not to get yourself mixed up in police work?"

"Holy Mother of God, would you let go of me," I exclaimed, shaking myself free of him. "I was only doing what any decent person would have done. If it had been my purse, I'd have wanted someone to alert me."

He sighed. "I suppose so. And with most pickpockets that would have been fine. Trust you to find the wrong one. Come on. I'll escort you home. We'll leave Nobby to cool his heels in a cell for a while and then release him."

"Release him? But he stole."

"Your word against his, as he said. The gangs employ good lawyers. They'd get him off and he'd come looking for you. Don't worry. We'll catch him when it matters."

"I suppose the Hudson Dusters pay you off, like the other gangs do," I said.

He glared at me. "Contrary to popular belief, the New York police force is not in the pay of the gangs. We just learn which battles are worth fighting and which aren't. If Nobby is charged with picking a pocket he'll be away for a few months at the most. I'd rather wait to pin the big one on him."

He attempted to steer me toward the curb.

"Wait," I said. "I'm not going home. I still have my shopping to do."

"I don't want you going back to that store." Daniel continued to scowl at me. "You go straight home and I'll have one of our men do your shopping for you. What was it you were buying?"

I wasn't going to let Daniel know that my finances were rather precarious recently, owing to a distinct lack of work, and that I was going to buy a couple of slices of cold tongue for our evening meal.

"It's all right. Nothing that can't be purchased in the morning, I suppose," I said. "But I'm a big girl now. I can cross streets by myself."

"Sometimes I wonder about that," he said and he smiled.

The aggressive Daniel was easier to handle than the smiling one. I went to pull away from him. His fingers slid down my arm until he held my hand in his, examining my fingers.

"No ring yet, I see," he said. "Not yet promised to the bearded wonder then?"

"If you are referring to Mr. Singer, we are not exactly promised but we have an understanding," I said stiffly.

"Molly—" he began in an exasperated voice.

"And I take it you are still affianced to Miss Norton?"

"I think she tires of me at last," Daniel said. "She told me I was boring and lacked ambition the other day. That's a good sign, wouldn't you say?"

"Good for whom?" I asked. "Really, Daniel, my life is too busy for idle thoughts about you and Miss Norton."

"Are you still pursuing this ridiculous notion of being an investigator?"

I nodded. "Doing rather well at it, if you want to know. Almost as good as Paddy Riley was."

"Paddy Riley got himself killed," he reminded me.

"Apart from that."

He crossed the street beside me and stopped at the entrance to Patchin Place, the small cobblestoned backwater where I lived. "I have to go back, but you'll be all right from here, won't you?" he asked.

"I was perfectly all right before," I said. "I really can take care of myself, you know, Daniel. You need not worry about me."

"But I do. And I think about you often. Don't tell me that you never think of me?"

"Never have time," I said briskly. "Good day to you, Captain Sullivan. Thank you for escorting me home."

I left him standing at the entrance to Patchin Place.

❧ TWO ❧

I did not look back as I walked down Patchin Place. I had handled
that encounter rather well; in fact, I was pleased with myself. I
had shown Daniel Sullivan that he no longer had a hold over
me. I had come across as a confident, successful woman. Maybe I
should change my profession instantly and ask my playwright
friend Ryan O'Hare for a part in his next play on the basis of that
convincing performance.

Because if truth were known, I wasn't exactly flourishing at the
moment. I can't say I was making a fortune as a private investigator.
P. Riley and Associates still received a good number of inquiries, but
when they found out the investigator was a woman, the interest
often waned. The general opinion was that you couldn't trust a
woman to be discreet. Women were known for not being able to
hold their tongues. That had been Paddy's opinion too, although I
think he was changing his mind about me when he was killed. I still
missed him. I was still angry that he had gone before he could teach
me all the tricks of the trade.

I put my empty basket down and fished for the door key. I always
felt a sense of pride when I let myself into my own house, and such
a dear little house too. Now I wondered how long I'd be able to
keep it. There had been no money coming in for a couple of
months. Seamus O'Connor, who shared the house with me, had
been laid off from his Christmas job at Macy's Department Store. It

was now May and he had yet to find other employment. His two children, Shamey and Bridie, were hearty eaters and money disappeared at an alarming rate. There was no reason why I should have been feeding children who were not even related to me, except that I owed my present life in America to their mother, who was dying in Ireland, and I had grown fond of them. By now they seemed like my own family.

I let myself in and looked around with annoyance. The remains of a meal littered the kitchen table—the bread sliced crookedly and drips of jam on the oilcloth. The children had clearly come home from school and gone out again. Well, they'd better be prepared for a good tongue-lashing when they came back. I started clearing away their mess. Seamus wasn't home, it seemed. I had to admire the way the man tramped the streets every day, looking for work. The problem was that he still wasn't strong enough to do the laboring jobs available to the newly arrived Irish—and not educated for anything better.

I sighed as I put the bread back in the bin. Something would have to be done soon if I was going to come up with the money for rent and food. Maybe the O'Connors would just have to squash into one room and I'd let out the third bedroom to a lodger. But the thought of a stranger sharing our home wasn't appealing.

I could always offer my services as an artist's model again, of course. I had to smile as I thought of Jacob's reaction to my posing in the nude for a strange man. For all his liberalism, I didn't think he would take kindly to that. Sweet Jacob; he was the one stable thing in my life at the moment. I had so far refused to discuss marriage with him, but I was weakening. I have to confess that the thought of being cherished and protected was occasionally appealing, even to an independent woman of commerce like myself.

Thinking of Jacob made me realize that I hadn't seen him for a few days and I needed some cherishing at this moment. It wasn't one of the evenings for his labor organization, the Hebrew Trades Association, so he should be home. He could take me to our favorite café, where we would have borscht and red wine. In spite of the heat that radiated up from the sidewalks, I almost ran across Washington Square, then down Broadway and into Rivington Street.

As I progressed into what was called the Lower East Side, the street became clogged with pushcarts and stalls selling everything from the lyrics of Yiddish songs to pickles, buttons or live geese. A veritable orchestra of sounds echoed back from the high tenement walls—the cry of a baby, a violin from an upper window playing a plaintive Russian melody, shrill voices arguing from window to window across the street, hawkers calling out their wares. It was a scene full of life and I savored it as I hurried past.

Jacob lived at the far end of Rivington Street, close to the East River. The pungent river smell wafted toward me on the evening breeze. He had one room on the third floor of the building, but it was big and airy, half living space and half studio for his photographic business. He was a wonderful photographer and could have made a fine living, had he not chosen to dedicate himself to social justice and thus shoot scenes only of squalor.

The front door of his building stood open. Two old men sat on the stoop, long white beards wagging as they gestured in earnest discussion. They frowned at me as I went past them. I was on my way to visit a young man, unchaperoned. Such things were unheard of in the old country. I grinned and bounded up the stairs two at a time.

At the top I paused to wipe the sweat from my face and to tame my flyaway hair. I could hear the sound of voices coming from inside his door. I tapped and waited. The door was opened.

"Jacob, I'm starving and I wasn't allowed to buy anything for dinner because . . . ," I started to say, when I realized I was staring at a strange young man. He wore the black garb and long curls favored by the stricter Jewish males and he was looking at me in horrified amazement.

"Oh, hello," I said. "I came to visit Mr. Singer."

The eyebrows rose even higher. "Mr. Singer. Not here," he said in broken English, the straggly beard quivering as he shook his head violently.

13

"Oh. When will he be back?" I asked.

He didn't seem to understand this. I had no idea what he was doing in Jacob's room, and who else was in the room with him, but clearly he wasn't going to let me in. I was about to admit defeat and go home again when boots clattered up the stairs and Jacob's face came into view.

"Molly!" He sounded surprised, pleased, but wary. "What are you doing here?"

"Do I need an appointment to visit you these days?" I asked, my eyes teasing.

"Of course not. It's just that"—he paused and glanced up at the black-garbed young man watching us—"It's rather difficult at the moment." He turned to the newcomer and spoke quickly in Yiddish. I had come to understand a few words of that language, but not spoken at any speed. The young man nodded and retreated. Jacob closed the door, leaving us standing outside.

"Who is that?" I asked, giving him an amused look. "Don't tell me it's someone sent from the rabbi because you keep company with a Shiksa?"

"I'll walk you downstairs again," he said and firmly took my arm. The afternoon seemed to be a progression of men taking my arm and walking me in directions I didn't want to go.

"What's this all about, Jacob?" I asked.

"I'm sorry, Molly, I really am," he said, talking under his breath even though there was nobody to hear us in the stairwell. "It's just that—it's awkward at the moment."

"You've already said that once," I reminded him. "What's going on, Jacob?"

He glanced up the stairs again. "That man, he's my cousin, arrived out of the blue from Russia. There are three of them, actually. My cousin and two friends. They had no money and nowhere to go, so naturally I had to take them in. In other circumstances I would have introduced you, but, as you saw, they are rather rigid in their religious views. Bringing an unescorted girl—correction, an unescorted, non-Jewish girl—into my living quarters would shock them beyond belief. So just for the time being . . . "

"You want me to stay away."

He looked at me with gratitude in his eyes. "I think it would be wiser. You know how I feel about all these antiquated traditions and customs, but they are newly arrived here. I can't spring too much on them, too soon."

"So how did you explain me away?" I asked icily. "The mad-woman from the floor below? Come to borrow a cup of sugar?"

He looked embarrassed now. "I said you were one of our union workers."

"I see." I turned away from him, feeling the flush rising in my cheeks.

He put his hands on my shoulders and tried to turn me back to face him. "Molly, I'm sorry. It was stupid of me. I just couldn't think of a way of introducing you without upsetting them."

"And upsetting me? That doesn't matter to you?"

"Of course it matters. I thought you'd understand."

"And is it always going to be like this, Jacob?" I asked coldly. "If we did get married, would I have to move out of the house any time your relatives came near? Or hide under the bed? Or have to live my life pretending to be one of your union workers?"

"Of course not. Everyone who has a chance to know you likes you. My parents like you."

"Your parents tolerate me."

Jacob sighed. "These things take time. When you have been raised in one culture and are suddenly thrust into another, with a completely different set of rules, it is not always easy to change. Me, I am a modern thinker. I am all for change. Many Jews are not." His grip on my shoulders tightened. "And forgive me. I haven't even asked you why you came to visit. Nothing's wrong, is it?"

"In your modern way of thinking is a young lady never allowed to visit her gentleman friend? Does she always have to wait for him to call upon her at his convenience?"

He laughed uneasily. "No. Of course not. On any other occasion I would have welcomed your presence."

"On any occasion unless one of your relatives or friends was visiting." I lifted his hands from my shoulders. "I'll leave you to your entertaining then, Jacob, and I'll see you when it is convenient to both of us."

I pushed past the old men who were still deep in earnest discussion on the front stoop.

"It's only for a little while, Molly. Just until I've found them a place of their own," he called after me.

I kept on walking. He didn't follow me. Anger was boiling inside me. I had first been attracted to Jacob because I saw him as a fellow free spirit. He was not bound by stupid rules of society. He wanted to change things for the better. Now it seemed he wasn't quite the free spirit I had thought him to be.

❧ Three ❧

I walked fast, pushing my way through the evening crowds along Rivington. As I came toward Broadway the street was completely blocked by a white wagon drawn by two horses. I drew level with it and saw the red cross on the side. An ambulance. You didn't see many of those on the Lower East Side. Most people here couldn't afford to be sick in a good hospital that cost money, and wouldn't want to go to a charity hospital, where they were liable to get even sicker. They stayed home and either got well or died. A couple of men in white uniforms were keeping the crowds back as a stretcher was carried out of the building.

"Another one," I heard someone saying. "That makes three on this street alone."

"What is it?" I asked.

The woman had a dark shawl draped over her head, in spite of the heat.

"Typhoid," she whispered as if saying it out loud would bring bad luck. "Dropping like flies, they are. They get taken off to the isolation hospital, but it's too late by then, isn't it? The damage is done."

Wailing came from the doorway as the stretcher was bundled into the back of the ambulance and the driver cracked his whip to clear the crowd blocking the street. They parted, suddenly silent, as if wanting to distance themselves as far as possible from the disease. I noticed some women had their shawls wrapped over their mouths now and others pulled the sheets up over the heads of their babies in their prams. I hurried toward more sanitary areas of the city, hoping, even though I was angry with him, that Jacob would be sensible enough to stay well away from those affected with typhoid.

Twilight was falling as I crossed Washington Square. The remains of a pink glow lit the sky behind the trees, and the air was sweet with the scent of jasmine growing in one of the flower beds. I didn't want to go home and face finding something in the larder to cook for three hungry mouths. The alternative was to visit my friends Augusta Walcott and Elena Goldfarb, usually known as Gus and Sid, across the street instead, which seemed like a much better idea. But I was halfway across the square when I heard shrieks of delight. I recognized those voices and turned around to see two bedraggled urchins, flicking each other with water from the fountain.

"Shamey, Bridie. Come here at once," I called, and they came, heads down and giving me sheepish smiles.

"What do you think you're doing, out this late, and running around in that state?" I demanded. When I saw them at close quarters, they looked even more disreputable. Their hair was plastered to their heads and their clothing was sodden.

"Holy Mother of God, what have you been doing to yourselves?" I demanded.

"Just playing in the fountain a little bit," Shamey said, not meeting my eye. "It was too hot."

"Do you take me for a complete idjeet?" I glared at them. "You've been swimming in that river again, haven't you?"

"Only just getting our toes wet," Shamey said.

"Getting your toes wet! Just take a look at the pair of you— soaked from head to toe. What did I tell you about swimming in the East River?"

"Aw, but Molly, it was hot today and our cousins do it all the time."

"I am not responsible for your cousins," I said. "And you know I don't like you visiting them. They're a bad influence. Come on. Home with you." I grabbed their wrists and marched them across the square to the street. "And you should have known better than to take your sister," I said to Shamey. "She doesn't even swim properly yet. She might have drowned."

"No, she wouldn't. We keep an eye on her. She just holds onto ropes and bobs from the dock anyway. She don't jump in or nothin'."

I sighed. In spite of all my efforts, Shamey was turning into a little New Yorker. We crossed Waverly and headed for Sixth Avenue.

"I don't jump in," Bridie said, looking up at me apologetically. "I just stay at the edge, honest, Molly."

"But I don't like you in that dirty water, sweetheart," I said, stroking back her plastered, wet hair. "God knows what is in that river."

"Sorry, Molly," Shamey muttered.

It was almost dark as we entered Patchin Place.

"I'm putting on hot water for a bath for the pair of you," I said. "And then it's bread and milk and straight to bed."

I bustled around, heating water and then filling the zinc bath for them. I was just heating up the milk when Seamus Senior came home.

"Sorry I've been out so long," he said, pausing to wipe his red, sweat-covered face with a dirty handkerchief. "I met some of the fellows I used to work with on the subway tunnel. They treated me to a couple of beers. They think it's shocking that I wasn't paid any compensation for getting myself buried alive. They say I should get myself a good lawyer and sue the bastards."

He was speaking with uncustomary belligerence and I thought it was probably the beer in him talking. That's often the way with us Irish. A couple of beers and we're ready to take on the world, single-handedly.

"Now where would you find the money for a lawyer?" I asked, wisely ignoring his use of a swear word in front of a lady. "You just put your energies into finding a job."

I realized as I said it that I was beginning to sound and act like a wife. I shut up instantly. Seamus still had a wife at home in Ireland, as far as we knew. And I wasn't about to volunteer to step into her shoes.

"I promised to stop in across the street," I said. "There's bread and milk for the little ones, and there's cheese in the larder if you're still hungry after all that beer."

Then I made my escape and rapped on the door of number nine. After a disappointing minute during which I thought they might be out, the door was thrown open and my friend Gus stood there in all her glory. She was wearing an emerald green silk kaftan with a matching band tied around her forehead and she held a cigarette in a long ebony holder in her free hand.

"Molly, my darling," she exclaimed. "What perfect timing. I sent Sid over to fetch you but you weren't home. Come in, come in, do."

I was half dragged inside.

"You'll never guess who is visiting and pining for you?" she asked.

I thought it wiser not to guess. You never knew who might be visiting Sid and Gus. She shoved me into the front parlor, which was brightly lit with candelabras to supplement the gas brackets.

"Here she is, I've found her," Gus announced in triumph. "You can stop sulking, Ryan."

I looked around me in delight. Lounging on the blue velvet sofa was my good friend Ryan O'Hare, wicked and fashionable Irish playwright. Next to him was another slim and lovely young man who gazed at me silently.

Ryan got to his feet. In deference to the hot weather he was wearing an embroidered cotton peasant shirt with frilly cuffs, opened down the front in comic opera fashion.

"Molly, my angel. I have been positively pining for you," he exclaimed in his smooth, well-bred tones. "How long has it been?"

"At least since last week, Ryan," I said, laughing as I accepted his peck on the cheek. "And I don't think you've missed me one bit." My gaze moved to his silent companion and Ryan laughed delightedly.

"Perspicacious as ever, my sweet. This is Juan. He's Spanish and speaks little English as yet. I'm educating him."

"I'll bet you are," Sid said dryly.

The dark young man continued to smile.

"Where on earth did you meet him, Ryan?" Gus asked.

"Waiter. Delmonico's. Thursday last." He patted my hand. "Juan. *Mi amiga* Molly."

Juan got to his feet and bowed. I nodded in return.

"So will you stay for dinner, Molly? We're entering a Chinese phase," Gus said. "Sid is experimenting with duck."

"I'd love to," I said. "I have just escaped from domesticity across the street."

"Very tiring. Ryan, pour Molly some ginger wine. It should be rice wine, but we couldn't find any," Sid said. "And excuse me if I have to return to my duck in the kitchen before it escapes from the pan."

"It's not still alive, is it?" I asked anxiously. One never knew with Sid and Gus.

Sid laughed. "Of course not, silly. But I'm frying it at an awfully high temperature. I should be watching it."

"I think I'd better come and help you, Sid," I said.

Ryan handed me the drink, then refused to let go of my other hand. "Hurry back to me, my sweet. You know I pine when you are gone," he said.

I laughed. "Ryan, you may not sound Irish but you know you're full of blarney. In fact you're just like other men."

"Don't say that, for pity's sake." He gave an exaggerated look of horror. "You strike daggers at my heart."

"Well, you are. Sweet and solicitous as anything when it suits them, and when it doesn't suit them, then we women don't exist."

"There speaks a voice of bitterness, Molly. Are you referring to Daniel the deceiver?" Sid paused and looked back from the doorway.

"No, to Jacob the spineless," I snapped.

"Jacob? Good, kind, sweet Jacob who could do no wrong? That one?" Gus asked innocently.

"The very same. I've changed my opinion of him." And I recounted the incident in Rivington Street. "I'm rapidly coming to the conclusion that men are an infernal nuisance," I concluded. "Life would progress more smoothly without them."

"Ah, but just think how boring it would be without us around to brighten your dull little lives," Ryan said, patting my hand.

Sid's gaze was suddenly riveted to the window. "Speak of the devil, Molly," she said.

"Don't tell me it's Jacob come to apologize!" I pulled back the curtain to look out.

"No, it's Daniel the deceiver, about to knock on your front door," Sid said delightedly. "Do you think he's finally given up his betrothed and a fortune for a chance at true love?"

"I hardly think so," I said. "I was with him only two hours ago and he was still betrothed then. Even the fastest automobile couldn't drive to Westchester County and back in that space of time. No, I rather fear he's come to deliver another lecture about the dangers of getting mixed up with gangs."

"Molly, don't tell me you've been doing foolish things again," Gus said as I stood fascinated at the window, torn between wanting to know why Daniel was visiting me and not wishing to confront him again.

"Not intentionally. I spotted a pickpocket and had him arrested, only he turned out to be a gang member with a rather violent nature."

"Trust you, Molly," Sid said, shaking her head. "Well, are you going to go over there to confront him or do you want us to hide you?"

"I suppose I'd better . . . ," I began.

"No need," Gus chimed in, joining us at the window. "Those sweet children of yours are directing him over here. Really, Molly, you must train them better in the art of lying."

I turned my back on their laughter as I went to intercept Daniel at the front door.

"If you have come to lecture me again—" I started as I opened the door before he could knock.

"I've come to invite you out to dinner with me," he said, recoiling from my unexpected attack.

"And you know very well what my answer to that will be. I'm not going anywhere with you until you are free and unencumbered. And since I don't think you've learned to fly since I saw you this afternoon—"

"This is strictly business." He cut me off before I could finish.

"Business? What possible business could you have with me?"

"I've a proposal to put to you." And that roguish smile crossed his lips. "A strictly business proposition. Now do you want to hear it or don't you?"

"I suppose I'd be a fool to turn down any legitimate business proposition," I replied frostily.

"Come on then." He reached out to take my arm. "I've a cab waiting on the street and reservations at eight."

"You were very sure that I'd come."

"I know you too well, Molly Murphy. I knew your curiosity would get the better of you."

"But I need to change my clothes if we're going out to dinner."

"You look just fine to me as you are. Say farewell to your friends and off we go."

He smiled as he escorted me to the waiting cab.

❧ Four ❧

S o what is this interesting proposition you are making to me?" I asked as the cab started off at a lively clip-clop.

Daniel gave an enigmatic smile. "All will be revealed later, "he said. "Tell me, are you really making a go of being a private investigator?"

"Why shouldn't I?" I replied, carefully skirting around an outright lie. "I've got a good brain, I'm observant and fearless. Why should I not succeed?"

Daniel nodded. "I'm impressed, Molly. When you first announced this madcap idea, I'd have said it was doomed to failure. I couldn't picture anyone entrusting a matter of great delicacy to a woman."

I chose for once to ignore the insult. "There are times when a woman is what's needed," I said. "No man could have gone undercover in the garment industry, as I did."

"You're right," he said, "which is one of the reasons I have an assignment I think will be right up your alley."

"You really do have a job for me?"

He laughed. "Why do you think I invited you out—to have my way with you?"

"That might have been interesting," I quipped before I reminded myself that this outing was strictly business.

"You're some girl, Molly Murphy." Daniel paused and eyed me

for a moment. "Any other lady would have blushed or fainted from shock." Then he wrenched his eyes away from me and went on. "All right. Let me ask you a question—what do you know about the Sorensen Sisters?"

"The who?"

"Sorensen Sisters—Misses Emily and Ella?"

"Never heard of them."

"Then you must be the only person in New York or the entire East Coast who hasn't," Daniel said. "They caused a sensation when they came on the scene a few years ago and they are still very much the darlings of society."

"What are they, actresses?"

Daniel smiled. "Who knows. Maybe they are. What they claim to be is spiritualists—they communicate with the dead. You must be aware that this city has experienced a real craze for spiritualism in the past few years and several spiritualists have made their fortunes through their ability to contact the dearly departed."

"How strange," I said. "In Ireland most families have at least one member who can talk to ghosts. It's considered quite normal."

Daniel laughed. "Unfortunately we Americans have lost that skill and yet apparently we have a collective longing to communicate with our dead. Hence the Sorensen Sisters. They used to hold mass séances in theaters and auditoriums. Now they have become so wealthy and famous that they only hold private affairs for the idle rich."

"And how does this concern me? Do you wish to contact a dearly departed?"

He leaned toward me and touched my hand. "I am sure they are frauds, Molly. My colleagues and I in the police force are convinced of it, but nobody has been able to catch them out. They are dashed good at what they do—the voices speaking as if from far away, the floating heads, the ectoplasm—"

"The what?"

"Ectoplasm," he said. "It's the vaporous, luminous substance that is supposed to emanate from a medium's body during a trance. I've seen it during one of their séances. It was quite impressive, curling around them all wispy and green."

"So why do you think they are frauds?" I asked.

"Because I don't believe in ectoplasm, it can't be possible to communicate with the dead, and because they have become so wealthy from taking in poor suckers."

"What exactly do you want me to do?"

"Expose them, of course."

The cab slowed as it was caught in the heavy theater traffic along Broadway. Bright lights flashed from marquees. The sidewalks were crowded with pedestrians.

I swallowed before I spoke. "And how do you think that I could expose them when the entire New York police force was apparently unable to?"

"For the very reason I just explained to you. They now only conduct their séances in private homes, where it should be easier to observe them at close quarters."

"And how do you propose I get myself invited to a private séance? Do you want me to enter a household as a maid?"

"As a guest, my dear," Daniel said.

I laughed. "Oh yes. I've a whole mantelshelf full of invitations from Vanderbilts and Astors."

"Don't worry. I'll arrange everything. You've heard of Senator Flynn, I take it?"

"I've read of him in the newspapers. He's supposed to be young and dashing, isn't he?"

"He looks a little like me," Daniel said, "though not quite as dashing."

"The conceit of the man!" I went to slap his hand, then remembered and withdrew at the last second.

Daniel peered out of the window. "Why aren't we moving? I declare the traffic in this city is becoming impossible. Has everyone in the world decided to attend the theater tonight?" He rapped with his cane against the roof of the cab. "Let us out here, cabby. It's quicker to walk."

"Very good, sir." The cabby jumped down and opened the door for us. Daniel stepped out first, then assisted me down the steps. The whole of Broadway was a seething mass of people, many of them finely dressed for the theater or restaurant. But at the edge of the curb beggars hovered, some selling things, some of them pitifully deformed and holding out twisted palms in desperation. I shuddered and averted my face. When I first arrived in this city, I could so easily have ended up as one of them. Had they come here with the same hopes and dreams?

Daniel finished paying the cabby and took my arm, steering me past toffs and beggars.

"So why were you telling me about Senator Flynn?" I asked.

"I have an assignment for you that involves him," he said. "Patience. All will be revealed when we reach the restaurant."

He guided me skillfully through the crowd until we came to a halt outside a discreet entrance flanked by potted palms. There was an awning over the door and the sign read MUSCHENHEIM'S ARENA. I was wondering what an Arena might be, since the only connection the word conjured up was gladiators and lions.

"Is this the restaurant?" I asked.

"This is it. One of the more fashionable establishments in the city."

"You didn't have to go to this trouble. An ordinary café would be enough for me."

"I want you to become accustomed to fine dining," Daniel said, "since you'll soon be dining at Senator Flynn's mansion on the Hudson."

"Senator Flynn's mansion?" I had to laugh. "And how do you propose to get me invited there?"

"You will be introduced as Senator Flynn's long-lost cousin from Ireland," he said.

"Buy a flower for the lady sir?" A half-starved-looking girl in pitiful rags blocked our way to the restaurant door, holding out a rose, her eyes pleading.

I thought I had noticed her among the beggars when we got

out of the cab and admired her tenacity at following us this far.

Daniel was about to brush her aside, then relented. "Oh, very well." He chose a rose for me and a buttonhole for himself and paid the girl. She didn't take her eyes off our faces for a second and was all thumbs as she fumbled over Daniel's coins.

"Oh, just keep the change." He brushed her aside impatiently. "Really, the poor thing is a half-wit."

"Maybe she doesn't get enough to eat," I said, glancing back at her. She was staring at us with a strange expression on her face.

Then the door was opened by a man in smart livery and we passed through. Inside was another world from the bustle and beggars of Broadway. It was a scene of comfort and elegance—white-clothed tables lit by tiny frilled lamps and the sparkle of glass and silver. An electric fan was turning in the ceiling, but it was still noticeably warm inside and Daniel requested a table by an open front window to catch what little breeze there was. He ordered what seemed to be a most extensive meal for us, then he was handed the wine list.

"A French champagne, I think," he said, handing it back without opening it. "Your best."

"So go on about Senator Flynn," I said, after the champagne had been brought, tasted and poured, and I had tried to give the waiter the impression that sitting in such establishments with a glass of French champagne in front of me was an everyday occurrence in my life. "I am intrigued. Has he something to do with the spiritualists you were telling me about?"

"You must be aware of the Senator's great tragedy?" Daniel asked. "I am sure it must have made the newspapers in Ireland. It was all the talk here for months."

I shook my head. "We had no money for newspapers, so I doubt that any news short of a French invasion would have reached County Mayo."

"It was about five years ago now," Daniel said. He paused, raising his glass to me. "Your very good health, Molly. Here's to success in all your ventures." We clinked glasses.

29

"Go on," I said, because any hint of intimacy was unnerving.

"Barney Flynn was running for the United States Senate for the first time. In the middle of his campaign his infant son was kidnapped."

"How terrible," I exclaimed. "The poor man. Was the child ever returned?"

Daniel shook his head. "No. It was most tragic. The ransom note announced that the child had been buried in a secret hiding place, somewhere on the Flynns' estate."

I gasped. "Buried alive?"

He nodded. "In a special chamber with a vent to provide oxygen. Barney Flynn gave instructions to hand over the money, no questions asked. Anything to get his son back. But he made the mistake of alerting the police. An overzealous policeman shot the kidnapper as he came to retrieve the ransom money."

"So they never found the hiding place of the child?"

"Never. They searched exhaustively with dogs, all over the estate, but the child was never found. The estate is huge, of course. Hundreds of acres of woodland and rocky mountainside."

"There was only one kidnapper then? He had no accomplice?"

"The police investigated thoroughly and no second kidnapper came to light, although it was suggested that the child's nurse might have been in on the plot. It was the Flynns' chauffeur, you see. And the child's nurse had been walking out with him."

"But she didn't know anything of where the child might have been buried?"

"She denied all knowledge of the entire scheme."

"How awful, Daniel. How very tragic for the Senator and his wife."

"Very." Daniel sighed. "Senator Flynn has thrown himself into his political work with extra vigor, but his poor wife has never really recovered from the shock."

"Did they have any more children?"

"A little girl, a year or so later, but the mother still grieves her lost son. She has recently turned to the Sorensen Sisters and has invited them to the house this summer, so that she can communicate with little Brendan."

"Ah." I looked at him over my champagne glass. "And you would like me to be there, as an observer."

"It's a perfect opportunity. I couldn't do it myself, as I am known to the Misses Sorensen, and to the Flynns. Splendid. Here comes the soup."

We broke off while we worked our way through a creamy oyster stew, then a salad, then a dish of smoked fish.

"Now how am I to pass as the Senator's cousin?" I asked in the pause before the main course was brought. "Surely he knows his own cousins?"

"Luckily for us," Daniel said, "the Senator comes from a very large Irish family. He was born over here, of course. His parents came over in the famine with nothing. Barney grew up in the worst slums of New York. Truly a self-made man. His fortune started when he hired a barge, sailed it up the coast to Maine and returned with it full of ice. He also played Tammany politics to perfection— going from ward boss to state Senate. And with Tammany's help he cornered the ice trade in the city.

"Now of course he's a millionaire. He married money, which didn't hurt either. But he has a reputation of being generous to any of his relatives who arrive from the old country."

"Yes, but surely such a shrewd man would do a little checking if I landed on his doorstep and claimed to be his long-lost cousin?"

"Of course he would, which is why your visit will be preceded with letters of introduction. I'll provide you with a complete family background and history. You must do your homework so that you don't make a slip. I have no doubt you can pull it off." Daniel toyed with his fork as a roast chicken was brought to the table and dismembered in front of us. It was accompanied by tiny new potatoes, pearl onions and peas. A generous portion was placed in front of me.

"Holy Mother. This is a feast," I exclaimed, before I remembered that I should be playing the successful lady detective for

Daniel—used to the good life. "And as a matter of interest, who will be paying my fee if I agree to accept the assignment?"

"The city, of course—just as the police pay for any undercover work."

"And you will be providing a retainer, if I take on the case?"

"Naturally. Fifty dollars up front, the rest when you return. A bonus if you succeed in exposing the sisters."

"It does sound very tempting." My mind went to that empty larder and next month's rent bill.

"Then be tempted for once. It's not often that I can tempt you these days."

His eyes met mine as he paused with a forkful of chicken just below his lips.

"This is a strictly business dinner, remember," I said.

Daniel grinned, that wicked, attractive grin. The first glass of champagne was going to my head. Champagne was still such a novelty to me that it had a strange and overpowering effect.

"Of course," Daniel said. "Strictly business."

I concentrated on attacking my chicken.

"This meal will seem like a light snack when you dine at the Flynns'," Daniel said, eyeing me with amusement. "They like to eat well, I seem to remember."

"Am I supposed to be used to such meals or am I a poor relation?"

"The relatives who stayed behind in Ireland are humble folk. But you shouldn't appear too much of a peasant, or Theresa Flynn won't take to you. It's important that you get along well with her, or she won't ask you to be present at her séances."

"Theresa—that's Barney Flynn's wife? Is she Irish also?"

"Yes, but her family came over to America before the Revolution. They own plantations in Virginia, so she was brought up as a spoiled Southern miss. One gathers that they weren't too thrilled about her marrying a peasant like Barney."

"So I have to become the bosom pal of Theresa. When is all this to start?"

"The Sorensen Sisters are invited to the mansion the second

week of June, after Barney comes home from Washington for the summer recess. If you arrive around the same date, that will give us sufficient time to collect all the information we need from Ireland, and write the necessary letters to secure you an invitation. I'm thinking also that the excitement of having the Sorensen Sisters in the house will subject you to less scrutiny."

"Very good," I said. The way I was feeling at this moment, bubbling with my third glass of champagne, I was ready to tackle anything. "And what should I do if I spot the sisters cheating?"

"I'll give you a telephone number where you can leave a message for me at all times. Call me right away. I'll come to the house myself."

That statement should not have made me absurdly glad, but it did.

"Would you believe it?" Daniel said. "We have got through a whole bottle of champagne. You're turning into quite a drinker, Molly Murphy."

"It was you who kept filling my glass," I said. "And you should know that it's having no effect on me whatsoever."

Daniel smiled. "I think maybe a little ice cream and a coffee will restore both of us to sobriety."

"I've never been known to turn down ice cream," I said.

The ice cream was delicious but it didn't do much to counteract the champagne. I still felt only vaguely tethered to earth as I floated out on Daniel's arm. I spied the flower girl, standing in the shadows beside the potted palm as Daniel hailed a cab. She was still staring at us and I wondered if she was recalling better times in her own life.

"A very satisfactory evening, Molly," Daniel said as he climbed into the cab beside me and slipped his arm around my shoulders.

"I really don't think that's proper, Captain Sullivan." I attempted to move away.

"Just to make sure you're not swung around too violently, Miss Murphy. I'll wager the dreary, earnest Mr. Singer doesn't take you out to dine at places like this."

"Let's not discuss my relationship with Mr. Singer," I said. "My personal life can be of no interest to you while you are engaged to someone else. We've been through this a thousand times, Daniel."

"It is of concern to me and you know how I feel about you," he said. "Dash it, Molly, you said yourself that you can't just shut off feelings for another person. You must still have feelings for me."

Without warning he took me in his arms and was kissing me with abandon. I knew I should tell him to stop, but the champagne had numbed my limbs. It had also dulled my willpower and I had always liked Daniel Sullivan's kisses.

"See, I knew it," he whispered as we broke apart at last. "You do still have feelings for me."

"What do you expect if you ply a girl with champagne." I attempted to recover the last of my dignity. "You don't play fair, Daniel. Stop the carriage. I'll get out and walk the rest of the way home."

He grabbed my hand as I reached up to attract the cabby's attention.

"You'll do no such thing. All right. I promise I'll behave myself for the rest of the journey. It's just too tempting, sitting here in the dark beside you. It's been too long since we've been alone together."

"And it won't be repeated in the near future. Next time you invite me for a business meal, I'll come in my own cab and I'll drink water."

"Think of tonight as good practice for Barney Flynn," Daniel said. "I understand he's something of a ladies' man himself."

"Surely not, with his wife present?"

Daniel just grunted.

"And you have no qualms about sending me into such a lion's den then?"

"If anyone can handle Barney Flynn, you can. And you are a cousin, after all."

The cab slowed and came to a halt. "I'd rather not take the horse up the alleyway, if you don't mind, sir," the cabby called down to us. "He don't like backing up."

34

"That's fine. I can easily walk the rest of the way," I said.

Daniel helped me down. "Allow me to escort you to your house."

"Probably better if you don't," I said. "You have a history of not taking no for an answer."

Daniel laughed. "Are you sure you're steady enough to walk on your own?"

"Quite steady. Not intoxicated at all. I'll look forward to your next instructions then, Captain Sullivan."

I started out and heard Daniel's laugh behind me as I teetered.

"It's these narrow heels on the cobbles," I said with cool dignity and made it safely down the rest of Patchin Place. He stood there watching me as I successfully negotiated my door key into the keyhole and let myself in.

"Good night, Daniel. Thank you for a lovely dinner," I called.

Thank heavens I hadn't let him accompany me. The way I was feeling at this moment I might well have weakened and let him come inside . . .

I put my purse down on the kitchen table. The lamp was still burning in the parlor and I saw the back of a head in our one armchair.

"You didn't have to wait up for me, Seamus," I began and then stared as the man rose to his feet.

"Jacob," I stammered. "What are you doing here?"

He came toward me. "I came to apologize for my behavior earlier this evening," he said in a voice that was frigidly polite. "I thought that the brusque manner in which I turned you away had upset you badly. However, I see now that I need not have worried. I obviously don't have the claim on your affections I had believed."

"I have just returned from a business meeting," I said.

"Really, Molly. I am not completely naive," he said. "Please don't lie to me."

"I'm not lying."

"You come home tipsy and in the company of your policeman friend and tell me you've been to a business meeting?"

"Believe it or not, it's true," I said. Part of me whispered that I

35

should smooth things over, but the champagne was all for a good fight. "I thought you were the one who promised not to put me in a cage. You loved my free spirit, I seem to remember."

"I didn't think your free spirit extended to midnight outings with other men."

"We are not engaged, Jacob."

"No, but I thought we had an understanding."

"We do. Although if you are going to question and mistrust me every time I leave my front door—"

"Surely I have a right to question and mistrust your assignations with other men?"

"No," I said. "You have no right at all. Either you trust me or you don't. I thought you were different, Jacob. I liked you because you respected my right to be an independent person. You didn't want to keep me wrapped in cotton, the way most men do. But in the end you are just like all the rest—devoted when it suits you, free-thinking when it suits you."

"If that's the way you feel . . ."

"I do." I held the door open for him. "I think you should leave now."

"Very well." He bowed stiffly. "Good evening, Miss Murphy."

With that he marched to the door. I experienced a strange mixture of sensations watching him go—indignation, guilt and maybe just a touch of relief. I wanted to get far, far away—away from Jacob and Daniel and all the complications in my life.

This assignment on the Hudson River could not start soon enough for me.

❧ Five ❧

When I woke in the morning, my eyelids heavy from those three glasses of champagne, I couldn't really believe that I had broken off my relationship with Jacob Singer. I had told myself that I never really intended to marry him, but I had become accustomed to relying on him and knowing that he was there. This assignment could not have come at a better moment.

I had barely finished sending the children off to school with a strict warning that they go nowhere near the East River or their cousins when there was a knock at the front door. If it was Jacob, come to demand an apology from me, he wasn't getting one. If he had come to smooth things over, I was still in no mood to talk to him. I opened the door, conscious at the last moment that I was still in my apron with my hair flying free around my shoulders.

It wasn't Jacob. Instead, a thin beggar woman stood there, her eyes somehow too large for her hollow face. 'I'm sorry to trouble you," she began, "but I have a favor to ask."

Beggars were a common sight in the city, but they didn't usually try their luck in the Village where most residents were immigrants or students or starving artists with no money to spare.

"I'm sorry," I said, "but I've a family here to feed and barely enough to keep body and soul together ourselves. I'll bring you out a cup of tea and a slice of bread, but other than that—"

"I haven't come to you for money," she said with dignity. "I think you can help me. When you stepped out of that cab and I heard you mention Senator Flynn's name last night . . ."

Then I remembered why she had looked vaguely familiar. The flower girl from outside the restaurant who had fumbled with the change.

"You sat at the open window," she went on. "I was able to overhear most of your conversation."

I eyed her warily, wondering what might be coming next. Had she found out that Daniel was engaged to another woman and wanted money to keep quiet about our assignation?

"It isn't polite to eavesdrop," I said. "And anyway, I don't see what interest our conversation could be to you."

"It was of great interest to me," she said. "In fact, it was like a miracle. Then, when I found out who you were and where you lived, I knew you must have been sent from heaven in answer to my prayers."

"I'm afraid I have no idea what you are talking about, Miss . . . ?"

"Lomax," she said. "Annie Lomax. You talked about the Flynn baby's kidnapping. You see, I was the child's nanny."

"Jesus, Mary and Joseph," I muttered. In spite of years of being a heathen and missing mass, my hand went toward my forehead to cross myself.

"I was not blamed at the hearing," she went on, as if a dam had broken and the pain and injustice of the past years was spilling out, "but I haven't been able to get another job since then. Everyone believed that I must have had something to do with it, you see, because the child was taken from his nursery in broad daylight, and because I was sweet on Bertie Morell. I've been reduced to begging on the streets and I don't think I'll make it through another winter. I've tried everything, miss, except I refused to consider prostitution, because I was raised to be God-fearing. Now I wouldn't have the chance to be a prostitute, even if I wanted to, the way I look."

"I'm very sorry for you," I said, "but I don't see what I can do."

She stared at me as if I was the simple one. "That man you were with, he's a top policeman, isn't he? And you're some kind of investigator. I want you to clear my name," she said. "Prove to them that I didn't do it."

I took a deep breath. "You'd better come inside."

I took her into the kitchen and seated her at the table with a cup of tea and some bread and jam. She must have been starving, but she ate like a lady, chewing each morsel daintily.

"You must be something of an investigator yourself, Miss Lomax," I said as she ate. "How did you manage to track me down?"

She looked up and smiled. "Oh, that wasn't too hard. I heard your gentleman friend give the address to the cabby when you came out of the restaurant."

I gave her a decent time to finish eating. "Now, Miss Lomax," I said, "I don't want to dash your hopes, but how do you think I can prove you innocent after all this time?"

"The police asked me lots of questions," she said, "but they never found anything I did wrong, except they said I was negligent for not checking on the boy more often. He always had a good long sleep after lunch and I'd have disturbed him if I kept opening his door to check on him, wouldn't I?"

I nodded. "But you were friendly with the chauffeur who kidnapped the child?"

"We stepped out together a few times. Bertie was a likable enough fellow. Good-looking, too. But I never imagined in my wildest dreams that he'd do anything like this. In fact, I still have trouble believing that he did it."

"But surely the police established that he was the kidnapper? They shot him when he went to collect the ransom money."

A tired smile crossed her face. "Oh, I can believe that Bertie would help himself to money that wasn't his, all right. I'm not denying he wasn't entirely straight. He liked gambling and he got himself involved in a few shady schemes in his life. If he had found out where a large sum of money was to be left for the taking, he might well have decided to help himself to some of it. But kidnapping little

Brendan? No, I can't believe it. He loved children. Little Brendan loved him. The prosecution said that was why the kidnapper had been able to take Brendan out of the house without a fuss—because Brendan was comfortable with him. Or because I was in on it too and I was the one who delivered the child to the kidnapper."

"Then if Bertie didn't do the kidnapping, who did?"

She shook her head. "I have no idea. That's what I want you to find out for me."

"It's been many years and the police investigated it thoroughly," I said. "They must have proved beyond doubt that Bertie carried it off alone."

"They proved it to their own satisfaction," she said. "The public was clamoring for justice. A dead body solved it very neatly for them, wouldn't you say?"

"So you believe that someone else was involved and let Bertie take the rap?"

She nodded. "If Bertie had thought up any scheme to extort money, it would never have involved putting a child in danger."

"And if anyone else had thought up the scheme and paid Bertie to help carry it out? What then?"

She thought for a moment, staring across my kitchen to where the sunlight came in dappled past the spindly ash tree in the back-yard. "I still don't think he'd have done anything that might risk little Brendan's life. He wasn't that kind, miss."

"Do you have any suspicions of your own as to who might have done it?"

She shook her head. "I've been over and over that day in my head. Mrs. Flynn had taken the train to New York for the day. The house was quiet. I put Brendan down for his nap as usual at one o'clock. I went to darn socks in my own room next door. When I checked on him at three, his crib was empty. He had just learned to climb out over the side, the little monkey that he was, so I went looking for him. But he wasn't anywhere to be found. I alerted the master, who was in the middle of a meeting in his study. He sum-moned all the servants and we searched everywhere—right down to the riverbank. Then that evening we found the ransom note at the front gate."

"If the child could climb out of his own crib and wander away, then anyone could have taken a chance and snatched him."

She shook her head violently. "He'd never have been able to wander off the estate by himself. It's a good half-mile to the gate, and that was kept locked and there's a gatekeeper at the lodge. It's always possible that the kidnapper came by river, I suppose. There are places along the shoreline where a small boat could land without being observed, but"—she paused as if weighing the options, then shook her head again—"it was broad daylight. There are lawns around the house, and there's never a time you don't run into a servant or a gardener. And how would the kidnapper know that little Brendan would choose that very moment to climb out of his crib?"

I had to agree with her. If I were going to kidnap a child, I'd hardly have chosen broad daylight in the middle of the afternoon at the child's own home, unless I were very sure of myself—which precluded, in my mind, an outsider.

I extracted my notepad and pencil from a drawer in the kitchen dresser.

"So who was in the house at the time?" I asked.

She frowned in concentration. "The Senator, of course, and Mr. Rimes."

"Mr. Rimes? Who's he?"

"The master's good friend and adviser. He started off by running Mr. Flynn's first campaign, for the State Senate, and then he was asked to stay on and keep giving advice when Mr. Flynn went to Washington. The master thought a lot of him. Can't say that I did. He was rather rude and blustering for my taste. Not from the top drawer, if you get my meaning."

"So they were in Mr. Flynn's study together, is that right?"

"And both talking away nineteen to the dozen, if I know them. Both liked the sound of their own voices."

"So they wouldn't have heard anything."

She nodded agreement.

41

"Who else?"

"Oh, the Senator's secretary would have been with them, taking notes."

"And her name?"

"The secretary was a he," she said. "A cold fish by the name of O'Mara. Desmond O'Mara."

I scribbled it down, then looked up expectantly

"That's all," she said. "Like I said, the mistress had gone to town shopping, which meant that her cousin would have gone with her. This cousin, a spinster older lady called Miss Tompkins, lived with them, as a kind of companion for Mrs. Flynn. Mrs. Flynn took her everywhere with her."

"So no one else was in the house that afternoon except for the master in his study with his cronies?"

"That's correct," she said. "Except for the servants, of course."

I was interested that she had hardly thought the servants worth mentioning, even though she had been one herself.

"And how many of them would there have been?"

She pushed her hair back from her face, resting her fingers on a grubby forehead. "Let me see—the butler, of course—Mr. Soames. English. Very proper. Then there was a footman and the master's valet, and the mistress's lady's maid, then just housemaids and parlor maids and cook and the scullery maid."

"What about their names and anything you can tell me about them?"

"No point," she said. "After the kidnapping, the mistress dismissed everyone. She said she'd never be able to trust them again, so they went. They'd all be new now."

"But did you suspect any of them at the time?"

"There was one gardener, called Adam. A local man employed for the summer. I never liked the look of him—" She dared to look up expectantly. "Does this mean you're going to do it? You'll try and prove my innocence?"

"I'm going to be there anyway," I said. "What harm can it do to ask a few questions?"

Her face lit up and I saw that she might have once been a very handsome young woman. "I've nothing to pay you with," she said. "Of course, you can see that, can't you? But you'll have my devotion and gratitude to my dying day if you can show them I had nothing to do with it. You'll have given me back my life."

"I really can't promise anything, so please don't get your hopes up too high," I said cautiously.

"If anyone can do it, I know you can." She was still beaming at me as if I was some kind of celestial being, which made me uncomfortable. "You've got that look about you."

"Where do you come from, Miss Lomax?" I asked.

"New York, miss. I was born in Yonkers."

"To Irish parents?"

She shook her head. "No, miss. Scottish Presbyterians."

I grinned. "Then for somebody without Irish blood, you've a good command of blarney."

She looked puzzled. I reached across and patted her hand. "No matter," I said. "But I will try my best for you."

She drained the last of her mug of tea, then got to her feet. My conscience was wrestling with me. Could I, should I just let her go back onto the streets?

"Thank you again, with all my heart," she said and opened the front door.

"Just a minute, Miss Lomax," I called after her. "How will I know where to find you if I have news? Do you have somewhere to stay?"

"You'll find me on my patch of Broadway, miss. Right where you got out of the cab is where I sell my flowers every evening."

"But where do you live? Do you sleep on the streets?"

"Oh no, miss. A group of us girls shares a room down by the docks, in an alley off Water Street. Not exactly what you'd call a respectable neighborhood. I wouldn't want you contacting me there." She looked up shyly. "I'll stop by your house from time to time, with your permission?"

The struggle with my conscience was still going on. I could take her in here, couldn't I? I'd be gone to the Flynns' mansion and she could maybe help look after the little ones. I knew it was a risk. She could, after all, be a complete crook. She could bring gangster cronies to take over my house. "Look, Annie," I began. "May I call you Annie?"

She grinned. "A darned sight better than what most people call me these days."

"Annie—I'll be gone to Senator Flynn's house in a while. You could stay here—"

She shook her head violently. "Oh no, miss. That wouldn't be right. You don't even know me, and besides, this fellow who supplies us with the flowers and lets us sleep in the room, he wouldn't take kindly to me sleeping somewhere else. He likes to keep us where he can see us, in case we do a bunk with more than our share of the profits. You're already doing more than enough for me. And if you can clear my name—well, I'll just tell that fellow what he can do with his flowers, right?"

And she laughed.

I watched her walk down Patchin Place with a lump in my throat. Why had I agreed to do something that might be beyond my capabilities? And of course I knew the answer. Because that pitiful figure might have been me. I too had arrived in New York with nothing but the clothes on my back. I too had faced starvation and it was only by luck that I was not selling flowers or worse on the streets of the city. I'd had more than my share of luck. Maybe it was Annie Lomax's turn.

❧ Six ❧

A s the train pulled out of Grand Central Terminal with much huffing and puffing on a sticky June afternoon, I rested my head against the velveteen upholstery and heaved a sigh of relief. I was finally on my way!

It had been an emotional scene as I left Patchin Place, with Bridie clinging to my skirt and Seamus gruff and teary-eyed as if I was setting out for the North Pole and not the Hudson.

"You will come back, won't you, Molly?" Bridie had asked. "You won't forget about us?"

"I'll be away for a week or two, you goose," I said, laughing as I ruffled her hair. "Who knows, in that time your father might have found a fine new job and have taken you all to live on Park Avenue." I glanced at Shamey, who held a half-eaten piece of bread and dripping in one hand. "But in the meantime, I've left a stocked larder for you and a little money for emergencies." Thanks to the retainer, I thought, as I prized Bridie's hands from my skirt. "And no swimming in the East River, remember?"

I had been itching to get going for three long weeks. I never was good at waiting. I had always been the one who stayed up on Christmas Eve to peek in my stocking the moment my mother had hung it at the foot of my bed, even though I knew it wasn't likely to contain much more than a sugar mouse and an orange wrapped in silver paper. I had found the waiting for this assignment particularly trying, for several reasons. First, because the city was engulfed in a most unpleasant heat wave and a rising typhoid epidemic, making a mansion on the Hudson River sound most appealing. And second, because I wanted to put enough distance between myself and Jacob. I had received a most polite letter from him, apologizing for acting hastily and asking for a chance to make things right between us. I sent an equally polite reply, indicating that I'd be out of the city for a while with plenty of opportunity to think over what I wanted for my future and whether it might include Jacob Singer.

Oh, and then there was the little matter of the Hudson Dusters. I had heard rumors that a certain notorious gang member, whom I had caused to be arrested for pickpocketing, had been inquiring about me.

I had found this out when I returned to Mr. Giacomini's store to buy groceries a few days later. When he saw me, he shook his head.

"That man was here again," he muttered in a voice so low that I could barely catch the words, "asking about you." He looked around the store as if a spy might have been lurking in a dark corner. "Of course I tell him I have no idea who you are. I never saw you before in my life."

"Thank you, Mr. Giacomini. I'm grateful, but I'm sure you're worrying for nothing."

He shook his head violently. "No, you don't understand, Signorina. He's a bad man. His kind make the Black Hand look like pussycats."

"The Black Hand?" I had never heard the term before.

Again he glanced around the store before whispering, "Italian gangsters. They collect protection money from businesses. If you don't pay up, something bad happens—business on fire, legs broken, child kidnapped, wife killed. Very bad. But this man, he's also a gangster. So please, Signorina, for your own sake, do your shopping somewhere far away from here, okay?"

I could tell that his concern was as much for himself and his business as it was for my safety, so I smiled and thanked him, even though it went against my principles to be scared off in this fashion. But it was another good reason to be out of the city.

The days seemed to drag on while Daniel wrote letters to Ireland and I finally received my invitation from dear Cousin Barney Flynn. During that time I tried to lie low, did my shopping, as instructed, over on the East Side, where at least I knew another gang held sway, and read about the Flynn baby kidnapping in back issues of *The New York Times*. I didn't learn much that I didn't already know. The paper, like the police, had decided that Albert Morell acted alone. But in one paper I saw a photograph of Annie Lomax. She had round cheeks and a fine plait of dark hair over her shoulder—not at all like the skinny wretch who had sat at my kitchen table.

When the day finally came that I could pack my clothes and head for the station, I could hardly wait for the arrival of the cab. I was finally about to fly away from my responsibilities for unemployed Seamus and his two wild children, away from the male complications in my life, and toward earning an honest penny again.

Of course I have to admit I was just a little anxious about what lay ahead of me. I'd been told often enough by my mother and folks at home in Ballykillin that I had the cheek of the devil and ideas above my station. I was about to put both to the test. I had to pose as Molly Gaffney, from Limerick, cousin of Senator Flynn. Fortunately for me, it turned out that the Senator did have a second cousin Molly, of about the right age, among the hundred and something relatives still living in the old country. It was a relief that I could answer to my own name. There was a risk, however, given the Senator's generosity toward his many Irish relatives, that someone would show up on the doorstep who knew the real Molly and I would be unmasked. Hopefully this time I wouldn't find myself in any personal danger when I explained my assignment—unless the Sorensen Sisters set their spirits on me!

Then, on that hot June afternoon, I was finally on my way. Nobody had come to the depot to see me off.

"You'll understand if I don't accompany you to the train station, won't you?" Daniel had said when he came to deliver final instructions the night before. "One never knows who might be traveling by train and it wouldn't do for us to be seen together."

I assumed this meant that he didn't want word to reach the ears of Arabella Norton, who lived out in Westchester County and thus might have friends traveling from this very station.

"Thus speaks the brave and fearless Daniel Sullivan who assures me his fiancée grows tired of him," I said, giving him my most withering stare.

He smiled. "That wasn't what I meant at all. It was your upcoming assignment that concerned me. If you are supposed to be the cousin newly arrived from Ireland, then there would be no reason why you should be accompanied by a New York policeman, especially one who is known to the Flynns and their neighbors."

"Oh," I said, and was annoyed at myself that I had exposed feminine weakness. "You're absolutely right, of course," I added for good measure.

"You'll be all right, won't you?" Daniel asked. "Able to manage your own luggage and all that?"

"Do I look like a weakling?" I asked. "Don't worry. I won't disgrace you by trying to carry my own luggage. I'll find a porter to manage my valise."

I glanced up at the valise now sitting comfortably on the rack above my head. Had I only been carrying my own possessions they would have fitted inside the hatbox; however, Gus had been her usual generous self and loaned me some delicious dresses suitable for a stay at a country house, as well as the valise in which to transport them.

When I protested that I couldn't take anything so fine, and would probably wreck them, she laughed. "Molly, my sweet. You know I'll never wear dresses like that again in my present style of living. They belonged to a time when I was still Augusta Mary Walcott, of the Boston Walcotts, and thus expected to marry well. I fear they are a trifle old-fashioned as they've been hanging in a closet for the past three years."

"They're lovely," I said, fingering the silk of the ball gown. "I've never worn anything so fine in my whole life. But maybe they are a trifle too lovely for a simple girl newly arrived from Ireland?"

"Then say they were lent to you by a well-meaning friend of good family, and that's the truth," Gus said. "The fewer lies you have to tell, the better, I've always found."

I had to agree with her on that point. I was going to have to keep my wits about me every moment I was at Adare, which was the name of the Flynns' mansion and also the name of the village in Ireland that Barney Flynn's parents had come from. It was fifteen miles outside of Limerick, where his cousin Molly, and about a hundred other cousins, still lived. I had never been to Limerick in my life, but I had done my homework well, reading the guidebooks that Daniel had brought for me and studying picture postcards until I felt I could give a pretty convincing tour of that part of Ireland.

The train picked up steam as we came out into the open, hurtling along between tall brick buildings that shut out the sunlight and prevented the smoke from escaping. It was stiflingly hot and stuffy in the carriage. I looked longingly at the closed window, but I couldn't risk getting a face full of soot. When the railway left the confines of the city behind, then I'd open the window. At present I was in the carriage alone, which was a blessing as I wanted to collect my thoughts. I opened my notebook and studied the family tree one more time. It was so broad and convoluted that I surely wouldn't be expected to know it all.

Then I opened and reread the letter from Senator Flynn. He welcomed me to stay at his home. He hoped I'd be like a breath of good Irish air and a tonic for poor Theresa, who hadn't been too well lately. It was only when I studied the signature at the bottom that I realized it hadn't been written by him at all, but by D. O'-Mara, secretary to Senator Flynn. So at least the odious secretary was one person who had remained in the household—one person I could pump for information.

To tell the truth, I was feeling more and more reluctant about taking on Annie Lomax's assignment. I should have liked to view the police files on the case, but I couldn't risk making Daniel suspicious about my intentions. If he knew I was going to be delving into a past crime, he'd have withdrawn his commission immediately. Poor Daniel—I must say he tries valiantly to keep me away from trouble.

"So what should I know about this kidnapping?" I asked innocently as he was going through one of his briefings.

"Nothing more than was in the papers," he said. "The chauffeur was shot on his way to pick up the ransom money. The child was never found. It was the most awful tragedy and I presume they'll be trying to shut it from their minds, apart from Mrs. Flynn and her séances, of course."

"So this chauffeur must have been a really wicked fellow," I said. "No conscience at all."

"Absolutely," Daniel agreed.

"You don't think he was in the pay of someone else then?"

Daniel raised an eyebrow. "What are you hinting at?"

"Just that it seems rather a dashing and ambitious crime for a humble chauffeur to carry off alone. I was wondering if he had been paid to take the child and to collect the money while the real villain lurked in the background—and has wisely kept quiet ever since."

Daniel shook his head violently, making those unruly curls dance. "Oh no, Molly Murphy. No! Absolutely no! I can read your mind like a book and you are not going to poke your nose into this. Trust me—the police carried out a most extensive investigation and came up with nothing, apart from the chauffeur. So put it from your mind and don't think of it again—and that's an order."

"Yes, Daniel." I lowered my eyes and attempted a good imitation of a simpering female.

The train rumbled over a bridge and we were off the island of Manhattan. On my left the river opened up with tall brown cliffs along the far shore. The river presented such a lively scene full of craft of all sizes, ranging from humble rowboats to barges laden with timber and granite and bricks to bright-painted side-wheeler paddle steamers looking most jaunty with flags flying. I had been given the choice between making the trip by steamer or train, but opted for the quicker journey. I didn't want too much time to sit and brood about what I had let myself in for and what might go wrong.

Not for the first time I wondered why I hadn't found respectable employment for myself instead of trying to establish myself in a man's profession, and a dangerous one at that. At this very moment I could have been selling ladies' hats, or serving tea and cakes in a genteel coffeehouse, safe and secure instead of never knowing what might happen tomorrow. Letting my thoughts wander like this and swaying to the rhythmic motion of the train reminded me of the occasion, a little over a year ago, when I had been forced to flee by train from a life of boredom, drudgery and unchanging certainty in Ireland. I had killed a man by accident, in circumstances that I won't go into now, but suffice it to say that it was a case of flee or be hanged. I had chosen the former. I had lived with my heart in my mouth ever since, but at least I had never been bored. Thus satisfied, I looked out of the window and enjoyed the view.

We stopped at neat little pastel-painted towns along the way. People got into my compartment and disembarked again further up the line. The river had opened into a wide, tranquil lake bordered by green meadows and willow trees. I caught glimpses of fine houses set in parkland and wondered if Adare would be as grand. Then we pulled up beside a great granite building. The sign on the station said OSSINING. I looked out of the window with interest.

"What is that, an army post?" I asked the two women who now sat opposite me.

They shook their heads and made clucking noises. "Dear me no. That's Sing Sing, the prison. They've got the most desperate criminals in the state locked up in there."

"I've a sister who lives in this very town," the other confided. "I tell her I don't know how she sleeps sound in her bed at night, knowing what depraved creatures are on her doorstep."

More clucking noises and shaking of heads. I studied the prison with interest as the train pulled out of the station, but could see nothing beyond the high wall. It didn't seem likely that any of the depraved creatures would find a way to escape from that formidable institution.

Soon the river narrowed again. Tall mountains loomed on either side as the river raced through its granite pathway. It was a scene right out of an Italian Romantic painting, complete with cliffs, rapids and valiant boatmen. I was so intrigued at watching little craft attempting to navigate upstream that I almost missed my station.

I was still gazing out of the window as we came to a halt. I leaped up as I heard the station master yelling: "Peekskill. All aboard," and had to make a great fuss to find a porter willing to lift down my valise. I suspect that I could have taken care of it myself, but was already into the part of helpless young girl newly arrived from Ireland.

"Where are you heading to then?" the man asked, depositing the case on the platform as the train steamed out. "Will you require the hack?"

I had no idea. I had written informing Senator Flynn the train I intended to take, but had received no reply. "I'm for Senator Flynn's residence: Adare," I said.

"Adare? That's on the other side of the river," he said, looking at me curiously, "and no bridge between here and Albany. I hope you're a good swimmer."

"Is there no ferry here?" I asked, wondering how I would contact a house on the other bank and how they planned to meet me.

"No public ferry. There's no real village on the other side. Just the few houses at Jones Point and then wilderness all the way to the military academy at West Point. Why the Senator chose to have a house over on that shore, miles from civilization, beats me. Are you expected at Adare?"

His expression indicated that I was probably a new maid. Why did nobody ever take me for a young lady of quality? I gave him my most haughty stare. "I'm the Senator's cousin, visiting from Ireland."

"Bless my soul." The man's look of embarrassment told me that I had exactly read his thoughts. "Well then, in that case, there should be someone to meet you. What's your name, miss?"

"Molly Murphy," I blurted out, then corrected myself immediately. "Molly Murphy Gaffney. Miss Gaffney." I felt my cheeks burning, furious with myself that I had failed the very first test. I surely wouldn't last long at this assignment if I couldn't remember my own name.

"Anyone from Adare here?" the man shouted. "I've a Miss Gaffney waiting to be picked up."

A small, wiry man with a shock of gray hair poking from under a cap came running up from the direction of the shore. "Hold your horses, I'm coming," he announced, then took off his cap to me. "Sorry to keep you waiting, miss. I got held up while a string of barges was coming past. Which is your luggage?" I pointed and he hoisted the valise onto one shoulder, while I carried the hatbox. "The skiff's this way, miss. If you'd be so good as to follow me."

I thanked the gentleman who had been watching over me and followed my valise down a rocky path to the shore. A small boat was tied up there and a second man, this one young and strapping, sprang to attention as we approached.

"You found her then, Tom. That's good," he said. "Here, miss. Ever been around boats before?"

I was just about to answer that I'd lived on the shore for most of my life when I remembered that I came from the city of Limerick and probably hadn't needed to go anywhere by boat. "Not really," I said.

"Take my hand then, miss, and try to step into the middle of the craft," the young man said and almost lifted me down. I was conscious of big, muscular arms and enormous strength.

"And your name is?"

"Adam, miss," he said. "Tom and I are gardeners at Adare, and also boatmen when the need arises."

Tom loaded in my bags, jumped down with an agility that I wouldn't have expected from his age, untied the rope and we drifted out into the stream. Immediately the current caught us and the two men had to strain on the oars, pulling strongly against the force of the current.

53

"So Adare is upstream from here, is it?" I asked.

"No, miss, not really," Adam said. "You can catch a glimpse of it through the trees on the other bank there. But with this current, if we don't start out heading upstream, we'd be back in the Tappan Zee before we knew what had hit us."

Adam, I thought, watching the burly one pull at the oar. Annie Lomax had mentioned a gardener called Adam. But she'd also said that all of the servants had been dismissed. Was this a new gardener with the same name, or had he somehow managed to escape the purge? I glanced at him with interest. If it were the same Adam, then Annie hadn't trusted him. I wondered now if that was because he was a sly individual or because of his way with women. He was certainly giving me the eye at this moment.

"So have you been with the Senator long?" I asked, addressing them both.

"Old Tom's been at Adare since before the Senator's time," Adam said. "The Senator bought the house about ten years ago, wouldn't you say, Tom?"

Tom nodded, grunting with the pull of the oars.

"And I came as apprentice about five years ago."

"Was that before the tragedy with the Senator's son?" I asked.

"A few months before," he said. So it was indeed the same man.

"That must have been so terrible for everyone at the house," I said. "His family in Ireland certainly felt it hard enough. My poor mother never stopped crying."

Adam nodded. "It was bad," he said. "A bad time. If you ask me they've never really gotten over it."

Tom glared at him. "You keep your mind on the rowing and forget about the gossiping. It was none of our business then and it still ain't now."

"You two must have been lucky or particularly good workers," I pressed on. "I heard that Cousin Flynn fired all his employees after the tragedy."

"Most of them, yes," Tom said. "But it just happened that Adam and I were away when it took place. I was laid up with pneumonia and Adam was visiting his sick mother, who lives on the other side of the river. So the master figured we could have had nothing to do with the crime and he kept us on."

I nodded. The western bank was fast approaching, but as yet I saw no sign of a house. A great hill rose up, clad in a shaggy coat of trees, with the occasional boulder showing through—as wild as anything I'd seen in Connemara at home.

"So from what we heard, it was the chauffeur did it?" I ventured as the two rowers negotiated us past a clump of swirling vegetation brought down from upstream. "He must have been a smart one to have planned something as cunning as that."

Adam looked up now. "Bertie? He never struck me as another Thomas Edison, nor as having an evil nature either. We often went for a pint at the tavern and—"

"Watch your oar, boy," old Tom snapped. "You'll run us aground and the little lady will be feeding the fishes."

They rowed in silence past some frightening-looking rocks. Then I looked up and gasped. The trees had parted. In front of me were green lawns and behind them a sprawling, gray stone house, rising three stories high amid the trees. It had a romantic look to it, with a round tower on the far right and painted shutters at the windows.

"Here we are," old Tom said, and took over both oars as Adam leaped nimbly onto a small wooden jetty. My bags were handed up, then Tom took me by the hand.

"You're a very curious young lady, by the sound of it," he said. "Let me give you a word of advice. It don't pay to ask too many questions around here."

Then he handed me up to Adam and I was ashore.

❧ Seven ❧

I had no time for thought as Adam picked up my bags and set off at a lively pace across the lawn. As I approached the house, I had a chance to study it more closely. I couldn't say I found Adare elegant. Solid. Imposing. Powerful—that was the word for it. The exterior was rough-cut granite. The style was definitely a mixture—a Southern type of veranda running along the side of the house that faced the river, but with that very Italian-looking round tower at the right, French shutters at the windows and a roof that looked more Dutch than anything. I wondered if the first owner had designed it himself and what had attracted Barney Flynn to buy it.

As we approached the veranda, I heard voices and noticed figures sitting in the shade at white-clothed tables. It was four o'clock. Obviously tea was being served. We came closer, unnoticed, until a servant tapped one of the women on the shoulder and pointed to me. Then all heads turned in our direction and a young woman rose to her feet.

"Molly, you're here at last," she exclaimed, coming to greet me with open arms. "We've been waiting impatiently all day. You must be exhausted, poor lamb. All that tiring travel. Do come and have a cup of tea before you drop."

"I've only come by train from New York today, not all the way from Ireland," I said, returning her smile. "And forgive me for asking, but you must be Cousin Theresa."

"How silly of me." She had a high, musical laugh. "In my excitement at seeing you, I completely forgot my manners." She held out her hand. "I am indeed Theresa. How do you do, Cousin. Welcome to Adare."

"You are most kind to ask me to stay," I said, taking her hand. It felt cold and so frail that I didn't dare squeeze it. She looked frail too, as if a breath of wind might blow her away. She had pale hair and her skin matched the whiteness of her summer gown. There were dark circles around her eyes and her collar bones stood up above a low-cut neck. But she had a sweet smile as she grasped at my hand.

"Another place please, Alice. And Clara, pour dear Cousin Molly some tea. She must be close to fainting in this heat."

"I assure you I'm just fine," I said.

Theresa patted my hand as I sat. "Would you listen to that accent?" she cooed. "Isn't it divine. Straight from the old country. Won't she do Barney's heart good?"

I looked around the group seated at table and gave what I hoped was a shy smile. A cup of tea was placed in front of me by a severe-looking older woman, clad in a high-necked dress of dark gray, in spite of the sticky heat of the afternoon.

"Please make the introductions, Thesesa," she said.

"Of course," Theresa Flynn said. "This is Molly Gaffney, Barney's cousin, newly arrived from Ireland. Molly, may I first present our other guests: Miss Emily Sorensen and Miss Ella Sorensen."

I screwed up my eyes to look from sun into shade and found myself observing the famous Sorensen Sisters in the flesh. The strange thing was that there was nothing unusual about them. They looked like two perfectly ordinary middle-aged women. Miss Emily was a trifle dumpy and Miss Ella on the bony side. They both wore their hair in an unflattering fashion of years ago, parted down the middle and rolled into large wings on either side. Their black dresses were unadorned and their faces calm and composed as they inclined their heads to me.

"Miss Sorensen. Miss Sorensen," I said. "I am pleased to meet you."

Theresa reached across and squeezed my hand again. "I must tell you all about them later when we are alone. They are so wonderful and we are so honored to have them here. You've heard of them, have you?"

"I believe I might have," I said. "Are you not the famous spiritualists?"

"We are." Miss Emily had a deep, masculine voice.

"Has news of their fame reached Ireland?" Theresa said delightedly.

"We are not at the ends of the earth, Cousin Theresa," I said, making her giggle again in a girlish way.

"The introductions, Theresa." The woman who had handed me a cup of tea tugged at Theresa's arm. "There are others present who need to be introduced before you chat with your new friends."

Theresa flushed. "Oh, of course. I'm sorry. Too much excitement after the normal reclusive nature of our lives here must have gone to my head like wine. Molly, this is my mother's cousin, Miss Clara Tompkins. She is kind enough to live with us and keep me company."

The older woman inclined her head without smiling, not taking her eyes off me for one second.

"And this is my sister Belinda Butler, making a fleeting visit to us on her way home from Europe."

The second woman was in direct contrast to the first. She was a pink-and-white gorgeous creature in a delightfully lacy creation with a cameo on a pink ribbon around her neck. She turned big blue eyes on me and gave me a sweet smile. "I'm pleased to make your acquaintance, Cousin Molly. What a delightfully quaint accent you have. Do all the people in Limerick sound like you?"

To be honest I hadn't a notion what the inhabitants of Limerick sounded like, never having spoken to one. "More or less," I said.

"How strange to think that Barney would have spoken like that if he'd been born there and not here," Belinda said. She fanned herself with a dainty carved ivory fan.

"A sandwich, Molly dear?" Theresa asked. "Or will you take an éclair? Cook is most gifted when it comes to pastries."

I opted for the sandwich, noting that the fast-melting chocolate on the éclair would no doubt wind up on my person or my dress. Even here in the deep shade of the veranda, the heat was oppressive.

"You've just returned from Europe, Miss Butler?" I asked Belinda. "Did you have a chance to visit my country?"

"I'm afraid not, Miss Gaffney. I was only away for a month and one only had time to visit the important places—you know, cities noted for their fine art and cultural heritage like Florence and Paris."

"We are not without a cultural heritage of our own in Ireland, you know," I said. "The castles and monasteries date back to the dawn of time."

She frowned, as if I was a sweet puppy that had unexpectedly bitten her. "I didn't mean to imply that the culture of your country was any less important, Miss Gaffney. Dear me, no. That was not my intention."

"I'm sure you didn't, Miss Butler." I smiled sweetly at her. "And given the chance, I would also have chosen Paris and Florence over Dublin any day."

Theresa laughed delightedly. "Isn't she a gem? She has Barney's wit, doesn't she? Molly—I may call you Molly, mayn't I?—I can't tell you what a joy it is to have you here. Life has been so awfully dreary and I haven't been well, you know. I have been so longing for a merry companion and now God has provided you in answer to my prayers."

"I trust you have not found my companionship too unutterably dreary these past years," Cousin Clara said in her prim little voice. "And if my presence is no longer required here, then maybe I should speak to your husband about returning to the bosom of the family in Virginia."

"Oh Clara, don't be so silly," Theresa said.

"So I'm silly now, as well as boring and dull. What a pathetic excuse for a woman," Clara said. She rose to her feet. "Maybe I should retire to my room until I am needed, since I only aggravate and bore."

Theresa grabbed her sleeve. "Clara, please sit down. Do. You're embarrassing my guests, and of course I am most grateful for your companionship. What would I have done without you in the bleak years of my despair? Have another éclair, do. You know how you love them."

She offered the plate and Cousin Clara took one, casting a black look in my direction.

"I shall not be staying long, Cousin Clara," I said, "and hope that my visit will not cause any disruption to the running of this household."

"How sweet you are, Molly." Theresa gave me her dazzling smile. "And I do hope that we can persuade you to stay for as long as you like. This house is on the wrong side of the river so we don't get as much company as I would like."

"Yes, it's certainly wild over here, isn't it?" I said. "Is there no settlement on this side of the river then?"

"There's a small hamlet about a mile down the road in one direction, and some farmhouses in the direction of the military academy, but there are only two great houses nearby—ourselves and our neighbors, the Van Gelders."

"You have neighbors?" I stared into the trees but saw no sign of another house.

"Riverside, the house is called. Van Gelders have lived there since the first settlements. Not exactly the friendliest of neighbors, since Mr. Van Gelder Senior was once Barney's political rival. But now they are no longer rivals, we are on social terms again. In fact, we are invited there to dinner tomorrow."

"I understand they have visitors from Europe," Clara said, looking quite animated for her. "Young men, Belinda."

"Clara, I am perfectly able to select my own beau, thank you," Belinda replied.

"Your dear mama has paid to send you all around Europe and

you've come back empty-handed," Clara said. "Not a count or a duke in sight."

Belinda laughed. "How quaint you are, Cousin. It was never my desire to marry into European aristocracy. A red-blooded American boy is all right for me."

"You sound as if you might have one in mind," Theresa said, glancing at her sister.

"As a matter of fact I do." Belinda gave a mischievous smile. "He doesn't know it yet, but he will."

"We mustn't bore Miss Emily and Miss Ella with our family gossip," Theresa said. "Where can Eileen have got to? I wanted them to meet her. Alice, run and tell Nurse that we are waiting to have the child brought down to us."

The servant curtseyed and went into the house.

"Your family is well, I trust, Miss Gaffney?" Cousin Clara asked.

"Very well, thank you."

"I believe your poor dear mother passed away recently?"

"Three years ago now, although it seems like yesterday," I said, lowering my eyes so that I looked suitably bereft. "And my father preceded her, and two little brothers from diptheria within weeks of each other." I paused. "So now I'm left with just the one brother and two sisters, both married."

"It's such a comfort to have a family though, isn't it?" Theresa said. "I know I'd never have survived these past years without the love and affection of my dear ones."

She looked up as we heard light steps on the marble flooring and a small girl emerged, holding onto the hand of a large, crisply starched nanny. Unlike Theresa, the child was dark-haired and had huge dark eyes, with which she looked around the company in alarm.

"Go to your mother, child." The nurse sent her across to us with a firm shove. "Give her a kiss."

The little girl moved slowly toward Theresa, who bent her cheek to receive a peck. "How are you today, Eileen?" Theresa asked.

"Very well thank you, Mama."

"And what have you been playing today?"

"With the doll's house that Papa bought me. Nursy made new bedclothes for the baby bed and she's going to knit a new shawl for the baby and . . ."

"We don't need to hear every detail, child. I'm glad you enjoy the doll's house. Now I want you to shake hands with our guests. These two ladies are both called Miss Sorensen."

Eileen was pushed across to them. She looked up seriously. "How do you know which one is which if you have the same name?" she asked, then looked confused at the titter of laughter.

"Eileen, that's not a polite way to greet people," Clara said. "You hold out your hand, drop your best curtsey, and say, 'Pleased to meet you.' Go on. Do it."

The little girl responded. Then she was directed to me.

"And this is Papa's cousin, all the way from Ireland," Theresa said. "Shake hands with Cousin Molly and give her a curtsey."

I took the little hand in mine. "Will you show me your doll's house later? I never had one of my own and I've always wanted to play with one."

Her eyes lit up. "Oh yes. I'd like that. Why didn't you have a doll's house? Were you very poor?"

"Eileen! Gracious, what will the child say next," Clara muttered.

"Don't scold her," I said. "It was a natural thing to ask." I squeezed her little hand and smiled at her. "I'm not as rich as you are, and doll's houses are a luxury. But I did have a favorite doll when I was growing up. Do you have a doll's pram? We could maybe take your dolls for a walk some day."

She was gazing up at me adoringly. I bent to kiss her little forehead. "We'll have some grand times together, won't we?"

She nodded and lingered hopefully at my knee.

"All right, Eileen. That's enough of you. Have you had tea in the nursery yet, Nurse?" Theresa's voice was sharp.

"Yes, ma'am. The child has already had a good tea."

"Then maybe just one cookie as a treat." Theresa reached across and handed a frosted ginger cookie to the child, who took it solemnly. "Off you go, then."

Eileen glanced back at me as she took her nurse's hand and they disappeared into the house.

"What a delightful little girl," I said. "I'm sure she gives you a lot of pleasure."

"Yes," Theresa said. "I'm sure she does."

But I got the feeling that the child gave Theresa no pleasure at all.

⚜ Eight ⚜

The child had only just gone and I was wondering whether it would be polite to take a second sandwich or a biscuit when masculine voices were heard from inside the house and three men appeared. I'd seen enough pictures to recognize my supposed cousin, Barney Flynn, but in the flesh he was even more imposing than his photographs. He was not very tall, but a well-built man, with a strong Irish cleft in his chin, a high complexion that indicated a life in the fresh air and a good head of red-brown hair on him. He was wearing a well-tailored light suit, although without an ascot at the neck. When he espied me, there was the proverbial Irish twinkle in his blue eyes and a smile that lit up his whole face.

"Well, would you look here. She's arrived!" he exclaimed in a voice that bore a trace of Irishness, even though I knew he had been born in New York. "My little cousin Molly, Cousin Rose's child. I'd have known you anywhere."

It was gratifying to know that I bore a family resemblance. I got to my feet. "I am indeed, sir, and I'm pleased to make your acquaintance."

"Would you listen to her talk," Barney said, turning to the two men with him. "Straight from the old country. Isn't she a delight?"

Barney grasped my hand and shook it firmly. "But let's have none of this formality. We're family here and you're as welcome as the

65

flowers in May to dear old Adare." He laughed at his own joke. "I hope you'll be happy here, and more to the point, I hope you can bring Theresa out of her doldrums."

"I'm sure she will," Theresa said. "I've already fallen in love with her completely, my dear. If all your cousins are this delightful, then I might decide to undertake a trip to Ireland some time."

"We live very simply compared to this," I said. "Not a great house among us."

"Wealth isn't everything, Molly," Theresa said. "Money does not buy happiness, as Barney and I know only too well."

"But I always say if you're going to be miserable anyway, it's better to be rich and miserable rather than poor and miserable." The man to Barney's right chuckled at his own wisdom. He had a loud, booming voice which matched his large person, his round, red face, piggy eyes and thinning sandy hair. Not the most attractive of men and probably somewhat older than Barney—although the latter had surprised me with the number of lines on his face. I had expected a young man, but his face was definitely careworn when he wasn't smiling. Who could blame him, having gone through what he had endured?

The large man came up to me and held out a beefy hand. "I'm Joseph Rimes, Miss Gaffney. Barney's adviser, strategist and right-hand man. I trust you'll enjoy your stay here."

"Thank you, Mr. Rimes. I hope so indeed." I nodded my head demurely, then glanced at the third member of the party. This had to be the pallid secretary Desmond O'Mara. Again not the most attractive of men. He had light hair, a pale face and the lightest of bulging eyes, giving the impression of a fish on a slab, and he wasn't regarding me with welcome in those codfish eyes.

Barney saw me looking at him. "Oh, and this is Desmond," he said, tossing him off with a wave of his hand. "My secretary."

"Miss Gaffney." The man inclined his head. I did likewise.

"So have you boys finished your hard work for the day?" Belinda asked.

66

"We came out for a breather," Barney said. "Have we missed Eileen?"

"Already made her appearance and gone again," Belinda said, smiling up at her brother-in-law in what might have been a rather flirtatious manner. I wondered if Theresa had noticed, then I suspected she had as she said, in a flat voice, "If you want tea, I think you'll find it stewed."

"No matter. I only wanted to see if our new guest had arrived and to say hello to my daughter," Barney said. "Was she in good form?"

"She says the most outlandishly funny things without meaning to," Belinda replied. "No sense of propriety at all."

"Definitely a chip off the old block, eh, Barney?" Rimes slapped him on the back.

Theresa frowned. "I'll ask Cook to brew another pot if you'd like." She rose to her feet.

Barney waved her aside. "Not necessary, my dear. I think we'll bring out the whiskey decanter instead, to celebrate a good day's work."

"I don't quite understand why you need to work in summer," Cousin Clara said. "Is the Senate not in recess until fall?"

"You understand correctly, Cousin Clara, but there is a small matter of an election next year," Joseph Rimes said. "Barney is up for reelection. The campaign strategy has to start now."

"But surely everyone loves Barney," Belinda said. "His reelection will be only a formality?"

"One hopes that will be true," Barney said. "But you never know with politics. This new fellow they're putting up against me—he's old money and will have the power of all those Vanwhosits backing him."

"And more charisma than the last opponent next door." Rimes nodded to his left.

"Watch what you're saying, Joe," Theresa scolded. "We still have them as neighbors, however our politics may differ."

"You think my voice is loud enough to carry that far?" Joseph Rimes asked, a grin on his large red face. "Or do they have spies, snooping in the shrubbery?"

This provoked general laughter.

"Aren't we supposed to be suffering through an evening with them some time soon?" Barney asked.

"We are dining there tomorrow night. I told you about it at breakfast. Honestly, Barney, you are hopeless. You never listen to a word I say." Theresa frowned again. "Tomorrow night, remember, so don't go making other plans or finding boring political people you just have to talk to." For a frail dove, she could be quite forceful if she wanted to, I noted.

"And you haven't forgotten about tonight, have you, Barney?" Theresa continued. "The séance? Miss Emily and Miss Ella are going to try and contact Brendan for us."

A spasm crossed Barney Flynn's affable face. "I'll leave that to you ladies, if you don't mind. If we're going to start chatting with the dead, there's a few fellows might want to come back and tell me what they think of me."

"It's no joking matter," Miss Emily said in her deep smooth voice, "but if you don't wish to get in touch with your little son, then that's entirely up to you."

Theresa reached out and grabbed Barney's hand. "Oh do come. Please do. You want to know that he's all right, don't you? You'd like to hear his voice again?"

"Of course I would, it's just . . ." He glanced across at the two women and left the rest of the sentence unsaid.

Miss Emily had risen to her feet and tapped her sister on the arm. "If you would please excuse us, Mrs. Flynn. We need to rest and prepare ourselves mentally if we are to contact the spirits tonight. The room must be set up to make the atmosphere conducive to their appearance."

Rigged up, more like it, I thought to myself and wondered if I might be able to spy on them. I also got to my feet.

"Would you also think it very rude of me if I went to lie down also? The rigors of the journey are just catching up with me."

"Of course, dear cousin." Theresa beckoned to the maid who stood in the doorway. "We are about to retire inside ourselves. You men are welcome to sit out here and be eaten alive by mosquitoes. Alice, please show Miss Gaffney to her room and bring her up some hot water. I trust her trunk has already gone up? Good." She smiled up at me. "We dine at seven-thirty, Molly. Nothing too formal. It is the country, after all, and then you are more than welcome to join us at the séance."

"I'd be delighted," I said, and departed with a polite bow.

"She's really quite civilized, isn't she?" I heard Belinda's clear voice floating after me. "Apparently all the Irish live don't in bogs."

"This way, miss," Alice said, hurrying me across the black and white marble-tiled entrance hall and up the wide main staircase. A stained glass window above the front door threw a rainbow of colors onto the dark carpeted stairs. At the second level a wood-paneled gallery ran around all four sides of the stairwell, with doors going off it. From inside one of these I heard a child singing in a sweet, clear voice. Little Eileen was relaxing after her teatime ordeal. Alice turned me to the left and headed around to the front part of the gallery. "The mistress thought you'd like to have the view," she said and opened a door at the end of the hallway.

It was a corner room with windows at the front and side of the house, giving me a view of the Hudson and the rocky hillside beyond the lawns. A writing desk sat in one window and the bed was placed to enjoy the best of the view. An electric fan turned lazily in the high ceiling. The room was delightfully cool. The scent of the flowering creeper climbing up the house, mingled with the smell of newly mown grass, drifted in through the open windows.

"Thank you. I shall love it here," I said, noting that my valise had already been unpacked and my dresses hung in the mahogany wardrobe. I was about to dismiss the maid when I remembered that I had a task to fulfill.

"So how long have you been with Senator and Mrs. Flynn, Alice?" I asked.

"About two years now, miss."

"Not very long, then. Are you fitting in well? Are the others making you welcome?" I gave her an encouraging smile. "It's not always easy fitting into a household, is it?"

"As a matter of fact it wasn't too hard," Alice said. "Most of the girls haven't been here much longer than I have. Mrs. Flynn doesn't seem to keep servants too long. I don't know why. She's been nice enough to me."

"I expect they all run off and get married," I said, giving her a knowing look that made her blush and giggle. "Any handsome male servants around?"

"Ooh, miss, you shouldn't talk that way. The mistress doesn't want us walking out with the male servants. We'd get dismissed on the spot."

"I suppose she doesn't want another Albert Morell on her hands," I said.

Alice put her hand up to her mouth to stifle a squeak of terror. "We don't mention him, miss. The devil himself, that man was, by all accounts. Cook says she knew he was up to no good when he helped himself to her meringues, after she'd made sure she'd done the right amount for a dinner party too."

"How disgusting," I said. "I wonder why Senator Flynn hired him in the first place if he was such a tricky character."

"I wouldn't know, miss. He had a way with automobiles, and with horses too, so they say."

"What else do they say about him?"

She looked around nervously. "I shouldn't be gossiping like this, miss. I'd get in terrible trouble if the mistress knew. Albert Morell was before my time, thank the good Lord. It's all over and past and they've put it behind them." She headed for the door as rapidly as possible. "Just ring the bell by the door when you're ready for your hot water," she said. "I'll have Cook stoke up the boiler to make sure it's nice and hot."

Then she curtseyed and was gone.

They obviously hadn't put it all behind them, I thought as I wandered the room, inspecting the furniture. If they had, there would be no need for tonight's séance.

I took off my hat, unbuckled my shoes, and flopped back onto the bed. Ring when I wanted hot water, indeed. I could easily adapt to this kind of life. Maybe I should just forget about earning a living and keep Theresa company all summer.

Oh to be sure, and I'd be likely to wind up in jail as an imposter, I reminded myself. I sat up and stared at my own face in the dressing table mirror, a face slightly worse the wear from travel with a smudge of soot on my nose and my hair blown by the river crossing. "You have a job to do," I said to the face, "or rather, two jobs. You'll need your wits about you, so no slacking off!"

I got up and rang for the hot water. When I had washed and attempted to tame my flyaway hair, I examined the dresses hanging in the wardrobe, wondering which might be suitable for a not too formal dinner. Gus had lent me one silk ball gown and a sea green formal taffeta dress that went well with my coloring and red hair. I tried it on and was pleased with the result. What a pity no eligible young men would be there to admire it. No men at all, apart from the overbearing Mr. Rimes and the fishy Mr. O'Mara. And, of course, the Senator, who was known to be one for the ladies. I wondered if my relationship would make me safe from his advances, and whether he behaved himself when his wife was present.

I could still hear the sound of voices floating up from the veranda. I managed to fasten the hooks on the back of my dress with much effort and difficulty. Clearly one needed a servant to get in and out of fashionable clothing, and also a corset too, I decided, as I tried to breathe in sufficiently to bring the waist together. Gus had also had the foresight to lend me one of those articles of torture.

"If a maid comes to dress you, Molly, she'll expect you to be wearing the correct undergarments."

I examined it again now, having no clue how one laced such a contraption. I had never worn a corset in my life and had sworn never to do so. In my present situation, however, it might prove to be a necessity. I wrapped it around me and wrestled with the hooks and laces.

Feeling very uncomfortable and unable to breathe, I stood in my doorway listening. No sounds came from inside the house. If they were all still on the veranda, this might be a good moment to snoop on the Misses Sorensen as they prepared for tonight's exhibition. I tiptoed down the stairs and began opening doors on the lower level. The first was a grand drawing room. The heavy red velvet drapes were drawn, but in the darkness I could make out the gilt mirrors and portraits on the walls and the plush sofas and armchairs, even a Greek bust or two on plinths. Behind it was a library, with tall mahogany bookcases covering the walls. Then came what must have been the master's study—a large desk with a round-backed leather chair at it and the smell of cigar smoke in the air.

"May I help you, miss?"

I spun around guiltily at the sound of the voice behind me. I hadn't heard anyone approaching. A distinguished-looking man in a frock coat was eyeing me with suspicion. He had sleek gray hair and a Roman nose that made him look like a bird of prey. I wondered if he was another relative or political adviser.

"I'm sorry," I said. "I was just trying to find my way around the house. I'm Senator Flynn's cousin Molly Gaffney, just arrived from Ireland. May I ask who you are?"

"I am Soames, the Senator's butler." He inclined his head in the barest hint of a bow.

"Soames? I believe I have heard my family mention you before," I said. "You have been with the Senator for quite a while, haven't you?"

"Ten years, miss."

"Then you were here before the tragedy," I blurted out before I had a chance to consider whether it was wise to do so. "We heard that Mrs. Flynn had replaced all her servants after it."

"Maybe I wasn't considered to be an ordinary servant, miss," Soames replied with such a withering look that I should have shriveled up on the spot. "Now what was it you were looking for?"

he went on, firmly closing the master's study door behind me.

"I understand there is to be a séance tonight. I am most excited, having never seen one before. I thought I might just take a peek at the room to see where it will be held."

"The spiritualist ladies have prepared the room and made it clear that they do not wish anyone to enter it," he said. "Now, may I escort you out to the mistress, who is still on the veranda?"

"No, thank you, Soames," I said. "I think I may go and write some letters home before dinner. There is a pretty writing desk in my room with a view of the river." I nodded gravely and felt his eyes watching me as I made my way back up the stairs. Clearly, snooping in this house was not going to be an easy matter.

❧ Nine ❧

I kept to my room until I heard the dinner gong. Sitting at that elegant little writing desk with its view down the Hudson, I jotted down my impressions so far.

Members of the household to be questioned about Albert Morell—Tom and Adam who had rowed me across. Of the two, Adam might be the more inclined to talk, if suitably encouraged with mild flirtation.

The same cook has apparently been working here since the time when Albert was employed. Ditto Soames the butler, although not likely to get anything out of him.

I wondered if Cousin Clara had been around in those days. Mr. Rimes and Desmond O'Mara had been working with Barney Flynn in his study on the afternoon of the kidnapping, but three men at work were not likely to notice a baby being carried past their window.

And then what? I asked myself. What was I hoping to get from any of these people? If they had had any suspicions, they would have shared them with the police years ago. If Bertie Morell hadn't been the kidnapper, then I would have to find out who was. And that was probably beyond my ability. The police had access to files and the right to question whomever they chose. I was just one very amateur investigator, staying at a private house. I rather feared that Annie Lomax had put too much faith in me.

But at least I would carry out my commission from Daniel. At the séance tonight I would be a keen observer.

I rose to my feet as I heard the gong echoing up from the tiled foyer and paused to examine my appearance in the glass. Not bad for someone who had been a resident of a peasant cottage in County Mayo until recently. I'd surely come a long way in the world. I smirked to myself and almost heard my mother's voice muttering that pride always comes before a fall.

The party was assembled in an oak-paneled room across the hall from the grand drawing room and master's study. It appeared to be a smaller sitting room, with several chairs and tables dotted around and a large marble fireplace, unlit at this time of year. A sideboard ran along one wall and apparently sherry was being served. I was about to slip in unnoticed when Soames stepped forward to usher me in.

"Miss Gaffney," he announced in sonorous tones, making everyone stop and look up at me.

I felt myself blushing, which is always unfortunate for one with such pale skin as mine. Theresa was seated in a dainty Chippendale-style chair. She held out her hand to me.

"Molly, my dear. We'd been wondering where you'd disappeared to. Barney wanted to send for you, but I didn't want you disturbed in case you were sleeping. Did you manage to take a nap?"

"I'm well rested now, thank you, Cousin Theresa," I said, taking the hand she held out to me. It was still very cold.

"How pretty you look," she said. "Don't you think she looks delightfully pretty, Belinda?"

The latter cast a critical eye over me. "I'm sure she does," Belinda said. "Are the leg of mutton sleeves still in fashion in Ireland? I suppose it does take a while for new fashions to travel so far."

I managed to keep my sweet smile. "Well, you know, in Ireland we're only allowed to change our fashions with the blessing of the Pope," I said. "And we don't like to disturb his praying too often."

The rest of the company laughed. "You've met your match there, Belinda," Barney said, eyeing me from across the room, where he stood with Rimes at the drinks table. The fishy Mr. O'Mara was not in evidence. Maybe he had to dine with the servants.

Belinda's sweet smile wavered for a moment, but I said hastily, "In truth, Miss Butler, I possessed no such fine clothes in Ireland. These have been loaned to me by a kind friend in New York so that I shouldn't disgrace myself at this great house."

"As if you could disgrace yourself, Molly," Theresa said. "Your youth and vitality are like a breath of fresh air. I suppose it is all that good Irish fresh air that does wonders for the complexion."

"That Irish fresh air is more like a gale, half the time." I smiled at her. "Especially if the wind comes right off the Atlantic Ocean."

"Oh, is Limerick on the ocean?" Theresa asked. "I always imagined . . . ."

"No, it's well inland," I said rapidly. "But the wind sweeps up the river from the ocean and we get our fair share of gales."

Barney came over with a glass of sherry in his hand. "Here you are, Molly. You'll need this if you're going to face the séance afterward."

I took it gratefully, glad to be occupied with sipping sherry rather than putting my foot in my mouth every time I opened it.

"Don't frighten her, Barney." Theresa frowned at him. "I'm sure the séance will be a wonderful experience for all of us."

"So where have your two voodoo ladies got to then?" Barney asked.

"Behave yourself." Theresa frowned again. "They have been preparing themselves." She glanced up. "Ah. Here they come now."

All conversation broke off as the Misses Sorensen came into the room. They were still dressed head to toe in black, but the dresses were now silk and Miss Ella wore a pleated silk turban. Apart from that, neither wore any other adornment and their faces looked deathly white against all that blackness.

"Miss Emily, Miss Ella. Do come in. I hope you feel up to joining us for dinner before the séance," Theresa said.

"One has to eat occasionally," Miss Emily said in her deep

voice. "It is important to keep the body in good condition if one is to be open to the spirits."

"How fascinating," Cousin Clara said. "So tell me, can you call up spirits at will?"

"Certainly not." Miss Ella had a sharper, higher voice. "My sister merely makes herself the vessel through which messages are received from the other side. It would be most presumptuous to think our role is anything more than that."

"It is Chief Ojuweca who does all the work," Miss Emily said, accepting the sherry glass from the butler's tray. "Our spirit guide, you know."

"How simply marvelous, isn't it, Theresa?" Clara said, beaming at Theresa. "They have a real spirit guide. Is he a Red Indian?"

"An Indian chief," Miss Ella said, looking smug. "We were most fortunate that he chose us, of all people."

I pressed my lips together and tried not to smile. It was almost as if they were discussing servants or even patrons.

"So we don't actually know whether your Indian chief will be able to get in touch with Brendan then?" Theresa asked in a quavering voice.

Miss Emily shook her head. "My dear, we cannot command the spirits. Those who wish to make contact, do so. But we shall keep trying until we do find your son for you. I am most hopeful."

Theresa let out a sigh. "Oh, I'm so glad. Thank you so much for coming. If only I can talk to him again, just once . . ."

Barney went over to her and put a hand on her shoulder. "Don't hope for too much, my dear. I don't want you hurt again."

"Senator Flynn has little faith in our abilities, I can see," Miss Ella said in her sharp voice. "It may be better if he doesn't attend tonight. The spirits can tell when they are not welcome. Some of them are very shy, you know."

"Don't worry, ladies. I have no intention of coming," Barney Flynn said. "Theresa can do the talking for both of us."

"I do wish you'd try to believe, Barney," Theresa said. "It would be so wonderful. I'm sure it would make you feel better too."

Barney shook his head. "How's dinner coming along, Soames?" he asked. "Shouldn't the second gong have rung by now?"

"I'll go and see, sir." Soames bowed and retreated gracefully. A few minutes later he returned to say that dinner was served. Barney took Theresa's arm to escort her down the hall and into the dining room. Mr. Rimes latched onto Belinda, who didn't look at all pleased. The rest of us followed, myself and Cousin Clara bringing up the rear. The long, polished table sparkled with chandeliers and silver and crystal. I was glad that Daniel had warned me about the size and extent of the meals or I might have eaten too much of the first courses and been completely full by the time the roast pork arrived. Each course was more delicious than the last. There were things I had never eaten before. I nearly put my foot in it again when I read the words "Seafood Mousse" on the gold-framed menu in my place and wondered if the next thing on my plate might be a mouse stuffed with shrimp!

Then there was wine to accompany the food—a different kind with each course. Remembering how tipsy I had been after Daniel's champagne and that I needed my wits about me, I took only modest sips.

"Drink up, Molly. Drink up. It will do you good," Barney exhorted from the head of the table. I noticed he was following his own instructions well. His face had definitely become flushed and his eyes wild.

"I'm not yet used to wine, Cousin Barney," I protested, "but it's very good. I'm sure I could develop quite a taste for it if I'm not careful."

"A very dangerous thing, wine," Miss Emily said. "It lowers the inhibitions and clouds the judgment. We never touch a drop."

I did note, however, that both Misses Sorensen ate most heartily and cleaned their plates at every course. And apparently sherry wasn't considered wine in their definition, as they had each drunk a couple of glasses.

At last the savory plates were cleared away and Theresa stood up. "We will leave you men to your cigars and port while we go to a higher calling." She glanced at the Sorensen Sisters. "Do you need more time to prepare? Shall we await you in the drawing room?"

"All is ready, Mrs. Flynn," Miss Emily said. "If you will follow us."

Belinda fell into step beside me. "I didn't think I'd be excited, but I am," she whispered. "Do you think they will make ectoplasm appear? I've always wanted to see it."

"I've no idea," I said, "but I'm very anxious to see what they do."

We were ushered into a small, dark room. The furniture had been hidden under black drapes so that only a circle of chairs was visible. One solitary candle was burning on a black-draped table. The pictures on the walls had been similarly black draped. For some reason it felt uncomfortably cold too. I shivered.

"Please be seated," Miss Emily commanded.

We sat. That one candle threw monstrous shadows and made our faces look hollow and deathlike.

"We will all hold hands around the table. Take care not to break the power of the circle. Nobody is to say a word. We will open our minds and invite the spirits to come."

I was sitting with Theresa on one side of me and Belinda on the other. I could feel Theresa's frail hand absolutely shaking. Belinda's didn't feel too steady either. And me? Even though I pooh-poohed the whole idea, I found that my heart was beating very fast.

Rubbish, I said to myself. There are no such things as spirits and any minute now I'll see how they are faking.

At that very moment there was a strong gust of wind that swept across the room, blowing the candle out and stirring the draperies on the walls. We were plunged into complete darkness. Cousin Clara wailed.

"Peace," Miss Emily said. "Someone is in the room with us. I can feel it. Are you with us, Chief Ojuweca?"

"I am here," said a very different voice. "I bring greetings from the other side to my friends."

Miss Emily has a deep, masculine-sounding voice, I told myself. Of course she blew the candle out so that we couldn't see her mouth move. And yet, this voice really did sound like a man's, and not only that, a man for whom English was not his native tongue. Also it seemed to be coming from the far right corner of the room, not at all where Miss Emily was sitting.

"Will you deign to show yourself to our friends tonight, Chief Ojuweca?" Miss Emily asked.

I felt Theresa's hand grab onto mine as I looked up and saw what she saw. In that same far corner of the room a head was materializing. It was too faint to make out the features clearly, but one could see the eyes and hooked nose and the mouth that moved.

"Here I am," it said. "State what you want of me."

How did they do it? They were sitting in the circle with us, holding hands. There was no light in the room and yet the head glowed with a faint light of its own. I felt the back of my neck prickling.

"There is a lady present who grieves for her son who has passed over," Miss Emily said. "She would like to contact him. His name is Brendan, Brendan Flynn. A little boy. Can you contact him for us?"

"I will try," Ojuweca said. "In the meantime I bring messages for others present. I bring a message for someone whose name starts with a C."

"That's you, Clara," Theresa whispered and Clara whimpered again.

"A message from someone you knew long ago. Someone who was dear to you once."

"Not Johnny!" Clara exclaimed.

"He says his name is John, yes."

"Saints preserve us. Johnny's come back to speak to me. How are you, Johnny?"

"He says he is fine and you don't need to grieve for him. He's in a better place, but he still misses you."

Clara gave a sob. "Young Johnny Parker. The only boy I ever loved. Taken from me when we were just seventeen."

"He died of pneumonia, didn't he?" the voice asked.

"No, he fell through the ice when we were skating."

"Because he was already weak with the pneumonia that was coming on."

"I never knew that," Clara whispered. "Poor, brave Johnny. He came skating with me, even though he was already sick with pneumonia. He really did love me." And she burst into tears.

"He watches over you, Clara, and waits for the day when you will join him," the voice said, "and now I have a very strong message coming through. It is for an M?"

"Molly, that's you," Theresa whispered.

In spite of the fact that I didn't believe, I thought my heart was going to jump out of my mouth. I didn't want to hear what any of my dead might say.

"It's your mother, Molly. She's been trying to get in touch with you for some time."

God forbid. My mother! She'd be here half the night telling me all the things I was doing wrong. I opened my mouth but no sound would come out.

"She says to tell you not to grieve. You are still her sweet and darling child. She's not suffering from those terrible headaches any more, and she's with your father and your little brothers, so all is well."

Suddenly it hit me—this wasn't my mother at all. It was Molly Gaffney's mother. My father and little brothers were still alive. And it was all facts that I had inadvertently given the Sorensen Sisters at tea that afternoon. If the spirits had been real, they would have known that the person in the room was Molly Murphy and not Molly Gaffney. I smiled to myself. They were fakes, after all!

❧ Ten ❧

There were no other startling revelations at the séance that evening. Contact was not made with little Brendan. I suspected that Miss Emily and Miss Ella would keep up the suspense for some time so that they could continue to enjoy the hospitality of this pleasant house on the river and the good food at table. The other women in the party were most impressed by the whole thing and went to bed babbling with excitement. Clara especially was like a new woman.

"Johnny came back to speak to me. Imagine that, Theresa. I was never really sure that he loved me as much as I loved him, but he did. He sacrificed everything for me. He gave his life so that I could go skating with him. Wasn't he a gem?"

"And you, dearest Molly," Theresa said, moving closer to me. "How blessed you must feel, knowing that your mother is beside you all the time."

I didn't answer that one. One person I didn't want beside me all the time was my mother. I didn't even want Molly Gaffney's mother! I smiled and nodded. Then I remembered why the séance had been conducted in the first place. "I'm only sorry that the Indian chief didn't manage to contact Brendan tonight," I said.

"I am too, but I have great faith in the sisters," she said. "I'm sure they'll contact my son for me before they go."

I was sure they would too—just before they were about to be

83

thrown out. A sudden thought struck me. "Maybe they need some help with the room?" I asked.

Theresa took my sleeve. "Oh good heavens no. The servants will do that in the morning," she said. "You have to remember that we have lots of servants here, Molly. You are not required to work for your keep—apart from amusing me, that is." And she smiled at me so sweetly that it melted my heart. If I don't find out the truth about Brendan's kidnapping or the Sorensen Sisters, at least I can do some good for Theresa, I thought, as I made my way up the stairs to bed.

I woke at first light. I had slept with the windows open and the sweet, soft smell of grass and river, mingled with jasmine, wafted in to me. I lay there for a moment, listening to the dawn chorus of birds, realizing how far from nature I was in New York City. I hadn't thought I'd ever miss the green hills and the lonely countryside, but it was good to hear the birds again and to smell the sweet air. Then, feeling energized and awake, I jumped up, washed in cold water and dressed. I opened my door but heard no sound. If the household was still sleeping, then I had time to do some snooping. I tiptoed down the stairs, holding my breath each time a floorboard creaked. It wasn't easy to pick out the séance room door from the many doors in that long wall. I counted them off. The dining room had been at the back. Then we had walked past two more doors to reach the séance . . . I grabbed the door and opened it.

And found myself staring at a charming music room. A white baby grand piano was in one corner. A pair of matching small armchairs graced a bay window, looking onto the lawns. The table between them held a crystal bowl of roses. There was no hint at all that a séance had been held here last night.

"May I help you, Miss Gaffney?"

Soames was standing in the doorway, impeccably dressed as usual, with that same haughty expression on his face.

"Oh, Soames, you startled me," I stammered. "I thought nobody else was awake."

"The servants rise at five," he said. "I rise soon after them. There is much to be done before the household stirs."

"I'm sure there is," I said. "Tell me, was this the room where the séance took place last night?"

"It was indeed, miss."

"The servants must have had to work hard to bring it back to normal this morning."

He shook his head. "The two lady spiritualists did most of it themselves last night. All the servants had to do was to remove the last of the black drapes and put the furniture back in place."

Of course, I thought. The sisters wouldn't want anyone to see how they managed those impressive tricks last night. I had tried to work out how they made that head appear, but I was still completely foxed by it.

"I'm quite confused." I attempted girlish laughter. "I thought I had left my fan in here."

"I will ask the maids if they found a fan when they straightened the room." He ushered me from it in the most gracious but firm manner. "I'm afraid breakfast will not be served for another hour, but I can have the maid bring a tray to your room."

"Oh no, thank you. I wouldn't want to put her to extra trouble," I said.

"It's her job, Miss Gaffney. All the occupants of this house are awoken with a tray of tea or coffee at their bedside."

"It's a lovely morning," I said. "I think I'll go out for a walk on the grounds. Do a little exploring."

"Very well, miss," Soames said. "May I suggest you stay away from the cliff path. It is very narrow and leads to a long drop."

"Thank you, Soames. I'll be careful," I said.

"I'll send one of the maids to fetch your wrap, Miss Gaffney. The early morning air has a chill to it."

"Nonsense." I laughed. "I'm used to the Irish mist. We grow up hardy."

"Very well, miss. I'll wish you a pleasant stroll then. Breakfast is served at eight-thirty."

As he spoke, he escorted me to the front door. "I'll be watching for your return, to open the door for you," he said. "The front door is usually kept locked."

I stepped out into the fresh morning air. There was dew on the grass that soaked into my light summer shoes immediately, but I was so glad to be out and free for a few moments that I didn't care. I crossed the lawn and stood looking down at the river as it sped between rocks. The rowboat was still tied to the little jetty below me. I made a mental note that a kidnapper could have come this way, but would have been in full view of the house for the whole time. It took skill to land a boat here, as I had seen. And anyone leaving the house would have had to get past a vigilant Soames!

On either side of this central lawn area the terrain rose to wilderness and a rocky shoreline. I was intrigued by the butler's warning about the cliff path. Where did the path lead? Did it mean that there was a way into the estate without coming along the road and through the main gate?

I turned to my left, leaving the smooth lawn for a shrubbery, and soon picked up a path between tall rhododendron bushes. As I followed it, the path grew narrower and I had to hold my skirts close to me to prevent their getting snagged on bushes. I realized that I was glancing around nervously, which wasn't like me at all. The tension I had felt since I stepped ashore at Adare would not go away. Then it came to me that Brendan Flynn had been buried alive somewhere on these grounds. At this very moment I might be walking over his grave. Not a comforting thought. I found myself glancing down at my feet as I walked. I had sensed a brooding presence about this place—more than just tragedy lingering in the air. I had been warned more than once to be careful here. But this feeling was enough.

There was a sudden movement and a squirrel dashed across the path ahead of me, making me give an involuntary gasp. Then I felt truly ashamed of myself. Some private investigator I was turning out to be, if I jumped every time I met a squirrel. I was reading too much into servants' natural caution when speaking about their

86

masters. Brendan's little body might be buried somewhere around here, but he was long gone. I didn't believe in spirits, did I?

At that moment I stepped around a large oak tree and a giant figure loomed up before me. I opened my mouth to scream but only a small squeak came out as he grabbed me by the wrists.

"Hey, steady on," he said, in a very human voice. "Don't scream. I won't hurt you."

I looked up into the face of a young man, rather good-looking in an insipid sort of way. He had fair hair, blue eyes and a somewhat weak chin. Although he was dressed in casual country attire with open shirt and breeches, I could see that he was a gentleman.

"I'm from next door," he said, and I realized he looked almost as shaken as I felt. "I was just coming to see Mrs. Flynn on an errand from my mother."

"Your mother?"

"Yes, I'm Roland Van Gelder. We live next door. Are you staying with the Senator?"

"Oh," I said, flushing and feeling foolish. "Mr. Van Gelder. I'm Senator Flynn's cousin, Molly Gaffney. Visiting from Ireland. I was just out for an early morning stroll. I wasn't expecting to meet anybody. You alarmed me."

"I'm sure I must have," he said. "I was equally alarmed when you floated around that tree at me. Especially since my mother has been babbling on about séances."

We looked at each other and laughed.

"Not exactly the intrepid white hunters, either of us, are we?" Roland said.

"You're right," I said. "It's all this talk about ghosts."

Instinctively we both glanced down at our feet.

"To tell you the truth," Roland said, "I don't much fancy coming over here, not since—well, you know."

"It must have been terrible."

He nodded. "I helped them search, you know. Poor old Barney Flynn was frantic. They never found the kid, of course, even using dogs."

I shuddered and wished I had let that maid bring my wrap after all.

"Were you going somewhere, or would you care to accompany me to the house?" Roland asked. "I'm never quite easy when Barney Flynn's around."

"Barney? He seems an amiable enough fellow."

"You're his cousin, my dear. And of course he's damnably amiable when he wants to be. Charm the hind leg off a donkey, so my father says. But he and the old man were deadly enemies until recently. Until he got himself elected to the Senate, in fact. Oh, they had some great shouting matches, the pair of them."

"Your father was running for the same office, I believe?"

Roland grinned. "He held the office in the state legislature, Miss Gaffney. Had done through five elections. Barney Flynn used every dirty trick in the book to get my father out. Every dirty trick known to New York Irish politics—bribery, bully boys, the lot."

"Oh." I couldn't think of anything else to say. I had lived in New York City long enough to have witnessed those things happening. The Irish in New York were known for dirty politics.

"Look, I'm sure it wasn't all his fault," Roland said. "He seems like a nice enough fellow. It's the Tammany machine. It kicks into gear when they've a candidate running. You should have seen the gears working when Barney decided to run for Senate—" He held a trailing shrub aside and we stepped out onto the lawns. "And lucky for him he had such a machine. The child was kidnapped a month before the election. Barney was in no state to get out and stump."

"Poor man," I said. "How terrible for him."

"Absolutely. But the sympathy vote didn't hurt him either. I heard he was behind in the polls until that happened."

I looked at Roland's affable face with distaste. Beneath that pleasant exterior there was clearly a deep-seated animosity toward Barney Flynn. "How did you manage to get in here?" I asked. "Is there a way between the properties?"

"Short cut." He grinned like a naughty schoolboy. "Not many people know about it. Mother would think it awfully common to squeeze through a hedge, but I wasn't about to walk miles to the road, or take the time to saddle the mare."

"Ah." I assigned that fact to my mental jottings. "And is that what the butler referred to as the cliff path?"

"Oh no. That's on the other side. There are no cliffs between our place and Adare. The real cliffs are between Adare and Jones Point. It's an absolute wilderness over there. Make your way up that mountain and you'd think you were miles from civilization." He looked up at the rocky crags, now glowing with the rays of the early morning sun. "I expect they buried the child over there. That's what I would have done."

I stared again at the tangled wilderness and shuddered. It was too painful to think about.

"I do hope you're coming to dinner tonight, Miss Gaffney," Roland said.

"If I'm invited."

"Oh, absolutely. That's why Mother sent me over. She wants to find out how many she can expect. It should be a jolly evening. We have visitors from your part of the world. A couple of eligible bachelors, in fact, over here looking for rich American brides."

"What about yourself?" I asked. "Are you an eligible bachelor too?"

He blushed like a schoolgirl. "Definitely, but please don't set your cap at me, Miss Gaffney, not unless you're terribly rich, that is. You see, the old man's fortune has gone downhill. We might even have to sell the place here. So it's up to me to snag an heiress if I want to keep up the style to which I'm accustomed."

"I'm afraid I'm not at all an heiress, Mr. Van Gelder. So I must remind myself not to be swept away by your charm."

He let the sarcasm wash over him and blushed again. "Gee, Miss Gaffney," he stammered.

A likable idiot, I decided.

As I was about to lead him to the front door, he grabbed my arm. "So have you had a séance yet?" he whispered.

"Yes, last night."

"And did things float around the room and heads appear and such?"

"Something of the kind, yes."

His face lit up. "I'm dying to see it for myself. So is Mother. She is most insistent that the Misses Sorensen know they will be guests of honor at our dinner. To tell the truth, she really had her nose put out of joint when she heard that the Sorensen Sisters had agreed to come to Theresa Flynn. They'd snubbed her invitations for years, you know. So between the two of us she's secretly hoping for a little séance over at our place. What do you think the chances are?"

"I really couldn't say, Mr. Van Gelder. I'm just a guest here myself. You'll need to speak to Cousin Theresa and I don't think she's up yet. No one was stirring when I left the house."

"Oh dear. Have I come too early?" He pulled a pocketwatch from his breeches pocket. "Oh dash it all, it is early. Mother's always been an early riser so we tend to think that the rest of the world is out and about at seven. Never mind, I'll sit here on the steps and wait. It is most pleasant in the sun, don't you think?"

"Very pleasant."

"Should we see if that Soames fellow will have some coffee brought out to us?" he asked.

I didn't like to tell him that I'd rather have died than ask Soames to bring coffee to me.

"Actually, I wasn't quite finished with my morning walk," I said. "If you'll excuse me, I must get my full constitutional. Once around the park, you know."

He smiled. "I say, that's dashed athletic of you. I suppose everyone in Ireland is fit and healthy? Lots of hunting and fishing and all that? At least that's what my friends seem to hint."

I laughed. "We have our share of weakness and sickness in Ireland, I assure you. Why, my own mother died of—" I broke off. "Of influenza," I added, quickly substituting the unknown Mrs. Gaffney for the too well known Mrs. Murphy. "But I intend to live long and stay healthy."

I gave him a polite little bow, then turned back across the lawn. As I glanced up at the house I saw one of the drapes on the upper floor hurriedly fall back into place. Someone was watching my progress.

☙ Eleven ❧

This time I headed in the other direction, to the right of the house and toward the wilderness area where I hoped to find the cliff path. I was in the middle of forcing my way through the bushes when I heard a great crashing through the undergrowth, as if a large bear was approaching. I spun around and snatched up a rock to defend myself, but instead of a bear, a red-faced Barney Flynn came storming through the bushes.

"Molly!" he cried. "Where on earth are you going? Roland Van Gelder told me that you had come this way. Not running away from us already, I hope?'

"Of course not," I said. "I told Mr. Van Gelder that I was taking my morning exercise. I had heard about the cliff path and I wanted to see if there was a view to be admired."

"Holy Mother of God," Barney said, sounding more Irish than the Irish born. "There is indeed a narrow path along the cliffs, but I wouldn't recommend it to any lady. It comes from the time when they had to portage canoes past the rapids here. Barely wide enough for a jackrabbit. Now, if you'd like to see around the estate, I'd be happy to show you around myself."

He took my arm rather firmly and I was escorted out of harm's way. Then he continued holding my arm as we recrossed the lawns.

"I'm glad to have a moment alone with you, Molly," he said. "I wanted to have a chance to talk to you about Theresa. How did you find her?"

"She seems very sweet," I said, not knowing what answer he wanted.

"It's true. She can be sweet when she wants to. But remote, wouldn't you say? Frail, sickly. Almost as if she'd given up on life?"

"Definitely frail," I agreed. "I was scared to shake her hand in case I crushed it."

"She's never recovered, you know," he said. "From the tragedy, I mean. You did hear about our tragedy?"

"Of course I did. It was in all the newspapers."

He sighed. "Theresa took it very hard. She loved that child. Well, I did too, of course. He was a darling little boy. The best." He coughed, trying to stifle the emotion in his voice. "I had hoped that Eileen would help Theresa out of her doldrums, but she's never really taken to the child. She treats her like a stranger."

I didn't quite know what to say. "It was the very worst thing that could happen to a person, Barney." I realized that I was addressing him by his first name, as if he really was a cousin and I'd known him for years. He didn't even seem to notice, but nodded his head in agreement.

"The very worst thing, but life has to go on, doesn't it? Theresa's making no effort."

"Ah, but you have a life outside the home," I reminded him. "You have your political career. Theresa is surrounded by her memories every moment."

"She could be a great assistance to me in my political future if she put her mind to it," he said, "but she's given up. We hardly entertain any more. I was surprised she agreed to have you at the house. No strange faces, no changes to her routine. It's enough to stifle a fellow and drive him away from home."

I looked up at him, wondering where this conversation might be leading. "You owe her your support, Barney," I said.

"Of course I do. But even a saint can only put up with so much. A husband has a right to expect certain—duties—from a wife. She

94

won't let me near her, you know. I'm a normal, healthy, red-blooded man with normal, healthy needs and she keeps her bedroom door locked at night. What's a fellow to do?"

Again I wasn't quite sure what he was hinting at. I was all too familiar with those so-called needs of red-blooded men, and their apparent lack of ability to control them. But was he suggesting that I might want to take Theresa's place? I'd heard about Barney Flynn's womanizing, but I hadn't thought it might extend to his own cousin. I didn't quite like the way he was looking at me.

"You made your vows in church," I said, primly. "For better or worse, in sickness or in health."

"I know." He sighed again. "I keep hoping. That's why I'm so glad you're here, dear Molly."

Again I glanced at him cautiously, not quite sure what he might be hinting at.

"I'll do my best to cheer up Theresa, I promise," I said hastily.

"I do hope so. You're so young and full of life. Maybe you're just what she needs, not that dreary Cousin Clara of hers who just drags her down, or her sister who reminds her what she might have been." He glanced around before lowering his voice. "To tell you the truth, I'm afraid her mind is going. Belinda wants her to see one of these new alienist fellows."

He looked at me for an opinion. Having never heard of alienists and having no idea what they were, I gave a sympathetic nod. "If he's going to help her . . . "

"What I'm afraid of is that the fellow might make her relive the details of that day and it might just push her over the edge. I wouldn't want her to wind up in an institution."

"Oh, I don't think she's headed that way, Barney. Her mind seemed quite bright and alert to me."

His face lit up. "You think so? I do hope you're right. It was a good sign when she mentioned she might want to visit Ireland. Should I plan a trip for us? Do you think it might help?"

"I could try to encourage the idea in her mind while I'm here," I said. "I wouldn't rush her or make her feel you were forcing anything on her." It was in my own interests that he didn't try contacting relatives in Ireland while I was still in the house.

"You're wonderful, Molly. I'm so glad you're here." He drew me into his arms and hugged me. Again I got the feeling it wasn't entirely a cousinly hug. I moved away from him, laughing uneasily.

"Do you think breakfast is ready yet? I'm starving after all this exercise."

"It should be soon," he said. "But I want to show you my pride and joy first. Come on." He took my hand and held it so firmly that it would have been rude to pull mine away. He led me behind the house, past an extensive kitchen garden and small orchard, then he stopped and pointed.

"There. What do you think of that?"

Amid a stand of chestnut trees stood a perfect Irish cottage. It had a thatched roof, whitewashed walls, just like the one I had left at home. A pang of homesickness shot through me. I had thought I'd never want to see Ireland again, but that cottage almost brought tears to my eyes.

"How did that come to be here?" I stammered.

"I built it." Barney was smiling with satisfaction. "When I took over this property, I built it for my parents. They were simple folk and didn't feel at ease in the grand house. So I built them a cottage like the one they had left. They spent their last days here."

"Who lives in it now?" I asked. I had seen a lace curtain twitch and fall back as we approached.

"Nobody. It's our guesthouse. The two spiritualist ladies are staying in it at the moment. They indicated they didn't feel comfortable in the main house. Not to the liking of their spirit friends, I understand." He threw back his head and laughed. He had a big, powerful laugh to match his build. "What a load of malarky, don't you think, Molly?"

"I saw them last night. They were rather impressive," I said. "A floating head that talks and blinks its eyes has to be explained, don't you think?"

"Some theatrical trick," he said. "But Theresa set her heart on having them here. If they can make her believe that Brendan is happy and she'll see him again some day, then they're worth the money."

"But you don't believe they'll contact your son?"

He shook his head. "My son is gone forever. I'll never see him again."

I was taking in the lie of the land as we spoke, noticing the gravel driveway that passed to the right of the cottage and went on, presumably up to the gatehouse and the gate. I hadn't realized how extensive the property was. Anybody kidnapping a child in broad daylight would have had to walk miles from the boundary and then cross exposed lawn in full view of the house. Carrying the child out of the house and across those lawns again without being seen seemed to me an impossible task.

Farther up the drive I spied a carriage house with a shiny automobile outside. A man in gray uniform was giving it a final polish. My thoughts went to Bertie Morell and I found myself blurting out, "If it was your former chauffeur who kidnapped your son, how on earth do they think he carried the child out of the house without being seen?"

"Easy," he said. "The child's nanny. She was sweet on him, you see. He was a likable fellow. She must have delivered the child to him. She swears she didn't, of course, but with the electric chair waiting, who wouldn't?"

"And if she's telling the truth and had nothing to do with it?"

He shook his head. "It had to be her. Do you think I haven't gone through this a million times in my head? There can't be any other explanation. And once she'd handed over the child, he'd have gone willingly enough with Morell. He was a friendly little chap, and he loved going for rides in the car. Morell always had candies for him. I thought he was genuinely fond of the child, but obviously he was just softening him up for the right moment." His voice cracked and he kicked savagely at a pebble in his path. "Anyway, it's a subject we don't discuss any more. Let's go and have breakfast, shall we?"

Again I was marched firmly away.

97

* * *

Back at the house breakfast was in full swing. Theresa, Clara and Belinda, as well as Mr. Rimes and the silent secretary were already seated at the table. Apparently Ronald Van Gelder had been asked to join them. He now sat close beside Belinda, trying to win her over with his charm. Her expression indicated that it wasn't working. There was a row of silver serving dishes sitting over hotplates at one end of the room, but not a servant in sight. I wondered whether I should go and help myself or sit and wait to be served. I certainly didn't want to upset the protocol of the house. As I hovered by the door, Theresa looked up.

"Molly, there you are at last! We were worried about you. Clara said you'd gone for a walk on your own."

"Only strolling around the grounds, Theresa, not scaling the nearest peak."

This produced polite laughter.

"But the estate is so large it's entirely possible to get lost, or to fall and hurt yourself. And you went out without a wrap."

"I'm used to Irish weather, remember. This is hotter than anything we've ever experienced. And I'm used to an early morning stroll at home."

"Alone? Molly, you are so independent. Anyway, you must be fainting from lack of food. Do help yourself and come and sit down."

I was glad for the instructions. I took off one lid after another and had to restrain myself from piling too much food on my plate. There was bacon and kidneys and eggs, tomatoes, smoked fish, flapjacks, potatoes . . . I reminded myself that I had to fit into some very small waists on those dresses and took an egg with one piece of toast. Then I sat between Mr. Van Gelder and Mr. Rimes. Almost as soon as I sat down Roland Van Gelder pushed his plate away and stood up.

"I must thank you for your early morning hospitality, Mrs. Flynn, but I should hurry back to Mother now. She'll be champing at the bit, wanting to know how many places to set at table."

"Of course." Theresa looked around the table. "Will you be joining us, Joseph? You, Desmond?"

"I think we'll politely decline," Joseph Rimes said, shooting a quick look at Desmond O'Mara who was concentrating on a congealed kidney on his plate. "A lot of work to be done."

"Well, you're not keeping my husband away," Theresa said, with just the hint of a frown. "I've already told Mrs. Van Gelder that Barney will be delighted to attend."

"Don't worry. We have correspondence to catch up on. Your husband can go and enjoy himself."

This time Theresa flushed. "Really, Joe, sometimes I think you forget that Barney is the employer and you the employee."

Rimes's face also turned red. He rose to his feet. "Back to work, I think, Desmond." And he strode from the room.

"Odious man," Theresa muttered. "I can't think why Barney keeps him on."

Roland Van Gelder coughed nervously, making Theresa exclaim, "Mr. Van Gelder. How extremely ill-mannered of me. Please tell your dear mother that we shall be seven for dinner."

"And what may I tell her about the possibility of a séance?"

"Miss Emily and Miss Ella take their breakfast in the cottage so I haven't had a chance to see them today, but I'll certainly do what I can to persuade them for your mother."

"You are most kind, Mrs. Flynn." Roland bowed his head. "Please excuse me if I run off. My mother doesn't like to be kept waiting."

As he closed the door behind him, Theresa turned to us. "He really is rather sweet, don't you think? Not at all like his blustering father."

"I think he's a crashing bore," Belinda said. "You obviously didn't observe him making sheep's eyes at me and trying to get me to promise him my entire dance card this evening. He does resemble a sheep, don't you think?"

"You could do worse," Cousin Clara said in her dry, sharp voice.

"Oh no, Clara. Not a Van Gelder." Theresa shook her head.

"For one thing, Barney wouldn't hear of it. They are still arch enemies, you know, for all their politeness. And for another, they haven't two pennies to rub together. Belinda needs to marry someone with money. She has expensive tastes, don't you, my angel?"

I didn't think that Belinda's smile was entirely friendly and wondered if Theresa Flynn's money had been financing Belinda's gorgeous outfits. As if in answer to my question Theresa went on, "Which reminds me. I had an idea in bed last night. Let's have the dressmaker come out this week and we can have a new wardrobe made for Cousin Molly."

I felt myself becoming hot all over. Posing as a cousin and eating their food was one thing. Having a new wardrobe made was quite another. "Oh no, Cousin. I couldn't possibly allow you to—" I began.

She waved a hand to cut me off. "Molly, I have quite made up my mind to find you a rich and handsome husband while you are in America, and your clothes, while charming, are a trifle passé. Please let me do this for you. It would give me such pleasure, like dressing a full-sized doll. What color do you think, Belinda? Not pink with that coloring. Pale blue? Lime green? What about buttercup yellow?"

I sat there, cringing with embarrassment, conscious that neither Belinda nor Clara was looking at me with favor at this moment.

"Please, Cousin, I beg you," I stammered. "Anyone would think I had come here to take advantage of your largesse."

"Why did you come, Cousin Molly?" Belinda asked. "Was it to avoid an unsuitable suitor at home?"

"No, nothing like that. Ireland's a small country. I wanted to experience a bigger one."

"Will you travel west and see the Great Plains, do you think?" Cousin Clara asked. "You must get your traveling in before winter arrives. Half the country is snowed in for the season and I'm sure you wouldn't want that."

"She's not going anywhere for a long while," Theresa said

firmly. "I'm keeping her here with me. You are my new toy, Molly, and I'll not relinquish you."

We looked up as Barney came in. "Any food left for me?" he asked. He lifted one lid, then a second. "Barely enough to feed a sparrow. Have you been stuffing yourself again, Clara?"

I could tell that the remark was a good-natured tease but Clara bristled. "Really Barney, sometimes you go too far. You know that I have a most modest appetite. I ate one of your eggs and two of your slices of bacon, if you really want to know, and if you'd like reimbursement for them then I'm sure—"

"Sit down, Clara. Relax. Can't a fellow have a lighthearted moment in his own home?"

"Not if it's at my expense," Clara said.

Barney spooned a good mound of food onto his plate. "So I gather I just missed the company of a Van Gelder?"

"Young Roland, sent over to see how many of us are coming to dinner."

Barney chuckled. "Sent over, my foot. Don't they have a telephone any longer? You know full well why he was sent. They want your voodoo ladies to hold a séance for them. She's been trying to snag them for years and now you've outsmarted her. Van Gelders can't allow themselves to be outsmarted by mere Irish peasants."

"Really, Barney." Theresa looked annoyed. "Must you see the basest motive in everything?"

"I've seen too much of human nature, my dear, just as you have seen too little, and I can tell you with utter conviction that the Van Gelders would never have invited us to dinner if the Misses Sorensen were not currently under our roof."

"Then if that's how you feel, why did you accept their invitation?" Theresa asked coldly.

Barney laughed out loud. "What, and miss a chance to eat old Van Gelder's food?"

Theresa got up and moved away from the table. Cousin Clara

followed her. I ate as quickly as I could, wanting also to make my escape. Only Belinda lingered on, chatting happily with Barney.

As I made my way back to my room, I heard voices through an open door.

"You shouldn't let him get away with it, Theresa. You should remind him that it was your money in the first place. Make him dance to your tune."

"Don't be so naive, Clara. You know full well that Barney is beyond dancing to anyone's tune. I just wonder how much longer I can take it."

❧ Twelve ❧

That evening five of us piled into the automobile to be driven across to the Van Gelders' house. The chauffeur was then to come back for Miss Emily and Miss Ella, who had graciously agreed to join the party, although they were a little reluctant on the question of the séance.

"The atmosphere does have to be right, or the spirits simply won't come," Miss Ella had said.

Meaning that the room needed a lot of black swathing and lack of light to perform their tricks, I decided. I was interested to see what they would do in a room that had not been rigged up first.

I sat beside Belinda and Clara in the backseat, feeling distinctly uncomfortable. I was wearing one of those instruments of female torture called corsets. Unfortunately Theresa had sent the maid, Alice, up to help me dress for the occasion. Since I didn't want the maid to swoon at the sight of an uncorseted woman, I had had to endure holding onto the bedpost while she tugged at various laces as if wrestling with a reluctant stallion and finally brought my waistline down to acceptable standards. Not without criticism, however.

"Why, miss, your waist is almost as broad as my own," she said in a disapproving voice. "The mistress's waist can be spanned by the master's hands, and she has delivered two children, you know."

"We don't go in for corsets much in Ireland," I said. "We find them too restricting."

"Mercy me. You just run around with your insides flopping all over the place?" She finished hooking the low back of my ball gown. "It must indeed be a wild, heathen place."

So now I was sitting in the car, trying hard to breathe. I certainly wouldn't be able to eat a morsel at dinner. And the corset was just the latest in a line of faux pas committed this day. I had been summoned to play croquet and had appeared on the lawn— gasp—without a parasol.

"Molly!" Theresa had exclaimed. "You'll get freckles." As if I didn't have enough already from a lifetime in the open air. Then I had whacked the croquet ball in an unladylike manner and—gasp again—sat on the grass, where I should surely get a chill and die of pneumonia. As we bumped up the driveway in the automobile, I found myself very glad that I was not a conventional young lady and that I had grown up wild and heathen!

All in all it had been a frustrating day. I was itching to get to work and question anyone who might have known Bertie Morell, or even do some snooping in the Sorensen Sisters' cottage, but Theresa had kept me close beside her every moment. She had babbled incessantly about plans for dressmakers and what colors really did justice to red hair, making me so hot and uncomfortable that I could hardly endure another moment. But she seemed so lively and animated that I hadn't the heart to stop her. Barney had hoped I'd be doing her some good and it seemed as if this was indeed so. I just wasn't doing the job for which I was being paid.

The driveway went on and on, with the dark shapes of trees looming on either side of us before we came to the gate—a tall, wrought-iron structure that was opened for us by the a burly gate- keeper. Then another half mile of darkness bouncing down an un- paved road with not a single light visible until we turned in at another fortresslike gateway to Riverside, the Van Gelders' man- sion. Riverside had none of its neighbor's extravagance of design. It was a square brick residence, with simple eighteenth-century lines and white shutters. As our wraps were being taken from us, Mrs. Van Gelder came out into the hallway to meet us.

"I am so delighted that you have agreed to grace our home, Mrs. Flynn," she said, embracing Theresa. "And you, Senator. We are honored."

While Theresa was presenting the rest of us, Mrs. Van Gelder's eyes were darting around. "You didn't bring the rest of your party? The Misses Sorensen are not coming after all?"

"We've sent the auto back for them," Theresa said. "It only seats five at the most and they were not quite ready."

"Ah, splendid. Do come and meet my husband. Theo—our neighbors are here!"

She led us through to a rather austere reception room where Roland Van Gelder and his father waited. The elder Mr. Van Gelder's face seemed to be frozen in a severe and permanent scowl. The scowl didn't waver as we came in.

"Mrs. Flynn. Senator," he said, inclining his head slightly. "Good to have you here. How's the reelection campaign going?"

"Hasn't really started yet," Barney said, "and how about you? Will you be running again, or are you thinking of handing your seat over to the younger generation?"

"Roland?" Van Gelder glared at his son. "He couldn't run an egg-and-spoon race."

"Really, Father, I must protest," Roland said. "You haven't exactly educated me for much, have you? If I'd studied law at Harvard—"

"You need brains to study law. Unfortunately, you've inherited your mother's scatterbrain mentality. Not your fault, I suppose, but not the stuff that politicians are made of."

Roland frowned at his father, helped himself to a generous amount of whiskey, and made his way over to Belinda. The rest of us stood around awkwardly.

"And where are the famous spirit ladies?" Van Gelder asked. "Did you decide not to share them after all?"

I couldn't recall meeting anyone so offensive and wondered who might have voted for him. But Theresa, sweet as always, merely smiled. "They are on their way. We only own one automobile, you know, and the chauffeur has returned for them." She slipped her arm through mine. "In the meantime, may I present our guests—my cousin, Clara Tompkins, my sister, Belinda Butler, and my husband's cousin, Molly Gaffney, newly arrived from Ireland."

"You're most welcome, ladies. How about a drink to counteract the chilly night air?" And he led us to a drinks table where he began pouring. Compared to the Flynns' establishment there was a distinct lack of servants.

"Roland mentioned you had some other young men staying with you?" Theresa asked, looking around hopefully.

"We do. Son of a friend of mine. English fellow. And his army pal. They're doing what all young Englishmen do—out to snag rich American brides. Where the deuce are they, Sophie?"

Mrs. Van Gelder scurried to his side. "They returned late from today's outing and will be down as soon as they have made themselves respectable. Such nice boys. You girls could do worse." She gave a knowing smile to Belinda and me. "Both have considerable properties over in England, so we understand."

"Why does everyone think we are desperate to be found a husband?" Belinda whispered in my ear. It was her first friendly overture.

"Like you, I intend to find my own husband some day," I whispered back, "but not too soon."

We exchanged a smile. Allies for a moment.

Noises in the entrance hall indicated the arrival of the Sorensen Sisters. Mrs. Van Gelder flew out to greet them and swept them into the room, gushing effusively over them. "And we'd be so honored if you'd just show us a small example of your powers. . . . Longing to meet you for years . . . such a wonderful gift. . . . The dearly departed . . . always feel their presence."

Miss Emily and Miss Ella both looked a little flustered, but accepted glasses of sherry when pressed.

"I really don't think—" Miss Emily began.

"Not really conducive to visiting spirits—" Miss Ella seconded.

Both were waved aside by the force of Mrs. Van Gelder's will. "I am sure that Riverside, being an older and more noble establishment than the recently built Adare, will be quite to the liking of any spirit worth its salt," she said firmly. "I have set up the morning room for you. I thought that since we had promised the young people dancing after dinner, we should have our séance now, while we're waiting for the young men to join us. I am sure they have no interest in contacting the dead. Why don't we go through?"

I had to watch with admiration. Mrs. Van Gelder was a small woman, not unlike portraits I had seen of Queen Victoria. She had the same force of personality as the old queen, I noted, as the two sisters allowed themselves to be swept out of the room again, followed by the rest of us.

Chairs had been set in a circle in an adjoining room.

"This will do, won't it?" Mrs. Van Gelder asked.

The sisters looked around. The rest of us held our breath.

Finally Miss Emily nodded. "We may be able to entice our spirit guide to manifest himself here. We'll just have to see. But no electric light, if you please. Just one candle."

A candle was lit. Grotesque shadows danced on the walls. We took our places in the circle. Miss Emily shook her head.

"We have unbelievers present. I can feel it. Chief Ojuweca certainly won't be enticed to come in the presence of those who mock him."

Barney nudged Mr. Van Gelder. "He means us, old sport. I suspect you don't believe in this any more than I do. Why don't we go and visit your Scotch decanter until the ladies are done?"

"Excellent idea." Mr. Van Gelder looked almost kindly toward his arch enemy. They departed. A hush fell upon the rest of us. The candle flickered in the draft from the closing door.

"Please take hands," Miss Emily instructed. "I sense a presence. Are you with us, Chief Ojuweca?"

The candle flickered, but there was no voice.

"If you are present, signify by rapping once."

A mighty rap made everyone jump.

"He's here," Mrs. Van Gelder said in an excited stage whisper. "I wonder if we are going to see him."

"Will you reveal yourself to us tonight, Chief Ojuweca?" Miss Ella asked.

Two loud and disapproving raps. It was hard to tell where they were coming from. I could see Miss Emily's and Miss Ella's hands. They were joined with the others in the circle.

"May we ask what has displeased you?" Miss Ella said.

"There are still unbelievers present," came a distant voice from somewhere up in the ceiling. "If they choose to stay, it is at their own peril. They may see what they would not want to see."

Even though I knew this was another trick, I felt sweat trickling down my bare back.

"Will no spirits choose to visit us tonight?" Miss Ella persisted.

"We shall wait and see," said the voice. "Patience."

We waited. Then five loud raps made everyone jump.

"Who is here?" Miss Ella asked.

Cousin Clara glanced across the room and gave a shriek. "Look, there on the table!"

A disembodied hand was moving across a side table, glowing with a light of its own. Then suddenly it vanished.

"Who are you?" Miss Ella asked, her voice now sharp and taut with fear.

"Peace. He is my messenger," said Chief Ojuweca. "He escorts the spirits you seek. Wait and see."

Then there came a tiny voice, no more than a whisper. "Mommy?"

Theresa jumped to her feet. "Brendan!" she gasped, shaking her hand clear of mine. "It's Brendan. Where are you, my love? Speak to me."

"Sit down, please," Miss Ella admonished.

"But I must speak to him. Tell him I'm here if he doesn't know. Brendan, my love, speak to me." She pushed her way out of the circle. A chair clattered over. Then silence.

"It's no good," Miss Emily said. "You've driven them away. They won't come back tonight. The spirits are sometimes very shy, you know. As I said earlier, I sensed that the atmosphere wasn't quite right this evening. The spirits do not like it if we try to make a spectacle of them or use them for our own benefit." I found this ironic coming from a woman who had done this on the stage until her finances permitted her to conduct only private séances.

"Turn the electric light on, please," Miss Ella commanded.

I was closest to the switch. As I got to my feet and walked toward the door, I became aware of a figure standing there in deep shadow. Suddenly I realized that I recognized him. It was Justin Hartley, the man I had killed a year ago.

❧ Thirteen ❧

My breath came in short gasps as I fought for air. The world was spinning around me, stars were dancing before my eyes. I believe that someone caught me as I fell.

I came to, coughing and spluttering, when smelling salts were waved under my nose.

"It's all right, Molly dear. Just lie still for a while," said a soothing voice.

I opened my eyes to find myself lying on a low couch. Theresa knelt beside me. Mrs. Van Gelder held the bottle of smelling salts in her hand and was looking at me with apprehension.

"What happened to me?" I asked.

"You fainted. Quite understandable, given the heat in the room and the excitement," Mrs. Van Gelder said.

"But I never faint," I protested and realized immediately why other women fainted so often when I didn't. When one is alarmed, one takes short breaths, which are not possible given the restrictions of a corset. As these thoughts went through my head, I remembered what had made me faint. I fought to sit up and looked around nervously. I was in a room bathed in strong electric light and there was no sign of Justin Hartley's ghost. The Misses Sorensen had promised they would make unbelievers change their minds and they had done so. I would have to write to Daniel and tell him that the sisters were quite genuine.

"How do you feel now, Miss Gaffney?" Mrs. Van Gelder asked. "Do you think you feel strong enough to join us at dinner?" She patted my hand. I sat up, feeling foolish.

"Quite well again, thank you. I'm so sorry for causing this trouble."

"Not at all. It happens to all young girls, doesn't it? Too much emotion."

I was furious at myself for being lumped together with emotionally unstable and weak young women, but I couldn't very well correct her. I had to smile wanly and allow myself to be lifted to my feet.

"And you, Mrs. Flynn?" Mrs. Van Gelder turned to Theresa, who had been sitting on a chair beside me. "Will you join us? I realize it must have been most emotionally distressing for you too."

"Oh no, quite the contrary." Theresa's eyes were shining. "I heard Brendan's voice. We all heard it, didn't we? That means Chief Ojuweca has contacted him and he'll come back to me when the time is right. At last I dare to hope!"

Belinda helped her to her feet. We came out into the hallway to find that the men had already gone through to the dining room.

"Ah, here come the casualties," Mr. Van Gelder said brightly. "Quite recovered, I hope. I always said that séances were dangerous things. Messing with the unknown. No good can come if it, you know."

"Nonsense, Theo. You don't know what you're talking about," Mrs. Van Gelder said. "Mrs. Flynn distinctly heard her son's voice. We all did."

"And we saw a creeping hand," Cousin Clara exclaimed.

"Whose hand?" Barney asked.

"Nobody's. It moved with a life of its own and it glowed with its own light," Clara went on excitedly. "Then it just vanished. Poof, like that. Most chilling."

"A disembodied hand? What next!" Barney took his wife's arm. "You are responsible for bringing this nonsense into my household.

Now you've got all the women in hysterics, even Cousin Molly, who seemed most level-headed to me."

"We're letting the soup get cold, Theo," Mrs. Van Gelder said. "Our two young adventurers have returned unscathed and are now champing at the bit for food, I'm sure. May I present Captain Cathers and his friend Mr. Hartley."

Captain Cathers had a pleasant, very English sort of face with light hair and rather protruding teeth. Then my gaze moved to the other man. For a moment the room swung again and I had to put a hand onto the back of a chair to steady myself. It couldn't be possible. The last time I had seen Justin Hartley, he was lying dead in a pool of blood on my kitchen floor. I hadn't meant to kill him, God's truth. But I'd kicked out with all my might when he tried to force me back onto the kitchen table and he'd hit his head on the corner of our cast iron stove. I suppose I panicked then and fled. I was sure I'd get no sympathy from the courts for killing the landowner's son. And so I had come, through a series of lucky breaks, to America, where I had almost forgotten that my adventure had started with killing another human being.

I glanced at the man again. He was pale enough to be a ghost, with dark, hollow eyes. Now dressed in evening attire, he looked like the model of a Romantic poet. Inside my corset my heart was thumping alarmingly.

"And gentlemen, may I present our guests, Senator and Mrs. Flynn and their party, Miss Butler, Miss Tompkins and Miss Gaffney."

The two men bowed politely. I saw Justin look at me and then his gaze moved on to Belinda. I was still holding my breath as I was escorted to table. Mr. Van Gelder took the head of the table with Theresa on one side of him and Miss Emily on the other. Roland was placed beside Miss Emily and I next to him with Clara on my other side. Justin Hartley had been put at the foot of the table, on Mrs. Van Gelder's left. He seemed more interested in getting to the bowl of soup in his place than in looking at me.

I sat, still holding my breath and trying not to look in his direction.

We ate soup. A maid was in attendance to clear away dirty dishes, but the Van Gelders didn't seem to have a butler. The food wasn't up to the quality of Adare, either, which was good, because I couldn't eat a thing. My gaze kept moving toward Justin, who was currently tucking into his food with relish. How could he be alive? How could he not know me? Then, of course, it hit me. It wasn't Justin at all. It was a family member who closely resembled him. I remembered how alike two of my brothers were, so much so that one had impersonated the other, for a fee, in catechism class. I knew Justin had no brothers, but a cousin, maybe?

The talk was all about the day's adventure.

"They went down the river by canoe, wasn't that brave of them?" Mrs. Van Gelder exclaimed.

"There was no bravery involved, I assure you, dear lady," Captain Cathers said in his lazy English drawl. "We went with the current until it petered out in the middle of the Tappan Zee, then we paddled to the side, caught the ferry and came back. A pleasant little ride, but not the least dangerous."

"So what do you think of our American countryside, Mr. Hartley?" Van Gelder asked.

"Quite amazing, what I can see of it," he answered. "Of course, as I told you, I had a severe riding accident which has robbed me of part of my vision."

"Oh yes, how terrible for you," Mrs. Van Gelder said.

"Not at all. I am lucky to be alive."

A wave of relief swept through me. Justin was alive. I hadn't killed him after all. And more miraculous still his vision had been damaged. He didn't recognize me. I was safe. I ventured a mouthful of roast beef.

After dinner we went into the drawing room where the carpet had been rolled up and the French doors were open onto the terrace.

"Young people always have to have dancing, don't they?" Mrs. Van Gelder asked. "I regret that we don't have anything like a pianola to accompany us, so we must take turns in playing. Now, who is familiar with a Strauss waltz?"

"I had better play," Cousin Clara moved toward the piano, "since I will not be taking part in the dancing." And she struck up a lively tune in three quarter time. Roland and Captain Cathers both made a beeline for Belinda. Roland got there first and so Captain Cathers was left with me.

"I must apologize in advance for any stepped-upon toes, Miss Gaffney," he said. "I am more skilled at hunting than dancing."

"I'm not much of a dancer myself," I replied.

He looked at me in astonishment. "You're Irish," he exclaimed.

"Yes, I'm the Senator's cousin, come to stay with him."

"What a coincidence. My friend Hartley is also from Ireland. Which part are you from?"

"Limerick," I said swiftly. "The Senator's whole family lives around that city."

"And how do you like America so far?" he asked.

"Delightful. I'm having such a lovely time and my cousin is making me so welcome."

"I'm glad to hear it."

"And you, Captain Cathers, how do you find America?"

"I'm dying to see the rest of it," he said. "The untamed West calls. The visit here is a courtesy call from my parents, but I'll be dragging poor Hartley off on a train as soon as possible and then across mountains and deserts. He needs building up, you know. Poor chap had a bad riding accident. Hovered between life and death for months. Only just back on his feet now."

"How terrible for him."

"Absolutely. Had to resign his commission, of course, and still gets dizzy spells. We're hoping that fresh air and exercise will bring additional improvement."

I glanced back at Justin, sitting alone at the table, and fought with a stab of guilt. Then I reminded myself how the accident had happened in the first place.

The music ended. Instead of escorting me back to my seat, Captain Cathers held onto my arm and led me to the table where Justin sat. "Come and meet my friend, Miss Gaffney," he said. "I hate to leave him sitting alone, but he doesn't trust himself to dance any more." I could think of no good reason not to comply.

"Justin, old bean. Here's a girl from the old country I'd like you to meet. Miss Gaffney from Limerick. The Senator's cousin. Miss Gaffney, this is Mr. Hartley."

"I'm afraid I don't dance any more, Miss Gaffney," Justin said, rising to his feet. "Lack of balance, I'm afraid. Maybe you'd care to join me in a stroll on the terrace."

Again I couldn't back down without looking rude. I just had to trust my luck a little longer. Maybe I looked so different in my grand ball gown with my hair up that he wouldn't recognize me even close up. He offered his arm. I took it. We strolled out through the French doors into the darkness. The cheerful notes of the Strauss waltz drifted out of the open windows. The lights threw shadows across the lawns to where the dark shape of the river flowed past. It was muggy outside but it was all I could do to prevent myself from shivering.

"You are from a good Irish Catholic family, I presume, Miss Gaffney?" Justin asked.

"I am indeed, sir." I stared out across the lawns, unable to look at him.

"In Limerick, that would be?"

"In Limerick, sir."

"Where a delightful drive to the south brings one to ancient Bunratty Castle?"

"No, sir, that would be a drive to the northwest." I had done my homework well and he was quiet for a moment. I wasn't sure where the conversation might be heading. Perhaps it was his way of making small talk. Then he blurted out, "And what would your good Irish Catholic family say if they knew how many of the Ten Commandments you had broken?"

I know I must have started. "What a strange thing to say, sir. Do you make a habit of insulting young women?"

"No, only young women who deserve it. Miss Gaffney from Limerick indeed! You are no more Miss Gaffney than I am the man in the moon!"

At this point I could confess and smooth things over or I could bluff my way out. I've always believed attack was the best form of defense. I stepped away from him, giving him my most haughty stare.

"I don't know what this is all about, Mr. Hartley, but I find you most offensive and your behavior extremely strange."

"So you deny ever having heard of Molly Murphy of County Mayo, do you?"

"There was a Molly Murphy in my class at the Sacred Heart Convent in Limerick," I said, still eyeing him coldly, "but I never heard that she moved to County Mayo."

I saw his expression falter. "I could have sworn . . . ," he muttered.

"An easy mistake," I said, nodding graciously, "since I understand that we Irish colleens all look alike to foreigners like yourself. And didn't I just hear you say that your eyesight is poor, following some sort of accident?"

We stood there staring at each other. Who knows where the conversation might have led, had not Captain Cathers come out through the French doors. "Oh there you are, Miss Gaffney." I thought I heard a snort from Justin. "Mrs. Flynn was wondering where you had disappeared to. She has a headache and is going home." He glanced from Justin to me. "I say, I hope I didn't interrupt anything."

"Not at all," I said, moving past him toward the room. "If Mrs. Flynn is going home, I think I'll accompany her. It has been a tiring day. Please excuse me, gentlemen."

I left them on the terrace and found Theresa. "I'm ready to come home with you, Cousin dear," I said, slipping my arm through hers.

❧ Fourteen ☙

By the time the chauffeur had brought the automobile to the front door, it had begun to rain—big fat drops spattering onto the granite steps. The chauffeur leaped out to pull up the canopy over the car and we hustled to its sanctuary. The canopy wasn't very good at keeping off the rain, and we huddled together, wet and cold. I was shaking as violently as Theresa was, although it may have been from shock as much as from the weather. I tried not to think about Justin and what he might be saying at this very moment. Then Theresa gave a little moan and put her hand up to her head. "If only I didn't get these awful headaches," she sighed. "I know Barney thinks I'm a poor weak creature for being ill so often, but when they come it's like having a knife cut through my head."

"It was the excitement of the séance," I said, resolving to put my own worries aside.

"I'm sure it was. Hearing my son's voice like that. I'm still trembling about it. You do think he'll come again, don't you?"

"I'm sure of it," I said. If the Misses Sorensen wanted to continue to enjoy Adare, that was.

Theresa patted my knee. "It was very sweet of you to accompany me like this, Molly," she said, "but you make me feel most guilty. I do hope I didn't force you away from a potential beau."

"Absolutely not," I said. "I was not feeling too well either."

"Mr. Hartley is good-looking, is he not? And I understand his family has several properties—one of them in Ireland, so I'm told."

"Mr. Hartley may be good-looking but I found him a bore," I said. "And we Irish have little love for our English landowners."

"Of course. How silly of me to have overlooked that fact. He wasn't at all the right man for you, Molly. Too frail-looking and never smiled."

"So you're saying I need someone jolly and healthy like Barney," I said with a smile.

A brief spasm of alarm crossed her face. "I wouldn't recommend Barney as an example of a good husband. Too many outside interests."

I had clearly distressed her, so I asked quickly, "And what about Mr. Van Gelder? Is he not a good catch? He seems quite smitten with Belinda and he's young, healthy and amiable."

"Roland Van Gelder?" She shook her head. "Not a good catch, Molly. As you saw from their household, they have no money to speak of and Roland is a queer fish."

"How do you mean?" I leaned closer to her.

"He's never managed to hold a job, in spite of his father's influence to find him a good situation, and I watched him lose his temper with his horse once and hit it most brutally. I've never felt the same about him since then."

"How terrible. He seemed so amiable to me, if not too bright."

"Not all men are what they seem, Molly. Choose your husband with care; don't be swept off your feet as I was."

"But Barney seems devoted to you and he has certainly provided well for you."

"Barney is devoted when it suits him," she said. "But I shouldn't be speaking like this. You're his cousin, after all."

"I know nothing about him," I said. "Only what we've heard in Ireland and that's all good."

"He is a good man in many ways, but like Roland Van Gelder, he has his not-so-admirable side. And he's very ruthless. He'll do anything to get what he wants."

"I suspect that is true of most powerful men," I said. "Weaklings don't get into the Senate."

She laughed and patted my hand again. "You are such a realist, Molly. You think almost like a man." I don't think she meant this as a compliment.

The chauffeur tooted the horn and the gatekeeper came running out of his lodge to open the big iron gates. I heard them clang shut behind us as we drove through. Soames met us with an umbrella and hot milk was brought to my room. It wasn't until I was finally alone that the full impact of my meeting with Justin Hartley hit me. I was cold and wet and shivered so violently that my numb fingers wouldn't unlace the hated corset. I cursed at it and sat on my bed, fighting back the tears that welled up. I was being just the kind of ninny that I despised, but I couldn't help it. Now that I knew he was alive, I could never feel safe again. What if he did some checking to prove whether I really was Molly Gaffney or not? What if he contacted Molly Gaffney's family in Ireland? If he told the Flynns the truth about me, I'd still have some fancy explaining to do. And even worse, one day I might open my front door to find someone with an extradition order, come to take me back to trial in Ireland.

A flash of lightning and a loud clap of thunder overhead startled me. Rain came in a solid downpour. I considered ringing for the maid to undress me, then was instantly ashamed of my weakness. I wrestled with the dratted corset until I was finally free. Then I climbed into bed and hugged my knees to me. I wanted to be away from this place and back to the safety and anonymity of New York, where I had friends to take care of me. I would have to find a way to free myself from Theresa and get on with the job I came to do.

The storm raged on and sleep wouldn't come. I opened my eyes, suddenly alert, at the small sound of my bedroom door opening. A flash of lightning illuminated a figure creeping toward me, glowing with a pale light. I sat up with a gasp of fear.

"Shhh!" The figure put a finger to his lips. "It's only me, Molly. Cousin Barney. I thought you might be frightened by the storm."

I watched him crossing the floor toward me. He was carrying a candle.

"It's kind of you to be concerned," I said, "but I'm perfectly fine. We get some pretty fierce storms in Ireland, you know."

"Yes, I suppose you do." He put the candle down on the small table beside my bed and perched on the edge of my bed itself. His speech was slurred and I could smell the alcohol on his breath. I wasn't sure what to do next and just sat there, hugging the bedclothes around me.

"I'm really all right, Barney," I reiterated. "You can go back to your own bed. I don't think Theresa would be happy if she caught you in here."

"Theresa has no doubt taken one of her sleeping powders and will hear nothing until morning," he said, "and as for my own bed, it's awfully lonely, you know. Cold and empty and lonely." His hand slid toward me and moved up my arm to my shoulder. "I told you before that I'm a normal man with normal needs, Molly. And I get the feeling that you're a hot-blooded woman. We'd go well together."

I had been frozen with fear and fascination until his hand moved to the neck of my nightgown and his fingers explored inside the thin cotton batiste. Then I was out of bed with one great leap.

"Are you out of your mind?" I demanded, half of me still trying to react the way I thought Molly Gaffney might while the other half wanted to hit him over the head with the nearest hard object. "Your own cousin. Have you no shame? Think of my poor mother, lying in her grave."

"Molly, don't throw me out. A fellow could go mad with desire, you know. Nobody needs to know."

He reached for me again. Again I bounded out of reach. "Cousin Barney!" I pushed away his hand. "It's the drink making you behave like this. You'll regret it in the morning. Now go back to bed before I scream loud enough to wake the entire household."

Without warning he sat down on my bed and started to sob. "You don't know what it's like," he mumbled. "She won't let me near her. Treats me like a stranger. I'm all alone, Molly. All alone."

I went to put an arm around him, then thought better of it. Instead, I lifted him to his feet like a child. "You'll be fine," I said. "What you need right now is a good night's sleep." I thrust the candlestick into his hand. "Go on, off with you."

This approach seemed to work. Maybe it kindled memories of his mother.

"I'm sorry," he muttered. "I don't know what came over me." And he ambled back down the hallway, leaving me shaken and wide awake. I put a chair under my door handle in case he had any more nocturnal wanderings before I crawled back into bed and lay there listening to the storm. Why did life have to be so full of complications? It was bad enough having Justin Hartley to worry about without having to bar my door against Barney Flynn. Marrying Jacob and settling down as a housewife didn't seem such a bad option after all. But then I remembered that dear, kind Jacob, who always asked my permission to brush his lips against mine, had been too weak to acknowledge my existence to his cousins. And then there was Daniel—whom I would probably never stop loving, but who was too weak to break off a loveless engagement.

What was the matter with men? I asked myself. Some of them were too weak to control their animal impulses, some too weak to go against society. And they called us the weaker sex! It seemed to me that we were braver and more steadfast than the lot of them. I resolved to steer clear of difficult male entanglements in the future. Having decided this, I fell sound asleep.

Next morning I woke to bright sunlight streaming in through my window. I came down to breakfast to find that Theresa was still feeling unwell and would keep to her bed for the day.

"That damned séance," Barney muttered. "I knew it would only upset her." He didn't look me in the eye as he came into breakfast.

We learned also that the Misses Sorensen were keeping to their cottage and having their meals sent over to them. Two séances in two nights had apparently taxed their strength and they needed time to rest and recover. This was not good news for me. I was free but unable to do any snooping around the Sorensen Sisters' cottage.

Instead I took a notebook and a folding garden chair onto the lawn by the river, on the pretext of writing letters home. Last night's storm had cleared the air, producing a clear cool morning. Birds twittered, bees buzzed, dragonflies darted over the water. There were cheery shouts from riverboatmen as their craft passed in the stream. Tom and Adam were working together, chatting as they cleared away tree limbs that had come down in last night's storm. All in all a peaceful scene, quite in contrast to the turmoil going on in my head.

Get a grip on yourself and start thinking like an investigator, I reprimanded myself. There was nothing I could do where Justin Hartley was concerned. I could only hope that his friend Captain Cathers would take him off on a westward journey as soon as possible, where, in uncharitable fashion, I hoped he might meet hostile Indians or charging buffalo. In the meantime I had two cases to solve. I picked up my pencil and analyzed what I knew about the Flynn baby's kidnapping.

Given the nature of the house, the number of servants and the visibility from the windows, it was either the nursemaid, Morell or someone else from the household who took Brendan out in broad daylight. Unless—I paused and chewed on my pencil, a bad habit and one for which I was caned across the knuckles in school, but which always helped me to think. Unless the child had somehow been drugged and carried out in some kind of container. A laundry basket? A grocer's delivery box? I would have to check what deliveries were made that day. There would be little point in asking Soames, who wouldn't talk to me, but I had yet to interview the cook. She must have been aware of all deliveries from her vantage point in the kitchen.

Speak with Cook, I wrote in my book.

I took my thoughts one stage farther. If it were a stranger who had carried Brendan out of the house, then why hide him on the property? Why not spirit him away in a laundry cart or on a delivery boy's bicycle and hide him somewhere less dramatic? I took this one stage farther. The very act of hiding the child on the property must have been an extra act of cruelty done to taunt the Flynns. The kidnapping might then have been done as much for revenge or spite as for money.

Look into those who might have a grievance against Barney Flynn, I wrote.

Another thought—preparing a chamber to conceal the child would have taken time and tools. It wouldn't have been easy for an outsider to find a way onto the property carrying spades and everything else needed to create a subterranean space. I thought of little Brendan, waking up to darkness, crying unheard, and shuddered. It was truly a horrible crime, not a simple act of greed.

I tried to push personal feelings aside. A good investigator never gets personally involved. That's what Paddy Riley, my mentor, had said. So far I hadn't managed to follow his advice once. The most logical suspect, I wrote in the notebook, would therefore have access to tools on the property. He would not arouse suspicion if seen moving around with tools. That meant Bertie Morell or the gardeners. Both Tom and Adam had been kept on because they had been absent that day, but could they have helped with the preparation?

Again the thought struck me that it was such an audacious, complicated and risky undertaking that it surely came from the mind of more than one person. Adam admitted to enjoying a beer with Bertie at the local saloon, and Annie Lomax had expressed mistrust for Adam. Had they hatched a plot together? But no, that was a ridiculous thought, because Adam would then know where the child was buried and would have spoken up to save him. Nobody would keep silent in such circumstances. Nobody except an unfeeling, inhuman monster. So, in the absence of such a monster, Bertie Morell had done the deed alone.

Still, if I were to help Annie Lomax, I had to keep trying. Joseph Rimes and Desmond O'Mara had both been here when Brendan was taken, although according to all reports, they had been working with Senator Flynn all afternoon. But even people hard at work sometimes look out of windows. I'd try to strike up a friendship with the unappealing Mr. O'Mara and maybe even the self-important Mr. Rimes.

But first things first. There were two gardeners at work within plain sight. I got up and made my way over to where Adam was swinging a wood chopper with alarming force at a dead limb that was hanging down from a buckeye tree.

"What a terrible storm last night, wasn't it?" I said.

They both looked up.

"Oh, good morning, miss. Yes, there was a bit of a storm, wasn't there?" old Tom said. "I hope you ladies didn't get too wet on your way home from next door."

"I survived it well," I said, "but Mrs. Flynn is still keeping to her bed today."

"There's no denying she's always been delicate and more so since you-know-what happened."

"You mean the kidnapping?" I asked.

They were both looking away from me, eyes on the ground.

"We try not to mention it, miss," Tom muttered.

"I find it hard not to think about it," I went on. "I mean, being here and knowing that a poor little helpless child—" I broke off. "Don't you find it impossible to believe that Mr. Morell acted alone? I mean, you two are out on the grounds all the time. Wouldn't you have spotted him digging the hole? Wouldn't he have had to borrow your tools?"

They looked perplexed about this, as if the idea had only just come to them.

"The policeman asked if we'd seen anyone digging on the estate and we told him no, we hadn't. But of course he could have done his evil work at night, couldn't he?" Adam said. "Living so far from the main house, he could come and go as he pleased."

"I told you before about idle gossip, boy," Tom reprimanded. "No good can come of speculating now. It's over, finished, and no amount of talking will bring the boy back. So you get back to your work, Adam. And you, miss, have been warned before about resurrecting the past."

"Thomas!" A shrill voice interrupted us.

Cousin Clara came striding across the lawns, waving a trowel. She was dressed in a gardening smock, sunbonnet and rubber boots, and carried a flat basket over one arm.

"Have you turned over that bed as I asked you?"

"What bed was that, Miss Tompkins?"

"I told you, stupid man!" Clara's face was as red as the cherry-colored smock she wore. "I said that Miss Henderson in the village had given me all these geranium cuttings and that they would be ready to plant out in a couple of weeks. They are now ready and I expected you to have prepared a bed for them."

"Sorry, miss. I didn't get no orders from the mistress." Tom faced her with an impassive stare. "But I expect Adam and me can find you a patch of ground, if you're set on putting them cuttings somewhere."

"A patch of ground? You speak me to as if I'm some child to be appeased. When I wanted to grow tomatoes last year you made all kinds of difficulties and found me a bed with no sun."

"Taking care of the grounds is our work, begging your pardon, miss. It's not something ladies should be doing."

Clara's face flushed even redder. "I happen to find gardening very healthful and growing things very satisfying. One of you will come with me immediately and help me find a suitable spot for these plants, or I'll have to report you to Mrs. Flynn."

Tom cast a quick glance at Adam. "Go with her, boy. There's room up against the back of the kitchen where that wisteria's past its prime. Geraniums can take a lot of sun. Off you go then."

Clara stomped off with Adam. Tom ventured to give me a grin. "Spinsters," he said. "I reckon something happens to them when they turn thirty with no man in their lives. Something goes wrong in their heads. Still, she's been company for the mistress all these years, poor soul. Now, if you'll excuse me, miss, I must get back to clearing this brush away."

I went back to my seat on the lawn, watching the two figures of Clara and Adam stomping side by side through the grass. Another person who had access to garden tools and who was, according to Tom, not quite right in the head.

Ridiculous, I muttered to myself. I was desperately searching for a suspect when everything still pointed to Bertie Morell. But I did write her name in the book.

❧ Fifteen ❧

I spent a few minutes writing a note to Daniel to report on my progress.

Dear Daniel,

I have been in the house two days now and attended two séances. While I don't believe in spirits, I have to admit that both were most impressive, with walking hands, talking heads and voices that seemed to come from different parts of the room. I am sure the sisters are fakes, however, as they conjured up Molly Gaffney's mother, not mine!

They are staying in a guest cottage and keep themselves to themselves most of the time. I haven't yet found a chance to snoop in the cottage but will take the first chance I get.

I signed it "Yours, Molly," before I remembered that I wasn't his, and probably would never be. So I added the word "Sincerely" and shoved the letter into an envelope, carefully addressing it to D. Sullivan at his home and giving no mention of his profession.

Then I decided that I had given Clara enough time to be fully engrossed in her plantings and made my way up to the house. I found her kneeling at a narrow bed beside the kitchen wall. A rather straggly wisteria was now showing the last of its purple blooms, but the bed below it had been empty except for some forget-me-nots.

Clara looked up suspiciously as I approached.

"I came to see if you needed any help," I said. "I was sure you must be upset at being spoken to so rudely by the gardener."

Clara pressed her lips together, then controlled herself and looked up. "It was most distressing, most. You have no idea what it's like, Miss Gaffney, always being the poor relation. Poor, dear Clara whom nobody really wants. They keep me on here as Theresa's companion, but she doesn't enjoy my presence and rarely includes me in her excursions. Only when she needs someone to carry her packages."

She looked away again.

I decided to take the plunge. "Do you often go into town shopping with Theresa?"

"She takes me with her whenever she goes into New York. As I said, she needs someone to carry her packages."

I started, as if an idea had just come to me. "So Theresa must have taken you with her that day," I said. "The day the baby was kidnapped?"

She looked up in horror that I should dare to mention it.

"I'm sorry," I said hastily. "I shouldn't have brought it up, but I've only just heard the details and I'm so shocked by it all that I need to talk to someone about it."

"It was awful," she said, shuddering. "A true nightmare. Theresa and I had taken an early train to New York. We arrived back at around five and were met with the horrible news that the child was missing. Of course no note had been found at that stage."

"Were you met at the station?" I asked.

"No, at the ferry. Theresa has a fear of small boats so we always rode the train as far as Garrison where there is a proper ferry across to the military establishment at West Point. The chauffeur always met us at the ferry dock."

"The chauffeur came to meet you?" I blurted out. "But I thought he was the one who—"

"It just shows what a cool customer the man was. He did seem upset when he met us, but of course, he had to break the news that the child was missing."

"Then he drove you back to the house?"

"At great speed. And even had the effrontery to join in the search."

"When were the police called in?"

"When the ransom note was discovered, later that evening. Even though the note stated that the police were not to be involved, Barney didn't care. He just wanted his child found quickly. But, of course, by not obeying instructions it cost him his son in the end. They staked out the spot in the forest. Morell must have seen a movement among the trees as he came to pick up the ransom money, because he started to flee. And a stupid policeman shot him in the back." She sighed and put her hand to her chest. "It is still as painful as if it were yesterday, Miss Gaffney. We all adored that child. He was the light of his mother's life, and his father's too. Everyone who knew him loved him. Even that devil of a chauffeur used to play with him and offer him candies, when all the while he was plotting to—" She broke off and put her handkerchief up to her mouth. "Forgive me," she muttered through the handkerchief. "I find this subject too distressing and my cuttings will wilt if I don't get them into the ground quickly."

I left her, feeling guilty that I had stirred up her grief again. I had learned nothing more than that the chauffeur came to meet them from the ferry as scheduled. I wasn't sure what this proved, except that the man had a cool head. But I'd already established that much.

I stepped into the coolness of the marble hallway and let my eyes accustom themselves to the darkness. From Senator Flynn's office I heard the sound of raised voices. "Dammit, Joe. I'll not stoop to that level."

"You're going to have to do something, Barney, and you're going to have to do it soon. Don't think that everyone loves you. They won't hesitate to use the scandal if they have to, you know."

"They can't have found it out. Nobody can have talked."

"There are no beans people won't spill for enough money. You should know that better than anyone, Barney. And I'm warning you that there are no lengths to which they won't go."

I tiptoed across the hall, not wanting to be caught eavesdropping, and made my way up the stairs. It occurred to me that I had never visited the first scene of the crime—the nursery. I had promised young Eileen a visit and she'd probably welcome a change from her very boring and restricted routine. I stood outside the nursery door and knocked before turning the handle.

The nanny looked up, startled at my entry, and scrambled to her feet. Eileen jumped up too.

"Have you come to see my doll's house?" she asked.

"Eileen, it's not polite to ask questions of adults. Speak when you are spoken to. How many times do I have to tell you? May I help you, miss?" Her large, severe face had no humor in it and I didn't think Eileen could have a very jolly life stuck in the nursery with her.

"I promised Eileen I would pay her a call," I said, "and she promised to show me her doll's house. Is it convenient? I haven't interrupted anything, have I?"

"I was just playing with my Noah's ark," Eileen said before her nurse could send me away again. "Come and see—isn't it beautiful?"

I didn't think the Noah's ark was very beautiful. It looked rather well worn. The paint had faded on the wooden animals and some of them were missing an ear or a leg.

"It looks very nice," I said. "Have you had it a long time?"

"A very, very long time," Eileen said. "It used to belong to my brother. Did you know I have a brother in heaven? His name was Brendan, but we don't talk about him because it makes Mama sad. So now it's my Noah's ark. It used to be his favorite toy and now it's mine."

"I don't know what she sees in it." Nurse sniffed her disapproval. "Her father buys her all these wonderful toys and she plays with that thing, day in and day out."

I sat on a nearby stool and studied the line of animals she had arranged going over one side of the fireside rug and down the other. "You've got the elephant lined up with the camel," I said, smiling at the child.

"That's because the other elephant and camel are lost and they'd be lonely." She looked up with her solemn little eyes. I realized I had yet to see her smile.

"Oh, in that case, I'm glad they've found a friend."

I got up and walked around, examining the doll's house and the rest of her toys. At the same time I noted that it was a corner room, with two windows, but no way down or up. The creeper didn't cover this part of the house. Through an open doorway I saw the night nursery with its small white bed. Whoever came to snatch Brendan would have had to come through the house, past Soames and all those watchful eyes.

The room would be any child's fantasy—a large china doll almost as big as Eileen herself, a small china tea set, books, paints, a doll's cradle and a magnificent doll's pram.

"What a beautiful doll's pram," I said. It was like a miniature real perambulator, compete with wicker hood and slung coach frame.

"Papa bought it for me. It's called a baby buggy."

I smiled. "In Ireland where I come from we'd call it a perambulator."

"That's a silly word. Buggy is better."

"All right. We'll call it a buggy then. It looks very new. Have you only just got it?"

"No, she's had it some time," Nurse answered for her. "She doesn't have much opportunity to take it out, seeing that my legs are bad and I can't walk far."

"Dear me, that's a pity," I said. "Maybe Eileen and I could go for walks together while I'm staying here?"

"Oh yes, please." Eileen ran over and hugged my skirt. "I'd like to go for walks with you and I can take my doll out in the buggy too. Can we go now?"

Nurse glanced up at the cuckoo clock on the wall. "Your lunch will be served in forty minutes. By the time we have one of the servants carry the buggy downstairs and we get you dressed in your outdoor shoes and sunbonnet, there would be no time."

"How about after your afternoon nap then?" I asked.

"Eileen has to go down to tea with her mother."

"Eileen's mother is sick in her bed today. I'm sure she won't want a visit if she's not feeling well."

"Is that right?" Nurse had obviously worked out that a walk with me would give her time for her own forty winks. "Well, there's no denying the fresh air would do her good, as long as she doesn't run around and get herself too hot."

"I'll be back around three then, Eileen," I said. "Make sure you have your doll dressed for an outing."

"I will." She nodded solemnly again and walked beside me to the nursery door. As I closed it quietly behind me a voice spoke in my ear, making me jump.

"Can I help you, Miss Gaffney? Did you lose your way again?"

I turned around to see Soames standing behind me, looking down his nose in that disapproving way.

"Soames, you startled me," I said. "I didn't see you coming up the staircase."

"That's because I came up the back stairs, miss Gaffney."

"Oh, is there a back staircase?"

"Just for the servants' use, miss. Servants are not allowed to be seen on the main stair. That door you were trying leads to the nursery."

"Yes, I know," I said. "I have just been visiting Miss Eileen."

Was that a look of alarm that crossed his face? "What for?"

I had had enough of the supercilious butler treating me as if I was a snooping stranger. "Heavens, Soames. Miss Eileen is my own cousin. Do I need a permission form from you to visit her?"

He backed away. "I'm sorry, Miss Gaffney. I didn't mean to imply—"

"Well, imply you did. I went to visit the child because she invited me to see her doll's house. And I should have thought you'd be glad for the poor little mite to have some company, stuck away on her own in there. It's not natural for a child to grow up shut away with just that sour-faced nurse as a companion."

"Nevertheless, that's the way it is done in the better households," he said smoothly.

"While I'm here, I intend to cheer her up," I said. "Will you ask one of the servants to carry down the doll's pram at three o'clock sharp? I'll be taking Miss Eileen and her dolls for a walk."

With that I walked toward my room. I waited until Soames had disappeared, then I sprinted down the hallway and discovered the back stairs off a side passage. They were narrow and uncarpeted and I crept down, holding my breath, half expecting Soames to be waiting for me at the bottom. Instead, the stairs ended in a similar side hall with the kitchen door at one end and various closet doors on either side. If anyone had carried Brendan down the back stairs, he'd still have had to make his exit through the kitchen or risk the entire length of the house and the front door. I hoped that lunch would be outstandingly good today because I needed an excuse to pay a visit to the cook.

❧ Sixteen ❧

I was in luck. It was Friday and Cook served a really delicious steamed turbot with parsley sauce for lunch, followed by an apple crumble and custard. Theresa remained in bed and initially just Clara, Belinda and I sat down at the long mahogany table. The men entered when we were halfway through our fish, did not apologize for their lateness and continued a conversation that had begun in Barney's study. It seemed to be a list of people Barney could count on to sway the voters in particular parts of the state. The notion of swaying voters had been quite new to me when I arrived in New York, but I had already witnessed such swaying, in one case amounting to kidnapping and threats of bodily harm if the voter didn't put his X in the right place. Since I was a female, and hence couldn't vote, I ignored them and they me.

"I am dying of boredom," Belinda announced, pushing her plate away with the fish half eaten. "After Paris and Florence I thought I'd welcome the chance to do nothing, but I'm too used to the whirl of high society. Do you know in London we dined with different people every single night, and went to theaters too. There's absolutely nothing to do here."

"We could play croquet," Clara suggested and got a withering stare in return.

"Clara, we always play croquet. I suppose I could go out for a bicycle ride. Would you like to join me, Molly? We could ride in the direction of the military academy and see if the young men are practicing any interesting maneuvers."

"Really, Belinda, I'm sure your sister wouldn't approve," Clara said.

"Don't be such an old fuddy-duddy, Clara," Belinda said, giving me a grin. "How about it, Molly?"

"I'm afraid I've never tried to ride a bicycle," I said, "and I don't have the proper clothing."

"It's not hard to ride a bicycle. I'm sure you'd master it quickly and you'd find it fun. And it's an excuse to wear bloomers."

Clara gasped and put her hand to her mouth. "You would never consider leaving the estate in those things, Belinda? And possibly being seen by the young men at the academy?"

"Of course. What else does one wear to ride a bicycle? Skirts get caught up in the chain."

"I'm afraid I don't possess bloomers either," I said.

"I'm sure Theresa possesses bloomers she would lend you," Belinda said. "She owns bicycles, so she must have the right clothing. I'll ask her maid for you."

"Belinda, as your older cousin, I must forbid it."

"Fiddlesticks, Clara, you're such an old stick-in-the-mud. This is now the twentieth century. I'm going to learn to drive an automobile when I get home."

"Speak to her, Barney," Clara insisted.

Barney looked up from his conversation. "About what?"

"Belinda insists on riding a bicycle, wearing bloomers, in the direction of the military academy."

A grin crossed Barney's face. "Asking for trouble, eh, Belinda? Going to drive the young soldiers wild with a show of leg?"

Belinda flushed. "Of course not. Just healthy exercise, dear cousin. And I'm trying to persuade Molly to come with me."

"But I don't know how to ride a bicycle," I added. "And I promised Eileen that I'd take her for a walk this afternoon."

"So tell her she can't go out alone, Barney," Clara said.

Barney glanced at Clara, then smiled again. "I'm sure you'll be just fine, Belinda. And you'll never make it as far as the military academy on a bicycle. It's all up and down, you know. I'll wager you'll only get as far as the Van Gelders, but perhaps it's Roland you're secretly hoping to visit."

"That oaf? Good heavens, no. Whatever gave you that idea?" Belinda said, but her cheeks had turned red and I realized that her secret motive might be to pay a call on one of the Van Gelders' visitors. I was glad I hadn't agreed to accompany her.

After lunch Belinda paraded through the house in her bloomers. I wasn't sure whether this was designed to shock Clara or flirt with Barney. Knowing that gentleman's personality I felt that she was playing with fire by encouraging him, but perhaps she already knew that.

"I've asked Theresa's maid to find you a pair," Belinda said. "Then I can teach you to ride a bicycle too. It's a skill every young woman should possess."

"I'd dearly like to learn," I said.

I waited until she had departed for the coach house and Clara had gone for her afternoon rest before I headed for the kitchen. A large, round-faced colored woman was sitting in a rocking chair by the open window, fanning herself with a newspaper as she rocked. Beyond the kitchen in the scullery I could hear the clatter of pots and pans as the scullery maid washed the dishes.

As I tapped politely on the door, the woman looked up and scrambled to her feet.

"It's all right, Cook. Please don't get up," I said. "I'm Miss Gaffney, the master's cousin, and I just came to tell you how delicious I thought the lunch was."

Cook's elderly face crinkled into a smile. "Well, isn't that kind of you, miss. I have to admit I do make a good, smooth white sauce and the master tells me my apple crumble is the best he ever tasted."

"It certainly was," I said. "I understand you've been with the family a long time."

"All my life, miss. I started in the kitchen with Miz Theresa's family in Virginia, and when Miz Theresa got married, they asked me if I'd like to go with her as cook. Of course I said yes. The chance to run my own kitchen doesn't come around every day."

"So you're one of the few servants they kept after the tragedy," I said. "I heard that they sacked everyone."

"That's right, miss," Cook said, her face growing serious. "Me'n Soames, we were the only two they kept on. Well, they knew they could trust us, having been with the family for so long. And on account of the master particularly liking my cookin'." She laughed at this joke, her large body heaving silently. "They take me everywhere with them. Why, they even took me when Miz Theresa was poorly and needed to go away to rest."

"After the tragedy, you mean?"

"When Miss Eileen was expected," she said, lowering her eyes modestly at the talk of such intimate matters. "She couldn't take the cold in New York so the master sent her to Florida for the winter. I was the only one she trusted to go with her." She gave a little smirk of satisfaction. "That's coz I know which side my bread is buttered."

"The Senator and Mrs. Flynn are lucky to have such a good cook," I said.

She preened then. "They even take me with them to Washington when they leave the rest of the servants behind. I've cooked for all kinds of famous folks, you know. Senators, generals—"

"Have you really? How wonderful." I looked suitably impressed.

"I'll tell you another who always praised my cooking," she said confidentially. "That devil. Albert Morell, the chauffeur. You heard about him, of course."

"Oh yes. We heard all about him, even in Ireland," I said.

"I warned Annie Lomax enough times," Cook said, shaking her head. "She was the child's nursemaid who was sweet on him. I said to her, 'You watch yourself, my girl.' If he was a sailor he'd have a girl in every port. He wasn't Irish but he could charm the hind leg off a donkey, just like the master can. Always hanging about in this kitchen, praising my cooking. 'Your food is fit for the gods, Beulah.' That's what he'd say. And I was fool enough to spoil him—save him tidbits from the master's table, you know."

"You said he wasn't Irish," I interrupted. "What was he? I think I read he was born locally?"

"Upstate New York, around Albany way, and he said his folks came from England. But you know what I thought?" She leaned closer to me, although we two were alone in the kitchen. "I always thought he had Italian blood in him. He had those dark flashing eyes and his skin in summertime used to go almost as dark as mine."

Of course, I thought. There was something about the name that hadn't fit. What if it was originally Alberto Morelli! I'd have to look into that.

"I should have known he was rotten to the core," Cook went on. "I should have suspected when he took one of my meringues. We were having a dinner party that night and I had made twenty-four meringue nests to be filled with strawberries and cream. When I came to fill them there were only twenty-three and then Fanny, the scullery maid, said she'd seen Bertie crunching something as he walked through the kitchen."

"Did he always come and go through the kitchen?" I asked. I looked out of the window. The kitchen garden began after a thin strip of lawn. I could make out the thatched roof of the guest cottage at the rear of the kitchen garden, then, to the right, there was a clear view of the gravel drive and the carriage house beyond.

"It was a short cut from the carriage house, wasn't it?" Cook said. "As a matter of fact he wasn't supposed to be in the main house at all, but he'd drop in here from time to time, and sometimes he'd sneak upstairs to visit Annie."

"That day the child was taken, did he come in through the kitchen then?"

She shook her head. "It was after lunch, wasn't it? I always take my forty winks in this chair, but I'd have woken up if anyone came to the door. I'd swear he didn't bring the child out this way."

"What about deliveries that day?"

"Deliveries?" She looked puzzled.

"Laundry? Grocery boy?"

"What are you getting at?" she asked.

"I was just wondering if the child could have been carried out in a laundry basket."

She shook her head. "The laundry is done right here, at that big copper in the scullery. Why do you think they keep all these maids?" She looked up at me. "There was no delivery that day and Bertie Morell didn't come through my kitchen. I reckon it was just what the police thought—he got his sweetheart, Annie Lomax, to bring the child to him."

I couldn't think of anything else to ask her. "I can see my main problem here is not eating so much that my corset won't lace properly." I smiled at her.

"You should be like Beulah, honey. Ain't never worn a corset and don't intend to. And always enjoyed my food, as I expect you can tell from this body!" Again she shook with silent laughter. A woman after my own heart!

I looked up at the kitchen clock and noted that Eileen would be expecting me soon. I left Cook, fanning herself and rocking again, and took a few minutes in my room to collect my thoughts before I went to fetch Eileen. I had learned nothing new from Cook, or had I? That Albert Morell was possibly Italian. That he sneaked in through the kitchen on occasion. That he could be very charming. But all of the above still pointed to his guilt.

Eileeen was dressed for her outing in a large-brimmed bonnet, trimmed with lace. Her petticoats were stiffly starched and she was wearing stout walking boots.

"You mind your manners with Miss Gaffney," the nanny said, "and don't go running and hurting yourself. Remember you're a lady."

Poor little thing, I thought, as I took her hand. I thought back to my own childhood when my brothers and I ran barefoot on beaches and climbed on rocks and slipped and skinned knees and came home freckled and dirty. Whoever said that money couldn't buy happiness was right.

The doll's pram was waiting for us outside the front door. Eileen took the handles and we set off across the lawns. She behaved like a perfect little lady, speaking only when spoken to and answering my questions in a small, grave voice. Even when I pointed out a flag-bedecked steamer going upriver and encouraged her to wave to it, it was a sedate wave with no joy in it.

The day was hot and muggy. Flies buzzed around us and I found myself wishing I had not suggested this outing. Clearly Eileen found pushing the pram heavy going over the grass, but wouldn't accept help from me. At last we reached the shade of the trees.

"Let's stop and rest for a while," I said. "I don't know about you, but I'm all hot and sweaty."

"You mustn't say sweaty. It's not polite," she corrected.

I sat on a fallen tree trunk and encouraged her to sit beside me. She did, cautiously smoothing her white dress.

"It's nice here in the forest, isn't it?" I asked. "Almost as if we're explorers in the distant jungle. We could be miles from anywhere."

In answer a squirrel ran across the clearing and up a big pine tree. Eileen jumped up excitedly. "Look, a squirrel. Can we pet it?"

"I don't think it will stay around long enough for you to pet it," I said, "but next time we come out, we'll bring some nuts or bread-crumbs and see if we can get it to come down and eat."

"Oh yes, let's do that." For a moment she was an ordinary little girl. "What other animals do you think there are in the forest? Are there bears or wolves?"

"I don't think so," I said. "Foxes maybe, and badgers and lots of rabbits."

"Will we see them?"

"If we sit very quietly, maybe we'll see a rabbit."

She sat, holding her breath in concentration. A jay screeched above our heads. A pigeon rose with noisy flapping of wings. Eileen was entranced. Then suddenly I got the strangest feeling. I could swear that we were being watched. Nothing moved in the undergrowth. I heard no sound, but I could feel the back of my neck prickling as if hostile eyes were on me.

I had not until now given a thought to the fact that another child had been kidnapped in broad daylight from this place. And hadn't Joseph Rimes given some kind of warning to Barney earlier today—something about no lengths to which they wouldn't go? Was it possible that the original kidnapping had some kind of political motive and that Barney knew more than he had told?

I stood up and jerked Eileen to her feet. "It's time to go back," I said.

"Oh no, please. I really want to see a rabbit," she protested.

"Another day. We'll come back another day." I took her by one hand and pushed the doll's pram with the other. She dragged behind me, protesting. "No, please. I don't want to go back. I don't want to . . ."

I didn't slow my pace until we were out on the sunlit lawn again.

❧ Seventeen ❧

I was in a quandary as to whether I should mention my suspicion to Barney. He'd surely want to know if his daughter was in danger. But by the time I returned to the house to find tea being laid on the veranda, I realized that I might have overreacted to what had been nothing more than a cool breeze from the river. Nevertheless, I decided not to take Eileen so far from help again.

Belinda didn't appear for tea, so it was just Clara and myself. Miss Emily and Miss Ella had also been absent all day and I inquired after their health.

"They've been having their meals sent over to them," Alice, the maid, said. "As if we don't have enough work to do around here without running up and down with food for them."

"Are they indisposed?" I asked.

"Not that I could see." She poured a cup of tea and placed it in front of me, giving me a look that indicated I probably wasn't worthy of being served either.

"I do hope nothing has happened to Belinda." Clara looked flushed from working in the garden all day.

"I'm sure she's fine. She probably stopped off to visit the Van Gelders and was invited to tea there."

"I do hope so." Clara fanned herself. "Young girls these days ask for trouble. Riding a bicycle to the military academy indeed.

145

There's no telling what those young men would do if they saw legs exposed to the knee!"

I went to my room to rest and change for dinner. By the time I came down again, Belinda was back and looking rather smug.

"Did you manage to ride as far as the military academy?" I asked.

"No, I didn't. Cousin Barney was absolutely right. It was much farther than I thought and the road is atrocious. I think it's a scandal there are no decent roads only an hour from New York City. What a backward country this is. There are fine roads all over France and England."

"So how far did you get?" Clara asked. "As far as the Van Gelders?"

Belinda tossed back her sausage curls. "Well, yes, as a matter of fact, I stopped off there for a glass of lemonade. It was devilishly hot work, riding a bicycle, you know."

Clara snorted. "Don't tell me you're getting sweet on Roland Van Gelder after all."

"Good heavens, no. Not if he was the last man on earth."

"Are their house guests still there?" I asked cautiously. "They said they planned to head out West."

"Captain Cathers and Mr. Hartley?" Belinda blushed faintly. "Yes, they were still there. And you made quite an impression on Mr. Hartley, Molly. He couldn't stop asking questions about you. He wanted to know all about your girlhood in Ireland. Of course I had to tell him that we knew nothing about Barney's numerous relatives in the old country." She gave me a wicked smile. "I'll wager he was trying to find out whether your family was prosperous enough to make a suitable match."

"Odious man," I said. "If he asks you about me again, please tell him I have no interest in furthering his acquaintance."

"I don't know why," Belinda said, and I thought she looked relieved. "He is quite good-looking. A little like Lord Byron, don't you think?"

"And just as brooding, I fear. I intend to pick a husband who can make me laugh."

"Then you should choose Roland Van Gelder," Belinda said, again tossing her hair. "His behavior is so pathetically comical that you'd be laughing every minute."

She swept ahead of me down the hallway.

We went into the drawing room together to find the Misses Sorensen had recovered enough to grace us with their presence. They were each sitting with a glass of sherry in their hands, working their way through a dish of cheese straws that had been placed between them.

"I was sorry to hear you were indisposed earlier today," I said.

"Our talent is very taxing," Miss Emily said. "Two nights in a row was too much for us. And we hear it was too much for poor Mrs. Flynn too. One does not meddle lightly with the spirit world."

"No indeed," said Miss Ella, her mouth full of cheese straw.

Cousin Theresa did not appear for dinner, neither did Barney or Joseph Rimes. I had thought we would be all women at the table, but then Mr. O'Mara appeared at the last moment, looking very embarrassed at the thought of sitting with a lot of women. He took a seat beside me and concentrated hard on eating his soup. It was leek and potato, on account of being Friday, but again Cook had done a wonderful job with it.

"So Senator Flynn has abandoned you to suffer through a hen party, has he, Mr. O'Mara?" I asked him.

He didn't smile. I hadn't expected him to, but he nodded seriously. "The Senator and Mr. Rimes had to meet with important backers. My services were not required."

I noticed Miss Emily and Miss Ella were scraping their bowls and looking around eagerly for the next course. On my other side Belinda was waxing lyrical about Paris fashions and the shocking amount of ankle that was being revealed on the Champs-Elysées. I took the opportunity to chat with Mr. O'Mara.

"How long have you been with Senator Flynn?" I asked.

"Almost six years."

"That's a long time for a young man like yourself. A secretarial position is all very fine, but I'd imagine you must be anxious to move on to something with better prospects."

"Beggars can't be choosers, Miss Gaffney," he said quietly.

"Have you ambitions to go into politics yourself one day?"

"Good Lord, no. Such a life wouldn't suit me at all."

"Then what kind of life would suit you?"

"I had thought to be a lawyer, when I graduated from Columbia University, but I now see that I am not suited to that profession. What about you, Miss Gaffney? How do you envision your future?"

"Aren't all ladies supposed to marry and have babies?" He noted my wicked grin.

"According to the young ladies at Vassar across the river, women can aspire to the law, to medicine, to vote, or to write witty novels if they put their minds to it."

"And why not?" I asked. "Is there anything in the male physique that would make a man more able to vote, practice law or write novels?"

"Stamina, Miss Gaffney. We are not prone to attacks of the vapors."

"That's only because we women are subjected to wearing ridiculous corsets. Apart from that, I would have thought we women were champions at stamina. Look at all those mothers who take care of twelve children. And take Mrs. Flynn—she's had to have stamina to bear the burden of reliving her tragedy every day for five years."

"I'd say she was buckling under that burden, Miss Gaffney."

"Maybe you're right. But what human being could endure it without buckling?"

"The Senator has had to get on with his life."

"That's because he has a life outside the home. Did you ever think that it was being cooped up, day in and day out, in a protective little cocoon that made women buckle?"

He looked at me as if I was a fellow human being for the first time. "You may be right," he said. "Under such conditions, even the strongest constitution can crack."

Later I wondered whether he had been talking about himself.

The next day Belinda informed me that Theresa was still feeling under the weather and would stay in bed yet again.

"She must have caught a chill when we returned home in the rain," I suggested.

Belinda shook her head. "It's all in her mind, Molly. There is nothing wrong with her body. She lives on the edge of sanity ever since that awful day. At one moment she appears bright and jolly, but the next she is plunged into the darkest depression. They have doctors these days who specialize in diseases of the mind. They're called alienists. We're trying to persuade her to see one, but she won't admit there is anything wrong."

"It must be very hard for you and Cousin Barney."

"Especially for Barney. You would not believe what he's had to endure since the kidnapping."

I nodded, wondering whether Barney had ever paid a visit to her room at night and whether she too had sent him away.

"So we are left to our own devices again today," Belinda went on. "I thought I might have one of the horses saddled up and ride over to the Van Gelders. I hear that Captain Cathers is a fine horseman. So was Mr. Hartley until his accident." She lowered her voice. "You know he was thrown from his horse during a hunt and landed on his head and almost died, don't you?"

"So I've been told," I answered.

"Poor man. Such a tragedy. No wonder he always looks brooding. He is lamenting what might have been. Do you want to ride over with me?"

I didn't like to admit that my riding was on a par with my bicycling skills.

"If you can find those bloomers, I think I'd like to practice riding a bicycle," I said. "But you go out riding by all means. I can have one of the groundsmen help me with my bicycle."

"If you really don't mind—" She gave me a sweet smile. "It's such a glorious day for riding, isn't it?"

The bloomers were found and I put them on, delighting in the lightness and freedom when I walked in them. I resolved to have a pair made when I returned to Greenwich Village and also, maybe, to buy myself a bicycle to carry me around the city. Both of these grand schemes would be dependent on my making some money, but I had been born an optimist. I collected the letter I intended to post to Daniel. It would be wiser if nobody in the house knew I was in contact with anyone in New York, I decided. Then I strode out onto the grounds, taking wonderful man-sized steps. As luck would have it, I ran into Adam, wheeling a barrowful of dead wood up the driveway.

"Just the person I was looking for," I said. "I was wondering, Adam, if you'd have a few minutes to spare to help me learn to ride a bicycle. I understand they are kept in the carriage house."

"Yes, miss, that's right," he said. "I'll be with you right after I've taken this load to the woodpile."

The big doors of the carriage house were open, revealing an automobile on one side and a grand-looking enclosed carriage on the other. Behind it were the mews and I heard the clip-clop of horse's hooves as Belinda rode out on a fine bay hunter. I looked around for the chauffeur but he was nowhere in sight. Stairs went up the outside of the wall to a door above which must be the chauffeur's residence. Formerly Bertie Morell's residence. I was sure the police would have searched it thoroughly. I wondered if the child had ever been held there.

"Here I am then, miss." Adam's cheerful voice cut short further musings. He wheeled a sturdy-looking bicycle out of the depths of the carriage house for me and dusted off the saddle. "Ever ridden one of these contraptions before?"

"Never. Is it hard?"

"Not once you get going. You just need to pick up speed and then you go straight enough. I'll hold it while you climb on."

I eased myself into the saddle and put my foot on the pedals.

"Now, I'm going to give you a push to start and then I'll keep hold of the back of your saddle for a while until you get going," he said. "Off we go then."

Suddenly I was moving forward. I turned the pedals and felt myself pick up speed. "Keep it straight, miss. Look straight ahead and keep peddling. That's it. You're doing fine." And I was moving on my own. Tentatively I turned the handlebars and rode in a circle. Then I slowed, wobbled and put my foot down just as Adam leaped to catch me.

"You did splendidly," he said. I noticed he was standing a little too close to me, one hand on the handlebars, the other on the back of the seat. "I've a feeling you're not quite as grand as the rest of these folks, or as least as grand as they'd like to be."

"You shouldn't talk that way about my cousin," I said, but I was smiling at him.

"Your cousin would still be living in a wooden house like the one my mother lives in, if he hadn't made a fortune in the ice trade."

"I heard about that," I said. "He bought a barge, sailed it up to Maine and came down with it full of ice, is that right?"

"That's how it got started," he said. "Then he set about getting a monopoly on the icehouses of New York City. Then, not content with that, he set about buying up all the ice along the river."

"How can you buy ice from a river? Nobody owns river water, do they?"

"There are ice-cutting leases up and down this river in wintertime," he said. "My father used to have one."

"Really? How interesting. He doesn't have it any more?"

"Flynn squeezed him out of it."

"Oh," I said, digesting this. "Then why do you work for him?"

"He pays good wages and it's convenient. My pa's dead now. My mother lives across the river and she's in poor health. So I'm able to help her out and see her real regular, which is good."

"And you were away visiting her the day the child was kidnapped?"

"That's right." But he averted his eyes.

"You say you and Bertie were good pals," I went on. "Did you ever think he'd pull off a thing like that?"

"Never in a million years," he said. "Oh, I'm not saying that Bertie was straight as a die. He'd cheat at cards, make himself ten bucks on a horse, that kind of thing. But nothing like that."

"So he never talked to you about his plans?"

He shook his head.

"He never talked big at all?"

"The only thing he ever talked about was going out West. Maybe to Alaska. 'There are plenty of suckers out there, Adam,' he'd say to me. 'I reckon I could make myself a mint in Alaska.'"

I took a deep breath before I asked the next question. "He never suggested that you go in with him then?"

"Me? Hey, I was on the other side of the river that day. If he planned something as evil as kidnapping that poor baby, he never told me about it."

"You know what I think," I said carefully. "I don't think it was his idea at all. I think someone was paying him, someone who had a grudge against the Flynns."

He was staring at me now, straight in the eye. "He never said a thing about that." He paused to consider. "Well, he wouldn't, would he? Anyone who knew who was behind it could wind up dead." He glanced around. "Look, I have work to do. You're doing just fine on the bicycle. Off you go then."

I set off up the driveway with quite a bit of wobbling to begin with, and also a lot to think about. If anyone had a grudge against the Flynns, it had to be Adam himself. His father had been cheated out of his livelihood. His mother lived in poverty. It only took a few minutes by boat to cross the river and I had seen how well he handled a boat.

The gatekeeper swung open the gate for me. "Go careful then, miss," he said. "Watch out for traffic on the road. Too many automobiles these days."

I smiled as I set off in the direction of the nearest village, away from West Point and the Van Gelders. The road was empty, with no sign of traffic of any kind, apart from a dog who trotted along, minding his own business. I had no idea how far it was but I assumed I would come to a hamlet of some sort before too long. At first it was a steep uphill climb as the road skirted the mountain above the Flynns' property. I had to dismount and push until I came to the crest. I was sweaty, red-faced and out of breath when I came to the top and I stood for a while, wishing I had brought water with me. Then I mounted again and started the long descent. It was delightful, feeling the cool breeze in my face and watching the trees flashing by me. I was about halfway down when I realized something rather vital—I didn't know how to stop. On the flat it was merely a question of not pedaling. Now I was not pedaling and going ever faster.

My straw hat flew off. Pins came out of my hair. By now I was definitely frightened and not at all sure how this could end safely, unless I met an uphill slope soon. Buildings appeared before me— the hamlet I had been seeking. If I shouted for help, maybe someone would rush to my aid, but I have always hated to look foolish. I'd choose disaster over embarrassment any day. I hurtled past the first homes. I was halfway down what passed for a main street when the disaster occurred. A young woman came out of the general store and started to cross the street. I shouted, but too late. She looked up to see me bearing down on her. I swerved to my right to avoid her. She dodged to her left to avoid me. The bicycle skidded and I struck her as I went flying.

❧ Eighteen ❧

The breath was knocked out of me as I hit the dirt road. For a moment I lay there, tangled up in my bicycle, too shocked to move. Then I remembered the young woman I had struck and tried to extricate myself from the machine. By this time the noise of our collision had reached the nearest houses. Large hands lifted the bicycle from me and helped me to sit up.

"Are you all right, miss? Easy now. Careful. Don't try to take it too fast."

Beside me the young woman had already scrambled to her feet and was brushing herself off. "Are you all right?" she asked me.

"More to the point, are you?" I stood up, somewhat shakily. "I am most terribly sorry. It was my first time on a bicycle and I couldn't stop the wretched thing."

"I always knew those contraptions were a bad idea," the local man who had helped me up grunted. "God expected humans to walk on their own two feet, not go racing through the countryside, mowing down innocent folk."

I examined my victim for signs of damage. She appeared to have come through the ordeal with no cuts or scrapes that I could see. But there was an ugly streak across the pale silk of her dress. "Oh no. I have ruined your lovely dress. There is oil on your skirt. How will we be able to clean it?"

"Please don't upset yourself." The young woman gave me an encouraging smile. "We have both survived with no broken limbs. Let us count ourselves lucky."

"Bring the young ladies inside, Homer," a woman instructed. "They'd probably like a nice cool glass of lemonade and a chance to rest."

We were led into the nearest building while the bicycle was wheeled behind us. I was grateful to sit in the cool darkness and it took me a moment to realize we were in a saloon. The young woman had obviously realized the same thing, because she looked at me and smiled. She had a delightful smile with dimples in her cheeks.

"I never thought when I set out for a walk today that I would wind up in a saloon," she whispered.

"It may be the only time in our lives that we are actually invited inside," I whispered back.

"With pure intentions anyway."

We shared a laugh. I examined the delicate fabric of her skirt. It was a fine silk, pale blue.

"Maybe they can find us some soap and warm water so that we can try to remove the worst of the damage to your skirt."

She put her hand onto mine. "Don't worry about it, please. I'll ask my landlady to tackle it, and if she can't, then I'll have my dressmaker put in a new panel."

"But I should at least pay you to right the damage."

"Fiddlesticks." She smiled again. "It was quite an adventure, wasn't it? I've never been run down by a bicycle before."

"And I have never hurtled down a hill on one." I held out my hand to her. "My name is Molly M—, Molly Gaffney."

"Margie McAlister," she said. "Goodness, you're bleeding," she added as she examined my arm. "We must ask our hostess for some water to clean your cuts."

My forearms and palms were starting to sting. Lemonade was brought, then our hostess returned with the hot water and gauze. Miss McAlister waved the woman aside and set about cleaning my grazes with precision.

"You'll live," she said. "Bathe them again in an antiseptic solution tonight and cover them with loose gauze pads."

"You seem very professional at the task," I commented.

"I have done some nursing in my time."

"Do you live around here, or are you a visitor?" I asked.

"A visitor. I live in Georgetown, just outside our nation's capital, where it is unpleasantly hot at the moment. I thought that the quiet atmosphere by the river might be beneficial to my health," she said. "And you?"

"I'm also a visitor, staying with relatives."

"You're from Ireland?"

"How could you tell, the accent or the red hair and freckles?" I asked with a laugh.

She gave me a wistful smile. "I understand it's a very beautiful country. Are you just over for the summer or do you live in America permanently now?"

"I'm just on a visit," I said, deciding I should stick to being Molly Gaffney, just in case. "I haven't decided how long I'll stay. My cousin Theresa doesn't want to part with me."

"Theresa?" I saw a flicker of reaction in those large dark eyes before she went back to the gauze she was wringing out.

"Senator and Mrs. Flynn. They have a house near here."

"Adare. I was aware of it," she said, folding the gauze neatly on the side of the bowl.

"This is not your first visit to the area then?"

"No, some years ago I used to live nearby." She looked up as the landlord approached and sat on a bench beside us.

"How are we doing, young ladies? None the worse for your little spill?"

"We seem to have been very lucky," I said. "Nothing worse than a couple of scrapes and bumps."

"I don't suppose you'll feel like riding that contraption home again," he said. "Are you staying far from here?"

"I'm staying with Senator Flynn at Adare," I confessed.

Miss McAlister had changed her mind about her dress and had

157

started dabbing at the worst of the marks with the damp cloth.

"Oh, well then, why don't I use the telephone at the police station and ask for their chauffeur to come and get you, miss?"

"Please don't," I said quickly. "I am sure I am quite able to make my own way home. I should feel such a fool if I had to be rescued."

"If you're completely sure, miss. I can have my man wheel the contraption for you if you'd like."

"You're most kind," I said, "but I came into the village to post a letter and I must do that before I forget."

"There's a post office in the general store across the street," he said. "Is it all the fashion at Adare to take bicycle excursions? You're the second young lady in two days."

"Really?"

"Oh yes. Another slip of a girl came down the hill at full tilt on her bicycle yesterday, only she didn't fall off. She went into the police station. I think she wanted to use the telephone."

So Belinda had lied about heading toward West Point. I wondered who she had wanted to call. Probably a suitor she didn't want her sister to know about.

Miss McAlister had risen to her feet. "I should be going," she said. "You have been most kind."

"Not at all, miss. Why don't you rest a while and have another glass of lemonade? I'm sure you must be quite shaken up. I'll have the missus bring out the jug. No, no. There's no need to rush. You take your time to recover. There won't be any men coming in here for a while yet. You're quite safe."

He shouted for his wife and our glasses were replenished. I was feeling fully recovered, but determined to make good use of the situation.

"The gardener at Adare has been telling me that he used to share a pint with Albert Morell, the chauffeur, from time to time. Would that have been in here or is there another tavern nearby?"

"It was here, all right." The landlord grimaced. "When I think how I called that scoundrel my friend. In here all the time, he was. Drank more than was good for him sometimes, but there wasn't any harm in him—or so I thought. You could have knocked me down with a feather when I heard what he'd done. My boy thought he was the cat's whiskers. Took him fishing on his days off, you know." He leaned closer to us. "Not that he wasn't what you might call slick. Many's the time I've seen him invite some poor sucker to a game of cards, and walk away with the poor man's cash in his pocket."

"Did you ever see him meeting shady characters in here?" I asked.

"Shady characters?" The man threw back his head and laughed. "You've been reading too many novels, miss. Like I told the police, Bertie Morell was an ordinary, likable fellow with no malice in him. From what he told me, I understand he had a way with the ladies. We used to tease him about it. Like master, like servant, that's what we always said."

Miss McAlister put down her glass and got to her feet. "I really must go. I thank you again for your kindness. Please excuse me."

"Miss McAlister, are you sure there's nothing more I can do for you?" I called after her.

"Nothing. Nothing at all," she called back as she pushed open the saloon door and hurried away.

It was a long, dreary slog back to Adare, wheeling the bicycle beside me. The climb up to the crest was too hard to undertake on a bicycle, especially with sore and grazed limbs, and once at the summit, I was not about to risk the downhill ride and a repeat performance of my last disaster. I should have to get some lessons in stopping before I took a bicycle out again. Fortunately the bicycle had suffered no apparent damage. That would have been most embarrassing!

The long way home gave me plenty of time to think. Disconnected thoughts and ideas ran through my mind—Bertie Morell, who was universally liked and took the landlord's son fishing, and Belinda, who had lied about bicycling toward West Point when she had instead used a telephone in the village, and the interesting Miss McAlister, who had once been a nurse and now wore an expensive silk gown and who had come to the mosquito-plagued river instead of the ocean for her health.

By the time I had delivered the bicycle to the carriage house, I had to rush to wash and change for dinner. Theresa once more did not make an appearance but her maid, a severe-looking Frenchwoman called Adèle, informed me that Mrs. Flynn would be most happy if I paid her a visit as soon as dinner was over.

I obliged and found her lying amid a mountain of pillows, her face as white as the cotton and lace around her.

"Molly, dearest." She held out a languid hand to me. "I am so glad you came. I have been so lonely up here."

"I would have come before if you had summoned me," I said.

She patted the coverings beside her, indicating where I should sit.

"My husband has no patience with my sufferings," she said. "In fact, he would have given up on me long ago if I didn't expect to inherit such a vast fortune when my parents die." She clutched at my hand. "To tell you the truth, dear Molly, I truly believe he only married me for my money in the first place."

"I'm sure that's not true," I said. "You are a beautiful and witty woman, Theresa. Any man would be fortunate to have you as his wife."

"You are such a sweet child. How could you know what it is like between a man and a woman? We were never suited, Barney and I. He has such strong—needs—and I have never been able to fulfill them. That has been our problem all along. And since Brendan died, I can't bear him to come near me. Naturally he is hurt and angry, but I can't help it. I live under this perpetual black cloud, Molly."

I followed her gaze to a dressing table where a large silver-framed photograph stood. It was of a beautiful child with long fair curls and huge bright eyes, sitting sedately in frills and petticoats on a straight-backed chair, holding a stuffed bear in one hand. In spite of the frills one could see he was all boy from the mischievous grin on his lips. It was the first time I had looked at Brendan, apart from the grainy pictures printed in the newspapers. And the first thought that crossed my mind was that looking at that sweet, impish smile every day would break any parent's heart.

"You have had to endure more than most women could bear," I said. "But you still have a lot to live for, Theresa. You have a husband who is handsome and successful. You could be the toast of Washington if you put your mind to it. And you have a lovely little daughter who would bring light into your life if you allowed her to. Would you like me to bring her in to see you now?"

Theresa shook her head. "You don't understand. I try to love Eileen, I really do, and I know she is a sweet child, but I can't. It was too much to ask of me. I should never have—" She broke off as Barney came into the room.

"Oh, I'm sorry, I didn't realize I was interrupting a chin-wag," he said. "I came to see how you were feeling."

"About the same," she said. "My limbs feel as if they are made of jelly."

"You should make an effort, my love," Barney said. "You will never get strong if you don't exercise in the fresh air."

"Fresh air, where is there fresh air on this accursed river?" she demanded, her voice suddenly strong. "I hate this house and everything about it. It has brought us nothing but trouble and grief. Why can't we go away, Barney? Let's get far away from this accursed place."

"You know we have to maintain a residence in the state which I represent in Congress," Barney said, "but I have offered many times to take you to Europe as soon as you are strong enough for the journey. You only have to tell me and I'll make the arrangements for you."

"And would you come too? Would you spend the summer in England with me, or France, or even Ireland?"

"I have work to do, Theresa. I'm a public servant, remember? Take Clara with you. Take Molly. You seem to tolerate her presence well."

"Oh yes," Theresa's eyes fastened on me. "You could show me around Ireland, Molly. You could introduce me to all the family."

I gave her what I hoped was an encouraging smile. "First you must make yourself strong enough to travel," I said. "Your limbs really will turn to jelly if you keep to your bed."

"I'll make an effort, I promise. I'll get up tomorrow."

"I'll have Adèle bring up your sleeping powder so that you get a good night's sleep." Barney leaned to kiss her forehead. "I think we'll leave her in peace now, Molly."

Theresa didn't protest as I was ushered from the room.

"You see how she is," Barney whispered as soon as we were outside her door on the upstairs landing. "She'll never be strong enough to travel to Europe. She's fine for a few days, then she collapses again. I should never have allowed those damned Sorensen women to come. It's the séances that have upset her."

"Maybe if you let them have one last séance and Theresa really can speak with her child, she'll be content," I suggested.

"How can she speak with her child? It's ludicrous." Barney's voice rose dangerously. "He was not quite two years old, for God's sake. Even if those charlatans could make him appear, he could scarcely say a word!"

"He may have grown more articulate in heaven," I said cautiously.

He looked at my solemn face and burst out laughing. "God, Molly, you're as much a cynic as I am." He moved closer to me. "You and I would make a great pair." He was so close now that I stepped away and found my back pressed against the railing that ran around the gallery. "Theresa wouldn't mind, you know," he whispered, so close to me now that his knee was forcing forward through my light skirts. "She'd be all for it. Keep it in the family. She likes it like that. Less complications."

His hands moved from my shoulders down my arms, his thumbs just brushing at my breasts. I put my own hands up to push him away. "Barney, I beg you, please stop this at once. Apart from the fact that you know it's not right, did you ever consider that I might already be promised to another man?"

He moved away, but not much. He was still dangerously close. "Oh, so you've had experience in the pleasures of the flesh, have you?"

"I have had experience in promising my heart, which is not the same thing," I replied stiffly. "There is a young man who waits for me and I wouldn't break my oath of fidelity to him for anything in the world."

"And who is this young paragon?" he asked.

"He's—" I tried to make my brain work rapidly. In all my preparation to take over the role of Molly Gaffney, a sweetheart had never entered into the picture. And worse still, a vivid image of Daniel Sullivan popped into my head and wouldn't leave. "He's a policeman," I said.

"A policeman? God's teeth, woman, you can do better than that for yourself. Isn't one of the reason you came over here to make a good match for yourself?"

"I didn't say the family approved of him," I said. "Now can we please drop the subject and let me return to the ladies in the parlor."

As he let me go I heard the sound of a door closing, very quietly, somewhere along the landing.

❧ Nineteen ❧

Sunday. Fifth morning of this even more complicated saga. I was nowhere closer to proving the Misses Sorensen were frauds. I was nowhere closer to finding out the truth about Bertie Morell. Theresa Flynn wanted to take me to Europe with her and Barney Flynn wanted to take me to bed. Then there was a man staying next door who would have me arrested if he found out the truth about me. Why on earth hadn't I chosen a simpler profession? And if I was bent on being an investigator, why on earth had I not stuck to divorce cases? I was tempted to take the next train home, until I realized that I had no way of reaching a station without being ferried across the river first.

I came down to find Clara already in her severe black crepe bonnet. "You'll be coming to church with us, I trust?" she asked. "I presume that Barney's relatives are good Catholics?"

"Catholics. I'm not so sure about the good part."

"No?" Her look of disapproval made me wonder if she was the one who had peeked from a bedroom yesterday evening when Barney had attempted to seduce me. To my surprise Barney appeared in a dark Sunday suit with hair well parted and slicked down. Theresa had announced that she was not up to the boat ride, so it was Clara, Belinda, Barney and myself, plus little Eileen and her nurse, who made the trip across the river and attended mass at the church in Peekskill.

After mass Barney was waylaid by well-wishers and friends. He made the rounds of handshaking like any good politician should. Eileen had been very good all through mass but I could see that she was getting bored with holding her nanny's hand.

"Come on," I said. "Let's you and I go for a little walk. Maybe we can see birds and squirrels in the park."

The nurse frowned but Eileen took my hand happily and skipped along beside me. A path led into the little cemetery behind the church. It was so peaceful and green up there, surrounded by trees, with a view of the river.

"Is this where dead people are buried?" Eileen asked, studying the tombstones.

"That's right. But just their bodies. Their souls have gone up to God in heaven."

She looked thoughtful. "My brother isn't buried here, is he?"

"No." It was better that she didn't know that her brother's grave had never been found. "But he's an angel in heaven himself now and he's watching down on you."

"Look, there's a squirrel." Eileen was off at a great pace, discussions of heaven quite forgotten. I ran after her, determined not to let her out of my sight for a second. At the far end of the cemetery, where the grass had not been cut and odd gravestones were dotted among pine trees, I spotted a boy, a little older than Eileen, dressed in his black Sunday best, climbing on a large grave monument. Eileen saw him at the same time and made a beeline for him.

"Hello, boy!" she called.

"Eileen, wait for me," I called. At that moment I noticed a woman who had been bent over a grave in the unkempt area. She rose hastily to her feet at the sound of my voice, grabbed the boy and yanked him down from the marble cherub. Then she shot me a glance, gathered up a bunch of dying flowers and dragged the protesting child away in the opposite direction.

"Why did he have to go so quickly?" Eileen demanded. "I could have played with him. We could have played hide-and-seek among all the lovely angels."

"His mommy must have been in a hurry, I suppose," I said.

Intrigued as to why she needed to rush away from what must have been a Sunday morning ritual, I made my way over to the grave. The small rectangle of granite bore the words ALBERT JOSEPH MORELL. I couldn't read the dates because there were now fresh flowers lying across it. Handpicked flowers from somebody's garden. I noticed rosemary and forget-me-nots among them. Somebody still remembered Albert Morell fondly apart from Annie Lomax in New York.

I took Eileen's hand to rejoin my party. As we made our way back to the boat, we had to pass under the railway to reach the river. A train was just pulling in from New York City. I looked up at the slamming of doors and saw what looked like the same woman getting into a carriage at the far end of the train.

We came home to find Theresa up and lying propped on a wicker chaise on the veranda, wrapped in a rug, although the morning was already warm. Roland Van Gelder had arrived and was perched on a chair beside her. A breakfast tray, hardly touched, stood on a round table and Roland was drinking a cup of coffee.

"Look who's here, Barney," Theresa called as we came around the side of the house. "Roland has been kind enough to keep me company."

"It's good to see you up again, my dear." Barney went up to her and kissed her forehead. "How are you, Roland?"

"Well, sir. And you?" Roland rose to his feet as we approached. "Ladies," he bowed to us, "you all look simply stunning this morning. Far too ravishing for church, I must say. You must have set the poor old priest's heart aflutter."

"Mr. Van Gelder!" Clara said in a shocked voice. "I must protest. You may not belong to our religion but I will not let you insult it. Our priests are pure and holy men, especially Father Conway at St. Agnes."

"Who is eighty if he's a day," Roland said, smiling in the direction of Belinda and myself. "I was wondering if you'd care to come out riding later today, Miss Butler?"

"Will your houseguests be accompanying us?" she asked.

"Captain Cathers may well be persuaded to. I think I mentioned that poor old Hartley doesn't ride much any more. Lack of balance, you know."

"Are they planning to stay with you much longer?" I tried not to sound too interested. "Captain Cathers spoke of wanting to go West."

"I think that is their plan," Roland said. He looked up at me. "And I must say you've made an impression upon Mr. Hartley. He spoke about you after you left the other evening and he says he plans to look you up when you return to Ireland."

"Did you hear that, Molly?" Clara asked. "Such a handsome gentleman too."

"He'll have to wait a long time for Molly's return," Theresa said, "because I have no intention of letting her go. In fact I made up my mind last night that she will come to Washington with us where I can introduce her to all the most eligible bachelors in the land. And we were going to summon the dressmaker, weren't we? Clara, I believe I asked you to do so—have you done it yet?"

"I'm afraid it slipped my mind, Theresa," Clara said, giving me a sideways glance. "I've been so worried about your health."

"My health is getting stronger by the minute, I can feel it. What do you think, Barney—should we ask Miss Emily and Miss Edith for another séance tonight?"

"Absolutely no," Barney said. "You are in no fit state for more shocks to your system. Let's get you back on your feet first and then think about séances."

"How are Miss Emily and Miss Ella faring?" I asked. "I hope they are finally recovering from their ordeal."

"How sweet of you to worry for their health, Molly," Theresa said. "But it's good news. They have already paid me a visit this morning and will join us for Sunday lunch. Will you also join us,

Mr. Van Gelder? Cook always puts on a really fine spread on Sundays."

"I would be honored, Mrs. Flynn." Roland's eyes didn't leave Belinda. "And after lunch maybe Miss Butler will satisfy my whim to go out riding."

Belinda crossed the veranda, trailing her gloves across the furniture. "I suppose riding would be slightly less boring than playing croquet with Clara," she said. "All right, Roland. But only if Barney lets me ride his new thoroughbred."

"I don't know, Belinda. He's very willful," Barney said.

"My dear brother-in-law, you know I can handle any horse in creation," Belinda said. "And if I don't ride the thoroughbred, I'm not going."

"Very well, only go carefully," Barney said.

"Don't worry. If Roland rides that old nag again, the pace isn't going to be exactly fast."

I saw a spasm of annoyance cross Roland's face. "Yes, I know what you mean. We're thinking of buying a replacement, but we—we haven't had time, what with all these summer visitors."

Lunch was everything that Theresa had promised. A huge joint of roast beef, surrounded by roast potatoes, sweet potatoes, baby carrots, beans, and peas, followed by a light concoction of whipped cream and fresh raspberries. Replete with food, we retired to our rooms, except for Belinda, who departed with Roland. I lay on my bed, watching the lace curtains stir idly in the summer breeze, listening to shouts from the river as pleasure craft passed. I found my thoughts drifting back to the strange encounter in the churchyard this morning. Surely Bertie Morell had been portrayed as a ladies' man, hadn't he? He had been walking out with Annie Lomax. There had been no mention of a wife and child. So who was the woman who came regularly to put flowers on his grave? I surmised she must be a regular visitor because the flowers she had removed were not yet quite dead—no more than a few days old. Would a sister be so loyal, or an old family friend? I didn't think so and resolved to delve deeper into Mr. Morell's family background.

Then a drowsiness overcame me and I must have drifted off to sleep because I woke with a start to hear voices below my window.

"What the devil do you think you're doing here?" A man's voice, barely more than a whisper. If there was an answer I didn't catch it. "You must be out of your mind," the voice continued. "You remember our agreement as well as I do. We're not going back on it now. I paid you well enough!"

I jumped out of bed and went to look out of the window. I waited but there were no more voices and nobody came out of the house. I was confused until I realized that I had probably been listening to one end of a telephone conversation. The telephone was kept in Barney Flynn's study and his windows were certainly open. Well, Barney's questionable dealings were no business of mine. I moved away from the window and pulled up a chair to the desk. I took out my notebook and jotted down what I had seen this morning—the strange woman who had left flowers on Bertie Morell's grave. The innkeeper in the village had hinted that he was one for the ladies. Was this one of Bertie's conquests? And what of the boy? I'd probably have no way of finding out, unless she came back next Sunday and I could find a way to engage her in conversation.

The question was whether I would still be here by next Sunday. I would have to make sure I left Adare before the embarrassment of a dressmaker's arrival and I still hadn't had any opportunity to unmask the spiritualist sisters. Since I had seen how fond they were of their food, it came to me that I could feign an indisposition and search their cottage when they were at lunch, although I had no idea what I was looking for.

Search cottage, I wrote in my notebook.

I looked up to see Desmond O'Mara hurrying across the lawn and disappearing into the undergrowth beside the river in the direction of the cliff path.

Apparently the servants always had Sunday afternoon and evening off, so the meal was cold meats and salad with the remains of the pudding. Most of us were too stuffed full from lunch to eat much anyway. The Misses Sorensen, however, made an appearance and worked their way steadily through everything.

"We are ready for another séance whenever you feel up to it, dear Mrs. Flynn," Miss Emily said. "In fact our dear Chief Ojuweca came to me in a dream last night and said he might have some good news for you."

"Good news? Really?" Theresa looked up. "Then let us hold a séance tonight."

"Not tonight, Theresa," Barney said. "I made it clear to you that you are not yet strong enough. If you insist on going ahead with this ridiculous business, then plan your séance for later in the week."

"But if Miss Emily and Miss Ella are willing and Ojuweca has news for me—" Theresa began.

"Not tonight. I forbid it and that's final. Now, why don't we retire to the parlor and play some cards."

"Cards, on a Sunday?" Clara asked.

"Clara, it's only Puritans who don't allow fun on the Sabbath. We Catholics have an understanding with our God. He wants us to enjoy ourselves whenever we please."

"Your God might, but mine forbids it." Clara said. "If you're going to play cards, I shall retire to my room."

Clara retired after the meal; so did the sisters.

"Do you play whist, Molly?" Barney asked.

"I'm afraid I never learned card games," I said.

"Don't tell me they are a bunch of Puritans back in Ireland!" Barney exclaimed.

"No, I'm sure they are not. It was just my family never went in for card games. But I'd be happy to learn."

"You can watch for a while then, until you get the hang of it."

"That's no use," Belinda said, "we need a fourth. What has happened to Mr. Rimes and Mr. O'Mara?"

"Both out," Barney said.

"Servants' night out?" Belinda asked sweetly. "You're so good to them, Barney."

"Wicked girl." Barney wagged a finger at her. "Never mind,

171

we'll teach Molly as we go along. I'm sure she's very quick on the uptake."

I was and we spent an enjoyable evening. Even Theresa seemed livelier and some color had returned to her cheeks. If I stayed long enough, maybe I could restore her to full health, I found myself thinking, and had to remind myself sharply that I wasn't really her cousin and I didn't belong here.

I was awoken by a loud banging noise and the sound of raised voices. Outside was a misty gray dawn. The first doves were cooing in the trees. At the sound of the raised voices, crows started cawing in alarm. I scrambled out of bed and hastily put on my robe before peering out of the window. Three men were standing there, humble folk by the way they were dressed, and they were gesticulating wildly.

"On the Senator's property," I heard one of them say. "We saw it clearly from the river, but we couldn't put in there because of those rocks."

"Somebody should go for the constable," I heard another voice say.

Then I heard doors open on the landing and footsteps running down the stairs. I opened my own door in time to hear Barney's voice shouting, "What is all this row at six in the morning? What is going on?"

"Sorry to disturb you, Senator," one of the men said, scrambling to take off his cap, "but we were out fishing and we spotted what looks like a body lying at the bottom of the cliffs on your estate."

"Because of the rocks we couldn't get near enough to see exactly, but it looked like a person lying there, sure enough," a second man added.

I didn't waste another second. I scrambled into the bloomers I had worn on the bicycle and put on my most sensible shoes. By the time I came downstairs Barney had assembled the estate workers and was in the process of sending the chauffeur into Jones Point to fetch the nearest constable. Mr. Rimes, still bleary-eyed and only half awake, stood at the top of the stairs in a plaid dressing gown calling, "What the devil is going on?" at the top of his voice. There was no sign of Desmond O'Mara.

Barney set off with the fishermen, along with Tom and Adam, plus two gardeners whose names I didn't know bringing up the rear. I gave them a head start, then followed. The river was hidden in a thick morning mist and strands of mist drifted across the lawns so that the men ahead of me disappeared and reappeared as they walked. We reached the wooded area beyond the lawns, where I had sat with Eileen that day and sensed somebody watching. The mist was thicker here and seemed to deaden all sound so that I felt as if I was all alone and miles from anywhere. I had no idea how far ahead of me the men were and hurried on, picking up the path beyond the clearing. It became ever more narrow and overgrown with brambles, making me glad I hadn't worn my usual skirts. At last it emerged from the undergrowth and I sensed rather than saw that we were high above the river. Then the mist parted, revealing a fearsome drop to the water that swirled and splashed over rocks below us. The path continued, hugging the very edge of the cliff, only wide enough for one pair of feet at a time as it skirted giant boulders. The mist had made the rocks slippery and I moved forward cautiously. Then I heard shouts ahead of me and tried to hurry.

"Go and get ropes and a board, Adam," I heard Barney commanding. "We'll have to find a way to lower somebody down there."

Through the mist I saw a pine tree, growing precariously at the very edge of the drop. I held onto this and peered down. The cliff was maybe a hundred feet high, with spray-drenched rocks at its base. On these rocks the figure of a woman now lay sprawled. I turned away, feeling sick. Barney had warned me about the dangers of this path. Some poor woman had chosen to ignore them and plunged to an untimely death.

Adam returned with the ropes that he tied to a tree before old Tom made the tortuous climb down the cliff face.

"She's dead right enough," Tom called back.

"Do you recognize her?" Barney shouted down. "Is she a local woman?"

"Hard to tell. The face is pretty bashed about."

"Then get a board under her and lash her down so that we can haul her up," Barney shouted.

I didn't think they should do anything before the constable arrived, but I could hardly give them instructions without revealing my presence. Besides, there was no way they'd listen to a slip of a girl fresh from Ireland. I watched as the board was lowered down and the poor woman's body dragged onto it. Then with shouts and encouragement she was hauled up the cliff, just in time for the arrival of the constable.

"Fell to her death, did she?" the constable asked, watching as hands reached out to grab the board with the woman on it and drag her the last few feet to the path. "Not the first time it's happened and won't be the last. One false step on that path and over you go. I wonder what she was doing here? Not a local woman, is she? And on your property too, Senator."

"Probably some tourist from the city out for a Sunday stroll," one of the men commented. "These modern women are too adventurous by half. Likely as not she didn't realize she was on private property."

"Even though there's that big notice saying, 'Private, Keep Out'?" old Tom said.

"Let's see if she has any identification on her." The constable began going through her pockets but produced only a lace handkerchief.

"Why don't we carry her back to the house?" Barney suggested. "Someone will have reported her missing."

I ducked back behind the rock as the procession made its way past me. I tried not to look at her, but I had to. Her face was a horrible black and blue sticky mess, hardly identifiable as a human being. One arm trailed in a pathetic gesture. Her sodden skirts left a trail of drips on the sandy soil. Suddenly I gasped. On that skirt was a recognizable streak of oil where a bicycle had collided with it two days ago.

❧ **Twenty** ❧

I ran after them, my heart beating so fast that I found it hard to
breathe.

"Wait," I called.

The procession halted and turned to face me.

"I know who she is," I said. "I had a slight accident when I was
riding a bicycle two days ago. I knocked her down. There was oil
from the chain on her skirt. Look—here it is. She didn't manage
to clean it off."

"And who are you, miss? A friend of hers?" the constable asked.

"No, this young lady is my cousin, visiting from Ireland," Barney said before I could reply. "Where did you come into contact
with this person, Molly?"

Come into contact was the right description and I would have
smiled, had not the situation been so tragic.

"In the village, right outside the saloon."

"Do you know her name then, miss?" the constable asked.

"I only know that she's a visitor to the area and she told me her
name is Margie McAlister."

"Sweet Jesus and Mary," Barney Flynn muttered.

"You know her, sir?" The constable looked up at Barney's oath.

Barney's face had turned pale. "She used to work for us. She was
my wife's nurse, when Theresa had a breakdown after our son was

177

kidnapped. But she left us three or four years ago. I have no idea what she was doing back in the area."

"Might she have come back to pay you a visit?"

"It's possible, I suppose, although I can't think why. I don't believe there was any particular bond established between her and my wife. She was an efficient nurse and she did her job, but we certainly didn't look upon her as one of the family, as we do our cook, or Tom here."

"Any idea where she might be living these days?"

"None at all," Barney said shortly. "As I say, we have a large staff and they come and go. When my wife recovered we had no further need of her services."

"I believe she said she was living somewhere called Georgetown," I said. "But at the moment she was staying in the area. She said she found it healthful beside the river."

"Did she tell you anything else?" Barney asked.

"Not that I can think of. We were both shaken up. We exchanged a few words while we recovered. It was strange, though. I mentioned that I was staying with you and she didn't admit to former service in your household."

"Maybe she had come up in the world and was ashamed to admit her former domestic employment," the constable suggested.

I realized this might have been true. I had noticed the good quality of her dress, and she had the money to take a summer trip for her health.

The constable lifted her left hand. "No wedding ring, I notice," he said. "Never mind. If she's staying locally we shouldn't have much trouble locating next-of-kin. What on earth made her come along that cliff path, instead of at the main gate like any normal person?"

"We'll never know that now, I'm afraid," Barney said. "Maybe we should carry her up to the carriage house until you can arrange transport to the morgue. It would be most distressing for my wife and the other ladies present if they saw her in this condition."

The procession moved on. I didn't follow them this time. Instead,

I waited until they were swallowed up into the mist, then I made my way back to the cliff path until I was standing above the spot where she had lain. The cliff edge had been disturbed by Adam bringing the body up, but I could still see the point at which the edge had crumbled as she lost her footing and slithered down. I stared at it with interest, picturing her body as it had lain on the rocks. So she had not been on her way to visit the estate at all. She had been on her way out. If she had lost her balance while going in the other direction there was a tree branch she could have grabbed onto to save herself. But heading away from the estate the branch would have been behind her. And the position of her body backed this up, even though she may have bounced off rocks on the way down. I shuddered and turned away. What a horrible end to such an attractive young woman.

Then a sobering thought struck me. What if she had not just lost her footing at all? Was it possible that somebody had crept along that path behind her and given her a good shove? For some reason that partly overheard conversation came into my mind, the man's voice whispering, "What the devil do you think you're doing here? . . . You remember our agreement. . . . I paid you well enough!"

Was that why Miss McAlister hadn't mentioned any ties to Adare? She had come to visit secretly and it could only be for one reason: blackmail. She knew something and was being paid to keep quiet about it. Was it about one of Barney Flynn's underhand deals, information which wouldn't look good if it came out during an election year? Or could it be about the kidnapping? Was it possible that someone still in the house had been involved in the kidnapping? Then I remembered Desmond O'Mara, hurrying across the lawn toward the cliff path. Desmond—the bright but penniless young man who certainly had the brain to hatch such a daring plot and who had stayed on in a menial situation for some reason. Was it because someone had a hold over him?

I walked back to the house deep in thought. I didn't know what to do next. I couldn't tell Barney, when everything was such pure conjecture. After all, it was possible that Barney was the one she had come to blackmail, but I had to admit that he had seemed genuinely shocked when I divulged her name and hadn't recognized her until that moment.

There was little point in mentioning it to the local constable, who seemed a nice enough fellow, but a little on the slow side. My only hope was to tell Daniel and let him take it from here. And risk another lecture on poking my nose into affairs that were none of my business, I thought. Daniel might decide that I was overreacting and jumping to wrong conclusions again. Margie McAlister's death could have been nothing more than a horrible and unfortunate accident and her reasons for visiting Adare nothing more than wanting another glimpse of the house of which she had fond memories.

As I returned to the house I encountered Barney, coming down from the carriage house. "Where have you been, Molly?" he asked.

"I wanted to see for myself where she fell," I said. "Morbid curiosity, I suppose. My mother always told me I was too curious by half."

"A tragic business," Barney said, falling into step beside me. "I can't think what she was doing here, and least of all why she was attempting to come along that cliff path. You saw yourself how narrow and dangerous it is."

"Maybe she just wanted another glimpse of the house and didn't want to disturb anyone at the main gate," I said. "It could have been the most innocent of reasons—maybe she wanted to take a snapshot to show her friends where she once worked."

I saw relief flood across his face. "Yes, maybe that was it." He shook his head, smiling sadly. "What a waste of a life for nothing." He leaned close to me. "Look, Molly, I'd be grateful if you didn't mention anything of this to my wife. You know how frail her health is. I don't want her upset again." We climbed the front steps together. "The way servants gossip she'll probably hear that there was an accident on the cliff path, but she doesn't have to know the identity of the victim."

"Of course not," I said. "You can rely on me."

He took my arm and squeezed it. "I knew I could," he said. "And now I must telephone for a doctor to come and sign the death certificate."

I opened my mouth to say something but thought better of it. Maybe I would have a chance to speak with the doctor when he arrived.

As Barney went into his study and closed the door behind him, I had another change of mind. I left the house again, heading up the driveway to the carriage house. The police constable had taken up a position outside the carriage house door. Presumably the body now lay somewhere inside. There was no sign of the gardeners.

"What a terribly sad affair, isn't it?" I said, going up to the police constable. "It gave me quite a shock when I realized that I had spoken with her only two days ago."

"I'm sure it would have done, miss. A delicate young lady like yourself."

Nobody could describe me as delicate with any stretch of the imagination, but I tried to look suitably pale and wan. "It can't be easy for you, either. Even though you must come across such things as part of your job."

"No, death is never easy," he said. "But it's not like we get murders out here every day, like the police do in New York City. That must be a terrible place with killings going on all the time."

"It must indeed," I said. "But I bet you've seen some excitement during your time on the force, haven't you?" I gave him what I hoped was an adoring look. "Were you involved when the kidnapping happened here?"

"I most certainly was," he said. "I was the one who got the first call that the child was missing. I helped them search the grounds all afternoon and then I was actually with them when the ransom note arrived."

"Really?"

"Oh yes. I was the one who handed it to the Senator. His poor hands were shaking so hard he could scarcely read the words."

"What exactly did the note say?"

"I can't remember the exact words now," he said, "but it was awful chilling stuff—all about the child being buried alive and how they'd never see him again if they didn't obey exactly what the note told them. Of course, one of the things it said was, 'Don't go to the police,' and I was standing right there."

"And of course he didn't obey, did he?" I said. "I understood that the police were there when the kidnapper came to pick up the ransom. Wasn't he killed by a police sharpshooter?"

"He was. And I was one of those policemen. But it was one of the federal marshals who did the shooting. Those guys always were trigger-happy, from what I heard."

"What a tragedy," I said. "And so unnecessary."

"I couldn't agree more, miss. If they'd only let him pick up the money, then we could have arrested him with no fuss as he came back to the main road. He'd arranged the pickup in the depths of the forest, you see. Bad mistake, if you ask me. Got himself trapped. That was why he tried to run for it."

"You're talking about the chauffeur, Bertie Morell, aren't you?"

"That's right, miss. You could have knocked all of us down with a feather when we saw it was him. We all knew him, see. He was a regular in the village, always at the saloon, laughing and drinking with the local boys."

"I wonder what made him do an awful thing like that," I said. "From what I hear, he liked children, and he was devoted to the Flynn baby."

"If you ask me, miss, he did it because he had to. I believe he was in the pay of someone or something."

"Something?"

He lowered his voice and looked around, even though we two were the only people in sight. "I saw the note, miss. There was a black hand on the bottom of it."

"A black hand?"

He nodded. "So I'm thinking that maybe the Senator wasn't

paying protection money where he should be and the Black Hand sent Morell out to put the squeeze on him."

"Holy Mother of God," I muttered. This put an entirely different complexion on things. But if the Black Hand had been involved, why hadn't it come out earlier? Unless Barney Flynn had been so frightened of them and what they might do next that he'd kept it a secret. Now I was definitely going to write to Daniel!

I left the policeman, promising to have a cup of coffee sent up to him, and hurried to my room. This explained a lot. If Bertie Morell was really Italian by heritage, then maybe he had become involved with the Black Hand and had no choice but to carry out their commands. Maybe he had family members who would have suffered if he hadn't obeyed orders. I positively ran up the stairs, free, for once, from the encumbrance of my long skirts, and sat at my desk to write.

"There is something strange going on here, Daniel," I wrote.

I know you wanted me to confine my efforts to two spiritualist ladies, but I noticed an atmosphere of tension in this house the moment I arrived. Since then another tragedy has happened. A young woman who used to work here has fallen to her death. I don't think it was an accident although it would be impossible to prove it. And I have just found out from the local policeman who was at the scene when the kidnap ransom note was delivered that the note was signed with a black hand. Was this known to the police? Did they ever do anything about it?

I signed and sealed the letter and decided to face the long walk into the village immediately after breakfast. Almost on cue the breakfast gong sounded. I tucked my letter into a book, just in case, and had just reached the bottom of the stairs when the front door opened and Desmond O'Mara came in. His hair was untidy and his face looked flushed as if he'd been running.

"Oh, Miss Gaffney," he stammered. "Is the Senator in his office yet?"

"I think he is, Mr. O'Mara."

"Oh dear, then I'm in for it." He gave an embarrassed laugh. "I went across the river last night and I missed the last ferry back."

❧ Twenty-one ❧

I went into the dining room where I found the women in the middle of breakfast.

"Molly, have you been out for a bicycle ride?" Theresa looked up from the toast she was spreading with marmalade.

"No, I think bicycles and I are maybe not meant for each other," I said. "Why do you ask?"

"Because you are wearing bloomers, my sweet." Theresa laughed. I had forgotten all about the bloomers.

"Because they are so wonderfully comfortable," I said. "I think I shall make a habit of wearing them."

A gasp from Clara, a giggle from Belinda. Even Theresa looked shocked. "Molly, be careful. No gentleman will marry a woman he perceives to be a suffragist and a bluestocking."

"I should think not," Clara said. "Revealing the limb all the way to the knee? What will they think of next?"

"I went out for a walk," I said. "I'll remove them after breakfast."

"Do help yourself and sit down," Theresa said. "And we have wonderful news."

"News?"

"Yes. Miss Emily had a dream last night in which Ojuweca came to her and said he had someone who wished to speak with me tonight. So we're having another séance."

"I thought Barney forbade any more séances until you were well again." Belinda wagged her finger, giving her sister a wicked smile.

"As if Barney could forbid her anything, after all she's been through," Clara said with a sniff. "After all she's done for him!"

There was a second of awkward silence during which the only sound was the two Misses Sorensen scraping their plates. Then Theresa smiled. "This has nothing to do with Barney. He's so busy with his stupid old campaign strategy that he will never notice anyway. The séance will take place tonight. I am not going to take the risk of missing a communication from my son."

Immediately after breakfast I went back to my room and reluctantly changed into more conventional garb. Which was a pity, because walking would have been so much easier in bloomers. But I didn't want to draw attention to myself at this moment. I told Theresa I was going for a walk and she was so caught up in the plans for a séance that she hardly heard me.

I slipped away and approached the carriage house with a mixture of anticipation and dread. The latter because I had no wish to look upon that poor woman's face again. The doors were now wide open and the chauffeur was outside, polishing the car. He looked up when he saw me.

"Morning, miss." He touched his cap.

"Oh," I muttered. "What happened to the body, and to the policeman who was here?"

"All taken care of, miss. Nothing for you to worry about."

"That was quick." So much for my plan of a private chat with the doctor. "Where have they taken her?"

He shrugged his shoulders. "I've no idea, miss. My job's not to ask questions. My job is to get this automobile ready for the master to go into town in ten minutes. So if you'll excuse me . . ." He went back to polishing.

I continued on my way up the drive. When I reached the gatehouse I was tempted to leave my letter with the gatekeeper, rather than face the long and arduous walk to the nearest post office. But I didn't want anyone in the house knowing I was writing letters to anyone in New York, especially that I was sending out a letter at this moment. And I wanted to find out where Margie McAlister had been staying in the village. So I set out bravely up hill and down and it must have taken me a good hour before I reached my destination. On the way I had ample time for thought. Had that poor girl come to meet somebody at the house or just to take another peek at a place where she had once worked? Had she slipped and fallen to her death or was she pushed? In which case, what did she know that was dangerous to somebody at the house? And most of all, where had Mr. Desmond O'Mara rushed off to and been all night?

I mulled over romantic assignations, but couldn't somehow put Desmond O'Mara in the position of ardent suitor. But there were other men on the estate that Miss McAlister could have found attractive. There was, after all, a handsome gardener. And if not romance, there was plenty of scope for blackmail. She had only come to Adare after the kidnapping was over, so that couldn't enter into it. I could indulge in endless speculation, most of it wild, and not a single piece of evidence to back it up. I'd just have to hope that Daniel took my letter seriously and did something about it himself.

I entered the village in somewhat less dramatic fashion than last time. It was sobering to think that only two days ago I had knocked that poor girl off her feet and then sat drinking lemonade and chatting with her. Now she was on her way to some morgue. I wondered what grieving relatives she had left behind.

When I went into the post office I wasn't sure whether the news of this latest tragedy had reached the village yet and how to broach the subject. I had underestimated the efficient telegraph system, superior to Morse code, that exists in every small community.

"You're the young lady staying at Adare, aren't you?" the woman behind the counter asked me as she handed me the stamps I had requested. "The one who had the nasty spill off her bicycle?"

"I am," I said. "And the other young lady I collided with—" I left the sentence hanging.

"Of course you would have heard about it up at the big house," the woman said, shaking her head sadly. "Poor Constable Palmer.

He's quite cut up about it. They say she lost her footing on that narrow path along the cliffs. What a horrible end."

"Did you know her?" I asked.

"I just spoke to her a couple of times when she came in here to buy something."

"I expect she needed stamps for letters home," I suggested.

"No. I can't recall her buying stamps. I think it was just candy of some sort, peardrops, I think, and maybe hairpins. But she seemed like a nice, pleasant and sober young woman. Well spoken."

"Yes, I thought the same," I said. "I wonder what loved ones she leaves behind."

"I don't think she was a married lady," the woman said. "I don't recall noticing a ring on her finger. But there's always someone to grieve, isn't there—some relative or friend whose heart will be broken. Likely as not there would be a young man. She was a pretty girl, if my memory serves me correctly."

"Yes, she was. I wonder where she was staying and whether her landlady would like help with packing up her things?"

"As to that, she was staying with Mrs. Brewer, down by the river. She runs a respectable, Christian rooming establishment. You go down past the church and it's the big redbrick house on the left with a white balcony running all around it. You can't miss it."

I thanked her and made my way to Mrs. Brewer's establishment. That good woman was concerned that Miss McAlister had paid two weeks in advance.

"What do you think I should do?" she asked me. "I don't rightly like to keep what isn't my due. Were you a friend of hers?"

"No, I only met her once," I said. "Did she mention her family at all?"

"I have her home address from our correspondence," she said. "But she lived alone, she told me that much. She said an aunt had left her a nice little legacy that had enabled her to buy her own little house and not to have to work any more. But I can't say she mentioned any family. No doubt the police will find out those things.

I don't like to touch anything in her room until Constable Palmer tells me to. What do you think, miss?"

I dearly wanted to take a look at her room, and was trying to make my brain work quickly enough to come up with a good excuse to do so.

"I can't see any reason why you should not pack up her things, ready to be shipped to her next-of-kin," I said. "After all, it's not as if a crime was committed in the room, was it?"

I shouldn't have said that. Her face turned white. "Whatever do you mean? The young lady met with a nasty accident—that was what we heard. You didn't hear to the contrary, did you?"

"No, of course not," I said rapidly. "She fell from the path. A nasty accident. Would you like some help packing up her things? I know you'll find it a distressing task and it would go quicker with two."

"Why bless you, my dear. What a sweet, Christian thought." She gave me such a wonderful smile that I felt guilty about my true motives. "It's up here, on the left." She started up the narrow stair. "I gave her the best room with a view of the river like she asked for."

"She asked for a view of the river?" I said as the woman led the way into a spotless, if Spartan room. The view from the window made up for the room's lack of adornment, with willows on the bank around a white gazebo and then the magnificent river beyond.

"Why, yes, she did. Requested it specifically in her letter."

"I can see why she wanted this view; it's delightful," I said.

Mrs. Brewer had opened a dresser drawer, then shut it again hurriedly. "It doesn't seem right for me to go through her things," she said. "No. I just can't do it."

"But it would help the constable if you found an address for her next-of-kin, wouldn't it?" I asked. "They'll want to know."

"I suppose so," she agreed and gingerly lifted items from the drawers.

There wasn't much. Some good-quality undergarments, neatly folded, a couple of summer dresses and a straw bonnet, some gloves, a novel and a sketch book. In a small brocade jewelry roll there was an enamel brooch in the shape of a bird and a locket on a velvet ribbon. The locket contained one small dark curl. That was about it. Whoever Miss McAlister was, she had left little of herself in that room. No letters from home, no postcards half-written to dear ones, no photographs.

"I hope the police where she lives will be able to trace her relatives," I said, "because she has no writing paper or address book with her. Did she receive any mail while she was with you?"

Mrs. Brewer thought, then shook her head. "No, I can't say that she did."

"Are you on the telephone?" I asked.

She looked shocked. "An instrument of the devil," she said. "Why do you ask?"

"I just wondered if Miss McAlister received any telephone calls while she was staying with you."

"If she wanted to use a telephone, she'd have had to use the instrument in the police station," she said. "That's the only one around here."

"You know what I've been wondering," I said, pulling back the lace curtain to stare out of the window, "and that's, what made her come here? Did she ever tell you why she came here?"

"For her health, that's what she said."

"But didn't you find that strange?" I asked. "I mean, why would she choose this of all places? The ocean is more bracing and if she wanted a river vacation, I understand there are resorts upstream in the Catskill Mountains."

"Maybe she wanted peace," Mrs. Brewer said. "And she wanted a Christian boardinghouse with no rowdiness or drunkenness, not a resort."

"Did she ever mention whether she had been in this neighborhood before?"

She was looking at me suspiciously now. "I thought you said you and Miss McAlister only met once. You seem awfully interested in her."

"Only because I'm anxious to help you trace her family," I said. "I can't get over them going about their lives, not knowing."

"Maybe it's better that way," she said. "Everything in God's good time. Now I'll just put these things in her valise and wait for instructions. Thank you for your help, miss. I hope you enjoy the rest of your stay at Adare."

And that was that. I was not going to find out why Margie McAlister had decided to visit Adare and whether she had concluded a meeting before returning along that cliff path.

The long road home seemed to go on forever. Sweat was running down into my eyes and flies were buzzing about me in the most annoying fashion when I heard the sound of an automobile coming up the hill behind me. Hope rose in me that the chauffeur had been sent out on an errand while I had been in the village. I stepped to the side of the road and waited expectantly. But it wasn't the Flynns' long, sleek car that came up the hill but a somewhat boxier, smaller model. I was about to step into the shade and let it pass when it slowed to a stop.

"Miss Gaffney, may we give you a ride, or are you out for another of your constitutionals?" Roland Van Gelder called to me.

"This time I'd most appreciate a lift, thank you," I said and was heading for the automobile when I noticed the occupants of the backseat. Captain Cathers and Justin Hartley were sitting there. I had no choice. I could hardly declare that I had changed my mind and preferred walking. Besides, that would let Justin Hartley know that I was afraid to be with him. I just had to bluff it out again. I climbed into the front seat beside Roland.

"This is most kind of you, Mr. Van Gelder. I must confess that I hadn't realized what a long, hot climb it was from the village." I took off my straw hat and fanned myself. "I'll never get used to this heat."

"Quite different from the cold winds of Ireland, isn't it?" Captain Cathers said pleasantly. "I went to visit Hartley at the property he owns in County Mayo. I swear I was never warm once. The wind blows right through one."

"Ah, but we Irish hardly notice it, Captain Cathers," I said. "We are born hardy."

"Especially those of us from Connemara, wouldn't you say?" Justin Hartley said.

I kept fanning myself with my hat. "I thought you were English, Mr. Hartley, and I personally have never ventured far from my home in Limerick, so I couldn't pass an opinion about Connemara, although I do understand it is quite lovely there."

The automobile bounced and lurched up the hill, making loud popping noises. As a comfortable means of transportation, I don't see how they will ever catch on. Give me a good enclosed carriage any day. We reached the crest and were just starting down the other side when we encountered a particularly large pothole. There was a lurch and a hiss.

"Damn," Roland muttered under his breath. "Not another flat tire. I keep telling the old man that we have to have a more up-to-date model. Everybody out, I'm afraid. Come on, Cathers. I'll need a hand with the jack."

We all got out. I went to stand in the shade. Captain Cathers rolled up his shirtsleeves in preparation. As the two men knelt beside the back wheel, Justin moved closer to me. His hand gripped at my forearm.

"It was dark the last time we met," he whispered. "I thought I might have been wrong about you. I should have known when you fainted upon seeing me. Then I thought that my eyes must be deceiving me. After all, how could a peasant from a tumbledown shack be dressed in such fine attire and acting like a lady? But now that I've seen you in daylight and heard your voice again, I don't doubt any more. I know exactly who you are, Molly Murphy."

"Why do you keep on with this strange notion, Mr. Hartley?" I demanded. I tried to keep my voice even and not let him see even the slightest spark of fear. "Please come with me to the house and ask my cousin Barney to verify my identity. That should put these flights of fancy to rest forever."

"Very well, let us go now," he said. "I don't think your so-called cousin will be too happy about harboring a wanted criminal in his house, and one who has lied to him about her identity to boot."

"A known criminal?" I said. "So I'm not only a lady with a different identity, but a gangster's moll on the run, am I?" I looked at him and laughed. "Be warned, Mr. Hartley—my cousin Barney has a nasty temper and he's very protective of his family. He may get out the horse whip to anyone insulting his cousin."

"I'm willing to chance it," Justin said.

"And what do you hope to achieve with this?"

"Justice, Miss Murphy."

"My name is Gaffney, sir. I'm sorry your eyesight is so poor and that I remind you of someone else you once knew."

"Hartley, don't stand there flirting with the lady," Cathers shouted over to him. "Be a good chap and give us a hand."

I took the opportunity. "I'm almost home, Mr. Van Gelder. Shall I not walk ahead and ask the Flynns' chauffeur to come out and help you with the tire?"

"I'd be much obliged, Miss Gaffney," Roland's red and sweating face appeared over the bonnet of the auto. "Much obliged."

"Then I'll take my leave, gentlemen. Thank you for the lift." I nodded and made my exit. I had escaped from Justin Hartley this time, but for how long?

I came home to find the Misses Sorensen going into the music room with swathes of black cloth to prepare it for the evening. I made up my mind that I was not going to miss what could be my last chance to find out the truth about them. After all, this was the one job I was actually being paid to do. I had to find a way to get into that room. Then it came to me. Just before dinner, I became suddenly unwell. I told Theresa that I must have come down with the chill she caught earlier. My head was swimming and I felt too nauseous to come to dinner. The only thing for it was sleep—uninterrupted sleep.

Theresa looked most concerned. "I am so very sorry, Molly dear. It means you'll miss the séance, too."

"Oh dear," I said. "But in the circumstances I think it's more sensible that I keep away, just in case I'm contagious."

"Let me have the maid bring you up a cup of beef tea, or some calves foot jelly at least," she insisted.

"Really not, thank you all the same. I'm sure I'll be just fine by morning."

I felt deceitful as she walked away. She couldn't have been kinder to me since my arrival and I was planning to prick her bubble of hope.

I watched from a vantage point on the landing as they all went in to dinner. Then I sneaked down the back stairs. Luckily there was no lock on the room where the séance was to be held. I entered, leaving the door just wide enough open to get my bearings, then I closed it and made for the piano in the corner, now disguised under its black swathe. I squeezed underneath and adjusted the cloth so that I could look out. I wasn't sure how much I'd be able to see, but I couldn't risk turning on an electric light. Then I sat and waited. My stomach growled with hunger and I wished I'd been sensible enough to ask for that cup of beef tea to keep me going. Now I had to pray that a similar growl wouldn't give me away during the séance.

Dinner lasted a long time. I became cramped and uncomfortable. My left foot went to sleep. Then at last I heard voices coming down the hallway. The door opened. The light was switched on and Miss Emily and Miss Ella came into the room first. They looked around and I held my breath, just in case they somehow sensed my presence. Had I replaced the folds in the cloth exactly as they had left them? What excuse would I give if I were unmasked?

At that moment Theresa, Clara and Belinda arrived and there was a scraping of chairs and whispers as they were seated around a black-clothed table with the two spiritualists completing the circle. The lone candle was lit and the electric light was extinguished. For a long time nobody moved, then suddenly there came the loud rap we had heard before. I jumped and barely escaped banging my head against the piano keys. Wouldn't they have been shocked to hear a sound they hadn't created or planned?

The rap came again. Even though I was sure they were somehow manufacturing it, I still felt those prickles at the back of my neck.

"Are you with us, Chief Ojuweca?" Miss Emily asked in her sonorous voice.

"I am here," came the deep reply and I could swear again that it came from somewhere above our heads.

"Do you have any messages for this company tonight?" Miss Emily asked.

"Perhaps," said the deep voice.

"Will you show yourself to us tonight?"

"There are other spirits that seek a chance to materialize so that unbelievers may believe," Chief Ojuweca's voice said. "They are all around us. All around us."

Then there was a gasp. A flimsy white shape flitted through the air and vanished. Clara uttered a scream. "Ectoplasm! Look, Theresa, ectoplasm!"

I watched with fascination as some kind of substance oozed out of Miss Emily's right ear. It was greenish, luminous, billowing, and as we watched it formed itself into the image of a face. It was hard to determine whose face, but it was young, with large dark eyes and a plaintive expression. It hovered about Miss Emily's ear for a moment before it too vanished.

"They are all around us," Miss Ella said.

I have to confess my heart was thumping. I had seen that face with my own eyes. I began to question whether the Misses Sorensen were indeed the real thing.

"Whose face did we see?" Theresa asked with quivering voice.

"Her name is Angelique. She is a spirit guide. She tells me she has brought someone with whom you wanted to communicate. Go ahead, my dear. Speak. Invite the spirit in."

"Brendan?" Theresa could barely speak the word. "My baby, my dearest boy, are you with us?"

"Mama?" Again it was the smallest of voices.

"It's him! Brendan, it's your mother who loves you, who has wept for you every day since you left us."

"Mama, do not grieve for me. I am an angel now."

I could swear it was a small child talking and I thought I saw something white fluttering again.

"I must go back now. I love you."

"I love you too, darling boy, with all my heart!" The words came out between sobs. "Don't go, please stay longer."

"I can't. Must . . . go . . ." The little voice faded away as if it was floating up through the ceiling.

"That was most gratifying," Miss Emily said. "I think we must thank Chief Ojuweca for bringing your son back on a visit."

"Oh yes," Theresa attempted to collect herself, dabbing at her eyes with a white lace handkerchief. "Of course—please thank the Chief for me,"

"Thank him yourself. He is still here."

Theresa took a deep breath that shuddered through her whole body. "Thank you, dear Chief Ojuweca," she said in a shaky voice. "I'll never be able to thank you enough for hearing my son's voice again and to know that he is happy. What a miracle. What a blessed miracle. If only Barney had been here to witness it."

"Your husband does not believe," the chief's voice said. "There are others who still do not believe. Others in this room. And I am not finished yet. I have a message from another child for someone in this room. Here she comes now—she's dressed all in white, and she's wearing a veil and carrying flowers and a prayer book."

Clara gave an excited squawk. "First communion. Now who do we know who would be dressed for her first communion?"

"What about Cousin Emmaline's daughter, Fanny," Belinda suggested. "Didn't she die right before she was about to receive the sacrament?"

"You're right," Theresa spoke in a hushed voice. "She did. She caught diphtheria the week before her first communion and they buried her in her communion dress. I went to the funeral; so did you, Clara."

"Be quiet, ladies," the chief's voice said. "The little girl wants to say something."

"Don't worry about me. I'm with my mother and I'm happy." The voice this time was of an older child, but soft and sweet enough to make you cry.

"She's with her mother, God bless her," Clara said in a cracked voice. "Emmaline died last year, and now they're together, praise the Lord."

I felt strangely moved by the young voice, even though I knew it had to be a trick that one of the sisters was pulling off. No more spirits appeared and the séance soon came to a conclusion. Theresa still seemed shaken and needed the support of both Clara and Belinda to escort her from the room. As they left, I suddenly saw the flaw in my plans. If the Sorensen Sisters decided to strip the room right now, they would find me hiding under the piano. I held my breath and looked for a way of escape. Of course there was none.

But luck was with me. Theresa paused in the doorway, her manners and upbringing winning out over emotion.

"Do come and have some strawberries and cream, Miss Emily and Miss Ella," she said. "You did not have time to finish your supper because of my impatience, I fear."

"We don't usually eat late at night," Miss Ella said. "Bad for the digestion."

"However, strawberries and cream does sound delightful," Miss Emily interrupted her sister. "And on this one occasion I think we might just . . ."

"Yes, why not," Miss Ella agreed. "We will join you as soon as we have composed ourselves."

I watched as they stood up, holding my breath in case they decided to strip the drapes immediately. Instead, I watched Miss Ella lean behind a chair and pick up something from the floor. It went into a pocket so quickly that I couldn't see what it was, but it was white and flimsy. They looked at each other and nodded.

"A satisfactory evening, I would say," Miss Ella muttered.

Miss Emily nodded. They left the room. I came out of my hiding place and gave the room a quick going over before creeping undetected up the back stairs to my bedroom. But I found nothing incriminating.

❧ Twenty-two ❧

When I woke on Tuesday morning, I considered breaking into the sisters' cottage while they were at breakfast, but missing dinner last night had given me a ravenous appetite and I wasn't prepared to forego that meal myself. In fact, I got through a large helping of oatmeal followed by eggs and ham and toast.

"Molly, I am amazed and delighted to see you so quickly recovered," Theresa exclaimed as she watched me tuck in to my food.

I had all but forgotten that I had been an invalid the night before and blushed. "I have a good constitution, Cousin. With me it's one evening of sickness and then I'm on my feet again."

"How fortunate you are, Molly. How I wish I had your blooming good health."

"Maybe you'd feel better if you didn't take all those confounded patent medicines and headache powders," Barney said as he came into the room, followed by Joseph Rimes.

"If I didn't take my medicines I should feel even worse," Theresa said coldly.

"Did you ever stop to think that the medicines might be negating each other?" Barney asked. "Powders to make you sleep, powders to wake you up, tonics to keep you regular, tonics to stop you going too often."

"Really Barney, I must protest," Theresa said sharply. "Such talk at the breakfast table."

"I've never understood why talk of bodily functions is so taboo in polite society," Joseph Rimes said, piling his plate with food as he spoke. "Everyone has to do them; even Queen Victoria had to visit the smallest room occasionally."

"Mercy me!" Clara fanned herself. "Mr. Rimes, I must remind you that there are ladies present."

Joe Rimes laughed.

"You do it deliberately, Joe," Barney said, also grinning. "You enjoy making other people squirm, don't you?"

"One needs a few simple pleasures," Joe Rimes said, "and I've had to abandon most of them in the cause of getting you elected to Congress and keeping you there."

"And I'm most grateful to you, as you know." Barney sat beside Miss Emily. "And how are you ladies this morning?"

"Well, thank you, Senator. We had a most successful séance last night."

The grin vanished from Barney's face. "You went ahead with a séance, after I specifically forbade you to?" he roared.

Theresa stuck out her chin defiantly. "Miss Emily had a message from her spirit guide. He asked me to attend last night and it was a good thing that I did because Brendan came and talked to me."

"You saw him?" Barney's voice was still sharp.

"No, but I heard him. His dear, sweet little voice. He told me he was an angel now and I shouldn't grieve."

"For God's sake, woman, he was a baby when he died. Not even two years old. He could hardly say two words. How can you possibly believe it was he who was talking to you?"

"But don't you see, he has continued growing as an angel. He's now seven. A dear little precious seven-year-old angel and he told me he loves me." Theresa started to cry.

Barney glared at the two sisters, who pretended to be very busy eating toast and jam.

"Well, let's hope you're now satisfied and this is an end of it,"

Barney said to Theresa. "No more séances, do you hear? They're not making you feel better, but worse."

"Don't send dear Miss Emily and Miss Ella away, I beg of you." Theresa reached out to grab his hand.

"I am concerned for the health of your mind, Theresa. No good can come of this ridiculous communication with a dead son."

"Maybe we should pack our things immediately if we are no longer wanted." Miss Emily rose to her feet. "We are snowed under with invitations from people who want our help. Perhaps it would be wise to move on to a place where we are welcome."

"Look, now you've upset them." Again Theresa started to cry into her handkerchief.

"Dammit, woman, I want you to be well again," Barney shouted. "I want a normal wife. Is that too much to ask?" He left his food untouched and walked out of the dining room, slamming the door behind him.

The rest of us sat uncomfortably. The Misses Sorensen stood up. "I really think it might be wise for us to leave, Mrs. Flynn. Spirits will not come where there is such hostility to their presence."

"At least you spoke with Brendan once," Clara said. "You heard his dear little voice."

Theresa stretched out her hand imploringly. "Please don't go. Let me reason with him. I'm sure I'll make him understand and appreciate what you've done for us. Please, don't be hasty—just in case my son wants to contact me once again. I couldn't bear it if he tried to contact me and I wasn't there."

"We only want to do what is right for you, Mrs. Flynn," Miss Emily said. "But I do sense the most hostile of vibrations coming from your husband. We will never make a believer of him."

With that they made their exit. I got up too. There was no time to be lost. If those sisters were about to pack up and leave, I had work to do. But before I could leave, Theresa grabbed at my sleeve. "Don't you desert me too, Molly. I need your comforting presence beside me at a time like this. You are becoming my rock, Molly. I shall cling to you."

So naturally I couldn't escape after an appeal like that, could I? Instead, I had to sit listening to Theresa play the piano and then share a book of poems with me all morning. I managed to keep a look of calm composure on my face every time she smiled at me, when I was just itching to rush out to that cottage before those sisters could pack up their things.

Just before lunch I feigned feeling sick again.

Theresa shook her head. "I didn't think it wise at the time when you ate such a big breakfast. I've always found one must treat the stomach most delicately after episodes like yours."

"I suppose I'm not as robust as I thought I was," I answered. "But if you will excuse me, I think I'll forgo lunch today. The sight and smell of food will only make me feel worse."

"But you will at least take some beef tea in your room today?"

"Later," I said. "For the moment I think I'll just lie down quietly. I may feel well enough to join you for tea."

I went upstairs and dutifully laid down on my bed, just in case she decided to check on me. Then, when the lunch gong sounded, I watched and waited until Miss Emily and Miss Ella arrived and they were all safely in the dining room. Then I crept down the stairs and out of the front door. Instead of taking the most direct route to the cottage, which would be up the driveway, in full view of the dining room windows, I went around the other side of the house, past the Senator's study and the library and then the back wall of the kitchen where Clara had attempted to plant her sorry-looking flowers.

From there I cut across the kitchen garden, finding a path between tall rows of beans and peas. It came to me that Bertie Morell, or whoever took the child from the house, could have taken the boy this way without being observed from any of the rooms except the nursery or the other back bedrooms, in which Belinda and Clara now slept.

The cottage door opened with a simple latch, like ours at home, and I tiptoed inside. I don't know what I expected to find—a den of black magic perhaps. I do know that my heart was thumping alarmingly. I think part of me still believed in that Indian chief and the floating spirits and the ectoplasm. And with all that inbred Irish superstition of fairies, ghosts and goblins, part of me also believed those spirits might be inhabiting this house.

Instead, it was a perfectly neat and tidy room that met my eye. It was comfortably furnished in a country cottage style, with a big whitewashed fireplace in the middle of one wall, two chintz-covered armchairs and a gate-leg table in the window. Apart from a book and a pair of spectacles on the table, there was no sign that the place was inhabited. A door at one side opened into a kitchen that the sisters had obviously not used, apart from a kettle on the stove, and off a narrow hallway behind it was the bedroom on one side, a bathroom on the other. These, at least, showed signs of being lived in. There were hairbrushes and pins and face powder on the dressing table and a pair of black lisle stockings over the back of a chair. The dresser and wardrobe both contained items of clothing—black silk evening dresses, shawls, shoes, all very ordinary things.

I went through one drawer after another, finding nothing. No walking hands, magic lanterns or any other devices for carrying out magic tricks. I rooted around some more, but came up with nothing.

The strange thing was that there was no sign of any trunks or suitcases. Surely they must have traveled with luggage? I prowled the cottage once more and even looked into the lean-to at the back, but found nothing. I was about to admit defeat and consider the possibility that the Misses Sorensen might be genuine spiritualists who really did communicate with the dead, when I noticed a trap door in the ceiling of that dark and narrow hallway. I pulled on the cord that hung from it and a crude ladder unfolded. I hoisted my skirts and climbed up into a dark and musty attic. Above me was the thatched roof, probably infested with all manner of creepy crawlies. One dormer window provided enough light for me to see my way and to make out shapes around me. There were various humps and bumps hidden under dust sheets.

I stood, breathing in the dusty air and wondering if this investigation was a waste of time. Surely the stout and aging Misses Sorensen would have had no reason to come up here. Then I noticed something. Neat footprints across the dusty floor. Someone had been up here recently. I followed the footprints and lifted the dust sheet from one of the objects. It was a trunk.

I held my breath as I lifted the lid, half afraid of what I might find, even though I fully believed that the sisters were fakes. The first thing I came across was black fabric, neatly folded, then a magazine with a hole cut from a page with a pair of scissors. There was nothing suspicious about cutting out a favorite article or recipe, so I put it aside and pulled out a cloth bag. The objects inside it were most intriguing: two round wooden disks with straps attached to them. As I held them up, they reminded me of cymbals and on impulse I clapped them together. The noise was so loud that I started and almost fell into the open trunk.

I stared down at the disks and smiled. I had heard that sonorous clap before, when Chief Ojuweca arrived. But the two sisters were sitting in a circle, holding hands with the participants. Unless—I perched on one of the dust sheets, pulled up my skirts, and strapped the disk to the inside of my knee. Then I did the same with the other one. Then I lowered my skirts and clapped my legs together. I wasn't as skilled at it as they obviously were, but it still sounded quite convincing.

Now that I had unmasked one trick, I felt a lot better. I lifted out the magazine with the hole in it and the damaged page turned to reveal what was on the other side—it had been a full-page picture of a young woman, only the face was now missing. I could guess what that face looked like—it had appeared from the side of Miss Emily's head, seemingly coming as ectoplasm from her ear. I had no idea how the ectoplasm was produced, but knowing that the face had an earthly origin made me feel much better.

Next to the magazine was a scrap of flimsy white fabric, which looked as if it had once been part of a petticoat or nightgown. I threw it up into the air and it floated down quite nicely. So that was the spirit that Miss Emily had quickly pocketed from behind the chair last night. I was dying to find out how the chief's face and the walking hand worked, but I had to be aware of time too. I went across to the window and peeked out. No sign of them yet.

Then I wondered if any of the other items in the attic were theirs as well. I turned back the sheets only to find a broken washstand and a hatbox full of outmoded hats. These had obviously been stored in the attic for some time. I covered them in their dust sheets once more and, glancing back across the room, I realized that my footprints were now all too visible. The Misses Sorensen would know I had been up here unless I found a way to wipe out my prints. The only thing I could think of doing was to give the floor a good sweep. But that would mean going down to the kitchen and finding the broom. Maybe if I dragged one of those cloths over the floor I could spread the dust around and make the prints less obvious. I went to the far corner to take the cloth from the most unobtrusive object and my foot kicked against something small.

I bent to pick it up. It was a toy wooden camel.

❧ Twenty-three ❧

I stared at the little camel, trying to come up with the implications of what I had found. Its mate was still living in the Noah's ark in the nursery. It had been Brendan's favorite toy. But he was a toddler. He could never have come up here on his own to drop the camel, unless . . . unless he had been brought up by someone else. My heart was racing so fast now that I could hardly breathe. Was it possible that he had been hidden up here instead of being buried on the estate, as the kidnapper said? In which case . . . I stood looking at the various humps and bumps around the room. Was it possible that he was still up here?

I shook my head against the absurdity of this idea. Surely they would have searched this place. Surely they would have heard him crying. Surely dogs would have smelled him out. But I had to know. I started pulling off one cloth after another, opening one box and trunk after another until I had gone through the whole attic and found nothing. He wasn't here. But I had an overwhelming feeling that Brendan had been kept here at some moment during the kidnapping and that might be important.

I had heard that the police had now come up with a way to remove fingerprints left on surfaces and to identify them. If only I could get Daniel up here, maybe he had that skill and he could find Bertie Morell's fingerprints, or not. Even if Brendan had only been held here briefly after having been spirited from the house, it would be one step in a puzzle that had never been solved. As I stood in the dusty twilight of the attic, an eerie feeling came over me. I could feel a little voice whispering, "Find me." We Irish are known for the second sight—not the hocus-pocus of Miss Emily and Miss Ella, but the real thing. Not that I professed to have it myself, but there had been occasions when I had sensed danger. I felt that same prickling at the back of my neck now, not danger this time, but urgency. Why urgency? I asked myself. Why should it matter when the child's body was found—unless? A thought that must have been lurking at the back of my mind took shape. Was there any possibility that the child was still alive?

I was so lost in thought that I had forgotten about the Misses Sorensen and why I had come up here in the first place. I jumped at the sound of voices and a front door closing. The ladder was still hanging down from the attic, clearly visible to anyone who came this way. I crept across to the trap door, wondering how I could haul the ladder up without being heard, or, failing that, what I could say when I was discovered. Could I pull it off if I claimed to be searching for an old book that Theresa thought might be stored in the attic here? Hardly, since I had pretended to be too sick to eat lunch. I could hide under one of the dust sheets and wait for them to leave the cottage again, but the whole place was now in disarray. They'd know that somebody had been here.

I crept across the floor and closed the lid of their trunk, pulling the dust sheet back over it. Then I decided that I didn't want to be caught up here with no way of escape. They might be middle-aged ladies, but there were two of them to one of me, and they were very good at sleight of hand. I had no wish to be stabbed with those scissors and to wind up under one of those dust sheets. I've often found that attack is the best form of defense. I brushed myself off, slipped the camel into my pocket and came down the stairs.

"Miss Emily. Miss Ella." I smiled and nodded as I saw their astonished faces. I made my way to the front door.

"Would you mind telling us what in heaven's name you were

doing in our cottage?" Miss Emily demanded. "I thought that sickness was feigned. Does Mrs. Flynn know that her cousin is really a common thief?"

The front door was comfortingly within reach. "As to that, I'm happy to turn out my pockets and you're welcome to check your things. The question I'm asking myself is should I tell Mrs. Flynn that you two are a couple of frauds and tricksters?"

"So that's why you came here—to try and catch us out? I'll wager you found nothing." Miss Ella glanced first at her sister and then at me.

"Oh, but I did, Miss Ella. I found all kinds of incriminating evidence, including the magazine from which you cut your ectoplasm picture, the disks you use to make your impressive claps with your knees and the wispy spirit that turned out to be nothing more than a piece of underwear."

Miss Emily was still smiling at me. "We often cut pictures from magazines for our scrapbooks, Miss Gaffney. And, being of a thrifty nature, we keep spare pieces of cloth for patching worn undergarments."

"And the wooden disks?"

"For pressing flowers. One places flowers between sheets of blotting paper, then straps the wooden disks tightly together. It works very well, I can assure you."

"You may be able to take in poor suffering creatures like Mrs. Flynn," I said, "but I was asked to watch you by a captain of the New York Police and he'll be most interested to hear what I have found out."

Miss Emily's smile didn't waver. "Go ahead, my dear. It won't be the first attempt to prevent us from carrying on our wonderful work. If it comes to a trial, there's not a jury in the land that would convict us. For every person like yourself who claims we are frauds, we can produce a hundred people who will attest that our communication with the spirits is real."

"We have satisfied customers all over the country, my dear," Miss Ella said. "We bring comfort to the broken-hearted and you want to stop us from doing that? Are you saying that Mrs. Flynn is less content now that she has spoken to her son?"

"Only you know and I know that it wasn't really her son at all. How can you ladies live with yourselves, deceiving the most vulnerable of people to make money?"

"You say that we deceive, but then we always knew you were a non-believer," Miss Emily said. "One day you might find that you have a change of heart."

"And as for making money," Miss Ella said, "we never charge a penny for our services. If satisfied clients wish to give us a small donation, we take it, but we have never asked for money."

Miss Emily opened the front door for me. "So go ahead, my dear. Do tell your policeman friend everything you've discovered. Tell Mrs. Flynn too if you wish to plunge her into her abyss of grief again."

I knew, as I walked back along the driveway, that they had won. They were right. There was no way I would risk hurting Theresa by telling her the truth. And with a hundred Theresas testifying on the witness stand, there was no way a jury would convict the Sorensen Sisters.

I made it safely back to my room, very fortunately, because Alice the maid appeared with beef tea soon after I had returned.

"The mistress's instructions are that you should stay in bed today and make sure you're not running around too soon," she said, talking to me as if I was a naughty five-year-old.

So I had to sit, fuming, by my open window, wondering what might be going on downstairs and up at the Misses Sorensens' cottage. I heard snatches of conversation as tea was taken on the porch. I heard Eileen's little voice as she came to make her daily visit. Then shortly afterward Theresa herself came to see me, bringing wafer-thin slices of brown bread and honey while the maid carried a cup of weak tea.

"Do get well again soon, Molly dearest," she said. "It won't do to have two wretched invalids on the premises and I am so relying on you."

I promised I'd feel as right as rain in the morning and even suggested that I might even feel well enough to come down to dinner,
but was met with stern instructions to stay where I was. I felt like
a complete fraud, seeing her so concerned about me. The evening
dragged on until Alice appeared with hot milk just as it was getting dark. Then there was nothing to do but go to sleep.

I woke to complete darkness and to the most awful cramps in
my stomach. I scarcely had time to find the chamber pot under my
bed before I was horribly and violently sick. The bouts of sickness
went on all night, leaving me weak and sweating. How my mother
must be enjoying this, I thought grimly. She'd always told me
about the dire punishments for lying. Well, I'd claimed to be
stricken with a mysterious illness and now it had come true.

By morning I was just strong enough to stagger across my room
and ring the bell for a servant. She must have given a vivid description of my condition because it brought Theresa herself, still
in her dressing gown, in to see me. She stood in the doorway and
eyed me with grave concern.

"Molly, my dear lamb, you look terrible. Let me call Dr. Chambers for you."

"I'm sure it's nothing more than something I ate," I said.

"But there are all kinds of dreadful illnesses going around at the
moment," she said. "There's typhoid in the city. We can't be too
careful, can we?"

Dr. Chambers arrived in due course, listened to my heart and
breathing and came to the same conclusion as myself—that it
must have been something I had eaten. I was put on a strict invalid
diet of slops and ordered to stay in bed for a few days. Strangely
enough I felt much better the moment he left and managed to eat
some gruel and a soft-boiled egg.

Theresa came to visit me again, looking most agitated. "Molly,
you'll never imagine what terrible thing has happened," she whispered. "Miss Emily and Miss Ella—they have gone. Apparently
they asked the chauffeur to drive them to the ferry early this
morning and they have left us without even saying good-bye."

She put her hand to her mouth. "Now I'll never get a chance to hear Brendan's voice again. I am so angry with Barney. It's all his fault."

"I'm so sorry," I said, feeling doubly guilty because I was sure the fault was mine and not Barney's that the Misses Sorensen had done a bunk. The day dragged on. I had always made a terrible patient. I got up and walked around my room, wondering what I should be doing. I had to admit that I felt shaky on my feet and soon had to lie down again. In fact I must have drifted off to sleep because I woke to find Alice shaking me.

"Sorry to disturb you, miss, but the mail has just arrived and Mrs. Flynn thought you might like to be cheered up." She handed me a letter.

It was addressed to Miss Molly Gaffney from Mrs. Priscilla O'Sullivan. The address, of course, was Daniel's.

"Oh, how nice," I said. "An old family friend in New York has written to me. I stayed with her briefly when I first arrived."

I waited until Alice had departed before I opened the envelope. I had recognized the handwriting. Inside was Daniel's black and angry script.

Molly,

Do not get yourself involved in anything other than the task you were asked to complete. For your information, there was no indication at the inquiry to suggest that Albert Morell had any connections to the Black Hand. That isn't to say that he wasn't working for them. Their squealers tend to wind up in the Hudson, so it's possible that they were behind the kidnapping. It is certainly the kind of brutal and heartless thing they would do. Which makes it all the more imperative—do not ask any more questions or poke your nose into this any further. Find out all you can about the Sorensen Sisters and then come straight home. And that is an order.

As to the other matter you mention. There could be something irregular with the woman's death you describe, but you are not going to investigate it, and neither am I. It is beyond my jurisdiction and if the local police decide not to pursue it, there is nothing I can do.

Destroy this letter as soon as you have read it. If there is an informant in the house you may be putting yourself in the gravest jeopardy.

Daniel

So that was that. I was being ordered home. In one way I was relieved; in another I was frustrated that I had managed to accomplish so little. I had caused Miss Emily and Miss Ella to bolt, and I had uncovered some of their tricks, but that was a long way from being able to stop their little game. And I was no nearer at all to finding out the true story behind the Flynn baby's kidnapping. It now seemed that Albert Morell was in the pay of the Black Hand, or that they somehow had a hold over him, and he had carried out their instructions. Why else would the note have been signed with a black hand on it? And I had not been able to prove that Annie Lomax hadn't played her part in it, bringing the child to the cottage. All in all, a dismal failure.

I lay feeling annoyed, frustrated and sorry for myself until the maid came up with a supper tray, containing a cup of beef tea and some thinly sliced bread and butter. I cleared my plate and fell asleep.

❧ Twenty-four ❧

That night I woke again to cramps and vomiting. I lay there suffering, rather than wake one of the servants, but this time it was even more severe and I became quite frightened. In my weakened state hallucinations danced in front of my eyes and it suddenly came to me that this was a curse, put upon me by Miss Emily and Miss Ella for standing in their way. I didn't believe in curses any more than I believed in spirits, but lying all alone in a dark room, listening to the owl hoot outside my window while my body was wracked with cramps, I was not at my most logical.

Theresa came to minister to me in the morning and again by midday I was feeling stronger. I kept down a little lunch, and that afternoon Theresa suggested I might feel up to joining everybody on the porch to enjoy the cool breeze from the river. A strapping footman carried me downstairs and deposited me on the wicker chaise. Theresa, Belinda and Clara were all sitting around the tea table and little Eileen was being grilled on her daily activities as I was carried out.

I noticed the others stayed well clear of me, probably not fully believing the doctor's diagnosis that I didn't have typhoid. I noticed Clara eyeing me suspiciously as she poured my tea. "Are you sure Cousin Molly would not be better off staying in her bed as the doctor ordered?" she asked.

"Oh, but Clara, it's so terribly lonely to be up there all alone all day," Theresa said. "I should know. I've spent enough lonely days myself in recent years. Molly needs cheering up."

"If you're sure it's nothing contagious," Clara said. "The child is with us, remember."

Eileen wanted to go up to me, but was restrained by her nanny. "Miss Gaffney isn't well," she said. "She won't want you disturbing her." And the child was hurriedly taken back upstairs.

I took a thin slice of bread and some tea with the others but felt as weak as a kitten. If this continued, when would I ever be strong enough to travel, and what excuse could I use to make my exit?

We were in the middle of tea when we heard the sound of horse's hooves on the gravel drive. Soon a horse-drawn cab came into sight and stopped at the front door. Teacups were put down and everyone watched with great interest as a slim, bearded gentleman got out of the cab. He was pale and light-haired, with round, wire spectacles like the kind that Jacob wore. His tweedy travel clothes were well worn and clearly designed for a cooler climate. In his hand he carried a black leather travel bag and he stood looking around nervously before marching up to the front steps.

"Who on earth—" Clara began, but Belinda had already leaped to her feet.

"Dr. Birnbaum—it's really you. How wonderful of you to come!"

The man shook hands with a curious little clicking of heels and bow. Belinda grabbed his sleeve and dragged him up the steps.

"Theresa, this is the Dr. Birnbaum I told you about. He's the one I met in Paris and he said he might be coming to America, so I said of course he had to promise to come to Adare and here he is."

I was intrigued by Belinda's choice. I should have thought that the pale and rather shabby doctor was not her type at all.

Theresa held out her hand. "Dr. Birnbaum. Any friend of Belinda's is most welcome," she said. "Do sit down and have some tea."

"How kind." The doctor bowed again.

"May I introduce two members of my family—my cousins Miss Tompkins and Miss Gaffney."

"Your servant, ladies." Another bow. He turned back to Theresa. "Then you must be Mrs. Flynn, the one I have come to help." He spoke English fluently but with a pronounced German accent.

"Come to help?" Theresa looked puzzled. "I don't understand. I thought you were a friend of Belinda's."

"He's my alienist friend, Theresa. I told him all about you and he said he might be able to ease your depression."

"An alienist?" Theresa's voice had grown sharp. "You brought him here to treat me? But I don't need an alienist. I'm not insane. You didn't imply that I was insane, did you?"

"Of course you are not insane, Mrs. Flynn." The doctor said, pausing to take a sip of tea, then wipe his mustache. "Anyone can see that. But depression is also a disease of the mind and can be cured. I told your sister of my work in Vienna with Dr. Freud."

"Dr. Freud is doing wonderful things, Theresa," Belinda said. "He has learned to analyze dreams and he can tell you what's troubling you through your dreams."

"I know what's a troubling me," Theresa said. "I grieve for my child. I don't need an alienist for that."

"But we have made great advances recently, Mrs. Flynn," Dr. Birnbaum said. "If you let me treat you, I can help you to let go of these terrible memories. Dr. Freud has worked very successfully with hypnotism and I studied under him for two years. You would be amazed at the cures he brings about. A girl who had not spoken for years is restored to sanity and health. It's like a miracle."

Belinda leaned across to her sister and placed her hand delicately on Theresa's arm. "You do want to feel better, don't you, Tessa dear? To be able to enjoy life again? To look forward to the future? If this man can make your black cloud go away, why don't you give him a try?"

"It would be wonderful to enjoy life again, I agree," Theresa said, "but he will have to treat me here. I am not going to be put in any institution."

"There's no question of an institution of any kind, Mrs. Flynn," Dr. Birnbaum said. "I may want to hypnotize you, with your permission, but other than that, we will just have little chats together. You will treat me like an old and trusted friend."

"Very well," Theresa said. "You seem to have come at an opportune moment, Dr. Birnbaum. I just lost my spiritualist friends who contacted my dead son for me. Maybe you have been sent to take their place."

"I'm sure I can guide you to the road to recovery, Mrs. Flynn," the doctor said. He accepted an éclair from the plate offered him by Alice, patting neatly at the sides of his mouth after each bite.

I watched him with interest. Until this week I hadn't heard of alienists. I hadn't even realized that diseases of the mind could be treated, apart from locking up lunatics in asylums. I hoped I'd have a chance to watch Dr. Birnbaum at work, if ever I recovered from this disease. In truth I was feeling dizzy and nauseous just from sitting propped up and after a short while I had to ask the footman to get me back to bed.

"Poor Molly, she doesn't seem to be getting better, does she?" I heard Theresa's voice float up from the veranda below. "I do hope Dr. Chambers was right and it's not more serious than we thought."

"I remember one of the Butler cousins contracted a similar ailment," I heard Clara, loud and clear. "Nobody could do a thing for her. She just wasted away before our eyes."

"How terrible. What do you think we should do for Molly?"

"If she really is dying, maybe she would want to go home to the bosom of her family," Clara suggested.

"Don't say that word, Clara. I couldn't bear to think of it," Theresa said.

"Of course Molly's not dying. You do dramatize everything, Cousin Clara," Belinda said. "You know how common food poisoning is in summer. She ate something that had gone off, that's all. She'll be right as rain in a few days."

"If she's not, I'm going to have Barney bring out a specialist from the city," Theresa said.

"Just in case you should perhaps write to her family," Clara suggested. "Better to prepare them for the worst."

I lay there agonizing over this. I would certainly have to get better before a letter had time to reach Ireland. I wasn't intending to die, either! I was feeling so weak after two nights of retching and my excursion down to the veranda that I fell asleep before it was dark and didn't stir until morning. I awoke on Friday morning feeling much better. I washed, dressed and came downstairs to find another mood of high drama.

Theresa and Barney were facing each other in the hallway.

"Honestly, Theresa, I have never heard anything more ridiculous," Barney was saying. "I agree that an alienist might be able to help you, but what do we know about this fellow? He could be some wandering quack that Belinda bumped into on her travels for all we know. Where are his credentials? And as for hypnotism—that is surely the stuff of fairgrounds and not medicine."

"Dr. Birnbaum says it has produced some miraculous cures. It brings out hidden fears and worries."

Barney's voice softened a little. "But we know what your worries are, don't we, sweetheart? If the fellow could give you a pill to cheer you up again, I'd be all for it. But if he hypnotizes you, I'm afraid of what he might unleash."

"You're just afraid the truth will come out," Theresa said. She turned on her heel and strode in the direction of the dining room, leaving me feeling embarrassed halfway down the stairs. I would have crept back to my room again, but Barney looked up as he headed for his study and saw me.

"Ah, Molly, you are on your feet again. That is good news! Theresa was insisting I write to your family about you—thought you were wasting away, I gather." He laughed. "We Flynns are made of sterner stuff, aren't we?" He came up the stairs toward me. "This alienist fellow," he whispered, "did you get a chance to meet him yesterday? What did you think of him?"

"I'm in no position to judge a doctor's qualifications," I said. "If he helps Theresa, what harm can he do?"

"That's just it," he said. "I'm scared he might push her over the edge. She's so fragile. Still, I suppose it can't hurt to let her talk to the man. I'm just not going to allow the hypnotism."

Having made up his mind to his own satisfaction, he ran down the stairs again in the direction of his study. I joined the others at breakfast and Clara kept commenting on my miraculous recovery.

"I thought you were for the churchyard, Molly. That terrible sunken look to your eyes—and now look at you, well on the road to recovery again. Did you pray to a particular saint? They say St. Jude can work miracles in the case of lost causes, but then St. Luke was the physician."

"No, I can't say it occurred to me to pray to a saint," I confessed. "I was feeling too sick to think of such things."

"Next time it recurs try St. Jude then," Clara suggested.

"I hope it won't recur," I said. "If it was food poisoning, as Dr. Chambers suggested, then hopefully it is now out of my system."

I ate sparingly at breakfast, not wanting to tempt fate, and sparingly again at lunch. Theresa had her first session with Dr. Birnbaum and apparently it went well.

"It is more complicated than I thought," he reported to us as Theresa went to lie down in her room. "She brings a lot of hurt and anger from her childhood—a father who could never show affection, a mother who was jealous of her beauty. Yes, I would say that the anger she keeps bottled up inside her is greater even than her grief."

"And how will you be able to release this anger?" Barney asked, and there was a tightness to his voice.

"I will strip away the layers, like an onion," Dr. Birnbaum said. "Then, when all the anger and hurts are brought out into the open, we will put her into a hypnotic trance to find if there are any angers and hurts that even she is afraid to admit to. She will awake like a newborn baby, with heart and soul pure and cleansed. You will have your wife back, Mr. Flynn."

"I just hope you know what you're doing, Birnbaum," Barney growled. "You're to keep me consulted at every step of the way, and you are not to attempt to hypnotize her without my permission."

"Naturally, Mr. Flynn. Your full cooperation will be needed for Mrs. Flynn's full recovery." He put out his hand to prevent Barney from walking past him up the stairs. "She is resting at present. I suggest we let her recover in peace until she is ready to get up."

Theresa stayed in bed until teatime. When she joined us, I was shocked at her appearance. I thought she looked paler and sicklier than ever before, with hollow eyes and ashen complexion. So did Barney.

"You call yourself a doctor, man?" he demanded. "Look at her. That's not getting better."

Dr. Birnbaum rose to his feet. "I assure you, sir, that the treatments will help Mrs. Flynn, but patience will be required. It will be painful to peel away the layers of this onion, as I described it. She may well suffer until she realizes that by speaking the words she fears most out loud, she will be free."

"I am feeling a little better, honestly, I am," Theresa said. "I know Dr. Birnbaum will be able to help me."

"I'm still far from convinced that this is a good idea," Barney said. "I'm sitting in on the next session whether you like it or not. I won't have my wife bullied and intimidated." He glanced across at Joe Rimes, who was standing in the doorway. "What do you think, Joe?"

"If you really want my opinion," Joe Rimes said slowly, "I think there are clinics that specialize in this sort of thing. I think what Theresa really needs is to get away from this place and all its memories. Send her to Switzerland for a few months. A healing process like this can't be rushed."

"I quite agree with you, sir," Dr. Birnbaum said. "A clinic in Switzerland would be ideal. I myself have been consulting physician at a fine clinic on Lake Geneva. I could write a letter of recommendation for you if you wished to pursue this."

Barney looked from Theresa to Joe Rimes and back again. "It might be worth considering," he said.

Theresa shook her head. "Don't send me away, please. I know that once I am locked up, I shall never return."

"There is no question of locking you up, my sweet." Barney put a hand on her shoulder. "These places are more like sanitariums. You would be restored to good health in no time at all."

"I'd go if you come with me," she said.

"I could come for a couple of weeks, to see you settled in," Barney said, "but then I have to be back here to return to Washington. I can't abandon my constituents, and I have my reelection campaign to think of."

"Then I won't go," Theresa said. "I have faith in Dr. Birnbaum. He and I will work together and he will cure me right here."

Barney sighed. "You can be very obstinate, Theresa. I wish you would understand that others are trying to do what is best for you."

"Are they?" she asked sweetly.

❧ Twenty-five ❧

Cook had outdone herself with dinner that night. Lobster followed by a soufflé followed by enormous steaks topped with mushrooms and pâté, and the meal culminating in a light mixture of brandied fruit and cream. I ate cautiously, as my stomach was still delicate, but the odors were so enticing that I tried a little of each course. I did ask Alice to bring me up a cup of peppermint tea in case I had overdone it. And obviously I had as the sickness returned that very night.

I lay there, heaving and groaning, remembering Clara's comments about the relative who had wasted away before their eyes. Was I never going to be able to eat proper food again without this sickness recurring? Was I never going to feel well and strong enough to escape from this place?

Dr. Birnbaum was sent to examine me in the morning. He tapped and prodded me all over, then smiled. "I think this is just an unhappy coincidence, my dear Fräulein. You ate shellfish last night, did you not? Most unwise. Shellfish spoils so quickly in this heat and one bite is all it takes. And you were already in a weakened state from your last bout of food poisoning. This time I warn you to be extra careful. Drink plenty of liquids, but take nothing else by mouth until your digestive system has had a chance to recover. I will have the cook make you a good veal bone tea for nourishment later.

Apart from that, barley water, remember. Nothing but barley water." He wagged his finger at me seriously.

"Thank you," I said. "So you don't think it's anything really serious? I'm not going to waste away and die, am I?"

"What rubbish. A young girl with your healthy constitution. You'll be back on your feet in a few days if you obey my instructions."

I lay back, too weak even to sip the barley water that sat on my bedside table. I didn't ever recall feeling so bad in my life. My head ached, my stomach felt as if it had been trampled by a herd of bulls. I was hot and clammy all over one minute, then cold and clammy the next. Lights danced in front of my eyes. Everything seemed to have a strange color to it. I couldn't help wondering if they were right and I really was dying. If that were true, shouldn't somebody be told? I managed to drag myself to the writing desk and scrawl a note to Daniel.

"I am very unwell," I wrote. "If you could find any way to get me out of this place and safely home, I would appreciate it. I don't want to die here."

Then I addressed it to Mrs. Priscilla O'Sullivan at Daniel's address asked the maid to have it taken to the mail right away. It would take at least twenty-four hours to reach New York and then another twenty-four for a response. I just hoped I'd be alive that long.

I had forgotten that the next day was Sunday. The week had passed in a blur of feeling terrible. So it would be more than twenty-four hours before Daniel even received the letter. I stayed away from any kind of nourishment all day on Saturday, as instructed by Dr. Birnbaum. In fact, I felt somewhat comforted by knowing there was a physician in the house, even if he was a specialist in diseases of the mind. By evening I was hungry but refused the calves foot jelly that was sent up to me and only took some sips of broth and barley water. Even that didn't seem to agree with me and I had another unpleasant night.

I woke to a clear, cool Sunday morning and I lay listening to the twittering of birds and the distant church bells on the breeze.

Theresa and Barney came to see me before they went to church.

"I just wish we knew what to do for you, my dear lamb," Theresa said. "Dr. Birnbaum suggested that you see a specialist, and wants us to send you to a hospital, but I don't want you in one of those terrible places."

"The man is a quack," Barney said. "I have little faith in anything he says."

"Oh no, you're wrong, my dear." Theresa touched his arm gently. "I really believe he is helping me. He wanted to have another consultation with me today, but of course it wouldn't be right on a Sunday. But tomorrow, maybe, and I think I may allow him to hypnotize me this time."

"I absolutely forbid it, Theresa," Barney said.

"It could help, Barney. You can come and observe if you want to."

"You looked ten times worse after that first session," Barney snapped. "I'm all for sending the fellow packing right now."

"It's Sunday, Barney. Let's not argue, especially not in front of poor, dear Molly. We'll say a prayer and light a candle for you, my pet." She bent to kiss my forehead. "Just ring for Alice if you want anything while we're at church."

They left me then and I heard their voices as they came out of the front door.

"Do you think we should bring the priest back with us?" I heard Clara asking.

"Really, Clara, you are being too morbid," Theresa snapped.

"Not the last rites, just to pray over her," Clara said.

They passed out of my hearing.

That afternoon they took tea on the lawn and played croquet. I lay staring at the plaster moldings on the ceiling, willing myself to get better. I longed for a cup of tea, but wasn't about to risk drinking one. To tell the truth, I was now seriously frightened. Should I try telephoning Daniel to have him come for me? Would I recover if I were in Sid and Gus's care? And of course the nagging worry behind everything else—did I really have typhoid?

In the evening a cup of clear broth was sent up to me, but I was too weak to drink more than one sip of it. I lay watching the sun set, feeling the cool evening breeze stirring the lace curtains and listening to the night noises. I was just drifting off to sleep when I heard a stirring in the vine below my window. I realized my windows were wide open to let in the breeze and wondered what wild animal, or even a rat, might be climbing up the trellis to find a way into the house. If so, I was too weak to stop it from coming into my room. I had just decided that I was imagining things when a foot came over my windowsill.

I watched in silent horror as the foot was followed by a leg and a dark shape hauled itself into my room. I wanted to scream but I couldn't make my mouth work. If it were only a burglar, I would feign sleep and maybe he would pass me by. The shape stood up, revealing itself to be a tall man. He crept forward, reaching out in the darkness, obviously not seeing as well as I could. There was a lead crystal vase on the dresser beside my bed. Currently it held no flowers and would be heavy enough if I had the strength to lift it.

I tried to ease myself into a sitting position so that I could grab the vase, but the room spun around as soon as I sat up and I must have moaned because the figure turned to face me.

"Take another step and I'll scream to wake the house up," I said.

"Molly? Thank God it's you," a voice said. "I was hoping I'd got the right window."

"Daniel?" For a moment I wondered if his presence was part of a fevered dream. "Is it really you? I'm not hallucinating, am I?"

He put a warning finger to his lips. "No, it's really me," he whispered. He came closer. "Are you all right?"

"Apart from the fact that I'm dying," I whispered back and tried to smile.

"I tried to see you this afternoon but they wouldn't let me," he said in a low voice. "They told me that you were indisposed."

"I am," I said. "Well and truly indisposed. But what are you doing here? I thought you wanted to stay well clear of the Flynns because they know you?"

"Oh, I told them I was staying in the neighborhood and I'd bumped into someone who knew you from Limerick and I promised her I'd give you the latest news from home."

"I see. That's good." I closed my eyes as the room swung around again.

"Can we be easily overheard?" he asked, prowling around the room.

I shook my head. "I don't think so. But other people will have windows open, and sound carries on still nights like this."

Daniel went across to the window and closed it. "That should do it, if we only talk in whispers."

"I can't talk louder than a whisper anyway," I said.

Daniel brushed my hair back from my face. "You're covered in sweat," he said. "Lie back. Have you seen a doctor?"

"Two of them. They both told me I had food poisoning and I'd be fine if I ate nothing, which I'm doing. But the moment I eat or drink anything it all begins again. I've been vomiting my heart out for several days now."

"That conjures up a pretty picture," he said, but he was still stroking my hair tenderly. "Is there any particular time of day it comes on?"

"At night," I said. "Always at night. I lie down and fall asleep feeling perfectly normal, then I wake up to the sweats and the cramps and the vomiting."

"Do you drink anything before you go to sleep?"

"Yes, they always bring up a milky drink or a cup of beef tea."

He gripped my shoulders. "Did you drink it tonight?"

"No, just a few sips. I felt too weak. It's still there on the bedside table."

He picked it up, dipped his finger into it and licked the finger. "Did you notice a bitter flavor?" he asked.

"Perhaps. I thought my sickness had upset my taste buds."

"I think it could be arsenic," he said. "We've got to get you out of here. I think you're being poisoned."

"Poisoned? But who would want to poison me?"

"Good question," he said. "Who brings the drink to you?"

"The maid. I have no idea who prepares it."

"Somebody who doesn't want you snooping around any longer, by the sound of it," he said. "I'll take a sample of the stuff and have it tested. Do you have something I could carry it in? A pill box? A little medicine bottle?"

I shook my head. "I don't take medicines. I've never been sick, until now."

"Don't women travel with an array of little boxes and toiletries?"

"Not me," I said. "I'm a poor Irish peasant, remember."

"You're hopeless," he said, but he was smiling. "I suppose for want of anything better—" He took out a clean handkerchief and dipped it into the cup. "I'll wring it out into a container when I get back."

"Ingenious," I said. "I must remember that."

He turned to glare at me. "I'm so angry with myself, putting you in harm's way like this, when I wanted just the opposite . . ."

"What exactly do you mean by that?"

"I meant that I thought this would be a perfectly safe assignment for you, and now if I hadn't arrived in time, you might be lying here dead. It was stupid of me . . ." He got up and started pacing the room.

"But I've been very careful, Daniel," I said. "They all think I'm harmless Cousin Molly. Nobody would know I've been snooping, apart from the spiritualist ladies, and they've done a bunk."

He stopped pacing and spun around.

"The Sorensen Sisters? They've gone, have they?"

"They have. Right after I confronted them and told them I'd found out some of their little tricks."

He shook his head in exasperation. "You weren't supposed to confront them, just report back to me."

"I didn't intend to. They found me snooping in their attic and I decided that attack was the best form of defense."

The head shaking continued. "So they fled, which is incriminating enough in itself. Do you think you've got enough to nail them this time?"

228

"To be honest, I don't think we'll ever nail them. They have too many believers who won't hear a word against them." I tried to prop myself up. "Do you think you could pass me that barley water. My mouth is like sandpaper."

Daniel poured from the jug, then tried the water first before giving it to me. "No, that seems to be all right," he said and perched on the bed again beside me.

"I still can't believe that someone here would want to poison me," I whispered. "They couldn't have been nicer to me."

"The Misses Sorensen obviously have a good reason to get rid of you. How long ago did they leave?"

"Oh, days ago. I'm a little fuzzy on time but the worst of the sickness came on after they went, so it can't have been them."

"Well, somebody obviously thinks you've been asking too many questions. Listen, Molly," he said, leaning closer so that his lips were almost touching my ear, "you had good instincts when you thought there was something not quite right about this place. I checked into your Miss McAlister. She bought herself a nice little house in the Washington area soon after she left service here, claiming it was a legacy from her rich aunt. By all accounts she lived quite well. The thing is that her only aunt is still living and not at all rich. Nobody in her family has died in the last five years and there have been no public records of any legacies."

"So it was some kind of payoff then?" I whispered. "She was blackmailing somebody and she came back here to get more and—"

"And somebody pushed her over a cliff," Daniel finished for me. "I went to see the spot for myself today and I think you were right. It wasn't a point on the path where she would have lost her footing easily or unintentionally."

"So somebody in the house has something to hide," I said.

"Any idea who?" he asked.

"I suppose it could have something to do with Barney's shady deals," I said. "He's known for them, isn't he? But I don't want to think that, because it would mean it was Barney himself who got rid of her."

Daniel shook his head. "Men like Barney Flynn don't do their own dirty work. He'd have had somebody else push her off the cliff."

"I find that hard to believe," I said. "I was with him when the body was discovered. He seemed genuinely shocked when he found out who it was. And genuinely surprised that she had come back, too. He said she'd only been with the family for a short while."

"Long enough to have found out something she shouldn't," Daniel said.

"I suppose it could have been something to do with the kidnapping of the Flynns' baby, but I don't see how. Miss McAlister didn't come to the house until the kidnapping was over."

"And the kidnapper was already dead," Daniel reminded me.

"Yes, but I've been asking some questions—don't look at me like that, I've been very discreet—and I don't think Bertie Morell had the brains or the character to mastermind such an audacious crime."

"You think he was just the pawn who carried out the deed?"

"Yes, that's what I think, if he did it at all. I did find one of the child's favorite toys in the attic of the cottage behind the house. So it seems possible that the child was held there for a while, although I can't see how Morell could have brought him there without being seen. And you know what else I have been thinking . . ."

Daniel put a hand on my shoulder. "Don't try to sit up. Lie back and don't talk too much. I don't want you overexerting yourself."

"But I have to tell you everything I know," I said. "When will I get another chance? It may be important."

Daniel sighed. "All right. I've never been able to shut you up yet. I don't suppose I'll be able to now."

I looked up at him and I can't tell you how wonderful it felt to know that he was here beside me. As a lady detective, I still had serious character flaws. I wrenched my mind away from personal feelings and back to business. "If there was a mastermind behind the kidnapping, and that mastermind wasn't the Black Hand, then there are several possibilities," I said. "My number one choice would be the secretary, Desmond O'Mara. He is well educated and brainy yet he has chosen to stay here when he surely could do better for himself. Smart and penniless. That's a dangerous combination, wouldn't you say? And I saw him leaving the house and heading for the cliff path the afternoon before Margie McAlister's body was found, *and* he was away all night, showing up innocently the next morning."

"Desmond O'Mara," Daniel echoed. "I'll check into him then. Go on. Who else?"

"One of the gardeners, called Adam. He was a close pal of Bertie Morell and he has a good reason to get revenge against the Flynns. Barney Flynn tricked his father out of his ice lease on the river. Why would Adam choose to work for the man who ruined his family if he has no ulterior motive? And then there's Roland."

"Roland? Another gardener?"

"No, the next-door neighbor. Roland Van Gelder. The Van Gelder family have been enemies of the Flynns ever since Roland's father ran for the same office as Barney Flynn."

"Oh, I'm well acquainted with the Van Gelders. Old money."

"Not any more," I said. "They claim they get along better with the Flynns now, but I'm not so sure. And Roland had a strong motive in needing money. He has expensive tastes but the family fortune has dwindled."

"Anyone else?" Daniel grinned. "I must say you do a thorough job, don't you? Any more dark secrets that you have uncovered?"

"No, only I overheard Joseph Rimes and Barney talking once about some scandal that could harm them if it came out."

"Joseph Rimes?"

"He's Barney's political adviser. I don't like him much. Bombastic and blustering."

Daniel nodded. "I really suspect that some political or business scandal may be at the heart of this murder, rather than the kidnapping itself. I can't tell you how thoroughly the police investigated every aspect of that abduction. We had pressure from the President himself, you know. But we came up with nothing."

"Was Bertie Morell married?" I asked.

"Yes, he was. Why do you ask?"

"Because I saw a woman putting flowers on his grave."

"Interesting, but I shouldn't think it was his wife. She was a much older woman and they separated years ago. Couldn't stand the sight of each other, so one gathered. I thought she moved to Chicago or somewhere out West. I did meet her once at a hearing—a large dragon of a woman with a mustache. She must have had money. There's no other reason he'd have married her."

"Then this definitely wasn't his wife," I said. "She was slim and young and there was a child."

"Interesting." Daniel nodded. "Morell had no children, or none that we know of. Another of his former conquests, who still retained a soft spot in her heart for him, maybe. Women tend to do these things, don't they?"

"Do what?"

"Retain a soft spot in their hearts for the man they once loved."

"Some women, maybe." Even in my weakened state I was not admitting anything to Daniel.

Daniel grinned. "There are probably quite a few of his former conquests dotted around. He had an eye for the ladies, so I understand."

"I wonder if she'd know anything," I said. I was feeling so much better already that I propped myself up on my elbow. "We could—"

Daniel put his hand firmly on my thigh. "You are not doing anything more. You're only going to drink and eat what everybody else is eating and drinking until I come and fetch you."

"Will that be soon?"

"As soon as I can arrange it. If this liquid tests positive, I'll be back with a warrant. If not, I'll find an excuse to come for you. In the meantime you are to do nothing but get well, is that clear?"

His hand on my thigh was very unnerving, even though the thigh was under the covers.

"You're very masterful when you want to be," I said.

He smiled. "For once I'm not about to take advantage of your weakened condition," he said.

"Oh, so you are a gentleman, after all."

"And you're not exactly looking your most desirable, my sweet." He leaned forward and kissed me very gently on the forehead. I nuzzled my head against his sleeve, taking in the familiar smell of his pipe tobacco. It didn't matter that Miss Arabella Norton would be waiting for him. He was here with me now. That was all that mattered.

He pulled me to him and cradled my head, stroking my hair gently. "Take care of yourself. Don't forget there is a very desperate person in the vicinity of this house. That person has already killed at least once. The next time will be easy. I don't want it to be you."

"I don't want it to be me, either."

"Good girl." He kissed the top of my head again. "I ought to go before I am discovered and your reputation is ruined forever."

"You take care of yourself as you climb down that creeper," I said. "You won't be much good to me if you're lying splattered on the trellis."

He smiled as he opened the window. Then he swung his leg over the sill and blew me a kiss. I heard the creeper rustling as he climbed down it. Then silence.

❧ Twenty-six ❧

S omething woke me just before dawn. It was still that gray, soft half darkness before the sun comes up, but I could hear activity going on in the house. Running feet past my door, raised voices and someone crying. I got up and reached for my robe and slippers. I had to hold onto the bedpost to steady myself but I made it as far as my bedroom door and opened it.

"Dr. Chambers is on his way," I heard Barney's voice. "Oh, do stop that wailing, woman. It's not doing any good."

I crept out, my hand on the railing to steady myself. Below me in the hall Soames ran to the front door—actually ran with coattails flying. This was such an unusual sight that I started down the stairs in my robe until I came upon Theresa's maid, Adèle, sitting on a side chair, crying her eyes out.

"What is it, Adèle?" I asked. "Is somebody ill?"

"Madame," she gulped between sobs. "She is dead, mademoiselle."

"Theresa is dead?" I hastily made the sign of the cross, reverting to the religion I had not taken seriously for years.

She nodded and burst into renewed sobs, holding her lace handkerchief up to her face. Barney came out of his office looking haggard.

"It's true then?" I asked him.

He nodded. "She killed herself sometime last night. Apparently she'd been hoarding sleeping powders and she took the lot. I knew that alienist was a bad idea. He drove her over the edge, that's what he did. I'll have him in court for it. I'll have him horsewhipped! And her stupid sister who brought him here—she can go straight home, and that interfering cousin. I want the lot of them out of my house!" His voice had risen to a distressed shriek that echoed through the two-story-high hallway.

I put a restraining hand on his arm. "Barney, I know you're terribly shocked and upset by this, but don't go blaming people. Theresa has been living under a black cloud, as she put it, for years. Let's pray she is finally reunited with her son and is at peace now."

"Yes, let's pray that," he said and made the sign of the cross himself. "God, Molly, I lived in fear that she'd do this and now she has." I could tell he was trying to master his tears. Then he shook his head in a defiant gesture. "That's it for me. I'm selling this house and moving right away from here. I was so proud when I moved in here—Barney Flynn from the Lower East Side slums has finally made it next to the Van Gelders. But it's brought me nothing but grief."

"I'm so sorry. If there's anything that I can do—"

"I'm glad to have you here, Molly. It's comforting to know that one of my family from the old country is with me at a time like this. All of Theresa's clan will come for the funeral, of course, and they'll all blame me."

"Why should they blame you?"

"Because I didn't treat her well enough. Because I couldn't protect our son. Because I put her through hell."

"Don't be too hard on yourself."

He sighed. "No, you're right. I'd better get dressed before the doctor gets here and then wake up Joe and Desmond to discuss what the press might do with this and what sort of statement I should make. It still seems like a bad dream."

"And what about your daughter? Should she be told?"

"I'll tell the nurse and she can decide the right way to do it."

"I think it should come from you, Barney. She's just lost her mother. She needs to know she can count on her father."

He sighed. "I suppose you're right, but I never know the right thing to say to children. I was too busy to get to know Brendan and now I've been the same with Eileen. And Theresa always kept her shut away in her own quarters."

"I expect she wanted to know she was safe," I suggested.

"Yes," he said. "I expect that was it."

"So you'll tell her?"

"I'll try."

"I'll visit her later this morning, if you like," I said. "She seems to like me. And at that age they have little concept of tragedy. I remember my own brother Thomas wanting to know if we could still go to the fair the day my mother died."

Barney managed a smile. "Lucky for them," he said. "We seem to carry around tragedy with us all the time."

He trudged back up the stairs like a man carrying a heavy load. I went back to my room, washed and dressed hurriedly. One glance in the mirror and I could see what Daniel meant about my appearance. I looked terrible, drawn and haggard—great hollow circles around my eyes, hair plastered to my forehead. Not exactly desirable. I rinsed my hair in the basin and brushed it back. I even wished I had been daring enough to bring rouge to put on my cheeks; at least that might have made me look more human. As I tied back my straggly hair, a chilling thought struck me. Everyone assumed that Theresa had killed herself, but if someone was trying to poison me, had that same person also succeeded in poisoning her?

The question was why. Had I stumbled upon a secret or a piece of knowledge I didn't even realize I possessed? In which case, had Theresa stumbled upon the same piece of knowledge? And why kill her now? I came up with a chilling reply to that one—the alienist. An outsider had come to the house who was about to probe Theresa's deepest thoughts and fears. He had suggested hypnotizing her, during which she would have no control over what she revealed. And it was Barney who had been so adamantly against hypnosis. I turned to stare out of the window, watching the peaceful river scene outside as I digested this thought. Could Barney have used the advent of the alienist as an excuse to do away with a wife who was no use to him?

I shook my head. I just couldn't believe that. I had been with Barney and his grief and confusion seemed so genuine. If he had masterminded the whole thing, then the man was a brilliant actor. But I had to admit that it did seem logical. He had set the scene beautifully—protesting the arrival of Dr. Birnbaum, claiming that Theresa was worse after his session with her and could easily be driven over the edge, then forbidding the hypnotism. I hugged my arms to myself, shivering in early morning chill.

They were not my family, I reminded myself, and yet in my short time there I had become fond of Theresa, and of Barney, too, in a way. And Theresa had come to rely on me. If she had had any suspicions about anyone in the house, she could have shared them with me when we sat reading poetry together.

I felt a wave of weakness and grabbed at the window ledge, sending pigeons flapping from the gutter above my room. Was that it? Did someone fear that Theresa had divulged a secret to me during the time we were alone together? Certainly my cramps and vomiting started immediately after we had spent the day in Theresa's room. But if someone wanted me dead, why not do a better job of it? Was this method designed to make it look like a natural death and not arouse suspicion—so that I'd get weaker and weaker until the final dose finished me off?

I shivered again. It was almost beyond belief that someone in this house was plotting my death. And yet I had seen evil and insanity before. I had faced murderers and guns and I knew what desperate men would do if threatened. It was just that this quiet country home was so removed from the back streets of New York.

I pulled out my notebook and sat at my desk, trying to harness my racing thoughts.

Baby kidnapped, I wrote. Margie McAlister killed. Molly slowly poisoned. Theresa dead. Four tragic events, the latter three of which would not be investigated as murders. People would say this was a cursed house, and find comparisons with other families who experienced more than their fair share of tragedy. But my year as an investigator had brought me to believe that not much happens by coincidence. If there were four deaths in one place and three of them within a week, then they had to be linked. Most probably there had to be one person behind them. The most logical assumption was that the circumstances surrounding the first of the events, the baby's kidnapping, led to the next three. And this came back to my next theory—that there was a master planner, a puppeteer behind the kidnapping, and Albert Morell was the puppet.

I turned at the sound of a tap on my door and Alice the maid came in. Her eyes were red with crying.

"Oh miss, you're up and dressed," she said. "Miss Clara sent me up to see if you were all right or you needed anything."

"I'm feeling better, thank you, Alice."

"Oh, that is good news, miss. The dear knows we need some good news around here. You've heard about the mistress, have you?"

"Yes. I've already spoken with Senator Flynn."

"Isn't it awful, miss? She was such a sweet lady. Adèle is beside herself. She came in with a jug of hot water, the way she always did, because Mrs. Flynn was an early riser, and there she was sprawled half out of the bed. Adèle went to lift her back into bed and she was cold." Alice put her hand to her mouth and turned away.

"It must have been a terrible shock for all of you," I said. "I'm quite upset myself and I had only known her for just over a week."

"I don't know what will happen now," Alice said. "The Senator is ranting and raving about the house being cursed and that he's going to sell up and take the child away from all this."

"Poor little thing," I said. "Now she'll grow up with no mother."

Alice sniffed. "It's not as if she'll want for anything. That child has always had the best that money can buy. And the Senator dotes on her. I think the two of them will get along just fine."

She went over to my bedside table. "Oh, you didn't drink your beef tea, miss. They had it made specially for you to build you up."

"No, I didn't feel like beef tea last night," I said.

"It would have done you good. There's nothing more nourishing than beef tea." She went to pick up the cup. "I'll take it away for you then, shall I?"

I realized that she would be destroying the evidence. "Oh no, don't bother. I'll bring it down myself. I'm just coming."

"No trouble, miss."

"I'd rather you took the chamber pot away first," I said.

"As you wish, miss." She picked up my chamber pot and nodded with satisfaction. "And a night without sickness too. That is good."

"Alice?" I asked as she was about to leave the room with the chamber pot.

"Yes, miss?" She turned back.

"Who gave you the beef tea to bring up to me?"

"Gave me, miss? It was on a tray in the kitchen and Cook said, 'That's to go up to Miss Gaffney when you've a minute.'"

"So you brought it up to me?"

"Well, miss, I was running an errand for Miss Clara and you know how she hates to be kept waiting, so I put it down on the table in the front hall for a minute or two."

"And was anybody else in the front hall at the time?"

"Just Mr. Soames. He ticked me off for leaving the tray there. Will that be all then, miss?"

"Yes, thank you, Alice. You've been most kind."

I sank onto my bed, my heart racing. I had never considered Soames before. He had always seemed like the perfect English butler, impeccable, invisible. I remembered mentioning that they had kept him on after the kidnapping when they had sacked all the other servants, and his haughty reply, "Maybe that was because I'm not like an ordinary servant."

A butler would have had the perfect opportunity to carry out any of the crimes—apart from pushing Margie McAlister off the cliff, maybe. But I remembered that overheard conversation with the man's voice asking, "What the devil do you think you're doing here?" and telling the other person that he or she had been paid off well. What if the voice I had heard was the butler's—if he was the one being blackmailed and he found a way to silence Miss McAlister? I tried to remember whether the voice I had heard spoke with an English accent. Soames had caught me snooping on a couple of occasions. I tried to remember the details. Once I had been opening the door to Barney's study, once to the séance room. What possibly could I have seen in either place that represented a danger to Soames?

Then I thought of something. Maybe he had caught a glimpse of the letter I had written to Daniel and he knew I was in touch with the police. I didn't think that was likely because I had kept the letter between the pages of a book until I posted it, but he could have an accomplice at the post office. I wished Daniel had not gone away again last night. I wanted him here right now. He should know about Theresa immediately and he would also be in a position to check into Mr. Soames's background. And to be honest, I would have liked someone around to protect me. It's not an easy feeling, knowing that someone wanted me dead. But Daniel had promised to come back for me, hadn't he? I just hoped I would still be alive.

⚛ Twenty-seven ⚛

I looked out of my window as I heard feet on the gravel and saw
the doctor arriving with the local police constable at his side
and Soames leading the way. I wasn't sure how to proceed. I
didn't want Theresa's death to be ruled a suicide without voicing
my suspicions, and yet suggesting her death might be murder
would make Barney the obvious suspect. And I didn't want Barney
to be the suspect, even if . . . I stopped that thought right there. If
only Daniel were here. He'd know what to do. But I couldn't sit by
and do nothing. Sitting by just wasn't in my nature.

I opened my door a few inches, watched and waited.

I could hear Barney's voice from the hallway. "What do you mean
by bringing the police into this? No crime has been committed."

"I'm sorry, sir, but we have to investigate any case of unnatural
death," I heard the constable responding. "We have to determine
it really was a suicide."

"Really was a suicide?" Barney was yelling now. "My poor wife
killed herself while of unbalanced mind. Ask anyone in the household. They'll tell you her mental state. Ask that ridiculous alienist
fellow. He's the one you need to arrest if you want to arrest anybody. He's the one that drove her over the edge with his probings."

"Calm down, Mr. Flynn. I can see that you're quite distraught,"
I heard the doctor's deeper, more educated voice saying. "All of
this is just a formality. Nobody is suggesting anything other than

the obvious. Now, if you'll lead the way to your wife's room?"

I watched through the crack in my door as the procession came up the stairs. Barney led the way. I noticed also that Soames followed them as far as the doorway. If Barney was going to insist on staying in the room with the doctor and Soames was going to hang around outside the door, I'd have no chance of speaking to the doctor alone without revealing my hand to the others in the house.

Then it occurred to me that maybe the time was right to reveal that hand. A police constable was within shouting distance, so I'd be quite safe. All the same, my legs were quaking as I came down the stairs, and it wasn't just from my weakness either. Order had broken down in this otherwise clockwork-running house. Servants were standing about in the hallway peering up the stairs or whispering together. Belinda and Clara, both red-eyed, were hovering about the dining room doorway, clutching each other for support. Clara was already wearing black and Belinda's flowery house robe looked garishly out of place. They looked at me as if I was a ghost coming down the stairs.

"Molly, you're up and around again. That is good news," Clara whispered. "So you've heard of the terrible tragedy that has taken place. God rest her poor tormented soul." She crossed herself. "This house is cursed. I always said it was from the moment they moved in."

"My condolences to both of you," I said as I approached them. "What a terrible shock for all of us. I hardly knew her and yet I had already become fond of her. It must be far worse for you, who had known and loved her for all of your lives."

Belinda put her handkerchief up to her mouth. "I feel so guilty. I should never have brought Dr. Birnbaum here. I truly thought he'd be able to help her. One hears such wonderful things about alienists these days, but it was obviously too much for her. It's all my fault."

"I don't think you should blame yourself, Belinda," I said. "Who knows the depths of despair that she had lived with for so long?"

"Maybe hearing her son's voice was enough to convince her she wanted to be with him again," Clara suggested. "She so wanted to have the spiritualists here, but that might not have been such a good idea either."

"What the devil is going on?" a large voice echoed through the stairwell. Joseph Rimes stood at the top of the stairs, glaring down at the huddle of servants. "What do you think you're doing? Where are your master and mistress? Where is Mr. Soames? Get back to your tasks immediately."

"Pardon me, sir, but an awful thing has happened." Soames stepped out of the alcove where he had been waiting and drew Joe Rimes aside. He muttered into Joe's ear and we watched Joe spin around, mouth open. "Good God, man. This is terrible. Why didn't somebody wake me? Where is O'Mara? Did anybody think of waking him up?"

Joe disappeared into Theresa's bedroom and soon afterward a bleary-eyed Desmond O'Mara appeared in a striped dressing gown. We stood below watching the drama unfold above us. My stomach reminded me with a growl that I was in serious need of nourishment. I turned to Clara.

"Might we suggest that Cook makes a big pot of coffee and some simple breakfast—maybe boiled eggs and toast, as befits the occasion? It won't help anyone if we become faint from lack of food."

Clara looked at me sharply, then nodded. "Yes. You're right. I'll go and speak to Cook. I suppose it is up to me to see that the household keeps on running. Barney has no interest in household matters and little skill with servants." She strode in the direction of the kitchen.

Belinda smiled. "You've made her day," she said. "Clara has been waiting for years to have the chance to boss somebody around."

"What will you do?" I asked. "Will you stay on?"

She looked horrified. "Good Lord, no. I only stopped for a brief visit on my way home from Europe and to tell you the truth I can't stand this place. Too out of the way and dreary. Not a single real ball since I've been here and the only male within miles is that awful

Roland Van Gelder. And having to put up with the uncouth behavior of Cousin Barney and Joe Rimes as well. I can't wait to go home to civilization." She looked at me as if she realized she might have said too much. "And you, Molly. What will you do?"

"I can't stay on any longer," I said. "It wouldn't be proper."

"Meaning you couldn't trust Barney's wandering hands with no Theresa to keep him in check?" she asked.

I blushed. "Really, I didn't mean . . ."

"Of course you did. We've all been through it. Barney can't keep himself away from women. That's just his weakness. Theresa never was the warmest of lovers in the first place and after Brendan she turned completely cold—" She broke off again. "I shouldn't be talking like this with poor Tessa lying stiff and dead upstairs. She and I were never close but I would never have wished this ending on her, never."

Clara reemerged from the kitchen, looking smug and satisfied. "I have ordered breakfast and it will be served shortly. Now to get those maids back to work. It will take their minds off things to keep them busy."

"I rather suspect Clara will want to stay on," Belinda muttered to me with the ghost of a smile.

Breakfast arrived and Joe Rimes and Desmond O'Mara came to join us. Nobody spoke as we sat at the big, white-clothed table. I don't know about the others, but I felt so much better with something finally in my stomach. Through the open breakfast room door I watched the police constable come downstairs and took the opportunity to invite him to have a cup of coffee.

"Is the doctor finished up there?" I asked.

He shook his head. "I've been sent down to use the telephone and call for transportation to the morgue," he said. "Second time in one week. Don't seem right, does it?"

"Precisely my thoughts, Constable," I said. I glanced back at the breakfast room, where the others were finishing their meal in silence. It was now or never. "So does the doctor really believe that she killed herself?"

He frowned. "What are you getting at, miss?"

"I just wondered if he can tell whether she did take an overdose of sleeping powders, or whether she might have been poisoned."

"Poisoned? Whatever gave you that idea?" He had lowered his voice, but I hoped it carried far enough in the dead silence of the household.

"Because I suspect that somebody has been trying to poison me," I whispered back, in what I hoped was a stage whisper. "I've been very sick this week, but only at night after I had a cup of hot liquid brought to me. For that very reason I didn't drink last night's beef tea, but I've kept it in my room so that it can be tested later."

"I can't believe what you're saying, miss." The constable shook his head. "Surely you must be imagining things."

"I only hope I am," I said, "but I tried to understand why I was only sick at night and I worked out that my nighttime drink was the only thing I didn't take communally with the rest of the household. Anyway, one simple test and then we'll know. But I mustn't keep you from your work. The telephone is in Mr. Flynn's office. Let me show you."

I went across the hallway and ushered him into the room. It was a dark and somber room with its book-lined walls, and even darker at this time in the morning when the early sun was on the other side of the house.

"The telephone is on Senator Flynn's desk," I said.

He leaned closer to me. "So do you think I should suggest that we take any cups or glasses from Mrs. Flynn's room for testing?" he muttered.

"I would think that they had all been carefully washed, but it couldn't hurt to take them for testing, and I would suggest to the doctor that he does a thorough autopsy."

He shook his head again. "Doesn't seem possible. Who could have done such a thing? There must be a mad person in the house."

"I may be wrong," I said. "I really hope I am wrong."

As I was talking I was taking in my surroundings. I saw that the room was made even darker by the creeper that half covered the window. Then I saw that it wasn't a window, but a pair of French doors. There was a way out of the house through Barney's study. And the study was on the side of the house away from the main living rooms, which meant that someone like Desmond O'Mara, or even Soames, could have carried the child out of the house without being observed. All he would have to have done was walk past the blank back wall of the kitchen, into the tall bean rows of the kitchen garden and up to the cottage.

Then I reminded myself that Barney and Joe Rimes and therefore also Desmond O'Mara were all overheard working in Barney's study that afternoon. So that shot down an otherwise good theory.

"I'll wait for you outside, Constable," I said loudly as I emerged from the room, walked purposefully in the direction of the front door, then doubled back and sneaked up the back stairs to my room. If my conversation had indeed been overheard I was hoping to draw the rat to the bait. I opened my wardrobe and stepped inside, half closing the door.

Then I waited. And waited. It was stuffy and cramped and the dust kept making me want to sneeze. After ten minutes turned into twenty and then half an hour, I began to think that this wasn't such a good idea after all. I was just about to come out and admit defeat when I saw my door handle start to turn. I held my breath. The door started to open and Cousin Clara came into the room.

She glanced around, then crept toward the cup and saucer still standing on my bedside table. I waited until her hand had almost touched the saucer, then I stepped out of the wardrobe. She gasped as she spun around.

"You're too late, Clara," I said. "Some of the beef tea has already been taken to the police for testing."

"What are you talking about?" she demanded. "What beef tea?"

"The beef tea on the table there that you flavored with arsenic for me last night. And several other nights before."

I watched the color drain from her face, then she collected herself. "Absolute rubbish," she said.

"Then what brought you to my room? And why that cup and

saucer? Have you taken over the maid's duties?" I went over to her and stared at her, eye to eye. I hadn't noticed before that she was almost as tall as me and for a moment I wondered if I was taking too big a risk. But she looked away, flinching as if I had struck her. "What I don't understand is what you hoped to gain from it. Why did you want to kill me?"

"I didn't want to kill you, you stupid girl," Clara snapped. "I just wanted to warn you off."

"Warn me off?"

"She liked you," Clara almost spat out the words. "I could tell that she liked you better than me. She was going to make you her new companion and then it was you she would take shopping and to Europe and where would that leave me? Where would I go if I was turned out of this house?"

Without warning she deflated like a balloon and collapsed onto my bed, sniffing pitifully. "I have nobody, no one who wants me in the whole world. At least Theresa needed me, until you came . . ."

"You foolish old woman," I said. "I had no intention of staying and becoming Theresa's companion. I was just here for a short visit, that's all—not trying to oust you."

"I didn't want to really hurt you," she sobbed. "That's why it was always such a small amount. Just enough to make you want to go back home to Ireland, that's all."

"But you nearly did kill me," I said. "I reckon one more night of that and they'd have found my body in the morning, just like they did Theresa's."

"Don't." She put her handkerchief up to her mouth. "Don't say that. I still can't get over . . ."

"Another thing I don't understand," I said, "is why you'd want to kill Theresa if she was all you had in the world."

She looked up. Her blotchy and tear-stained face was not a pretty sight. "Kill Theresa? You don't think . . . You can't possibly think . . . ?" she stammered. "Theresa took her own life."

"I'm not so sure," I said, "and since you've confessed to one poisoning, you'd be the obvious suspect to me."

Her face went ashen. "No!" she exclaimed. "You can't believe that. Theresa was all I had in the world. I loved her. I would have done anything for her—I would have drunk poison on her behalf."

"That's not how the police will see it," I said. "When they find the arsenic in that beef tea sample, they'll immediately put two and two together and come up with you."

She reached out and clutched at my skirt. "I really meant you no harm."

"But you did harm me, Clara. You almost killed me. You'll almost certainly be arrested for attempted murder."

"I didn't mean it." She was sobbing now, a harsh, ugly noise coming from her throat. "I only wanted to feel secure and now I don't know what's to become of me. They'd send me to jail or the insane asylum. Please, I beg of you, tell the police it was an accident. Tell them I didn't mean it . . ."

"Tell me one thing, Clara—if you didn't kill Theresa, do you have any ideas about who did?"

"It was suicide. It had to be suicide. Everybody loved Theresa. She was the sweetest, kindest . . ."

"I'm not talking about her personality," I said. "It may have been something she knew that was dangerous to know."

"I'd look no further than her no-good husband," she said; "only he had more to lose than anybody. Theresa was a rich woman when she came to him, but she stood to inherit a large fortune on the death of her parents."

"But Barney's done pretty well on his own account, hasn't he?" I asked. "He owns the ice monopoly and has fingers in lots of pies. Do you really think he'd have given up the chance of a future fortune to get rid of a wife who was not able to gratify his wishes?"

I could see that she was digesting this new thought. Then she shook her head. "Why would he worry about getting a new wife when he could get what he wanted on the side? Barney never could keep his hands off women. Theresa knew what went on, of course, but she put up with it in silence. That's what makes me think that she took her own life—the life she led was more than any human being should endure."

"You may be right," I agreed. "So we'll just have to wait for the doctor's autopsy results and then maybe we'll know more."

She got up, cautiously. "And about the other matter—won't you please forgive me? I'm truly ashamed of myself. I'll go to confession and do penance, but please don't let anyone else know. And if you told the police that it was a horrible accident and you weren't going to press charges?"

I stared at her for a long while, then nodded. "I'll think about it," I said. "Now we'd better go downstairs and see what we might have missed."

"Thank you, dear cousin. I'll never be able to thank you enough." She attempted to hug me. I stood like a tree and let her wrap bony arms around me. As she did so I felt something melt inside me and suddenly I realized what it must be like to be Clara—never hugged, never loved, always the companion tagging along in someone else's life. Against my will, my arms came around her and I hugged her back.

❧ Twenty-eight ❧

B y nine o'clock the doctor had departed, but the constable stayed on, awaiting the arrival of a vehicle to take Theresa's body to the morgue. I tried to play the investigator and observed each member of the household. Obviously I wasn't very good at this investigation business, as everyone seemed to be acting normally, except for Clara, who was being too effusively nice to me. Barney, Joe and Desmond O'Mara disappeared into Barney's study to discuss strategy. It seemed strange to me that men like Joe and Barney could be so concerned about what the press might say at a moment like this, but then I suppose politicians live or die by the press.

Desmond O'Mara definitely seemed paler than usual, if that were possible, but that meant nothing. He may have been rudely awoken and I know I never feel my best in such circumstances. I also watched Soames carefully. He certainly would have had the ideal opportunity to commit any crime in the household. He moved silently from room to room and blended in like part of the furniture. If he had carried a sleeping child downstairs, I doubt anybody would have noticed. If he had crept up to Theresa's room and somehow put poison in her drink or messed with her sleeping powders, nobody would have noticed either. But what I needed for Soames was a motive. I knew nothing about him. He spoke like a refined Englishman, which might mean that he was possibly highborn and fallen on hard times—which might give him the motive of wanting revenge against Irish peasant upstarts for usurping a position that should have been his. Still, this was all supposition. I now knew that he hadn't poisoned my drink, so it was possible that he hadn't kidnapped Brendan or killed Theresa either. But somebody had.

The more I thought about it, the surer I became that Theresa did not take her own life. She had been optimistic during the past days. She had talked about getting strong enough to go to Ireland and having clothes made for me. But then who knows what the alienist said to her and what deep fears he might have brought to the surface again?

It was strange, but the second I thought about the alienist, I realized that we hadn't seen him around this morning and wondered where he was. Surely nobody could have stayed asleep through the commotion that had been going on since six o'clock? But a few minutes later we had assembled out on the veranda, none of us wanting to be in the house while Theresa's body still lay there, when we heard the tap of feet on the marble floor and the alienist himself appeared, neatly dressed in tweeds and yellow waistcoat.

"I appear to have missed breakfast," he said, clicking his heels to us. "I must apologize to our hostess. Where is she, please?"

"You haven't heard?" Belinda demanded. "You've been asleep all this time?"

Birnbaum bowed again. "I'm afraid I am a very sound sleeper once I get to sleep. I was up reading until well past midnight, then my mind was active and I probably didn't doze off until two or three."

"I regret to inform you that Mrs. Flynn died last night," Belinda said.

"Mrs. Flynn died? But that is terrible," Birnbaum stammered. "May one ask how she died?"

"She took her own life, apparently," Belinda said quietly. "An overdose of her sleeping powders."

"*Mein Gott!*" Birnbaum struck his own breast. "I am a doctor—I am trained to work with such people as your sister and I did not see this coming. I am ashamed of myself. I am not fit to be called alienist. How could I have missed the signs? I would have said that she was on the road to recovery, becoming more optimistic in her outlook."

"I don't suppose we can ever know what goes on in the deepest recesses of the human mind, Doctor," Clara said. "Mrs. Flynn had been suffering for many years. Maybe she realized that she had endured enough."

Dr. Birnbaum was still shaking his head. "But usually patients give some sort of indication to me—they throw out little suggestions. They say, 'Sometimes I wonder if it is all worth it. . . . Sometimes I wonder if I would be better off dead.' Always some hint. But from her, nothing."

I had been sitting in silence watching this current drama unfold. But as they spoke, something was going through my mind. "Dr. Birnbaum, you say you were awake for most of the night," I said. "Did you not hear anything unusual?"

"Unusual?" He looked puzzled.

"I wondered if Mrs. Flynn might have cried out or fallen from her bed?"

He shook his head. "I don't think I heard anything strange. When I read, I am in deepest concentration and I am able to shut out the world around me."

He broke off as he observed Barney come out onto the veranda, followed by his faithful minions. Barney stiffened when he saw that Birnbaum was with us. "Oh, the great alienist who was supposed to be helping my wife get better!" he boomed. "How many patients do you lose a week, Dr. Birnbaum?"

"I assure you, Mr. Flynn, that nobody could feel worse than I do about your tragic news," he said. "I could have sworn that your wife was on the road to recovery. I sensed no suicidal tendency in her. Depression, yes, but a depression that could eventually be cured."

"It doesn't help to blame anyone, Barney," Joe Rimes said. "Theresa is gone. May she rest in peace."

There was a moment of awkward silence.

"I should go up and pack my belongings," Birnbaum said. "I can see that my presence among you will only heighten your grief, so if you could perhaps telephone for some kind of conveyance to take me to the ferry?"

"We can have a couple of the men row you across the river to Peekskill," Joe Rimes said. "That is the easiest way of hooking up with the train. I'll have Soames arrange it."

"And I'll come up and help you pack, if you'd like," Desmond O'Mara said suddenly.

"That will not be necessary," Birnbaum said. "I can see you wish me to leave. I can assure you I have no desire to stay here any longer. It will only take me minutes to pack my small suitcase and then I shall be out of your lives. Please excuse me." He bowed, clicking his heels, and went into the house. Desmond was left staring after him.

It occurred to me that I had never heard Desmond O'Mara volunteer to do anything helpful during my time at Adare. Why was he anxious to help Dr. Birnbaum pack his case? I watched and waited, and the moment Joe Rimes had gone indoors to arrange for river transportation, Desmond quietly slipped inside the house as well. I was curious and also alarmed. I got up and excused myself, feigning a need to lie down, then I followed Desmond into the house. Sure enough, he was going up the staircase and I watched him hurry around the upper gallery to the second stair that led up to the tower bedrooms where Birnbaum had been sleeping. Whatever he had really wanted to do, he was thwarted, however, as he met Dr. Birnbaum already coming downstairs, his grip in his hand and his hat on his head. He nodded to Desmond and went on down the stairs and out of the front door. Desmond hung around for a moment, then sighed and turned to follow him down.

I stood in the hallway wondering what to do next. What had Desmond hoped to accomplish up in Dr. Birnbaum's bedroom? There were two possibilities I could think of: one that he suspected Birnbaum of being the person who killed Theresa and that he had been brought to the house for that purpose; or the opposite—that

Desmond was Theresa's killer and was afraid that Birnbaum knew too much. I remembered that Barney and his entourage had arrived just when Birnbaum had been telling us about being awake for most of the night. Had there been a telltale noise? Had Birnbaum passed Desmond in the hallway while heeding the call of nature? In which case, exactly what had Desmond planned to do in that tower room? I shuddered and wished again that Daniel had not returned to New York. The sooner I was out of this house, the better.

As I walked along the gallery in the direction of Theresa's room, I remembered that she was still lying there. I told myself that any good detective would have wanted to view the scene of the crime and examine Theresa's body. There was nothing I would have less wanted to do. To see that sweet, pretty woman lying there stiff and cold would surely break my heart. But would she be counting on me to find out the truth? Everyone else wanted to call it a suicide, especially her murderer. That could mean that vital evidence might be destroyed before the police got a chance to look at it. I couldn't trust the thick Mr. Plod to know what to look for and I doubted that a detective would be summoned.

I steeled myself and crept to her door. A notice had been affixed to it: DO NOT ENTER, and the door was locked. But surprisingly the key was still in the lock. I glanced around, turned it, and went in. The blinds had been drawn and the room had that sickly-sweet smell of death that I had experienced before in my life. I couldn't exactly identify it, but it was the smell that lingered when my mother passed on and I knew it now. In the half darkness I could just make out the white shape of Theresa's body lying under a sheet on the bed. I tiptoed across the room, as if I might wake her, and switched on the electric light.

Apart from the white mound on the bed there was nothing out of place that I could see. Theresa's silver-backed toilet set was perfectly arranged on her dressing table. The clothes she had been wearing had been removed by Adèle and only her dressing gown was draped over the back of a low chair, in case she should need it in the night. I went around the bed to her dressing table. There were various bottles of French perfume on it, a gorgeous cut-glass eau de cologne spray with a pink silk-covered bulb, and the sort of toilet preparations I supposed that all rich women used. Then I noticed something interesting—a jar of face cream was on the bedside table with its top off. This struck me as significant. I took out my handkerchief to wrap around it, lifted it to my face and smelled it. It smelled like face cream—slightly perfumed but with no underlying bad smell. For a second I had wondered whether it was possible to administer poison in a face cream, since she had obviously used it last night. But I wouldn't know what poison smelled like anyway and it seemed a rather elaborate way of killing somebody.

Then I realized a second significance of the open jar. Theresa had put cream on her face last night. Would a person who was contemplating death decide to give her skin one last treatment of a cream that "guaranteed to restore your youthful complexion in a week"? I could only draw one conclusion from it: Theresa had not intended to kill herself last night.

With some trepidation I turned to the bed and lifted the sheet. I was so surprised that I almost dropped it again. Theresa lay there as if asleep, eyelids closed, mouth in peaceful repose. I fully expected her to open those eyelids and give me that sweet smile. This definitely damaged my theory that someone had poisoned her. I had never seen a poisoning victim but I had read of the dreadful grimaces of agony imprinted on their faces. Swiftly I covered Theresa again and crept into her dressing room. Here there was a washstand, a large flowery jug of cold water, a cut-glass water jug for drinking, and a whole shelfful of patent medicines. There were also, scattered on the floor, empty packets on which a prescription had been scrawled, "Take one powder to aid in sleeping. Do not take more than prescribed dose," and a doctor's scrawled signature. I counted seven of them. Assuredly enough to end a life—which made me think I might have been mistaken after all. Theresa could have woken in the middle of the night in a black fit of despair and decided to end it all. And if someone else had administered those sleeping potions to her, there would be no way of proving it that I could see.

I was about to make my way back to the bedroom door when I saw the handle start to turn. I had no time to dodge into the dressing room or behind the wardrobe as Desmond O'Mara came in. He started when he saw me.

"Miss Gaffney, what are you doing in here?"

"I might ask you the same thing, Mr. O'Mara," I said, sounding a lot braver than I felt.

"I watched you go along the gallery and then you vanished. I was curious as to why you would want to enter a room which was clearly forbidden to you." He closed the door behind him. "In fact I have been intrigued by your behavior since you came here. You arrive out of nowhere and start questioning everybody, then there are two deaths within one week. Can that be simple coincidence, I ask myself?"

I had an instant decision to make. I could come up with a perfectly innocent excuse or I could attack in my turn. I chose the latter. "As to that, I am asking myself the same question, Mr. O'Mara, especially when I observed you hurrying toward the cliff path on the afternoon when Miss McAlister plunged to her death. And you did not return to the house until the next morning, thus establishing your alibi, I've no doubt."

I saw his eyebrows raise. "I must say you are very different from most young women, who only seem to notice who is wearing what and which young man smiled at them. But I have a word of warning for you, if I may, Miss Gaffney. Are you aware of the old saying, 'Curiosity killed the cat'?"

"I am quite aware of it, Mr. O'Mara."

"Then I beg you take it to heart, Miss Gaffney, or you may be next in line."

"Is that a threat, Mr. O'Mara?" I was amazed how composed I sounded.

"Please take it as a friendly warning from someone who is concerned for your welfare." He glanced around the room, then back at me. "You have landed yourself, I fear, in a—" He broke off abruptly as the bedroom door opened yet again. This time Joseph Rimes was standing there.

"What the deuce do you two think you are doing? Can't you read the notice on the door? Nobody is allowed in this room."

"I'm sorry, Mr. Rimes," I said meekly. "I'm afraid I am to blame. I didn't want dear Cousin Theresa to be taken away before I had a chance to say my good-byes to her. Mr. O'Mara noticed me creeping into the room and was naturally suspicious about my motives."

Joe Rimes sighed impatiently. "She's already dead, Miss Gaffney. You can't say good-bye to a corpse."

I smiled at him. "You've obviously never lived in Ireland where most of us carry on the most spirited conversations with the dead." I moved past him and out of the room, then I looked back at the sheet on the bed. "Don't worry, Cousin, we'll give you a grand old wake," I said.

❧ Twenty-nine ❧

I heard Desmond and Joe Rimes discussing Dr. Birnbaum's departure as they went down the stairs, then I stood alone, holding onto the banister and looking down at the black and white tiles of the front hall while I took some deep breaths and tried to digest what had just happened. I had suspected there was something not quite right about Desmond O'Mara from the beginning. I had wondered what kept him here and was no closer to finding the answer. But now I had good reason to fear that the motive wasn't a good one.

Now he had actually warned me to keep my nose out of his business, hadn't he? I had to find a way to let Daniel know. Had I mentioned Desmond O'Mara to him? I wasn't sure what I had said during his surprise visit through the window. My weakness at the time and his very closeness as he sat on my bed must have addled my brains.

I wondered if I could find a chance to sneak into Barney's study and use the telephone, then I decided it would be too risky. Even if Barney and Joe Rimes went out, they didn't always take Desmond with them, and there was always the ever-lurking Soames sneaking around. So it would have to be the long slog to the village and back, which I wasn't looking forward to as the day had become especially muggy and sultry. And I was still feeling weak from my illness. Then I remembered the Van Gelders next door. They should be told about our tragedy and I could volunteer myself to be the bringer of the bad news—and ask to use their telephone at the same time. Justin Hartley was possibly still there, but I had to take that risk.

I was about to go downstairs when I heard a little voice coming from Eileen's room. "London Bridge is falling down," the child was singing, but the song broke off abruptly. My heart went out to the poor little thing, shut away up there with her nurse, probably wondering just what was going on and what would happen now that she had no mother. I just prayed that Barney had visited her as promised and had told her the bad news. I didn't want to be the one to break it to her.

When the door opened, I could tell instantly that she had been told. She was wearing a plain navy blue dress with no adornment and her hair had been pulled back into two pigtails. What's more, she was wearing black stockings and shoes.

"Oh, Miss Gaffney," the nurse said, looking startled, "I hope you haven't come to complain about the singing. I've tried to teach the child decorum but she doesn't seem to take in the seriousness of the situation."

"Why would she?" I asked, smiling at Eileen as I came into the room. "The poor little mite hardly knows her mother from the Queen of the May. And the very young have no concept of death."

Nurse nodded. "You're right about that. She keeps asking me when her mommy will be coming back from heaven and can she go there to visit."

"I'll try to talk to her if you like," I said. "At any rate I thought she might welcome a visit. You too."

"I won't deny it gets awful lonely stuck up here," the nanny agreed. "She's a sweet child, affectionate and bright for her age, but I do miss the company of women. Sometimes Cook comes up of an evening and we have a nice little chat together, but that's about it. The maids are just fly-by-night girls except for that Adèle, who thinks she's too grand for the rest of us—as does Mr. Soames."

"Mr. Soames is an interesting man," I said. "Does he ever talk to any of you about himself? He speaks such a beautiful upper-class English I'm wondering whether he started out life in service, or if he's come to reduced circumstances?"

Nurse shook her head. "If he's said anything, it's never been to me," she said. "He keeps himself to himself. I couldn't tell you if he was born in England or Timbuctoo."

Eileen had come up to me and was tugging at my skirt. "Come and play with me," she said. "Nurse says I'm not to play because of Mommy going to heaven, but it's boring just looking at my Bible pictures."

"We won't be allowed to play anything too rowdy," I said, stroking her sleek, dark head, "but I don't think Nurse would mind if we played a quiet game."

"With my Noah's ark?" she asked, glancing up at Nurse, who nodded silently.

I knelt on the floor beside her as she took it out and I remembered something. I put my hand into my skirt pocket and it was still there. "Eileen, I have a surprise for you," I said. "You'll never guess what I just found." And I produced the camel.

Eileen's eyes opened wide for a moment, then a beaming smile spread across her face. "You found it—the missing camel! You are so clever. Now the other camel doesn't have to be lonely." She took the camel from me and placed it tenderly beside its mate.

I hardly noticed what she was doing because I was staring at her as if I'd been struck by a thunderbolt. Until this moment I had never seen her smile. Now she had smiled and it was enchanting. Her whole face lit up, those dark eyes flashed and two adorable dimples appeared in her cheeks. And the amazing thing was that I had seen those dimples and that smile somewhere before, as I sat with Margie McAlister on the bench inside an inn, after I had just run her over on my bicycle.

"Miss Gaffney?" Eileen tugged at my sleeve. "Miss Gaffney, you can be Mr. Noah if you like today. I'll be the man who brings the animals to the ark."

"Are you all right, Miss Gaffney?" Nurse asked. "You've gone quite pale. I understand that you haven't been at all well."

I got to my feet. "You're right. I've had gastric troubles all this week. Maybe I should go and lie down and come back to play with Eileen when I feel better."

"Oh no, don't go," Eileen wailed. "I want you to stay and play with me."

"Where are your manners?" Nurse scolded. "You say, 'Thank you for coming, Miss Gaffney.' You don't go wailing at her like some heathen child."

"I promise I'll come back and play later," I said. "Only I just don't feel in the mood to play right now. You can introduce the camel to all his old friends and have a party for his safe return."

"All right," she said in her high, sweet voice and was happily chatting to the animals before I got to the door.

Once outside I had to pause and catch my breath again. In this morning of surprises this had been the most incredible. I could hardly have been more shocked if Theresa herself had sat up and spoken to me when I was in her room. Now so much made sense. No wonder Theresa had been so indifferent to Eileen. She had confided in me once that she had tried to show maternal feelings to the child but hadn't been able to. Understandable. What woman could learn to love the child of her husband's mistress? The clues had been there all along—I just hadn't seen them. Both Belinda and Barney himself had told me that Theresa hadn't wanted him near her since Brendan's kidnapping. And Barney was a man of healthy appetites— he had demonstrated that clearly enough to me! So what more natural than to turn to the pretty nurse while his wife lay languishing. When they found out she was expecting, Barney must have paid her off and kept the child, pretending it was his and Theresa's, while Miss McAlister went to live comfortably in a house in Georgetown and kept her mouth shut.

I realized something else too—she hadn't come back to ask for more money. She had wanted to catch a glimpse of her daughter. Hence my feeling that we were being spied on when I played with

Eileen in the woods. But somebody had seen her as a threat, even if she hadn't asked for money. With a sinking feeling in my stomach I decided that the only person could be Barney himself, unless it was Theresa . . . and Theresa now lay dead.

My heart was racing so fast that I could hardly breathe. I had to get out of the house this minute. Even if Barney thought I was his cousin, I no longer felt safe. I would go to the Van Gelders, put in a telephone call to Daniel and ask him to arrange to have me picked up today, not tomorrow. I tiptoed down the stairs. I heard Desmond's voice saying, "The mail has just arrived, Senator. Do you want to go through it in your office?" and Barney's voice mumbling some sort of reply. So at least they were all safely busy and not able to witness me slinking out of the house.

The constable was still standing on duty outside the front door. I was tempted to talk to him, but I couldn't really think what to say. Everything I knew was pure supposition, apart from Eileen's smile. It would surely be taken as female hysterics and would put me in even greater danger. I'd have to leave it to Daniel to decide what should be done and who should do it. This was a task too big for me.

I glanced down at the river and saw Dr. Birnbaum being rowed across to the train, sitting up straight and correct in the skiff. Belinda was still at the table on the veranda, writing letters. She looked up as I passed her.

"Oh, Molly, there you are. I wondered where you had gone."

"Where's Cousin Clara?" I asked.

"In the kitchen, bossing Cook around, I should think," Belinda said. "She's the only person who is actually enjoying herself. Doesn't this all seem unreal to you? Almost like watching a play and not knowing what's going to happen next?"

I nodded. "That's exactly how I feel."

"I'm writing to our relatives," she said, "but I can't seem to find the words. It doesn't seem possible. I keep expecting to see her coming down the stairs any moment." She sighed and patted at her hair although the sleek coil around her head was perfectly in place. "I feel so terrible, Molly. I wasn't really a good sister to her."

"You were a fine sister," I said. "You came to visit, didn't you? And you brought Dr. Birnbaum because you thought he could help her."

"That's part of the reason I feel so terrible," she said. "My action brought about her death. I'll have to live with that on my conscience for the rest of my days."

"You did what you thought was best," I said softly. "We can't do any more than that. I'm sure Theresa doesn't blame you. And you know as well as I do that she wanted to be at peace. Now she is. Let's pray she's with Brendan."

She tried to smile. "Yes, do let's pray that."

"I think I'll go for a walk," I said. "I can't stay in the house."

For a moment I thought I had done the wrong thing and that she was about to volunteer to come with me. She put down her pen beside the inkwell, then shook her head and picked it up again. "No, it's no good. I have to finish these letters whether I want to or not."

"I should write to my family in Ireland," I said, "but I just can't do it now. Like you, I just can't seem to get my thoughts in order. Some good fresh air might help."

"I'd hardly call it good fresh air today," Belinda said, peering out from the veranda. "In fact it feels thundery to me."

"It does," I agreed. "But I'll make sure I'm back before it rains."

I passed the constable, who gave me a hard stare. "Where are you off to then, miss?" he asked.

It took all my self-control to answer politely, "Just for a stroll around the grounds."

"I've been thinking about what you said and it's made me a mite uneasy," he muttered. "I'll not rest until our detective has had a look at things."

"You have a detective coming?" Suddenly I felt a whole lot better.

He nodded. "I put in a request when I called about the morgue wagon. So with any luck we should have both of them showing up soon. At least I hope it's soon. I'm sweating like a pig, pardon my French, standing out here and getting eaten to pieces by mosquitoes."

"I'm sure the family wouldn't mind if you sat on the veranda," I said, "or even in the front hall. When you see one of the servants, tell them I said you should have a glass of lemonade."

"Most thoughtful, miss," he said. "Watch where you're going now, won't you?"

I wasn't quite sure what he meant by that. Did he have his suspicions too? But Belinda was sitting within earshot so I couldn't say more. I started across the lawn and down to the river. It was all I could do not to run or to look back to see if I was being observed. I didn't want to take a direct course to the Van Gelders in case anyone was watching me. Once I reached the riverbank I pretended to admire the view. The skiff with Dr. Birnbaum in it was no longer in sight and the river was deserted apart from a family of mallards paddling along the shallows, while down toward New York City a paddle steamer was pulling into the dock at Peekskill.

I tried to calm myself down and collect my thoughts, but it wasn't easy. I was beginning to put two and two together and I didn't like the conclusion I was reaching. Barney was the only one who would have known the truth about Margie McAlister, apart from Theresa. And Theresa herself was now dead. Barney was the only one for whom she would have been a threat, which must have meant that he was the one who killed her, unless he had had one of his minions do it for him. Desmond O'Mara had slunk out of the house and not accounted for his presence until the next morning. Did Barney have some sort of terrible hold over him, which made him do evil things at Barney's bidding?

This is rubbish, I told myself. You really are suffering from female hysterics! I made myself calm down and think things through with logic. But each thought came back to Barney. He was a nice enough fellow, if one ignored the groping hands. But more than one person had told me how ruthless Barney was, how he would stop at nothing to get what he wanted. In spite of the perspiration trickling down my back, I shivered. Had he stopped at nothing to get rid of a wife who shut him out of her bedroom and was no longer any use to him?

I began to meander along the bank in what I hoped was aimless fashion. Then, the moment I gained the safety of the trees, I picked up my skirts and made for the path to the Van Gelders. The wretched skirts kept getting caught on brambles and bushes and I wished again for those bloomers. When I got back to New York I'd see about having a pair made for myself. Then I'd be like Sid and Gus and not care a fig what anyone else thought about me!

Thinking of Sid and Gus brought on a powerful wave of homesickness. It was a feeling I'd never experienced before. I was only too glad to get away from my home in Ireland. But I missed Patchin Place and Sid and Gus and yes, I even missed Seamus and the children. I'd have given anything to be back there with them right now. I wondered how they were doing and whether Shamey and Bridie had wrecked the house and eaten all the food yet. I hoped Shamey had obeyed me and not taken Bridie to swim in the East River again. I hoped Seamus had found a job. I wondered whether Sid and Gus had held any exciting parties in my absence. It was stupid really, as I'd only been gone a little over a week, but I felt as if I'd been away for months. And I longed for the safety of my own little world away from intrigues, murders and Justin Hartley.

The path led me around the big oak tree where Roland Van Gelder had startled me that day, so I knew I was heading in the right direction. The forest was silent. Not even a bird chirped from the treetops today, as if they too found the weather too hot for them. Even out of the sun the air was muggy and oppressive. Midges buzzed around my face and I brushed them away. As I came around the tree a figure loomed up in front of me and I opened my mouth to scream.

"Don't be afraid, Miss Gaffney, it's only me." And Roland Van Gelder stood there in a repeat performance of our first meeting.

"Mr. Van Gelder," I gasped. "Do you make a practice of lurking behind this tree to scare poor helpless females?"

He grinned like a wicked schoolboy. "Not a practice, I assure you. I came over today because Mother is having a house party and I hate having to make polite conversation with people I don't know. And if I climb up onto that branch," he added, "I have an excellent view of Adare and Miss Belinda sitting on the veranda."

"You've been spying on us?" I demanded.

He blushed. "Not all of you. Just Miss Belinda. Don't you think she's the loveliest creature you've ever seen?"

"I hope I don't look at her in quite the same way as you," I said.

"She doesn't return my affections," he muttered. "I know why too."

"You do?" Could he possibly know that she found him a boorish oaf?

"It's because we no longer have a family fortune. Belinda is used to the finer things of life. We are reduced to meager circumstances, and I don't have a head for business, I'm afraid. My parents despair of me. All in all I'm a terrible disappointment to everyone."

He was speaking in his soft, calm voice but suddenly I felt most uneasy talking to him. We were far from both houses, too far for anyone to hear me scream. I remembered Theresa telling me how Roland had a foul temper. And there was something chilling about a grown man who climbed trees to spy on people, wasn't there?

"I really should go," I said. "I have to tell your mother important news."

"News?" he asked innocently.

"Yes, I'm afraid that—" I broke off. "I'm afraid that we have had a spate of sickness at the house. We just hope that it isn't infectious and we haven't passed it on to you," I added lamely.

"I see." The way he was looking at me made me feel that he knew more than he was letting on. How long had he been spying from his tree? Had he seen the constable and the doctor arriving? Had he seen any of us weeping?

"Maybe you'd be good enough to show me the way through the hedge that you always use," I suggested. "I have no wish to walk all the way up to the road on a day like this."

"Okay," he said affably. "Follow me."

He took off at a brisk pace between bushes and past brambles until at last he squeezed through a gap in the tall cedar hedge. "Don't ask me to come any farther with you," he said. "And please don't mention to Mother that you've seen me. I don't want her to know where I am."

"Of course not," I said. "I thank you for your assistance, Mr. Van Gelder."

I let out a sigh of relief as he turned back into the forest. My heightened imagination had turned everybody I met into a potential killer.

❧ **Thirty** ❧

s I approached Riverside, the Van Gelders' solid brick house, I heard voices and saw that tables had been set out on the lawn and a game of croquet was going on. Several ladies stood under parasols, while one young lady concentrated on her croquet shot and her beau followed her, holding the parasol. I heard the thwack of mallet against ball and then a man's voice calling, "Good shot, Emily," and polite applause.

I skirted around them, hoping to make for the house without being noticed. And indeed, nobody looked up from the croquet game until I was about to enter through French doors and almost collided with Mrs. Van Gelder as she rushed out calling, "Roland—where is that wretched boy when I need him?"

She gasped and stepped back as I loomed up in front of her. "Miss Gaffney! What a pleasant surprise. You must have read my mind."

"Read your mind, Mrs. Van Gelder?"

"As you can see, we're having a little house party here. They've just finished breakfast and were keen to play croquet before it became too warm. Nothing like the grand affairs we used to have in the summer, just a few old family friends, but I thought it might provide a little entertainment for you young people next door. Poor Miss Butler is used to a much livelier scene, I fear, and you too. So I wanted to send Roland over to Adare to invite you all, but I can never find the useless boy when I need him."

"I'm afraid we won't be able to accept your kind invitation today," I said. "In fact I have come to bring you the most terrible news. Mrs. Flynn died during the night. We are a house in mourning."

"That poor dear woman dead? God rest her soul. Still, it wasn't exactly unexpected, was it? She didn't look well when you dined with us a week ago and I gather she took to her bed the next day. And the poor thing was in torment about her son. And so delicate too."

I nodded silently.

"Well, dear me," she went on, putting her hand to her ample bosom, "this changes everything. I was planning to have dancing tonight, but it wouldn't be right now, would it?" She looked across in the direction of Adare. "And what about the croquet? Do you think I should stop them from playing?"

- "I am sure Senator Flynn wouldn't expect your house to go into mourning, as long as no loud music comes in our direction," I said. "You do have guests, after all, and they will expect to be entertained."

"How thoughtful you are, my dear." She smiled at me. "And how kind to come all this way to tell us the news."

I flushed with guilt as my motive had not been at all unselfish. "I wondered—" I stammered, "if I could possibly use your telephone? Senator Flynn is busy in his office and I didn't like to disturb him, but I do have a very important call to make."

"But of course," she said. "Come this way. And afterward you must at least come and meet my guests and have a glass of lemonade with us."

"You're most kind." I followed her into the house and was led to the telephone in the master's study. I fervently hoped that she wouldn't stand behind me listening, but she was tact itself and closed the door behind her. I picked up the receiver and asked the operator to connect me to police headquarters in New York City. No, I didn't know the number, but it must be one that she could find out easily. She did and soon came on to say that I was connected and could go ahead.

"I'd like to speak with Captain Daniel Sullivan," I said. "It's very urgent."

"Captain Sullivan? Hold the line please." I heard a muffled conversation, then the voice came back on the line again. "Captain Sullivan is off duty today. Would you like to speak to one of the other officers, or the sergeant on duty?"

"No, thank you," I mumbled. "You don't happen to know if Captain Sullivan is at home, do you?"

"I'm just an ordinary constable, miss. He don't keep me informed of his social engagements." He ended with a chuckle. "But there are plenty of other officers here who could help you if it's urgent."

"No. No, thank you." I hung up and dialed his home number. It rang and rang. I put back the receiver and stared at it for a long moment. Tears of frustration welled up in my eyes. I had counted so much on being able to talk to Daniel and now I'd have to wait until he came to rescue me. I would have to go back to a house where there was at least one murderer present. I supposed it was possible that the person who pushed Margie McAlister to her death was not the one who administered an overdose of sleeping powders to Theresa Flynn, but that really did seem like a surfeit of murderers in one location. Besides, in my limited experience one murder inevitably led to another.

I had just put down the telephone into its cradle when the study door opened. Justin Hartley came in and shut the door behind him.

"Finally we're alone, Molly Murphy," he said.

"Really, Mr. Hartley, we've just experienced a great tragedy at Adare and I'm in no mood for your extraordinary games," I said. "Now please stand aside and open this door before I start yelling."

"I wouldn't do that, if I were you," he said. "I don't want to upset my hosts by summoning the police to their residence, but I will if I have to." He moved toward me. "I must say, Molly Murphy, that I'm most impressed with your transformation. Quite the elegant lady, aren't we? I knew my mother made a mistake when she educated you with my sisters. I told her it would lead to nothing but trouble and it has."

"I can take your nonsense no longer," I said and went to push past him. He grabbed my arm and spun me around.

"I can prove that you are not the Senator's cousin," he said, "but a peasant girl from Connemara. A peasant girl who tried to kill me."

He has written to Ireland, I thought, and he saw the fear flash across my face. I was furious with myself immediately, but it was too late. "And how can you prove it?" I asked.

"Molly Murphy had a little scar on the side of her neck. She got it from falling out of a tree on our estate. I noticed it the other day when you were fanning yourself with your hat. So I no longer have even a shadow of doubt." He was gloating. "I must say you've played a good game, Molly. Quite impressive. I like a woman with spunk. In fact, if circumstances were different, I might find myself quite attracted to you."

"I, on the other hand, would not be attracted to you if you were the last man on earth," I said. "Now let go of me this instant. My relatives are waiting for me at Adare."

He was smiling now, such an unpleasant smile. "Goodness me, Molly Murphy—won't your newfound relatives be surprised when they find you arrested and dragged home in chains?"

When I had left Ireland, I was a peasant girl with no one to speak on my behalf. But I'd had to stand on my own feet ever since and I'd learned a thing or two in the process.

"And why do you think that I might be arrested, Mr. Hartley?" I turned to face him.

"For attempted murder, of course. You're damned lucky that it wasn't for murder itself. If my dog hadn't run home and raised the alarm, the doctors say I should have bled to death. Instead, I had to endure months in the hospital and I'll never be truly fit again."

I didn't let my gaze falter. "It's strange that you should see it that way, Mr. Hartley. I saw it as trying to defend myself against attempted rape. And if it's any consolation, I never meant to hurt you.

I was just trying to push you away from me. It was purely accidental that the floor was slippery and you went over backward and hit your head on our stove."

"No matter what the circumstances, it was a vicious attack that left me almost dead. People have swung for less."

"In Ireland maybe, where we are ruled by foreign invaders and where we Irish have no voice. But this is America, Mr. Hartley, where all are equal in the eyes of the law and where forcing your attentions on a young woman against her will earn you a trip to Sing Sing across the river. So it would be your word against mine, and"— I challenged him with my eyes—"I happen to have a very good friend who is a senior captain in the New York Police, who will come to my aid at the snap of my fingers. If you want to risk it, Mr. Hartley, go ahead, but I warn you, I'm not the helpless little peasant girl who ran away a year ago. I have plenty of powerful friends in these parts."

With a thrill of recognition I saw that he was surprised, alarmed even.

"And I suppose you'll be telling me next that the Senator really is your cousin?"

"Why should I not have discovered a newfound cousin in America?" I demanded, not wanting to resort to the outright lie. "As you know yourself, we Irish breed like rabbits. I probably have cousins all over the place. Cousin Barney Flynn has been very good to me, and he's another powerful man, one who would not take kindly to any rogue who attacked me."

I could see that I had him. His eyes darted nervously toward the door.

"You exaggerate," he said. "It certainly wasn't an attack. How was I to know you didn't welcome my attentions?"

"I thought the words 'no' and 'get out of my cottage' were quite self-explanatory."

"I thought you were just playing hard to get." He laughed nervously.

"You ripped the front of my dress," I said. "You told me that you

275

owned me as much as any of the animals on the farm. You forced me onto the kitchen table and you would have raped me. It was an attack. And it wouldn't go down too well in an American court of law."

"I'm sure I didn't—" he began.

"If you want to put it to the test, I'm game to take you on," I said. "Go on. Call in Mrs. Van Gelder. Admit to what you did to me in front of all of her guests. Then come over to Adare and tell my cousin Barney who is grieving the death of his wife."

Justin's mouth dropped open. "Mrs. Flynn?"

"Died last night. And I'm needed by my grieving relatives. So if you will excuse me—"

I opened the door and he didn't stop me. I came out of the study to find Mrs. Van Gelder hovering by the French windows.

"Ah, Miss Gaffney. There you are. It must be such a strain, having to convey such bad news. You look quite pale, my dear. Would you like to sit down? Should I have the chauffeur drive you home?"

"No, thank you. I can walk back the way I came, along the river," I said.

"At least take a glass of lemonade with us before you go," she said. "We will have to break your news to my guests, and I'd appreciate your support. I fear the poor dears will be so disappointed when they hear there is to be no dancing tonight."

I really didn't want to have to face a bevy of strangers at this moment but I had no alternative. Mrs. Van Gelder took a firm grip on my wrist and I was literally dragged out to the terrace. The croquet game was still going go and more guests were watching from the terrace steps. It seemed that the Van Gelders had invited an impressive number to their house party.

"Your attention please, everybody!" Mrs. Van Gelder clapped her hands as if she was bringing a class of schoolchildren to order. "I'd like to introduce you to Miss Gaffney from Ireland. Miss Gaffney is a cousin of Senator Flynn who lives next door and she has come, I'm afraid, with the most tragic news."

The croquet players froze in mid-action so that they resembled a French painting by one of those delightfully modern Impressionists. Everyone was staring at us. Mrs. Van Gelder nudged me and I realized that she expected me to deliver the bad news myself.

"I regret to inform you," I said, finding it hard to deliver the words with all those eyes upon me, "that my hostess, Mrs. Flynn, passed away last night."

There was a collective gasp. A couple of the women began to swoon and were caught by attentive males. An older woman fanned herself. Nobody made the sign of the cross, indicating that this was entirely a Protestant gathering. Nobody cried or wailed, indicating that it was entirely non-Irish.

I hoped just to slip away at this point but they had surrounded me. Was Mrs. Flynn in ill heath? It wasn't typhoid, was it? They had come from the city for that very reason . . . Questions were peppered at me. Mrs. Van Gelder placed the glass of punch into my hands. "Drink this, dear. It will make you feel better."

"Mrs. Flynn's death—was it an accident?" a voice asked. I turned to answer and found myself looking straight at Daniel Sullivan. What's more, Miss Arabella Norton was standing at his side, looking as lovely as ever in a pink lace dress with matching parasol. No wonder he had been able to reach my bedroom window so easily the Sunday night after church. He had been staying with the neighbors as part of their house party. I forgot about tragedy and intrigue as I fought back anger and jealousy. He hadn't come all the way from the city because he was concerned with my welfare. He had only bothered to check on me because he was staying in the house next door with his fiancée. Would he have given me a second thought if he hadn't been so close by? I fought with my emotions and tried to remain calmly professional. I had, after all, been hired to complete an assignment.

"No accident, sir," I replied and saw his eyebrows react to my meaning.

"I must come to pay my respects to the Senator," he said. "He is an old and good friend of my family. May I escort you back to Adare, miss?"

"Daniel, we have to finish our croquet game first." Arabella tugged at his arm. "You can't just desert our team, especially not when we're winning."

"Arabella—Mrs. Flynn has just died. Where is your sense of decorum?" Daniel frowned.

Arabella gave a silly giggle and tossed back her head. "It's not as if I knew her well. I only met the woman once, I'm sure. Indeed, I'm very sorry for her, but life has to go on, doesn't it, and I don't see how our not playing croquet can make anything better for anyone."

"If you'd care to take a seat and wait, Miss Gaffney?" Daniel said. His eyes were imploring. I chose not to be implored.

"Please don't concern yourself with me," I said stiffly. "I can find my own way back, and I choose to be alone at a time of such grief. Please excuse me, Mrs. Van Gelder, but I am needed at Adare." I handed her my untouched glass of lemonade, nodded politely to the assembled company and made my exit.

As I left I heard Arabella's high, clear voice saying, "Do tell me, Daniel, does every girl in Ireland have red hair? They all look the same to me."

If it had been a happier occasion, I would have smiled.

❧ Thirty-one ❧

I reached the gap in the hedge and squeezed through. There was no sign of Roland anywhere near the big oak tree. Maybe he had other vantage points from which to spy on Belinda. I was reluctant to go back to the house but I realized that I had to act normally until Daniel arranged for my departure. He had promised me he would get me out and I didn't think he would forget that promise—unless Arabella was in the middle of another stupid croquet game. I felt tears stinging at the back of my eyes and angrily brushed them away. I knew perfectly well that Daniel was engaged to another woman. I thought I had learned to accept it by now, but it was always a shock to see them together. At least he would come over to Adare as soon as he could. That was a comforting thought. And once he appeared, I would find a way to share my suspicions with him and he would take charge. Thus reassured, I made my way back through the undergrowth.

A twig cracked on the path ahead of me. I looked up and found myself face to face with Barney Flynn.

"Why, Cousin Barney, you startled me," I said. "Is something the matter?" He kept on coming until he was only inches away from me. I cried out in alarm as he reached out and grabbed my wrist.

"Do you mind telling me who the hell you are and what you are doing in my house?" he demanded.

The way he was glaring at me was frightening. This was the

other Barney Flynn, the one who had been described more than once as ruthless.

"Cousin Barney, what on earth has possessed you?" I fought to stay calm. "What are you talking about?"

"This morning's mail brought a letter from my family in Ireland." He almost spat the words. "Lots of news, including a tidbit about my dear cousin Molly who has now been in the convent for the past two years. What do you have to say to that? Or do Mother Superiors let their nuns out on little jaunts across the Atlantic these days?"

I realized that I was alone in the woods with a man who had possibly killed two women and was no fool. What I told him had to be as close to the truth as I could manage without alarming him.

"Senator Flynn, I'm deeply sorry for deceiving you and I ask your forgiveness," I said. "My motive was entirely in your interest."

"Go on." His eyes were still glaring at me.

"I'm a sort of private investigator," I said. "I was sent here to spy on the Sorensen Sisters. The New York Police thought that they were charlatans but nobody had been able to catch them at their tricks until now. Since my face was not known to any of you, it was thought I might just have a chance of exposing them."

"And did you?"

"They left in a hurry, didn't they?" I asked. "I found out enough to make them uncomfortable but probably not enough to prosecute them."

"Would it not have been more correct to let me in on the secret? It is my house, after all."

"For all we knew the entire household was composed of devotees of the sisters who would not have taken kindly to my efforts to expose them."

He nodded as if this made sense, but his eyes never left my face for a second, nor did he let go of my wrist.

"If you had completed your assignment, what made you stay on after they had departed? How do I know you're not a thief or some damned magazine reporter?"

"If you want proof of my credentials, I can show you my card. I have associates with the New York Police who can vouch for me. And as to why I stayed on—if you remember, I became sick the day the sisters departed. So sick that I wondered whether they had put a hex on me."

He looked at me and suddenly he laughed. "You're a rum one, and that's the truth. Full of Irish blarney. So are you telling me you're not from Ireland after all?"

"Oh no, sir, I'm newly arrived from Ireland, only not from a convent."

I saw his expression change in a way that made me uneasy. "Not from a convent, eh? That much was obvious. And not a relative either. Well, that does change the situation, doesn't it? And nobody need know except for the two of us."

He jerked me into his arms. I was so surprised and taken off guard that I didn't have time to react before he was kissing me roughly. I tried to push him away but he was like an animal, grabbing at me, attacking me.

"Stop it! Leave me alone!" I managed to gasp as I wrenched my mouth free of him. "Your poor wife is not yet cold. Holy Mother of God—have you no shame?"

"My poor wife kept me out of her bed for five long years," he muttered. I could feel his heart thudding against my chest. "And I've wanted you from the first moment I saw you." His hands started moving down my body. He was panting like a caged beast.

"Barney, stop this, please," I pleaded. "You'll regret this later."

"No, I won't. I haven't regretted one moment's pleasure in my life so far and you owe me some return for my hospitality, Miss Whoever-you-are."

With that he attempted to throw me down onto the grass. I tried to bring up my knee but was trapped by my own petticoats. It was as if the scene with Justin Hartley was replaying itself in front of my eyes.

"I owe you nothing," I shouted, hoping in vain that someone

would hear me. "Get away from me this instant. I'll summon the police and have you arrested!"

"I don't think so. The police are in my pocket. You should know that. And there isn't a woman yet who has been dissatisfied with my lovemaking—and a whole string of them who can vouch for me."

He was still attempting to throw me down, while I fought to get free of him. I tried to bring my hands up to his face but he grabbed my wrists easily in his big hands. A large oak tree was behind us and he forced me up against it, nuzzling at my neck and grunting as his knee thrust in between my legs and he tried to pull up my skirt.

"Damned stupid skirts," he muttered.

I couldn't have agreed with him more. If women wore sensible clothing, they'd be able to defend themselves better in the first place. I was just about thinking that there was no hope for me when an indignant voice demanded, "Barney—what in God's name are you doing? Have you lost your senses, man?" And Joe Rimes stood behind us. He grabbed at Barney and dragged him away from me.

"You must be out of your mind, man. Your own cousin?" Joe took my arm. "I'm sorry, my dear. The Senator is out of his mind with grief—"

"She's not my cousin, she's an imposter." Barney was still breathing heavily. "She's a little spy, that's what she is."

"What do you mean, a spy?" Joe's voice was suddenly sharp. His grip on my arm tightened.

"An investigator, sent here to spy on us."

"Good God. By whom?"

"The police, so it seems."

"Then get rid of her. Now. While we've got the chance."

"What do you mean, get rid of her?"

"What I say. Find a large rock and drop her into the river and no one will be any the wiser."

"What?"

"You heard me."

"You're crazy, Joe," Barney shot him a look of alarm. "We're not killing anybody. We'll pay her off. That works."

"Like the last one, you mean? Money didn't keep her away, did it? She kept coming back, didn't she? And she threatened to let out the secret too. If I hadn't—"

Barney turned on him abruptly. "What are you talking about, Joe? When did she threaten to tell?"

"When she was here last week. She wanted to see you. I warded her off with promises that you'd meet her later."

Barney was staring at him. "And then, Joe? What happened then?"

"She had to go. She was a constant danger to you. She didn't learn her lesson."

"So you followed her and pushed her off the cliff?"

"You couldn't afford another scandal, Barney. Any breath of scandal now and they'll not reelect you. And nobody can prove that her fall wasn't an accident."

They stood staring at each other and I could see Barney trying to digest the weight and implications of what he had just learned. Joe Rimes's grip was still firm on my upper arm. I considered breaking free and making a run for it.

"I can't believe you'd do a thing like that, Joe," Barney said at last. "How many years have I known you, and I still can't believe it of you."

Joe Rimes glanced across at me. "Oh, it's easy enough after the first time," he said. "I won't have any trouble with this one."

I realized instantly that my one hope was to get Barney onto my side as an ally against Joe Rimes. "And what about Theresa?" I demanded. "Did you kill her too?"

Rimes smiled then. "Like I said, it's easy after the first time. The first time the guilt burns at your very soul, but when you realize that you're damned already, what does it matter? You can't burn in hellfire more than once."

Barney let out a roar of rage and grabbed him by the lapels. "You killed my wife?"

Joe dropped his hold on my arm and put his hands up to defend himself against Barney's onslaught. "Oh come on, Barney. Don't try to pretend that you wanted to be married to her any longer. What kind of marriage was it? If she'd satisfied you, you wouldn't have had to keep grabbing anything in skirts that walked past you. I did you a good turn. You should be thanking me."

"Thanking you?" He started shaking Joe Rimes as if he were a rag doll. I began to back away.

"You're crazy," I heard Barney spit out the words.

"I'm not the crazy one," Rimes shouted. "Your wife was. You were tied to a madwoman. And if you'd let her be hypnotized by that quack, she'd have told him everything—about the child, about Margie McAlister—everything!"

"You killed my wife." Barney's voice dropped to a whisper and he let go of Joe Rimes.

"She didn't suffer, Barney," Rimes said quietly, putting his hand on Barney's shoulder. "She went the best way possible. She fell asleep and didn't wake up. Isn't that what you wanted for her? And there will be an added bonus. You'll get the sympathy vote again. Poor Barney Flynn whom tragedy keeps striking but who soldiers on bravely, in spite of everything."

"Wait a minute." Barney looked up suddenly. There was total silence apart from the sound of two men breathing and the gurgle of the river passing the rocks. "My son . . . my boy. . . . Was that the first time, Joe? Tell me that wasn't the first time."

Joe Rimes's red face flushed the color of beetroot. His eyes darted around wildly. "For you, Barney. I did it for you. You were behind in the polls, weren't you?"

Barney went for him again like a madman. "You killed my child because I was behind in the polls? What kind of depraved monster are you?" He struck Joe a great blow to the head, sending him sprawling.

"I didn't want to hurt him, Barney." Joe Rimes started to blubber as he staggered back to his feet. "I swear I didn't want any harm to come to the child. I arranged the whole thing with Morell. I'd put a sedative in the child's milk and I'd bring him to Morell. After that it was up to him. He'd hide the child where he couldn't be found. He'd collect the money and be well on his way out of the country when the child's hiding place was revealed. He was a good man. The boy liked him. I knew he'd take good care of the boy."

"But he didn't, did he? He buried my son alive and left him to die." Barney's voice broke and he turned his face away to hide his emotion.

"How was I to know the stupid policeman would shoot him before he could tell us where the child was? You should never have brought in the police. The note told you not to. You were warned."

"And whose idea was it to bury him?"

"Mine. Morell didn't want to, but I said it had to look terrible. It had to evoke public sympathy and make every parent's heart stop beating from fear. Morell said he'd make sure the child stayed asleep and had plenty of air. He'd take care of everything, he said." Rimes gave a great, heaving sob. "God, Barney, do you think I haven't suffered a million times over? I'd have done anything to take back what I did—anything."

"Get away from me." Barney yelled and gave him a great shove. "Get out of my sight now, before I tear you apart with my bare hands!"

"But I did it for you, Barney," Joe said again. "I've devoted my entire life to your career. You'd never have gotten elected in the first place if it hadn't been for me. I only wanted what was best for you."

"You're a depraved monster, Rimes." Barney was screaming now, half out of his mind with fury. "You make me sick. Start running before I call the police. The least I can do is give you a head start."

Rimes spotted me, still standing within reach in the dappled shade. "We have to get rid of the girl, Barney. Don't you see that?

She knows everything now. She's dangerous. She can ruin you if the truth comes out."

They were standing between me and the path to the house. I considered trying to run to the Van Gelders and Daniel, but I knew they'd soon catch me. It was so tempting to promise them that I'd keep my mouth shut and behave like a good little girl, but I couldn't.

Then I heard Barney say, "There has been enough killing, Rimes. No one else is going to die to keep me in the damned Senate. I'm resigning today. I'm selling Adare and taking my daughter abroad. I'm through with public life."

"No. No, you can't." Rimes's voice was shrill. "I won't let you. Not after all this. Not after everything I did for you. I'd rather have you dead first."

He pulled a gun from his right pocket and aimed it at Barney. But before he could pull the trigger, I heard footsteps crashing through the undergrowth and Daniel came running toward us.

"Daniel, he's got a gun!" I screamed as a shot whizzed past Daniel's head.

"Hold it right there," Daniel shouted and produced a gun of his own. "Drop the gun at once."

But instead Joe Rimes leaped at me with remarkable agility for his size and dragged me in front of him, his arm tightly around my throat. "She's coming with me," he said. "Stay back. Don't try to follow us."

He started dragging me backward down the slope, toward the river. His grip on me was so tight that I couldn't breathe and I coughed and choked as I fought for air. Lights flashed in front of my eyes. I was only half aware of Barney and Daniel watching helplessly as I was borne away, Daniel's gun at the ready, but aimed directly at me. Slowly, carefully, Rimes pulled me down the steps to the landing stage, then he yanked me like a rag doll into the skiff, which rocked wildly and I thought would tip us both into the water. But he managed to right it and cast off while he kept me in front of him. He took an oar and gave a mighty shove, sending us out into the current.

The current was flowing fast through these narrows and bore us out into the stream. With one hand around my neck and the other clutching his gun, Joe Rimes couldn't use the oars and had to rely on the strength of the current to bear us away. I had no idea where he might be taking us. I don't think he knew either. Rocks approached and he had to put down his gun while he picked up an oar to fend them off, but he was still holding my throat too tightly and I couldn't turn my head to see where he had placed the gun.

When at last we were far from either bank, he threw me down onto the floor of the boat and waved the gun at me. "No funny business, understand? You lie there and don't move. I need both hands for the oars but I've still got the gun right here if I need it."

Then he started to row. He was not a man of athletic build and his rowing was terrible. He jerked, splashed and caught crabs. After a few minutes his face was bright red. Sweat streamed down it, and he was puffing and panting. The current was still strong and swept us between towering banks. If we didn't hit a rock first or weren't swept into the undergrowth along the shoreline, we'd probably make it to the Tappan Zee—that wide lake into which the Hudson spreads. But I didn't know what Joe would do without help of the current. I knew that he couldn't row all the way to New York City and I was afraid that he'd decide he had to get rid of me—or that the police would start shooting at the boat. I remembered too well the last occasion when a police bullet had caused an unexpected tragedy.

I glanced up at him, wondering if he could be reasoned with. Then I reminded myself that this was a man who had caused three deaths and for whom a fourth killing would be no problem. And I had heard his full confession. I could never be let go alive.

I lay there on the floor of the boat, my eyes going from Joe Rimes's face to the gun. It lay on the seat beside him, within easy reach of his right hand. I'd have no chance of reaching it first. My one hope would be to tip the boat over and throw us both into the water. But with the swirling current and the rocks, I didn't like our chances. I didn't think drowning wouldn't be a preferable death to being shot.

We continued. The shoreline began to open out. We were almost to the Tappan Zee. The midday sun came out from behind hazy clouds and beat down on us. Joe was clearly tiring at the oars. Then suddenly a loud siren brought me up to my knees and made Joe jump and spin around. The pleasure steamer had left its dock in Peekskill and was bearing down on us, closing rapidly in the narrow stream. Joe grabbed the oars and fought to row us out of harm's way. But the more he struggled, the more he splashed, and we were getting nowhere. Then he reached forward for a mighty pull, missed the water entirely and went over backward. This was my chance. I scrambled to my knees. The gun had disappeared somewhere beneath Joe. One oar had floated away. The steamer was closing on us rapidly. The siren sounded again and warning shouts came to us over the thrashing of the two great paddle wheels. Joe struggled to right himself, and came up, grasping for the remaining oar.

The giant bow cast a shadow over the rowboat as it loomed above us. I could hear women screaming.

"Jump!" I screamed and dived into the water.

"I can't swim!" Joe's voice came to me as I broke the surface.

I could hear shouts and bells as the steamer changed course and the bow swung to the left of the rowboat. For a moment it looked as if it might pass him by. I was still too near those mighty paddle wheels and had no wish to be dragged under them. I felt my wet skirts wrapping themselves around my legs as I attempted to swim away. I turned on my back, hitched up my skirts and kicked out. The current caught me and swept me out of harm's way.

I raised my head and watched as the prow of the steamer grazed the rowboat. Then the great wheel approached him. At first it seemed that it too would pass him by. Instead, it drew the small boat in, like a fisherman reeling in his catch. Joe threw himself down as the boat was tossed around, then dragged into the path of the wheel. It rose up and flipped before the blades came down on it. On the bridge above the captain cut the engine, but it was too late. The wheel had smashed the tiny craft to matchwood. I waited for Joe's body to appear, but it didn't.

❧ Thirty-two ❧

Minutes later I was on board the steamer, wrapped in a blanket and sipping brandy from a flask. We waited in midstream until a police launch boarded us, having been summoned from Riverside by Daniel. I had hoped to see Daniel himself, but Joe Rimes had taken the only boat at Adare. Daniel would probably have to drive to the nearest public ferry, and that would take time.

Small boats circled the area, but Joe Rimes's body never surfaced, for which I was grateful. After a while the search was called off and the steamer limped on to the next port of Croton-on-Hudson. I was taken to the police station to make a statement. I wasn't sure what would happen to me after that. My clothes were still at Adare, but I didn't fancy going back there to face Barney again. I was wet and miserable and close to tears. Someone at the police station was kind enough to give me a drink of coffee and a blanket from the prison cell to wrap around me.

The sergeant who took my statement was not the brightest nor the most patient and I was becoming so frustrated with having to explain and repeat what had just happened to me that I was about to explode, when I heard voices outside the door. The door burst open. The sergeant got to his feet muttering, "What in blazes do you think—"

But Daniel strode past him as if he was invisible. "Thank God!" he exclaimed. "I've been worried out of my mind. It took ages to get a boat launched from the Van Gelders and when we finally crossed the river we heard about the accident and people kept telling me that the boat was crushed and they found no survivors."

"That's because I jumped overboard in time," I said. "Joe Rimes couldn't swim so he was scared to jump. It was horrible to watch."

"I'm sure it was," he said. "My God, woman, you're freezing cold."

"So would you be if you'd been dragged from a river," I said.

"This is a police interview room," the sergeant interrupted. "May I ask what you think you're doing, barging in here?"

"Captain Sullivan, New York Police," Daniel said. "This young lady was taken hostage by a ruthless killer. I'll get a report to you later, but at this moment she needs dry clothing and a chance to rest. I've already spoken with your chief." And with that he put an arm around me and led me from the room.

I looked up at him admiringly. "It must be nice to be a captain."

"It has its benefits." He smiled at me.

We stepped out into hot sunshine. Several reporters were milling around. Daniel brushed them aside. "There will be a statement later, fellows," he said. Then he took my arm and led me firmly in the direction of the station platform. "Another of your nine lives gone, I fear," he said as we ascended the steps to the platform, followed by a crowd of curious onlookers. "How on earth did you stumble upon Joseph Rimes?"

I wasn't about to admit that stumbling was exactly what I had done. "Call it female intuition," I said.

"But your female intuition didn't warn you not to confront him alone?"

"I didn't intend to," I said. I was about to tell him about Barney's assault on me and Joe Rimes's arrival, but I found that I couldn't. "It's all rather complicated," I said. "I encountered him on the path back from Riverside."

Daniel shook his head. "If only you hadn't been so darned

impatient and waited for me as I suggested, then none of this would have happened."

"If only you hadn't been so darned weak and not wanted to spoil your beloved's croquet game, you could have escorted me home right away," I countered.

I saw him stifle a smile. "Molly, what am I going to do with you?" he said. "I send you out on what I consider to be a nice safe assignment and you wind up being taken hostage by a madman. Flynn told me that Joe Rimes confessed to killing Theresa."

"And to pushing Margie McAlister over the cliff," I said. "And to organizing the kidnapping of Brendan Flynn."

This was clearly news to him. He stared at me in disbelief. "He kidnapped the Flynns' baby? Why, for God's sake?"

"Because Barney Flynn was running behind in the polls and he wanted to get him the sympathy vote."

"Good God. The man really was mad."

"He claims he never intended to harm the child."

"Never intended to harm him? They buried the poor kid alive. Why do that if he meant him no harm?"

"He told Morell it had to sound really terrible, to put fear into the heart of every parent. Morell promised the child would be safe and stay asleep."

Daniel shook his head in disgust. "And he didn't tell Rimes where he had hidden the child?"

"Rimes didn't want to know any details, in case he was questioned by the police, I suppose. He was a strange man, Daniel. Very ambitious, but without any of the qualities that would make a charismatic leader. None of Barney Flynn's charm or good looks. So he put all that ambition into Barney's career."

"But why did he have to kill the girl and Mrs. Flynn? Was the McAlister woman blackmailing Barney?"

"Not exactly," I said. "She was his ex-paramour and Eileen Flynn's real mother. She'd just come back to see her child." As I said this, I wondered weather there had been any love between her and Barney or whether he had taken advantage of her as he had tried to do of me. I felt deeply sorry for Margie McAlister.

"The child's real mother? How did you find that out?"

"Eileen had her mother's smile," I said. "And Theresa showed no maternal feelings for the child at all."

Daniel nodded. "I'm impressed," he said. "I wonder if any male detective would have picked up on that."

I realized there was another point I needed to clear up. "Exactly why did you send me on this assignment, Daniel?" I asked. "You've made reference to it a couple of times. Did you really want to nail the Sorensen Sisters so desperately?"

He shook his head and smiled. "I can't lie to you, can I?" he said. "All right. I admit. I did it to get you out of the city. Two reasons actually. I was concerned about the typhoid epidemic and also I wanted you well away from the Hudson Dusters in case they discovered who you were."

"So it was nothing to do with my detective skills at all?" I asked flatly.

"Your detective skills are just fine, my dear. Nobody is disputing them."

"But you wouldn't have selected me for a police undercover assignment if you hadn't had an ulterior motive?"

"Probably not."

"I see."

"But now I have to admit that you've probably achieved more than most police detectives. I'm genuinely impressed."

"You are?"

He nodded. "Only don't think I'm about to hire you to snoop on gangs and crooks."

The train came puffing into the station and pulled to a halt with much squealing and grinding of brakes. Daniel opened the door and helped me inside. As he did, so he muttered a curse and hastily removed his jacket.

"What is it?" I asked.

"Quickly. Put this on," he commanded.

"Why?"

"My dear, that muslin you are wearing becomes quite transparent when wet. No wonder the crowd was following us and ogling."

I glanced down at myself and saw the shape of my leg, clearly outlined as I climbed into the carriage. "Jesus, Mary and Joseph," I muttered and had the grace to blush before I laughed. "Well, I better not show my face in this town again, had I?"

Daniel smiled too. "You won't be needing to show your face in this town again any time soon. I'm taking you home."

Doors slammed, a whistle sounded and the train pulled out of the station.

"If you're taking me home, we're going the wrong way," I said.

"We're going back to Adare first, of course."

"I don't want to go back there," I said. "Barney Flynn knows I'm not his cousin. He was—" I broke off, unable to say the next words even to Daniel. "He was very angry with me for deceiving him."

"You'll have me with you. I'll shield you from Barney Flynn's anger," he said. "Besides, it's only to pick up your things, then I'll arrange to have you taken straight back to the city." A thought struck him. "So how did he discover that you're not his cousin?"

"His real cousin Molly has been in the convent for the past two years," I said, giving Daniel a haughty stare. "Your informants certainly slipped up on that one."

He started to laugh. "They certainly did."

"It's not funny, actually. It might have cost me my life."

He nodded. "You're right. I'm sorry, really I am. Well, that's it."

"What is?"

"I've learned my lesson. I'm not sending you out on any more assignments, however tame they may seem. I'll find you a nice safe job in a hat shop."

"Now can you see me working in a hat shop?" I had to smile. "I'd jab hat pins into difficult customers." I shivered suddenly and wrapped Daniel's jacket more tightly around me. It was easy to joke and make light of things, but I could have been fished dead from the Hudson. I suppose shock was beginning to set in. Home sounded particularly good to me—Bridie rushing up to wrap her little arms around me, Sid and Gus waiting to spoil me, Ryan to amuse me. Back to being myself again with no need for pretense. For a moment I wondered if I was really cut out to be an investigator. Then I thought of that hat shop again and decided that on the whole I liked the excitement of my life.

I stared out of the train window, watching the Hudson slip past, and thought how peaceful it looked. Who would ever guess that so much tension and misery went on in the great home on its bank? Much as I distrusted Barney Flynn and would make sure I was never alone with him again, I did wish him some peace. His haunted face came back to me, the despair in those eyes as he shook Joe Rimes.

As the train slowed, coming into Peekskill, I looked out and saw the little church and a picture flashed into my mind: the young woman bending over Albert Morell's grave and placing fresh flowers on it, then fleeing when she saw me coming.

"I can't go home yet," I said, sitting up suddenly. "I have to see this through to the end."

"But you have seen it through. Joe Rimes is dead."

"But I'm not sure that Brendan is," I said.

"What are you talking about? He was buried alive five years ago. He can't still be alive after all this time."

As we pulled into the station, my gaze went to a woman standing on the platform with a sleeping child in her arms. The child was almost invisible under a white blanket with just little feet sticking out.

"Daniel?" I demanded. "Was a search ever made for him outside of the property? Was it ever considered that the ransom note might not have been telling the truth?"

"What do you mean?" Daniel opened the door for me and helped me alight.

"Didn't it seem strange to anyone that the child's body was never found? If the underground chamber was built, as Morell promised, with a good air supply, then wouldn't dogs have been able to pick up the child's scent? Even if the child had been drugged, wouldn't he have eventually woken and cried? And wouldn't someone have smelled a decomposing body?"

Daniel looked at me with surprise. "For a sweet-looking young girl, you can discuss remarkably macabre subjects," he said.

"You haven't answered my question. Was there ever any conjecture that the child might have been hidden away somewhere else?"

"What would that matter now? The child would still be dead."

"Not necessarily," I said. "Daniel, I've had this nagging doubt ever since I saw that woman. And the more I think of it, the more sense it makes. From what I've heard of Albert Morell, I can't believe that he would do that to a child. Everyone agreed that he loved children. I love children and no amount of money in the world would make me bury one alive, even if I was sure he'd be safe."

"So you are suggesting that he spirited the child away?"

"It's possible, isn't it?"

"But his relatives and friends in Albany were questioned to see if any of them might be involved," Daniel said. "All inquiries came up blank."

"I'm still thinking of the woman who puts flowers on his grave," I said. "She must live quite close by and she must have been very fond of him. I just wondered who she was. And she had a little boy with her who would have been about the right age—"

"Come on, Molly," Daniel exclaimed, shaking his head. "You're not suggesting that the child with her was really Brendan Flynn?"

"He didn't look anything like him," I admitted, "but the pictures of Brendan as a baby all show him with long fair curls and dressed in petticoats. His hair could have darkened by now, and he could have turned into a sturdy little boy like the one who was climbing on the graves that day."

"This is the wildest conjecture, Molly," Daniel said. "I am sure no stone was left unturned to locate the Flynns' child."

I glanced back at the train. Doors were slamming and a whistle was blown. "I just have a feeling we should find out about this woman, Daniel," I said. "I can't explain it but I think she's important.

Where would we start? Albany? Isn't that where Morell lived and worked before he went to the Flynns?"

"We're going back to Adare to get you changed and rested," Daniel said. He reached out to take my arm. I shook him off.

"I'm almost dry and with a comb through my hair I should look reasonably respectable," I said. "And it's still early. Let's take the train on to Albany. How long does it take from here anyway?"

"A good two hours, and this is foolishness. We can just as easily go tomorrow or the next day. I can telephone the Albany Police and let them pursue the investigation."

I shook my head and yanked open the train door. "You don't understand. I have to do this for Brendan. I could swear I heard his little voice one day, telling me to come find him. Please, Daniel, let me see this through."

"Tomorrow then." He reached for my arm again. "You've just had a bad fright and you were being poisoned, for God's sake. You need rest, Molly. You're hysterical."

"No, I'm not. Fine. If you don't want to come with me, I'll go by myself."

"Now you're being ridiculous."

"You don't think I'm capable of taking a train to Albany by myself and asking a few questions when I get there?"

"Not at the moment," he said, "unless you have hidden money in the pockets of that dress, because you're not carrying a purse."

"Oh," I hadn't considered this. "You could lend me money. You could advance me the rest of my fee."

"All aboard!" Another whistle was blown. The station attendant had the green flag in his hand.

I hesitated, then at the last moment I jumped up onto the train. "If you're not coming with me, I'll go to the police in Albany and get them to advance me money, based on your good name," I shouted.

Daniel sighed and swung himself aboard as the train started to move. "What an annoying woman you are, Molly Murphy. Now you've got me going with you on a wild goose chase and you've still got bits of weed in your hair and you look like the madwoman of the Hudson."

"Thank you for your compliments, kind sir." I gave him a haughty stare and he burst out laughing. "Molly, what am I going to do with you?"

"You've asked me that before and I still can't answer it for you," I said.

He sat down opposite me. "I suppose I can't ignore your female intuition or your Irish second sight, can I? You've been right before."

"I appreciate this, Daniel," I said. "You won't be sorry, I'm sure."

He smiled back. "What the heck. It beats having to play croquet," he said and reached into his inside pocket. "But here's my comb. The least we can do is to get half the vegetation of the river out of your hair."

With that he set to work yanking the comb through my matted tresses. Again I was unnerved by his closeness and he must have felt the same because he suddenly handed me the comb. "I expect you can do this better than I can," he said. "I'm bound to hurt you."

I didn't answer that one.

❧ Thirty-three ❧

W e should make a plan of campaign for when we get to Albany," I said, and promptly fell asleep. The next thing I remember was Daniel shaking me and telling me that we were about to arrive. I had slept all of two hours. The remaining dampness in my garments had dried, leaving me redolent with the rather unpleasant smell of riverwater.

Two hours good sleep had worked wonders and I found myself starving hungry and ready for anything. I forced Daniel to stop at the station buffet for a ham sandwich and a glass of sarsaparilla before we got down to business. I had expected Albany to be another little sleepy riverside town and was amazed to find it a big, bustling city with tree-lined boulevards and an impressive capitol building.

Our first stop was the police headquarters, where Daniel was obviously well known and well received. We learned that Morell now had no family living in the area, no family at all in the States except for a sister in Ohio. But we came away with the address of the carriage builder where Morell had learned about automobiles and worked until he became Senator Flynn's chauffeur. We took a cab there right away and from that grumpy, taciturn individual we learned where Albert Morell had boarded.

Bertie's landlady had clearly fallen under his spell. "He was a dear boy, if a bit of a rogue, if you get my meaning," she said, "But why are you asking now? He's been dead a long while, God rest his soul."

But she clearly loved a good gossip and mentioned that Bertie had been sweet on a girl who worked, of all places, in a hat shop. He had once bought her a locket and had it inscribed with her name: Johanna. "I don't know why that fell through," she said.

"He was married, you know," Daniel said.

"Married? I never knew that about him." She put her hand to her ample bosom. "Well, mercy me. Who'd have thought it?"

Obviously the charming Mr. Morell had kept his secrets well. She could give us no more details. We noticed the lace curtain of the parlor window tweak back as we departed.

Daniel muttered about foolish women and wild-goose chases as our cab clattered around the millinery establishments of Albany. It was close to five o'clock when we entered a little shop beside a park. The shop itself was cool and dark and smelled of perfume. Madame was a distinguished-looking Frenchwoman with hair pulled back into a severe bun, a beaky nose and lorgnettes.

"Johanna Foreman?" she asked. "*Oui*. She once worked here, but she is now gone, many years."

"She left you to go where?"

"To get married, mademoiselle. She left me to marry a great brute of a farmer. Amos Clegg, he was called. She was a delicate little thing and I did not think she would make a good farmer's wife, but beggars can't be choosers."

"What do you mean by that?" I asked. "She was an attractive girl, I understand. She could presumably have chosen from a selection of beaux."

She leaned closer to me. "She was unwise, mademoiselle. She got herself into trouble and the man who trifled with her affections could not marry her. So this Clegg person was willing to overlook the circumstances and she went off to live on a farm in the middle of nowhere."

"In the middle of nowhere? Far from here?"

She shrugged in that remarkably Gallic way. "Me, I do not concern myself with the geography of the New York countryside."

"So she hasn't been back to visit then?"

"On one occasion, but it is again several years ago now. I'm afraid I can be of no more help to you."

Our next dash was to the county courthouse where Daniel had to do some fast talking to get us inside as they were about to close. But once in the department of records we unearthed a helpful clerk and within half an hour we knew that Amos Clegg's farm was outside a place called Rhinebeck, back along the train route to New York City.

We grabbed another quick bite to eat as we waited for the down train. "We'll have time to go there tonight, won't we?" I asked. "At this time of year it shouldn't become dark until almost nine, which gives us at least two more hours of daylight."

Daniel shrugged. "Anything to get this over with and get you out of my hair."

I tossed back my head. "Fine, if you want to get me out of your hair," I said. "After today I won't be bothering you any further."

"I didn't mean it like that," he said, went to ruffle my hair and thought better of it. "And how is the earnest Jewish photographer bearing his separation from you? Have you received ten letters a day, full of yearning?"

"Not that it's any of your business, but I've told Mr. Singer that I need time to consider what is best for my future," I said. "I thought I'd have time to mull things over on this assignment, but I hadn't banked on people getting killed and me being poisoned."

"One never does," Daniel said, making me laugh.

It was just under an hour by train back to Rhinebeck, one of those pleasant, sleepy towns on the banks of the Hudson. We attempted to secure a cab at the station; upon being told that the only hack was out on a job, we were able to rent a horse and buggy from the local livery stables. Then we set out through rolling countryside, along leafy lanes, up hill and down dale. It felt about as remote as my part of Ireland and it was hard to believe that it was within a train ride of bustling New York City. Moments after we set out, the first raindrops spattered onto the buggy. The promised thunder could be heard rumbling in the distance and the sky became heavy.

"Our timing couldn't be better," Daniel said dryly. "It looks like you'll have the chance of getting yourself soaked twice in one day."

"You could have found us a wagon with a hood," I answered. "Still, there is a carriage rug under the seat and they said it wasn't too far, didn't they?" I leaned down to reach for the rug and draped it around us.

Daniel didn't answer but sat looking miserable as raindrops landed on his straw boater. Luckily the brunt of the storm was still to the south of us. We could hear distant rumbles of thunder but we experienced no worse than a few raindrops. After stopping to ask for directions several times, we finally found ourselves bumping up a farm track while black and white cows scattered and a horse neighed a warning.

It was a small gray stone farmhouse, set stark and unadorned in the middle of the fields. There was a red barn to one side and a field of corn growing tall to the other. As we pulled up outside the front door, it opened and a woman's anxious face peeked out. She looked from Daniel to me and I saw a flash of recognition register.

"Are you the former Johanna Foreman?" Daniel asked her.

"Yes. What do you want?" She was hugging her arms to herself as if she was cold, even though the air steamed with the heat of the day. She looked thin and undernourished, but maybe that was just because of her hollow cheeks and pallor.

"Just to ask you some questions, if you don't mind." Daniel jumped down and assisted me.

"You'd better come in, I suppose." She led us through into a small, dark kitchen. The remains of a recent meal still littered the scrubbed pine table.

"Do you have any idea why we might have come?" Daniel asked.

"I don't know who you are."

"I'm Captain Sullivan, New York Police. This is Miss Murphy, who's been assisting me."

Johanna's eyes darted nervously to the door and back.

"You used to know Albert Morell," Daniel said.

"Albert who?"

"Morell. From Albany."

She shook her head. "Never heard of him."

"But you go to put flowers on his grave every week," I said. "I saw you."

"What do you want with me?" She sounded close to hysterics. "Why can't you let the dead rest in peace? Albert is gone. He paid, didn't he?"

"I realize he's gone, Mrs. Clegg," I said. "We're here for another reason. I think you can guess it, can't you?"

Again she shook her head. "I've no idea."

"You have a son?" I asked.

I saw her eyes momentarily widen, then she nodded. "Yes. I have a son."

"Can we meet him?"

"What for?"

"Is there any reason why we shouldn't?" Daniel asked.

"None at all. Billy!" she shouted. "Come down here at once."

There was a clatter of boots on bare wooden stairs and a sturdy lad came into the kitchen. I recognized him too. Last time I had seen him, he'd been climbing on gravestones.

"What do you want, Ma?" he asked, eyeing us suspiciously.

"My boy, Billy," she said. "Anything else you want with me?"

The moment I had a chance to observe him closely, I saw that he could not be Brendan Flynn. Indeed, I saw only too clearly who his father was. The boy had Albert Morell's dark Italian good looks. At the moment this registered, I heard Daniel say in annoyance, "That certainly isn't Brendan Flynn."

"Brendan Flynn?" Mrs. Clegg demanded. "You're looking for Brendan Flynn? He's dead and buried years ago."

"Do you have any other children, Mrs. Clegg?" Daniel asked.

She shook her head. "I had problems with this one and they said I couldn't have any more."

I could see how awkward that would be for her husband.

"Mrs. Clegg," I said, holding her gaze, "we need to know

whether Brendan Flynn is dead or alive. If there's any chance he's still alive, you have to tell us."

She seemed to deflate before our eyes and hugged her arms to herself again. "Do you think I haven't asked myself that question, day after day?"

"What happened to the Flynn baby, Mrs. Clegg?" I asked. "Didn't Albert Morell bring him to you?"

"We didn't know, did we?" Johanna Clegg whimpered again. "Bertie knew I'd do anything for him, but I never dreamed . . . he said it was a little girl, his cousin's child, and his cousin had died and he was going to take the child to his sister in Ohio, only he had to work all weekend first. Would we just keep the child there overnight and he'd make sure we were well paid for our services? We had no idea—the child had long fair curls and was dressed in a bonnet and petticoats. Bertie must have thought we were very stupid, because the moment I had to change him, of course I could see it was a little boy. Then we heard the news and Amos says to me, 'You know who we've got here, don't you?'"

She looked at us, her eyes begging us to understand. "I was all for turning the child in at the nearest police station. But Amos wouldn't let me. He said we'd be arrested for aiding and abetting. They'd think we were in on the kidnapping and just got cold feet. Whatever we did now, we'd be in for it. And Amos had a record from his earlier years. He got in a couple of fights, you see. He said he wasn't going back to jail for all the tea in China."

I felt a sudden chill of apprehension. "So what did you do, Mrs. Clegg?"

"He did it, not me." Her voice rose alarmingly. "I didn't want him to, but he wouldn't listen. He cut the boy's hair and dressed him in our boy's cast-off clothes so he wouldn't be recognized. Then he set off with the child and returned without it. I said, 'Did you leave the child where he'd be safely found and taken home?' And he said he wasn't risking that, wasn't risking the child being traced back to us, so he took him into Albany. He said he was planning just to dump him on a city street, but one of those orphan trains was in the station and when no one was looking, he put Brendan with all the other orphan boys."

I heard Daniel gasp. My heart was beating so loudly I expected the others to hear it.

"What is an orphan train?" I tried to make my voice obey me.

Daniel was frowning. "They gather up orphans from the cities in the East and take them to families out West. It gives them a new chance at life, so they say."

"So Brendan could be anywhere in the country?" I stammered.

Johanna Clegg nodded. "I've prayed for forgiveness every day, but that won't bring him back, will it? Those poor people. That poor couple, not knowing their son is alive."

"It's too late for his mother," I said. "She died this week."

Johanna gave a great choking sob. "Oh, Lord have mercy. What did we do? I didn't want him to—I begged him, but you don't know Amos—"

Without warning the front door was thrust open and a hulk of a man filled the doorway. "I thought I told you no strangers on the property," he bellowed. "Who are they? Get rid of them."

"I'm a New York City policeman," Daniel said, "and we're here about the Flynn baby."

"They know," Johanna Clegg whimpered to her husband.

"They wouldn't have found out if you hadn't opened your big mouth, you stupid cow!" Amos Clegg raised his arm as if to strike her. Daniel stepped between them.

"That wouldn't be wise," he said, "not unless you want to spend the night in jail."

"You can't stop a man from hitting his own wife," Amos Clegg said with a sneer. "It's the law."

"Go ahead and try if you want," Daniel said. They faced each other—two big strapping men, eye to eye.

Amos Clegg lowered his arm, still glaring at Daniel.

"Get out of my house," he said. "Go on. Out with you. My wife is soft in the head. She rambles. There's no way you can ever prove that we had anything to do with the Flynn baby."

"I think there is," I said. I had been watching young Billy Clegg sitting in a corner, eyeing us shyly while he pretended to play with some toy soldiers. Among the soldiers was a red wooden elephant.

❧ Thirty-four ❧

I need to take this, if you don't mind," I said to the child as I bent to pick up the wooden elephant. "It came from Brendan Flynn's Noah's ark and I know one little girl who will be very happy to see it."

"Out! Now! Before I get my shotgun!" Amos Clegg roared. He opened the front door wide. The rain had now started in earnest, great fat drops thudding down onto the dirt.

"You can't send them out in this, Amos," Johanna begged. "There's going to be a storm any minute."

"It was their choice, coming here," Amos said. "This ain't the Bible. I don't have to offer shelter. You folks had better make a run for it before the creek rises."

I wondered if Daniel was going to attempt to arrest them and was glad when he turned and said, "We'll be back, Mr. Clegg, with a warrant for your arrest."

"You can't prove anything. I ain't done nothing wrong," Amos blustered, waving his fist dangerously.

"Threatening a police officer will do to start with," Daniel said. He led me outside and assisted me aboard the buggy and cracked the whip. As we started off, we could hear Amos Clegg yelling at his wife. Probably hitting her, too. My mood matched the foul weather. I felt plunged into gloom. I should have been jubilant that Brendan was still alive, but the odds of finding him were slim. And I couldn't stop thinking about the cowering Johanna, who had chosen marriage to that brute rather than bear a child in shame. Maybe she had had no choice. It was an unfair world where women were punished and men went their merry way.

It was the last of a gloomy twilight and thunder now rumbled over the mountains across the river. I draped the rug over us, but it soon became sodden and we huddled together miserably. Heavy splatters of rain soon turned into a solid, drenching sheet. We couldn't see more than a few yards ahead of us. Then the horse stopped so abruptly that I was almost thrown over backward.

"Oh no," Daniel groaned.

What had once been a gentle ford was now a raging torrent, wide and fierce.

"We can't risk crossing that," I said.

"Even if I could persuade the horse to try, which I don't think I can," Daniel agreed.

"So what do we do now?"

Daniel shrugged. "Go back and try to find an inn or some kind of shelter until the water goes down."

It took long weary minutes to back up the wagon and turn it around. The horse clearly thought little of Daniel's horsemanship and eyed him with disdain out of the corner of its eye. In the end I had to jump down, take the bridle and sooth the animal into backing up. I had just got the wagon turned around and was attempting to climb back aboard when there was a brilliant flash of lightning right overhead, accompanied almost simultaneously by a mighty crash of thunder. The horse neighed and took off at a full gallop. I was thrown down from the buggy and landed in the mud. By the time I had picked myself up, they were out of sight.

I ran in the direction they had disappeared, but I had little hope of catching a galloping horse, especially as my skirts became sodden and weighted with mud. I was soon soaked through, shivering, and feeling very sorry for myself. Darkness had now fallen and there was no sign of any light indicating a place where I might take shelter. I slithered and trudged along the muddy track until I could make out a shape lying to one side. I made my way toward it and found Daniel lying there, unconscious.

"Daniel, are you all right?" I knelt beside him and cradled his head in my arms. He felt cold.

"Daniel. Speak to me, please!"

He still didn't move.

I fought to remain calm. "Daniel. It's Molly. Wake up, please."

I put my cheek to his mouth but was able to detect no warm breath on those cold lips.

"Please don't die," I begged. "You can't die. I won't let you. Please."

I sat there while the rain beat down on us. I tried to shield him with my body, but it was hopeless. Tears streamed down my face and mingled with the raindrops. I had never felt more lost and alone in my life. I didn't know what to do. I didn't want to leave him to go for help. I didn't know where to go. Then lightning flashed again and it occurred to me that I was likely to be struck if I stayed where I was. I wasn't doing Daniel any good sitting here crying. I dragged him to the side of the road and laid him under some bushes. "You'll be safe here until I come back," I whispered. "I don't want to leave you, but I have to. I'm going to get help, Daniel."

But I felt as if I was talking to a rock. I started to walk away. At the next flash of lightning, I looked back. He hadn't stirred. I kept walking. Then there was a great gust of wind followed by a moment's silence, during which I heard quite clearly, "Why am I having a cold bath?"

"Daniel!" I ran back to him.

He was sitting up holding his head. "My head hurts," he muttered. "What am I doing here?"

"The horse bolted. You must have been thrown out and hit your head."

"I couldn't have been thrown. Not an experienced horseman like me. It must have been a branch that knocked me down."

The old cocky Daniel. I threw my arms around him. "Saints be praised, you're all right."

311

"Of course I'm all right. What happened to the horse?"

"Long gone," I said. "And we're in the middle of nowhere."

"You'd better help me up," he said and staggered to his feet, letting out a yell of pain.

"Go carefully now. Is anything broken?"

"My legs seem to be okay," he said, "but you yanked me straight into some thorns." A swift thought crossed my mind that men are much better in theory than in reality!

We staggered together along the track, hoping that the horse had recovered from its fright and was standing waiting for us. No such luck. It was the most gloomy and desolate side road that I had ever seen. The half darkness had now turned to absolute blackness and we stumbled over rocks and stepped into deep puddles.

"This is madness," Daniel said at last. "We need to find shelter."

"Show me a light and I'll take you to shelter," I snapped, my sweet nature wearing remarkably thin at this point.

As if in answer, a flash of lightning illuminated a structure in a field to our left. We managed to climb over the wall and stumbled over tussocks of grass until we reached it. To our disappointment it wasn't a house but a disused barn, half tumbledown by the looks of the lumber that lay around it. We got in easily enough and found a dry corner at the back where some hay was still stacked.

"At least there isn't a bull in it," I said, and started to laugh.

He went to put his arm around me, then grunted in pain.

"What is it?"

"My shoulder. Ahhgh. I've definitely done something to it. What I need now is a good shot of whiskey to take away the pain. You wouldn't like to run to the nearest saloon for me, would you?"

"Fat chance," I said. "My devotion only goes so far. And if I found a saloon, you don't think I'd be coming back, do you?"

I helped him off with his jacket, with many groans and protests, and eased him onto the bales of hay.

"It's going to be a long, weary night unless somebody finds us," I said. "This is the second time in one day that I've been soaking wet. I'll be lucky if I don't wind up with pneumonia."

"Here, come and sit beside me," he said. "I can put my good arm around you."

I sat. His arm came around me and he pulled me close to him. "I'm glad you're here with me," he whispered, and kissed me gently on the forehead.

"I don't think we should start that kind of thing," I said. "Maybe I should move away."

"I don't want you to move away from me, ever," he said.

"I don't think Miss Norton will welcome my presence in your happy home," I said stiffly.

"Damn Arabella Norton! I want you, Molly. I've wanted you from the moment I saw you."

Then he was kissing me and it was no gentle kiss on the forehead this time.

"What about your shoulder?" I whispered.

"Damn my shoulder."

I'll have to put the rest of what happened down to my weakened state and the heightened emotion of the day. For next thing I knew I was lying in his arms, his lips crushed against mine, feeling his heart thudding through the wet fabric of my dress. I was giddy with desire as his lips moved down my throat.

"We shouldn't," I whispered, but I could hardly make the words come out.

"I'll tell her, I promise," he whispered back as his hand moved down my thigh and pulled up my skirts. I think I helped him get them out of the way. I know I didn't protest enough.

When I realized the next step was inevitable, a brief thought flashed through my mind that twenty-four was awfully old to be a virgin anyway. Then a moment of fear and uncertainly and then it wasn't at all like the old wives had whispered. When I cried out, it was in pleasure, not pain.

"I love you, Molly Murphy," were the last words I heard before I fell asleep in his arms.

I awoke to a bright shaft of sunlight falling across my face. It took me a moment to realize where I was and when Daniel sighed

gently in his sleep, I jumped a mile. He was lying beside me, looking so peaceful that I just stared at him. Then, of course, the full
memory of last night returned. A silly grin crossed my face. I was
with Daniel Sullivan and everything was going to be just fine.

When he awoke and gazed at me, a big smiled crossed his
face too.

"Don't look at me. I must look awful," I said. "I've no hairbrush
and I fell in the mud and . . . "

"You look beautiful," he whispered and kissed me tenderly.

When we went outside, we discovered that the trees behind
the barn concealed a farmhouse. In no time at all we were riding in
the farmer's wagon back to civilization, where we learned that the
horse and buggy had been found, unharmed, and there had been a
search going on for us during the night. I was rather glad they
hadn't found us.

By midday we arrived back at Adare.

"Why don't I wait out here at the gate while you give Barney
the news?" I said, loathe to have to face the embarrassment of seeing Barney again.

"You've just found out that his son is still alive," Daniel said.
"Who could remain angry with news like that? You should be the
one to tell him." He took my hand. "And when were you ever
afraid of an angry male?"

So I had no option. I was feeling distinctly nervous as Soames
opened the front door, but I need not have worried. Barney
seemed as anxious as Belinda and Clara and grateful to know I was
still alive. Only patchy news had reached them of Joseph Rimes's
drowning and my apparent disappearance. As we gave Barney the
news about Brendan, a look of wonder spread over his face.

"My son alive?"

We nodded. "We have every reason to hope so."

"My son alive," he said again, then he sank his face into his
hands and started to weep.

"Poor Theresa. If only she'd been alive to hear this. That rat
Rimes—may he rot in hell for this." I realized then that he cared

314

for his wife more than I had thought. When he looked up, his face was resolute. "I'll find him, Sullivan. I don't care how much time and money it takes. I'll search this country from top to bottom. I'll offer the biggest reward in the history of mankind, but I'm going to find my son again."

His gaze focused on me. "You brought this about," he said. "I said terrible things to you yesterday, but now I'll forever be in your debt. There will be a welcome for you at my home any time."

"Thank you," I said, noting that he had conveniently forgotten the circumstances under which Joe Rimes discovered us. If I came to his home again it would be under the escort of a good strong male, preferably Daniel.

"You are certainly some investigator, for a woman," he added. "I don't know what gave you the idea my son was still alive and how you tracked him down."

"Albert Morell's character," I said. "He loved children. And I always thought there had to be a mastermind behind the kidnapping—although I have to confess that I suspected your secretary."

"Desmond?" He sounded surprised.

"Why else would such a bright and qualified young man choose to stay out here when New York City is just down the river?"

"Ah," he said. "I think I can explain that. His father, you see, is in Sing Sing. Guilty of embezzlement. Desmond visits him whenever he can. And with that disgrace hanging over his head, a lot of jobs are barred to him. Since I've done a few crooked things in my own career, his family history doesn't bother me. He's a fine secretary."

He broke off as two automobiles came down the driveway, bearing the occupants of Riverside. Someone must have telephoned to tell them of our arrival. I glanced nervously to see if Justin was among them. He wasn't. Neither was Captain Cathers. I watched Arabella as she was assisted out of the car, looking delicate and lovely, her elfin face framed beneath a mauve silk parasol.

"Daniel," she cried, and ran toward him.

I held my breath.

"We were worried sick about you," she said. "Where were you?"

"We were following a lead about the Flynn baby," Daniel said "and as you can see, we got trapped by the storm."

She took in his crumpled suit, liberally caked with mud, then her eyes moved past him to where I was standing in the doorway.

"We?" she said icily.

"Miss Murphy was with me."

"Miss Murphy? I understood this was Miss Gaffney."

"Ah yes. Well, she was working for me. Undercover operation."

"She seems to keep popping up with boring regularity, Daniel." Arabella was eyeing me with distaste and suspicion. "What exactly was she doing with you?"

I held my breath.

"I told you, Arabella," Daniel's voice was harsh. "She's an investigator. We were on a case. The creek rose and we couldn't get back. Please don't make a scene about nothing."

I wanted to start breathing again but my breath wouldn't come. *About nothing*. The words resounded through my head. Nothing. I was nothing. I had let myself be fooled by the circumstances last night. Mrs. Van Gelder began cross-questioning Daniel and Barney. I chose the moment to slip away unnoticed. Once inside the house, I ran up the stairs, threw my belongings into the valise, then, while everyone was still chatting out in front of the house, I let myself out through the French windows in Barney's study. I lugged my case along the cliff path all the way to the village, where I got a boat across to Peekskill and a train home.

❧ Thirty-five ❧

I t was a long train ride back to the city. I felt like a coward for running out without saying good-bye to anyone at Adare, but truly my nerves had been stretched to breaking point. If I had had to be around Daniel and Arabella Norton for one more second, I would have cracked. Let Daniel finish sorting out matters with Barney Flynn. As far as I was concerned, I had done what I came to do—more than I came to do, in fact. Hopefully I had given Barney Flynn back his son. And Annie Lomax her good name, I realized. Joe Rimes had confessed to removing the child from the house and delivering him to Albert Morell. I would make sure the newspapers published this fact. Being able to tell her the good news was another reason I couldn't wait for the long train ride to end.

I thought of going straight to Broadway and seeing if I could locate her, but the draw of home was too strong. Patchin Place had never looked more inviting when I stepped out of the hansom cab. The cabby carried my heavy case to the front door of number nine, then I opened it and walked in. Nobody was home. The place was quiet and orderly. No half-eaten jam sandwiches or toys on the floor. I put down my case and went across the street to Sid and Gus.

Their front door was opened immediately by Sid, wearing a Japanese kimono.

"Molly!" she exclaimed and I fell into her arms, fighting back tears.

"It's so good to be home," I managed to say.

"My dear girl, what have you been doing with yourself? You look as if you've been dragged through a hedge backward."

"I have, and more."

"Come on, into the garden where it's pleasant today." She took me by the hand and led me like a child. "Gus has made lemonade."

Gus was sitting in a deck chair, fanning herself with a large Oriental fan, and she jumped up as she spotted me.

"She's come home at last," she exclaimed, flinging her arms around me. "I can't tell you how much we missed you. Not so much as a postcard, Molly. Shame on you."

"I'm sorry. I wasn't exactly in a position to write postcards."

"But we thought you were staying at a mansion on the Hudson," Gus said, pouring lemonade as she spoke. "We used our spies to try to find which one, but nobody seemed to have heard of you."

"That's because I was under an assumed name."

"Ah. Clandestine, of course." Sid and Gus nodded to each other. "So did it go well? Did you return bathed in glory?"

I shook my head and felt again that I might cry at any moment. "I suppose I did what I set out to do, but—"

"She's tired, Sid. Let her sit and rest before we grill her," Gus said, patting my hand.

I sat in the shade of their plane tree and sipped lemonade.

"Where is everyone at number nine?" I asked. "Don't tell me that Seamus finally has a job?"

Then I saw their faces. "What? What's wrong?"

"They tried to contact you, Molly, but nobody knew where you were. Bridie caught typhoid. They took her to the fever ward at St. Vincent's Hospital."

"Oh, no—is she going to be all right?"

They looked at each other.

"It's a terrible disease. People have been dropping like flies."

I jumped up. "I must go to her right away."

They tried to dissuade me but I ran past them like a madwoman. If I had been here, this wouldn't have happened, I kept telling myself—although I knew that she wasn't my child and not even my responsibility. As I came out of Patchin Place and turned past the Jefferson Market, I opened my mouth in horror as I realized something. The Sorensen Sisters were not fakes after all. That child in the veil at the séance—it wasn't somebody's niece at first communion. It was a little girl dressed as a bride so that I would recognize her. The message had been for me. Bridie was now with her mother in heaven and she had come to tell me she was all right.

I fought back tears all the way up Seventh Avenue to the hospital. It was a futile mission. If she had really been dead since the séance, then she would no longer be lying in a hospital bed. She'd have been buried days ago. But I kept on running, pushing my way past crowds of people, out shopping for their evening meal.

Stories don't really have happy endings, I told myself. I had gone from the heights of elation to the depths of despair in one day. To have been betrayed by Daniel the coward and then to have lost this precious child was almost more than I could bear. I forced my way in through the front door of St. Vincent's Hospital and heard a crisply starched nurse shouting at me as I ran down a tiled hallway. She grabbed me and shook me to my senses.

"Where in heaven's name do you think you are going?"

"I've got to see her," I babbled. "She wouldn't have died if I'd been there. I have to see her."

"See who?"

"Bridie O'Connor. She had typhoid."

"You'll most certainly not be allowed anywhere near the typhoid ward," the nurse said. "Go back to the waiting room. Someone will deal with you."

She forced me around and shoved me back down the hallway. As I entered the waiting room, I heard someone calling my name. Young Shamey came running down the hall toward me.

"Molly, you're back!" He flung himself at me with uncharacteristic affection.

"I came as soon as I heard," I said. "Where is she? They haven't buried her yet, have they? I do want to see her."

"They won't let you see her," Shamey said. "Nobody's allowed in the contagious ward. But she's doing better. They say she's sitting up and eating broth."

"Sitting up?" I stammered. "You mean she's not dead?"

"No. She's doing fine. Getting better every day."

Seamus came running to meet me. "You've heard the grand news then, have you? Sitting up and sipping broth." He wiped a big hand across his face. "I tell you, Molly. I thought we'd lost her for a while there. She hung between life and death for a couple of days. We tried to contact you, but nobody knew where you'd gone."

"I'm sorry I wasn't here, Seamus," I said, "but it is indeed grand news."

"We certainly needed something cheer us up," he said. "We got another piece of news while you were away. My dear Kathleen died last week."

I crossed myself. "Out of her suffering at last, God rest her soul."

So the Sorensen Sisters might just have been right after all— maybe Bridie did meet her mother during those days when she hung between life and death. The important thing was that she had come back. There was still hope. Life seemed to be one succession of good news and then bad. Ups followed by downs. But there was always enough hope to keep on going. I'd survived a lot before. I'd live through this latest setback. I'd get by without Daniel Sullivan. After all, I had a little family who needed me, friends who loved me, and an ex-nanny who was going to be very pleased to see me. I resolved to take the trolley to her patch on Broadway this very minute and give her the good news.

"Molly, where are you going?" Shamey asked, grabbing my hand.

"I just have to go and see a lady and tell her some news," I said. "I'll be back right away."

"But Molly," he said, clutching my hand more tightly, "I'm starving. Couldn't we go home first and you make me some bread and dripping?"

I smiled down at him. "Come on, then," I said. "Let's go home."

Historical Note

The mansion, Adare, does not exist. I decided to create a fictitious house for Senator Flynn as I didn't want any real history attached to it. I also needed it to be on the side of the Hudson where there is no railway line!

The spiritualist movement in the late nineteenth century was extremely popular and produced some incredibly slick mediums. I read every book I could find on the subject and was disappointed that many of their most spectacular stunts were never explained. These included disembodied hands writing messages, talking heads, violins playing by themselves—all at a time when the most primitive phonograph had only just been invented.

"If you are one of the few on the planet yet to discover Molly Murphy, created by Rhys Bowen, now is the time to take the plunge. Molly is sassy, saucy, brave, and smart."
—*The Huffington Post*

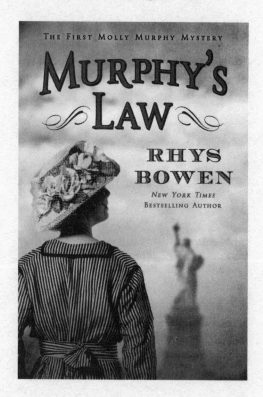

Read the Entire Molly Murphy Mystery Series